Dear Mystery Reader:

There are those who think the history of the United States is the story of its expansion westward: manifest destiny as our *raison d'etre*. Certainly there remains a rugged individualism amongst the people of those lovely, wide open places out west. In this novel, Chief of Police Harry Starbranch learns that the same independent spirit that made this country great has a definite downside.

The events chronicled in *Long Shadows in Victory* are the stuff of current headlines. Gregory Bean writes knowledgeable and exciting prose about the right-wing militia members that refuse to accept the authority of the government. In this book, Harry Starbranch finds that leaving the Denver police force for small-town life doesn't necessarily mean a quieter or calmer existence. So sit down and enjoy yourself: Harry Starbranch makes for good, exciting reading.

Westward Ho!

Dana Edwin Isaacson
Senior Editor
St. Martin's DEAD LETTER Paperback Mysteries

Other titles from St. Martin's
Dead Letter Mysteries

WIN, LOSE OR DIE ed. by Cynthia Manson & Constance Scarborough
MORTAL CAUSES by Ian Rankin
A VOW OF DEVOTION by Veronica Black
WOLF, NO WOLF by Peter Bowen
SCHOOL OF HARD KNOCKS by Donna Huston Murray
FALCONER'S JUDGEMENT by Ian Morson
WINTER GAMES by John Feinstein
THE MAN WHO INVENTED FLORIDA by Randy Wayne White
WHISKERS AND SMOKE by Marian Babson
FLY FISHING CAN BE FATAL by David Leitz
BLACK WATER by Doug Allyn
REVENGE OF THE BARBEQUE QUEENS by Lou Jane Temple
A MURDER ON THE APPIAN WAY by Steven Saylor
MURDER MOST BRITISH ed. by Janet Hutchings
LIE DOWN WITH DOGS by Jan Gleiter
THE CLEVELAND CONNECTION by Les Roberts
BIGGIE AND THE POISONED POLITICIAN by Nancy Bell

PRAISE FOR THE PREVIOUS HARRY STARBRANCH MYSTERY *NO COMFORT IN VICTORY*

"Bean packs a lot into this debut."

—*Publishers Weekly*

"Bean has a nice, easy style and an appealing tough-sensitive hero."

—*Kirkus Reviews*

"Some seriously nasty villains, a collection of colorful Wyoming characters, and authentic locales that are wonderfully familiar to this Wyoming native. A real read."

—Gerry Spence

"If you like quicksilver prose that challenges your senses, characters that do things to your mind, and a high-voltage story line guaranteed to jolt, *No Comfort in Victory* is the book for you. If it doesn't win an Edgar, there's no justice."

—Andrew Coburn, author of *Voices in the Dark*

"A mature, polished, and powerful first novel that bodes very well for the future of both Starbranch and his creator."

—*Booklist*

"A tautly written novel."

—Charles Levendosky, poet laureate of Wyoming

ALSO BY GREGORY BEAN

No Comfort in Victory

LONG SHADOWS IN VICTORY

GREGORY BEAN

St. Martin's Paperbacks

LONG SHADOWS IN VICTORY

 For information address St. Martin's Press, 175 Fifth Avenue, New York, N.Y. 10010.

Library of Congress Catalog Card Number: 96-2070

ISBN: 0-312-96217-7

Printed in the United States of America

St. Martin's Press hardcover edition/August 1996
St. Martin's Paperbacks edition/June 1997

10 9 8 7 6 5 4 3 2 1

For Phyllis Harris

All civilization has from time to time become a thin crust over a volcano of revolution.

—Havelock Ellis

Old sins cast long shadows.

—Anonymous

ACKNOWLEDGMENTS

The Posse Comitatus is a real organization. The manner of Gordon Kahl's death and the frightening growth of right-wing paramilitary groups in America are well documented. Beyond that, this novel is a work of fiction and any resemblance between the characters in the work and real individuals is purely coincidental.

I owe many people my heartfelt thanks for their help and support in getting this novel to print. Thanks to Sam Sherman, Rosemary McIntosh, Bob Turner, and Lloyd Fordyce, who read the manuscript and provided valuable insight and suggestions; Sherie Posesorski, who worked as my editor through the first draft; Neal Bascomb, my editor at St. Martin's; Helen Rees and Joan Mazmamian, who make it happen; Phyllis and Cloyd Harris, who keep the Wyoming home fires burning and have worked tirelessly throughout the entire process.

As always, thanks to my wife, Linda, who has read this manuscript so many times she knows most of it by heart. Without her love, encouragement, keen eye, and tolerance for many late nights and weekends at the typewriter, this novel would never have been possible.

1

It was 10:30 on a glorious October morning, and the dusty streets of Victory, Wyoming—population 650 and counting—were bathed in the rich, curiously yellow light of early fall in the Rockies. I poured myself a second cup of coffee from the ancient Mr. Coffee, rocked back in my chair, and propped my battle-scarred cowboy boots on my desk.

I closed my eyes, felt the warm sun coming in the window of the police station on my face. The crisp breeze from the foothills of the Snowy Range drifting through the open window brought with it the scent of wood smoke and pine. I might have looked like I wasn't paying attention to the conversation of the two other men in the room, but I was. It's hard to ignore people who are having fun at your expense.

"He couldn't have been any closer to that deer if he was makin' love to it," said Mike O'Neal, one of my so-called friends. He'd dropped by the office, apparently for the sole purpose of besmirching my reputation as a marksman in front of Frankie Tall Bull—Frankie Bull for short—a three-hundred-pound, six-foot-four-inch Teton Sioux and the only officer on my police force. Frankie had heard it all before, but he was plenty willing to hear it again.

I opened one eye a crack, peered at the ruddy-faced O'Neal through the slit in my eyelids. If he thought he'd get a rise out of me, he was wrong. "Yes sir, old Harry Starbranch was this close . . . ," O'Neal said, held his fingers an inch apart, ". . . but he hadn't counted on catching a dose of Buck Fever. He could've bagged that deer with a slingshot, but not with a .30-06 and a twelve-power Bushnell scope. No, by God! Four shots, all of them under fifty yards, and the Great

Hunter missed every stinking time." He paused for dramatic effect. "Blamed it on lousy ammunition!" he hooted.

I opened my eyes wide, tried to stare him down. "That buck was running serpentine," I said. "It knew what it was doing. And that ammunition *was* bad. . . ."

A wide grin split Frankie's face, crinkled the laugh lines at the edges of his brown eyes. In his early thirties, Frankie Bull was aging gracefully. Unlike many big men who start turning doughy as soon as they reach the beginning of their third decade, he kept his huge body in shape with a strict regimen of weight lifting, boxing, and some kind of martial-arts mumbo jumbo. I'm not the best judge of such things, but I suppose you'd call him handsome in a world-worn sort of way. His long, braided black hair was just starting to gray at the temples, which accented the tawny, weathered skin of his cheeks and forehead. His face was strong but battered by sun, wind, and hard living—his nose broken at least once, a half-inch scar through his left eyebrow, a series of small, white scars around the corners of his eyes, put there by a long series of flying fists.

Even though he was happily married to Frieda, his wife of five years, the women in Victory liked him—a lot. The men, at least those who didn't know him well, gave him plenty of room. "Won't wash, Harry." Frankie chuckled. "That's the same excuse you used last year."

With the two of them cackling, it didn't seem like the time to remind them of certain facts. First, I'm a competitive marksman with enough trophies to put their buck fever—the shivery anxiety that causes novices to flinch when they pull the trigger—theory in some doubt. Second, it didn't bother me that I'd missed my buck the week before, because I don't really subscribe to the standard theology of hunting, which holds that you have to kill something to be judged a success.

"I got my deer last year," I finally offered. "Neither of you did."

"The deer that ended up in your freezer only got there because he jumped in front of your pickup and bonked his head on your grill," O'Neal howled. "That doesn't exactly count. . . ."

"I missed my shots on purpose," I grumbled. "I told you a thousand times, I—"

"Missed 'em on purpose!" they jeered in unison, ecstatic that their taunting was finally showing results.

Morons. I slammed my coffee cup on the desk, stood up, pulled my Stetson from the peg where it hangs by the door, and jammed it low over my eyes. "I hope you both get piles," I muttered. "Big, red, excruciatingly painful piles."

Then I banged out the door and onto Main Street, careful not to let them see my grin. If the truth be known, I kind of enjoy the ribbing I take every year after hunting season. I go hunting because it gives me a chance to get into the mountains for a few days every October, which is the most beautiful time of year in this country, and the excuse to spend some time around the campfire playing poker with my friends. I don't go for the actual killing, and I guess I really don't trust anybody who does.

I jammed my hands in the pockets of my jeans and steamed down the sidewalk on Main. At the first corner, I leaned against a building and listened to the quiet heartbeat of my town—the far-off buzz of someone's chain saw as they cut wood for the coming winter, snippets of conversation from the opened door of the barbershop, Paul Harvey's voice from the radio in the hardware store, someone playing piano at the First Christian Church, the soft hum of tires on pavement as an occasional motorist accelerated away from the town's only traffic light.

Midmorning in Victory, and nothing going on—just the way I liked it. I'll concede the lack of activity is enough to drive some people crazy. I once heard a tourist describe Victory, Wyoming, as a place so dull, "you can throw a harmonica in the air, and it will land on someone who knows how to play it." From the vantage point of someone with an urban background as a primary point of reference, I suppose that observation is true—as far as it goes.

Between late June and late October—when the tourists, out-of-state fishermen, and hunters pass through by the thousands—Victory is a fairly lively place. Naturally, as chief of police, I'm generally busiest during that season, when it's my job to help relieve them of some of their money so that Victory's municipal coffers will be plump enough to see us through the winter.

I do that by ordering Frankie to park his cruiser out of sight near

Victory's lone four-way intersection and write a well-deserved $25 ticket for anyone who fails to notice that the speed limit plummets from forty mph to fifteen mph in a little over sixty feet.

We also supplement the town's income by paying careful attention to whether the cars parked at any of Victory's fourteen parking meters are local or from out of town. And while several disgruntled visitors have complained to His Honor, Mayor J. B. "Curly" Ahearn—who also owns my favorite Victory watering hole, the Silver Dollar Saloon—that perhaps $20 is a tad much to be penalized for being five minutes late in plugging one of our municipal revenue enhancers, we do give offenders an occasional break, especially if their station wagons and pickups are sporting our own Albany County plates.

When we're not busy in the summer writing tickets, there's always the odd fight to break up at Gus Alzonakis's and the Trail's End, the two competing steak houses a couple of Eastern entrepreneurs decided to build right across the street from each other. And, of course, there's your run-of-the-mill small-town police work—drunken rodeo cowboys who need a place to sleep it off before they go home to their wives, toddlers whose parents have misplaced them at the rest stop on the way to Saratoga, lost dogs, etc., etc.

All in all, you can see why I prefer late autumn.

Around the end of October, the living gets downright agreeable. The tourists have gone home for the most part, and about the only real traffic enforcement we need is the old black-and-white Chevy that Frankie and I park behind Millie Henderson's hedge on the main road into town from Laramie. We set a red coffee can on top of the Chevy, and if you're not looking real close, it looks exactly like Frankie hiding back there, waiting to write you a ticket.

Through trial and error, we've found this simple ruse provides almost all of the off-season traffic control we need in Victory. Which leaves Frankie and me time to spend on really important things, like trying to catch the joker who keeps stealing entire condom machines off the men's room walls at the Silver Dollar and Victory's three other cowboy saloons, and trying to survive eight months of winter.

For his part, Frankie uses the slack time to fine-tune his skills as a gourmet chef, enjoy his collection of classical music, read trashy romance novels, and work on his sculpture: beautiful, haunting bronzes of Plains Indians at the hunt and war that are eventually going to make him famous—and rich.

I spend it tying flies, listening to my Ry Cooder collection, fishing—when the weather permits—reading mysteries, and fighting with one woman who wants me and wooing one who doesn't.

It's not any kind of a life for someone with great ambitions, I know, and lots of my friends and loved ones have accused me of settling for less than I'm capable of. And if you're looking at things from halfway up a career ladder, I guess they have a point.

I'd been both a fast-track detective with the Denver Police Department and the sheriff of Albany County. If I'd wanted to stick with either, I could have carved out a very comfortable life for myself. Trouble was, it had become clear to me that in spite of my idealistic notions to the contrary, one cop can do little to protect the citizens in his care and almost nothing to guarantee that the criminals who prey on them will see justice—even when he's lucky enough to catch them. I'd become disillusioned with the whole system, to tell the truth. And too many times, I'd found myself breaking the rules to make sure the bad guys got their just desserts.

I was unhappy, drinking too much, tearing my family apart. If I'd continued down that rocky trail, I imagine I'd have wound up with cirrhosis of the liver and an overpowering desire to sneak down to the kitchen for a midnight snack of .357 Magnum.

I don't figure I'll ever get that hungry in Victory—and if you squint at things through my admittedly rosy glasses, it even begins to look like I've realized a sort of ideal. I've chopped my damned career ladder into a gazillion pieces and made a bonfire of the rubble.

My sun-drenched reverie was broken by the grumbling in my stomach, so I pushed away from the building, dusted my palms against the legs of my jeans, and made the two block trek to Mrs. Larsen's Country Kitchen for breakfast. A ramshackle joint that seems to miss most of the tourist trade, Ginny Larsen's makes up for it by maintaining the undying loyalty and devotion of the locals. Her restaurant is the kind of place where the chairs don't match, where the kitchen noise mocks any sophisticated notion of ambience, and where the food is fantastic.

"Mornin', Harry," Ginny called cheerfully as I came through the door, breathing in the heady aroma of fresh-baked bread and deep-dish apple pie. A short woman with unruly wheat-colored hair, pink cheeks, and a toothy smile, Ginny was wearing a crisp apron over her usual uniform of denim shirt, blue jeans, and low-topped white running shoes with fluorescent pink laces. There was a long smudge of flour over her left eyebrow. "I saw O'Neal go in your place a while ago, and figured you'd be headin' this direction before long."

The stories of my amazingly poor marksmanship are known by all of Ginny Larsen's customers, but it's considered bad form in Victory to harass people while they're eating, particularly if they're armed.

"The usual?" she asked. She slid the morning edition of the *Laramie Boomerang* down the counter and steamed off in the direction of the kitchen before I had the chance to answer. Not that she needed an answer. I've been eating the same breakfast almost every morning for the last five years, and most days, I have the same lunch—a big bowl of Ginny's soup of the day and a thick, juicy grilled cheeseburger with a huge slab of sweet Vidalia onion and beefsteak tomato. It varies only on those days when Ginny divines something off center in my being, and brings me whatever medicinal concoction she's determined will put me to rights.

As I skimmed the headlines and sipped my coffee, I looked out through Ginny's window from time to time. A couple of old pensioners strolled arm in arm up the cracked Main Street sidewalk, the first aspen leaves of fall swirling around the soles of their sensible shoes. Down the block, at Willard Feed & Seed, a couple of horse ranchers stood by their four-by-fours, arms crossed comfortably across their chests as they jawed and enjoyed the warming October sun on their foreheads.

At Shapiro's Hardware, Billy Sun, the stock boy, helped Janice McPherson wrestle a new Maytag washing machine into the back of her Toyota van. There was fresh white paint on Shapiro's storefront, courtesy of the townsfolk who pitched in to clean up after some asshole spray painted anti-Semitic bullshit there a week or so before. The real pisser, Shapiro noted then, was that as proprietor of the only hardware store in town, he probably sold paint to the jerk who used it on his building. Frankie and I were still looking for a culprit.

When my breakfast came, I stuffed my cheeks full of scrambled eggs, buttered toast, and jam and attacked the sports section in earnest. The columnist thought the Broncos had a chance of going to the Super Bowl. Hope springs eternal.

"Telephone, Harry," Ginny called, breaking my concentration. "It's Frankie."

"Tell him I'll be back in twenty minutes," I grumbled. "I'm not in the mood for any more of his stupid jokes."

"He says it's important," Ginny said. She slammed the receiver on the counter and marched back into the kitchen. She didn't have time to argue. I sighed loudly in self-pity, folded the paper, wiped my face with a napkin, and picked up the receiver. "Starbranch here," I growled. "And if you're disturbing my breakfast because you and Mike O'Neal couldn't wait until I got back to jab the blade in a little further—"

"Nah, Harry," Frankie interrupted. "There's something here I think you should come back and see."

"What is it?" I asked. I set the *Boomerang* on the counter and pulled a pack of smokes from my pocket, winced in disgust as I lit one up. I'd quit smoking almost three years ago but had recently picked it up again, against my better judgment.

"It's Sonny Toms," Frankie said. "He just showed up here with something that looks like a jawbone, and says the rest of the body is stashed in an old mine shaft on Encampment Creek. Says it looks like the victim was shot in the head."

Scrawny and wild-eyed, Sonny Toms lived in an old Airstream trailer about fifteen miles west of town and made his living as what we used to call a jack-of-all-trades. If your pickup or your hay baler broke down, you called Sonny, who came out and patched it together. If you needed a replacement sheepherder, Sonny was your man. And if you just needed someone to feed the dogs and water the stock once a year when you went on vacation, Sonny was happy to oblige.

He rambled around the foothills of the Snowy Range in his 1967

International Harvester truck, one door wired shut and the driver's window patched with cardboard, looking for odd jobs and, when he had time, for the treasure he was certain the U.S. Army buried somewhere near Victory in the summer of 1868 when the Southern Cheyenne were making life hot for the frontier posts and the settlers' roads.

That morning, Sonny looked even wilder than usual, and was pacing the small office of the police department like a baited badger. His wiry brown hair poked out from underneath an oil-stained baseball cap, and there were long gashes in the knees of his coveralls and mismatched laces in his scuffed work boots. His hands fluttered like hummingbirds as he talked. "It was the God damnedest thing," Sonny began before I'd had the chance to hang my hat. "I played the light across the side of that shaft . . . and there she was, propped up against one of the supports, looking right at me like she'd been waiting for me to come."

Frankie was hunched over his desk, poking a brown mandible with the eraser end of a pencil, the same curious expression on his face he wears when he's checking his malamute for ticks.

"What makes you think it's a woman, Sonny?" I asked, peering over Frankie's shoulder. It didn't take a forensic specialist to deduce that we weren't dealing with a violent act that happened in the recent past. The jawbone was dry and brown with age, missing teeth here and there, and lacking any of the gristle or connective tissue that clings to bone, sometimes for years, after the soft tissues have decayed. I guessed it had to be at least ten years old, and if the mine shaft had been dry, maybe a lot older.

"Because of her shoes," Sonny said, his hands still shaking. "She had woman's shoes. And little feet. Jesus, Harry, I feel like a grave robber."

I took the mandible from Frankie's desk and picked it up for a look. "Why did you only bring this much back?" I asked. "What happened to the rest of her?"

Sonny looked like he wanted to cry. "I was gonna bring her back, but when I moved her, this fell off. I guess I just grabbed it and ran like hell." Sonny shrugged miserably. "I can take you back there if you want," he said.

It sounded like Sonny would rather walk into a nest of black-widow spiders than back into the maw of that mine shaft. But even so, he'd told us he believed the victim had died as a result of foul play, in this case a bullet between the eyes, and all bodies fitting that description fall, at least temporarily, under my jurisdiction if they're found in reasonable proximity to the Victory city limits. Since this particular body had turned up on Encampment Creek, right on the eastern edge of town, I was responsible for its care and for notifying the proper county and state authorities—the coroner, the Albany County Sheriff's Department, and the state Department of Criminal Investigation—of its discovery.

I opened the top drawer of the file cabinet and dropped the jawbone inside, slammed the drawer shut with a bang. "Sorry, Sonny," I said. "That's exactly what I want."

It was only a five-minute ride from the police-department office on Main Street to the road that would take us to the mine shaft where Sonny had discovered the bones. At the edge of town, Frankie nosed the cruiser through the front gates of the Bauer estate, the big, white, plantation-style house nestled about seventy yards off the main drive in a silver grove of aspen. To get to Encampment Creek and Sonny's mine shaft, you have to drive smack through the heart of the Bauer estate on the county's road and circle back toward town and the parcel of public land where Encampment Creek runs into the Laramie River. The road has been a bone of contention between the Bauer clan and the county for generations, with various Bauers trying, so far unsuccessfully, to close it to through traffic.

For its part, the county points to the fact that when the Bauers bought the land, the easement had already been granted in perpetuity by the previous owner, and fishermen need access to this productive stretch of the creek. Besides, there's an unwritten rule in this part of the country that says simply: "Rich people like the Bauers are used to getting what they want everywhere. This isn't everywhere."

It's not that the locals dislike folks like Werner Bauer and his offspring out of some kind of mean reverse snobbery. It's just that down through the years the Bauers have proven themselves to be a thoroughly cantankerous and pushy bunch. Old Werner Bauer bought the estate at foreclosure auction in the 1930s because he needed some place to go to escape the pressures of owning a wildly profitable Chicago brewery. And after displacing the bankrupt family whose forebears had been trying to eke out a living there since homesteading the spread in the 1880s, he couldn't have been surprised to discover that he and the mansion he built weren't exactly going to be welcomed into Victory's society with open arms.

Neither side has warmed much in the last fifty years. While they're in residence at the estate during the summer months, the Bauers ignore the natives. The natives ignore the Bauers. We've found this approach is comfortable for everyone involved.

As we eased the stiff-springed cruiser onto the washboard road at the end of the Bauer corral, the Jeep trail that would take us the last quarter mile to where Sonny said we'd find the entrance to the mine, I noticed the nose of a new brown-and-white Blazer peeking from the barn. I'd seen it around town several times during the summer and knew it belonged to Wolfgang "Tad" Bauer II, Werner's grandson and eventual heir to the brewery fortune. The Bauers generally packed up and left for Chicago around Labor Day. It was unusual for them to be at the estate as late as October.

"Looks like that snowbird hasn't flown," I told Frankie, who was fiddling with the radio, trying to pick up KOWB, the country station out of Laramie.

He finally found what he was after, Dwight Yoakam's "Since I Started Drinking Again." He cranked it up loud. "That's not the half of it," he said over the music. "It looks like he's goin' native. I saw him last weekend at the Cowboy Bar in Laramie, with his arm around some sweetheart's waist. I've seen her around, Harry. She's local."

"Oh, Christ," I muttered. "The next thing you know, he'll be livin' here year-round."

"And there," Frankie chuckled, "goes the neighborhood."

From the back of the Bauer corral, the road drops into one of those Rocky Mountain picture-postcard meadows they use in ads to entice tourists to hop a plane and drop in for a visit. Lodgepole pine, spruce, and quaking aspen, turning bright orange and yellow in honor of fall, dotted the streambed, and the air was filled with the pungent aromas of sage and red dust. In the summer, this meadow would be alive with lupine and Indian paintbrush, and of an evening, the deer and elk would sneak down at sunset for a cool sip of sparkling water from the Encampment.

"It's up there," Sonny said, pointing up a steep, rocky incline that bordered the north end of the meadow. "The entrance is just to the left of that lightning-struck pine."

I'll have to say this much: whoever sunk a mine shaft on the side of that hill had a decent sense of humor. From where we sat in the cruiser, it was less than a hundred yards to the entrance as the crow flies. As a Starbranch walks, though, it might as well have been a thousand miles. I looked up at a wall of granite, boulders the size of Volkswagens, and treacherous scree. "Holy shit, Sonny," I said, "you didn't tell me we'd need a helicopter. What were you doing up there, anyway? Scouting locations for Marlin Perkins?"

He poked his scrawny legs out of the backseat. "It ain't as bad as it looks," he said. "There's a trail that starts in them scrub cedar and goes up easy as you please."

Frankie and I folded ourselves out of the cruiser, stretched our legs, and fiddled with our gun belts. I adjusted my hat and my sunglasses, poked around under the seat of the vehicle until I found my trucker's flashlight, jammed it in the waistband of my pants, and the three of us began our ascent of the hill.

As we pushed our way into the scrub cedar, I noticed that both Frankie and Sonny had dropped back a few yards—standard survival procedure in these hills, although a chickenshit method of demonstrating one's friendship, if you ask me—the theory being that if you walk far enough behind the trailblazer, you'll have plenty of time to haul ass if a rattler pops up and bites him on the shin. I didn't have time to worry about snakes, though, because I had a more pressing concern in the form of what threatened to be a massive heart attack. Maybe starting to smoke again wasn't such a hot idea after all. "Don't worry about the fucking snakes, Frankie," I wheezed. "Carrying me out of here will probably kill you."

"Carry you, my ass." Frankie laughed. "You die up here and we bury you where you fall."

In relative terms, the trail was fairly gentle, winding its way through the boulders and brush. It topped out on a little bench littered with a carpet of pine needles from the huge dead tree that stood sentry at the shaft of the mine—an opening scarcely three feet wide and four feet high, wedged between two massive granite slabs.

"Can you see this opening from the road?" I asked Sonny, who was beginning to leak at the armpits, in spite of the chill breeze sliding down the slope.

Sonny's eyebrows wriggled like flatworms over a couple of eyes that seemed to be moving in opposite directions. "Nah," he said. "I found it on accident. Well, I'd heard it was around here, but I didn't know exactly where. Took me a couple of hours this morning to move the rocks and brush out of the entrance.

"Listen, Harry, you don't mind if I wait here? That woman gives me the creeps."

Of course I didn't mind. I wouldn't have gone in myself if I didn't absolutely have to. There are two things in this world that scare the living crap out of me. One of them is the IRS, and the other is being confined in a closed, dark space. That's what really bothers me about my eventual demise. Being in a casket. Trapped. No way out. I flicked on the flashlight. "Let's make this quick," I told Frankie. "I don't like it any better than Sonny."

As I crabbed through the opening of the shaft, the strong beam of my light danced off the blizzard of dust particles floating like eiderdown on the musty air. Lurking beneath the scent of mold and the slight hint of moisture, though, was another, more pleasant aroma, the odor of campfires. That's common in old caves and other underground spaces that have been used, sometimes hundreds of years ago, as a place to get out of the elements, a shelter from the raging prairie storms, a place to build a small, cheery fire and keep the darkness and the cold at bay. At one point in its history, this shaft, with its smooth floors, had been used for that very purpose.

Lining the walls of the shaft as we inched deeper into the darkness were stout, eight-inch timbers studded with the six-inch, square-cut nails upon which a miner might hang his coal-oil lantern. Here and there, the sandy floor of the shaft was dotted with the bones of small rodents, owl feathers, bat droppings, and the discarded skin of a snake.

And beside one of the timbers, perhaps twenty feet inside the shaft and just where he said it would be, was what appeared to be a human skeleton, her back resting against the sturdy pine as if she had just sat down to catch her breath. Thin wisps of black hair still clung to her jawless skull, now resting at a crazy angle on her backbone. Her arms were crossed over her belly, and as Sonny had reported, there was a small, black hole in her forehead. On her feet were a cracked and dry pair of ladies shoes, the kind my mother wore when I was a kid in LaJunta, Colorado: three-inch heels, ankle straps, and big, velvet bows. Her clothes, what remained of them, were mostly decomposed and rotting, scattered like the brown petals of a faded rose on the ground around her legs.

"Do you think we ought to move her?" Frankie asked. He squatted down on his haunches beside the skeleton and took one of her delicate wrists in his calloused hand. The light from my flashlight reflected on his hammered silver armbands, the bone handle of the bowie knife on his belt.

"Nah," I said, "this didn't happen on our watch. She'll still be here tomorrow for the county boys."

As I spoke, the beam from Frankie's flashlight tracked slowly down her spine to the heavy bone of her pelvis. And there, lying among the tattered bits of cloth from what had been her dress, was another, much tinier skeleton, upside down and curled in upon itself, its small fingers pressed to the sides of what was left of its partially formed cranium.

She'd apparently been pregnant at the time of her death. Whoever killed her had gotten two for the price of one.

2

It seemed like I barely had time to shake the dust off my boots, brew a pot of coffee, and begin the humanitarian process of comforting Sonny—who was feeling guilty because he didn't think we should have left that poor dead woman and her baby alone for the night—when all three lines on the police-department phone started ringing at once.

I can't say I was especially surprised, considering the speed at which rumor travels through a town like Victory.

If you've ever lived in a small town, you know how it is. You know, for example, that one of the reasons weekly newspapers aren't always taken very seriously is that they seldom tell people anything they don't already know. Try as he might, there's no way that Ron Franklin, editor of the *Victory Victor*—which comes out on Wednesdays—can hope to compete with the local gossip pipeline, through which information flows at warp factor eight. By the time interesting and important news appears in the *Victor*, everyone has known all of the basic details for days, as well as the really interesting rumors the newspaper wouldn't print, even if it had them.

In small communities, people sense a rare and unusual event in the same unexplained manner that horses often know hours in advance that a lightning storm or a tornado is likely to sweep through their corner of the universe—and it doesn't take the gossips long to start accumulating particulars. Judging from the number of people currently trying to reach me by phone, it looked like the news—that the skeletal remains of a pregnant murder victim had been discovered by the local eccentric in an abandoned mine shaft on Encampment Creek—had nearly beat the three of us back to town.

I rolled my eyes at Sonny in a "what can you do?" pantomime, picked up the receiver, and punched the first line. I was only slightly relieved to find Mayor Curly Ahearn on the other end.

"What can you tell me, Chief?" Curly said in his officious voice, the one he always uses when he's got people sitting in his office listening to his end of the conversation. If he was alone, Curly would have addressed me by my Christian name, the way he does when we're drinking beer and grilling a couple of steaks at my farm on Saturday evenings.

"Well, Curly . . . excuse me, Mr. Mayor," I said. "At this point, about all I can tell you with a reasonable degree of certainty is that the victim is stone dead. Beyond that, it's pretty much conjecture."

"Come on, Harry," he broke in. "Give me something to go with here. People are worried."

Curly Ahearn is a good mayor, a good friend, and a boss who cuts his employees, myself included, a lot of slack. But he's still a politician, and it always irks me a little when when he puts on that particular hat. I should have given him a break and answered his question like an appropriately subservient municipal employee, but I didn't. "Who's worried, Curly?" I asked testily. "Hell, they haven't had time to get worried. We only found her a little while ago."

"Well, someone heard you talking about it, and now it's all over town," he said. "Was she murdered?"

"Do you want me to guess here, Curly?"

"Whatever."

"Well, then yeah, it looks like someone shot her."

"Any idea who did it?"

"Christ, Curly," I said in frustration. "For all I know, this woman could have been killed before you or I were even born, and the killer didn't drop his wallet or anything to give me a place to start. It could have been anybody, Curly. Maybe we'll hire us a psychic, because that's about the only way I'm going to pick up a scent at this stage in the game."

"So what are you going to do?"

"You want the official line, or the truth?"

"Start with the latter."

"Are we on the speaker phone?"

"No, of course not, Harry. What do you—"

"Okay," I broke in, "first, I'm going to pour Sonny about four fingers of bourbon, and see if I can't get him to quit sweating and shaking. Then, I'm going to have Frankie drive him home. While he's doing that, I'm going to call the county sheriff, the DCI, the coroner, and maybe one of those forensic anthropologists over at the university. Then, I'm going to dump the whole shitaree in their laps and forget about it."

"I see," said Curly, all business now and probably running a rough hand over his bald head. "Now, please tell me about the former."

"You can tell Ron Franklin, who I imagine is sitting within spitting distance of you even as we speak, that we're pursuing a number of leads and should know a great deal more in a few days."

When I finally got off the phone with His Honor, I ignored the beeping phone lines and poured Sonny a healthy dollop of fragrant Kentucky sour mash in a gas-station gimme tumbler, topped off with about six drops of water—branch, as we call it here in the Wild West. Sonny grabbed that glass like he'd just spent a week in the desert, drained the four-ounce ration of sippin' whiskey in a single swallow. As far as I could tell, even that eighty-proof jolt to his system didn't have much calming effect.

I put my hand on his gaunt shoulder. "Sonny," I said, "I know you don't come on something like that every day, but there's nothing to worry about. Whatever happened to her wasn't your fault."

"We shouldn'ta left her," Sonny gurgled. He pulled off his ball cap and ran his fingers through his wiry hair, licked his lips nervously as if they were dry. "Disturbin' the dead is bad enough, but leavin' 'em alone and uncovered is worse."

I would have poured Sonny a second bracer, but I didn't want him getting any more hinky on me than he already was. I put my arm around him and walked him to the door, told him the mystery woman was in professional hands now; someone else would see her to her final resting place. Then, I motioned for Frankie to take him out to the cruiser and drive him home.

"Go home and get some rest, Sonny," I said. "I'm going to call in the authorities."

Who, by the way, showed a remarkable lack of interest in the whole affair.

When I got through to the DCI office in Cheyenne, they said they'd pass the information along to one of their investigators and asked me to make sure they got a copy of the coroner's report. The sheriff's department in Laramie said they'd have a deputy drive out for a look sometime the next afternoon. The coroner was unavailable, and when I told his assistant why I needed to talk to him, I was informed that he'd gone to Old Baldy in Saratoga for a round of golf with the Kiwanis.

The assistant officiously assured me the coroner had left word he wasn't to be disturbed unless it was an emergency, which this wasn't, on account of the fact that the victim had likely been dead longer than the Lindbergh Baby. "I'll have him call you tomorrow," he rasped before hanging up.

The forensic anthropologist from the university, Dr. Walter Kottke, was the only one of the bunch, in fact, who expressed more than a passing curiosity, and said he'd have one of his graduate assistants swing out first thing in the morning, if that was all right with me.

"We're studying how long DNA fingerprinting works in a victim who's been dead for a long while," he explained. "And since it sounds like we can establish an approximate year of death from the shoes, this might give us an opportunity to monitor the accuracy of our procedure. If nothing else, it'll give the student a little experience in the field."

He didn't, I noticed, express the slightest interest in the victim or the nature of her death. He didn't even ask if there was any skeletal evidence he could use to pin down her race, age, or social standing.

I disconnected and picked up the dry and brittle jawbone, turned it over in my hand. Oh well, I thought, I didn't really expect this to excite anyone but Curly, and all he was huffy about is looking good when he's quoted in the next edition of the *Victor.* If none of them was going to worry about the dead woman and her baby on Encampment Creek, then neither was I.

I had more important things to worry about, anyway, like whether I'd lose the $40 bet I'd made with Gus Alzonakis on that night's football game—Broncos versus the Raiders—and whether I had enough clean underwear and socks to postpone the thirty-minute trip to the Laundromat in Laramie until Saturday. I certainly had enough groceries to last me until then, and if I didn't, I could always borrow a loaf of bread and some peanut butter from Edna Cook, my landlady.

As I set the jawbone atop that morning's editions of the *Boomerang* and the *Rocky Mountain News* and pulled my sheepskin coat and my hat from the peg on the wall, it was my firm intention to head for the farm, pull on my Wyoming Police Training Academy sweats, warm up a can of Dinty Moore beef stew, pop the top of an ice-cold can of Coors, and settle back into my battered La-Z-Boy for a relaxing evening of football.

I almost quivered with anticipation. Sometimes, life can be almost unbearably pleasant.

What I didn't count on, of course, was finding Karen Hall's Camaro pulled up next to the front door when I came home.

As I locked my Bronco and loaded up my arms with the beer I'd purchased before heading home, I wondered briefly about the occasion of her visit. I didn't have to wonder long, because she met me at the door wearing a tight, shiny, blue sheath dress, high heels, patterned black stockings, and her blond hair swept back in flowing waves. She stood up on tiptoe to plant a warm kiss on my cheek.

"Hi, Harry." She smiled. "I was driving through the neighborhood and thought you might like one of the T-bones I just happened to have in my car. I used one of your bowls to make a salad. Hope you don't mind."

With that, she shimmied off in the direction of the kitchen, shaking her marvelous derrière in unmistakable invitation. Football? To hell with football.

I'd met Karen about eight months before when, during round five of a heavyweight marital spat, her soon-to-be ex-husband reached across the table at the Trail's End and dumped a strawberry margarita on her head. She responded by grabbing his tie and pulling him, face first, into a huge plate of baby back ribs dripping with very red and sticky barbecue sauce. Her husband couldn't think of a witty rejoinder—not being an especially clever or original thinker when it came to problem resolution—and punched her in the nose. Before long, they were actually wrestling on the floor, sending the patrons of the steak house scattering lest they be accidentally clawed by one of her slashing nails or rendered impotent by a misplaced knee to the groin.

Robbie Moore, realizing that his furniture was at risk, called the cops to come out and restore order, the cop on duty that evening being my own self.

If I tell you what actually happened that night—that I threw Paulie Hall in the slammer after he took a swing at my nose, then took his wife home and made love to her three times—it sounds a bit sordid. But that's basically what happened, although I should mention that the actual physical consummation of our affair came at her suggestion, as well as some of the more acrobatic maneuvers that accompanied our lovemaking.

The next morning, I let Paulie out of jail and didn't see his wife for two months, until she showed up at the Silver Dollar one evening in jeans that had to be restricting her lower-body circulation, to tell me that her divorce was final. It was over a double shot of Old Granddad that she came to the real purpose of her visit. She was thirty-two years old, she said, with two daughters, a lousy car, and a ton of bills. She'd been married to the same spoiled man since she was sixteen, and she was finally rid of him—she never wanted to be responsible for a little boy in a man's body again.

"I'm not looking for a 'real man' to take his place, either, Harry," she told me. "What I would like to do is fool around a little, and you and I have some brief, but very memorable history. You wanna give it a shot?"

As it happened, I was semi-unattached at the time, my latest attempt at reconciliation with my ex-wife, Nicole, having temporarily been derailed by the same old thing, my disinclination to live in a larger community and travel a more promising career path. That being the case, I took Karen up on her suggestion, and we started seeing each other, the twist being that we were a nearly perfect example of the approach-avoidance syndrome. Whenever we started getting along too well—say, for example, after an especially satisfying encounter in the sack—one of us went into the avoidance mode and invariably picked a fight over something totally ridiculous.

Going through an emotionally wrenching divorce, as we both had, often brings out this kind of unsavory behavior in otherwise sane individuals, and that's why pugs like Karen and me wind up together so often. The normal people, the ones who have had time to get over the pain of their divorces, or better yet, had the good sense to stay single, usually avoid people like us like herpes.

After settling Ry Cooder's *Chicken Skin Music* on the stereo, I made my way in the general direction of the kitchen, where I could hear Karen singing along with "This Is the Way We Make a Broken Heart," her voice low and raspy. It was a voice so sexy it made little teeny bumps stand up all over my arms, and I was already thinking about dessert, even before we'd gotten to the main course. I slipped my arms around her waist from behind, pulled her fanny close to my middle. "This is a nice surprise," I said. "To what do I owe the pleasure of your unexpected company?"

As she squirmed out of my lecherous clutches to turn the steaks, I could smell the faint traces of her perfume, Opium. I didn't know which smelled better, Karen or the T-bones, which were giving up the first of their fragrant juices and making a joyous noise.

"I don't know," she said. "I guess I was just missing you and thought we might spend some time. The girls are staying at Sarah's."

"All night?"

"All night, cowboy," she chirped. "You have some wine around here?"

I did indeed, a nice little bottle of Napa Valley red—arrogant, with just a touch of unpredictability. I filled our jelly glasses to the brim.

I don't remember much of the food that came after we'd finished the bottle of wine, although I've never met a steak I didn't like. What I do remember, vividly, is how Karen excused herself from the table as soon as we'd finished and came back about five minutes later wearing nothing but the top half of a lacy white camisole set and those wonderful stockings. With a wicked look in her wide blue eyes, she swung one of her long legs over mine and sat facing me on the kitchen chair, her firm breasts pressing against my chest, her fingers fumbling with the buckle on my belt.

She was like that sometimes, very goal oriented, and it would take a foolish man indeed to suggest that she slow down and enjoy a bit of foreplay. Karen didn't mess around when it came to orgasm, and she wasn't shy about letting me know what she wanted and how to go about giving her pleasure. We were very good together in bed, and it's a damned shame we couldn't find a way to get along better out of one.

After a strenuous and insistent screw on the kitchen chair, I left my clothes jumbled on the floor and we stumbled, arm in arm, toward the bedroom. When the edge of our need was gone, we made leisurely and friendly love, laughing with each other at the sometimes ridiculous sight we made, our various limbs twisting together like a ball of worms.

"Do you think it would be as much fun to watch us make love as it is to do it?" I asked when we'd finished, my finger tracing a line from between her shoulder blades to the small of her back.

"I don't know," she murmured. "I don't know how much fun it would be to watch someone make love with his socks on, although actually making love to him has its entertaining moments."

Smiling, I pulled her close and closed my eyes, the warmth of afterglow more comforting than an old quilt. I suppose I had nearly fallen asleep, my mind drifting in that hazy land between waking and dreams, when Karen pulled herself up on one elbow and said something that tripped my early-warning radar, the alarm that goes off whenever conversation begins to wander onto dangerous ground. "Harry," she said quietly, "do you remember when you told me that you wouldn't mind if I saw other people?"

"Huh?" I said, stalling, hoping to gain three or four seconds to collect my wits.

"Do you remember when you told me that you wouldn't mind if I saw other people?" she said, her voice a bit more firm.

"Yeah," I said, noncommittally, "I guess I remember that."

"Well, would you mind if I saw someone else?"

The pang of hurt and fear that lanced my stomach at that moment was surprising. I certainly hadn't anticipated it, hadn't thought that I'd feel much of anything if this moment came. "Are we talking theoretically, or practically here?" I asked, still stalling, but stalling in a way that made it seem like I was taking part in the discussion.

"Theoretically," she said tentatively.

"Then I guess I wouldn't mind. We're not married to each other, Karen, and I can't tell you who to see and who not to see. I don't think you'd make that kind of demand on me, so what right would I have to make it on you?"

"All right," she said, pulling the sheet up to cover her breasts, "how about in practice?"

There are watershed moments in every relationship, and I knew, even as I considered my answer, that this was a watershed in ours. My answer would determine where our romance went from there, or whether it would go anywhere. On the one hand, I didn't want to lose her, and I suspected that this line of questioning might be her way of determining if I was ready to make a more long-lasting commitment, whether the wounds of my latest split from Nicole had healed over enough to take the strain of living with a new, full-time night woman. A part of me, therefore, wanted to tell her that hell yes, I'd mind if she saw someone else. But there was another part of me, the part that was scared to death of letting another woman get close enough to hurt me, that wanted to extract a bit of revenge for the dull ache her question had aroused in my gut.

I reached for my cigarettes on the nightstand, and my hands shook almost imperceptibly as I struck a match and drew the harsh smoke into my lungs. "Is there someone you want to see?" I asked.

When she answered, her voice was almost a whisper. "Well, I met a guy at school—an assistant English professor—and he's asked me two or three times to go out with him. I guess it might be fun."

"Then I guess I wouldn't mind," I said. Even as the words left my lying lips, I knew I'd just said the most mean-spirited, most ignorant thing a man ever said to a woman. Karen looked away from me then, and when she turned back, I could see, even in the dim glow from the yard lights through my curtains, that she was crying.

"I didn't think you would," she said softly. She swung her long legs out of the bed and padded off toward the kitchen, where she'd left most of her clothes.

I hoisted my own legs out of bed and fumbled around for my shorts. "Karen, I'm sorry," I said. "That's not how I meant for that to sound. Can we talk about this?"

"You made yourself clear, Harry," she called back. There was steel in her voice. "I don't think there's much more we need to say."

In less than three minutes, I heard the sound of the front door closing and the deep-throated rumble of her Camaro as she started the high-performance Detroit engine. You simpleminded son of a bitch, I thought to myself as I heard her rear tires catch gravel at the front of the house. If you let her go now, she may never be back.

I would have gone after her, too, but when I stumbled into the kitchen to find my pants, I found that she'd thrown them right out the front door as she left, spilling the contents of my pockets, including my car keys, into the dust, the cactus, and the sagebrush of my yard. Only a bloodhound could have found them in that mess, so I didn't even try.

I don't think I slept much after that, tossing and turning, replaying our conversation in my mind. And every time, I came up with a response that ended with us making love again instead of causing pain. Eventually, I must have drifted off into a grudging sleep, because the sound of the phone ringing by my bed at 8:30 the next morning was enough to cause my heart to thump in my tired chest.

"Harry Starbranch," I grumbled, my mouth cottony and rancid. "What do you want?"

"Sorry to disturb your beauty rest," clucked Frankie, "but I think you should come down to the office as soon as you can. Somebody broke one of the windows last night and came in."

"Why the hell would anyone want to break into that miserable office?" I asked. "The only thing worth stealing in there is the Mr. Coffee."

"Unfortunately, the Mr. Coffee's still here," Frankie said, "but it looks like they were after something else."

"What?" I sat up, squinted while I fumbled on the nightstand for my smokes.

"That dead woman's jawbone, Harry," Frankie said. "It's gone."

3

I shaved, showered, popped a handful of Excedrin, scrambled around the front yard until I found my keys, and made it to the police department in a little over twenty minutes. The place was a mess—papers strewn on the floor, files and drawers hanging open, wastebaskets tipped. We'd been burglarized, all right, but why we'd been burglarized was anyone's guess. I certainly had no clue. "Have you ever heard of anyone breaking *in* to a police station before?" I asked Frankie.

He jammed files back into one of the cabinets, shoved it closed with a metallic crash. "Nah," he said angrily. "This is a definite first."

According to Frankie, who'd arrived at the station at around 8:00, the burglar had gotten in by smashing a fist-size hole in the glass of one of the alley-side windows and reaching in to undo the latch. Then, it had been a simple matter of pushing the window up and wiggling in. The whole operation carried with it a certain amount of risk, because everyone who's been in town for more than a couple of weeks knows that both Frankie and I keep irregular hours. While we officially close the station at 6:00 in the evening, we split up night duty, making rounds of town and checking in to the station two or three times each evening. We don't keep a regular schedule after closing, so robbing our office would be a dicey proposition. I don't know about most criminals, lacking in brainpower as many of them are, but I sure as hell wouldn't want to be caught by the giant Frankie Bull in the act of ransacking our office files and strewing them all over the floor. With his size and obvious strength—not to mention the sidearm and bowie knife he wears on his belt—Frankie is not the sort of person you trifle with.

Still, that's the gamble this burglar had taken, and all for what looked to be a questionable payoff. I checked the lock on the gun cabinet, which was still secure. "You're sure all he took was the jaw?" I asked.

"That's all I can tell for sure," he said. "But why would anyone want it?"

It was a question with lots of possible answers, none of them very convincing. The pains the burglar had apparently taken to paw through our files indicated that there might be something in them he believed worth stealing, or at least worth knowing about. Maybe he came looking for something else and picked up the jaw as a kind of morbid souvenir. Then again, it might have just been kids who broke in on a lark, trashed the place out of spite, and took the jawbone with them when they left. If it was just the work of teenage thrill seekers, the break-in was nothing more than a nuisance.

I explained my theories to Frankie, who shook his head skeptically. "Maybe so," he said. "But it still doesn't make much sense."

I poked through the debris and came to the same conclusion Frankie had reached. Beyond the jawbone, nothing else seemed to be missing from the office. I picked up a pile of newspapers and police reports that had been swept from the surface of my desk to the floor. When I had them reassembled in a relatively neat pile, I reached tentatively for the phone. "Did you call the sheriff's department to see if they'd send someone out to take fingerprints?" I asked.

Frankie dropped to his knees to peer under my desk. "Done deal, Harry," he said. "They say they'd already planned to send a deputy out this afternoon to look at those bones, and he can dust for prints while he's here."

That was fine with me. I could have dusted myself, but that kind of fine-detail forensic work has never been my strong suit, and I smudge more prints than I save.

I had moved on to another pile of debris in the corner when I heard Frankie blow air threw his teeth and mutter a stunned "Oh, shit."

He stood up holding several pieces of broken-ceramic something in his big hands, shaking his head sadly. "Man, Harry, you're not going to like this one bit. The bastard smashed your coffee cup!"

* * *

Since ours is a small office, it didn't take us long to restore a semblance of order, order being a relative term where Frankie and I are concerned. My I HAVE PMS coffee mug, however, appeared to be a total loss. With Frankie out making rounds, I was sitting at my newly tidied desk, pondering the missing jawbone and trying to glue the shattered mug back together, when a blast of prairie wind and brittle leaves through the open door announced the arrival of a visitor.

"Chief Starbranch?" the woman asked, offering me her hand. "My name is Ellen Vaughn. From the university anthropology department. I hear you found some bones?"

I took her hand, felt a grip that was stronger than I'd expected. "Glad to meet ya, Ellen Vaughn," I said.

About five-six and 115 pounds, she looked to be in her middle twenties, with the shoulder-length dark curly hair, milky skin, and freckled nose that often indicates a Celtic background. Although she would never be called beautiful, Ellen Vaughn was a striking young woman, with an angular face and a healthy-looking runner's body. The kind of woman Norwegian farm kids like me always seem to spend our lives pursuing, unless we're nearly old enough to be their fathers. When we're that old, we just trip all over ourselves trying to be nice. "You couldn't have come at a better time," I told her truthfully.

As I busied myself at the Mr. Coffee and rambled on about our morning's excitement, Ellen shucked her anorak, ran her fingers through her mane, and took stock of our tiny office. It seemed to meet with her approval, because by the time I had brewed enough to fill two cups, she had made herself comfortable on one of our swaybacked chairs and was smiling at the photo of Lloyd Baxter's tombstone on my office wall. HERE LIES LLOYD BAXTER, the tombstone reads. SELF ABUSE KILLED HIM.

She nodded in the direction of the photo. "Is that for real?" she asked.

"Sure enough," I said, sipping the rank coffee. "His brother, a friend of mine, put that on his grave as a practical joke. At least one of them is still laughing about it."

Ellen smiled at the kind of person who would give his own brother such a send-off, but the smile faded perceptibly when she got around to the subject of her visit. Professor Kottke, she said, had given her the assignment of having a look at the skeleton we'd discovered and taking some bone samples for DNA tests. As far as she was concerned, it was busywork, since the procedure had already been thoroughly tested. Still, one didn't argue with the tweedy old coots in Laramie's ivory towers, especially if the tweedy old coot in question was one's thesis adviser.

I pushed my chair back and pulled my hat on my head, tilted it to what I hoped was a rakish angle. "Then I'll make you a deal," I said. "I'll take you out there right now, and then I'll show you where to get the best lunch in Wyoming. My treat."

She showed me that pleasant smile one more time. "Chief Starbranch," she said, "you have yourself a bargain."

The best way to get over losing a woman, my old granddaddy used to say, is to get yourself another woman. And while my intentions toward Ellen Vaughn were professional and honorable, I can honestly say that just having her next to me in the Bronco that morning went a long way toward loosening the knot that had been in my stomach since Karen's stormy exit the night before. As we drove, she told me a little about herself.

A Casper girl, she'd gotten her B.S. in anthropology at the university and upon graduating had been offered an assistantship that would pay her tuition and bring in a little spending money while she worked on her master's. Kottke, she said, was a pompous ass and a slave driver, but he was also the only forensic anthropologist on the faculty, and since that was her chosen field, it was Kottke or nothing. Pompous or not, she admitted, she was learning plenty from him about old bones, about the people the bones belonged to, and what might have caused their former owners' demise.

I'd like to tell you that I engaged her in an informed and erudite discussion about how similar our professions are, both of us adding up evidence and then coming to a conclusion, and how I found it purely fascinating that just by looking at a couple of hoary fibulas and dibulas a person who knows her stuff can tell you whether its owner had the scurvy, rheumatism, or gout. I'd like to tell you that instead of acting like some frustrated, adolescent poonhound, I acted like a mature, forty-something professional law-enforcement officer.

But that would be a lie. Truth is, I couldn't keep my eyes off her, the way the light caught her hair, the way her taut, round bottom worked beneath her jeans, the way her legs flexed as we climbed the hill, me wheezing and wanting to die with every step, trying to hide it.

I'd also like to tell you that after showing Ellen Vaughn the bones of the mystery woman and her fetus, the sharp-witted grad assistant was able to take a quick tour of the immediate area, poke a little here, prod a little there, and announce, in a completely confident voice that, "What we have here are the bones of a certain Bessie May Colter, who died, by the looks of things, in the year 1946 at the age of twenty-two, the victim of a traveling salesman named Jesse Carp, who lived in Omaha, Nebraska and, unless I miss my guess, drove a late-model Buick with a ding in the right front fender."

But that would be a lie, too—because when we got there, we found a lot of nothing. Well, the lightning-struck tree was still there. The mine shaft was still there. The snake skin was still on the floor of the shaft. But against the massive timber where the woman's body had rested in death, there was nothing at all. The skeleton was gone, and all that remained were the tattered remnants of the woman's clothes. There were drag marks in the sand on the floor of the mine shaft, and in places I could make out the waffled imprint of a heavy work boot, the kind Sonny had been wearing the day before.

"That damned Sonny," I grunted as I swept the entrance to the shaft with the beam of my flashlight. "He must have come back here last night and taken her home so she wouldn't feel lonesome."

It wasn't an especially brilliant deduction, but it seemed to make sense at the time. Say what you want about Sonny Toms, the man was unpredictable. Legend around Victory has it that during the Arab oil embargo, Sonny actually pushed his old truck into town by hand to save gas, loaded it up with groceries, and pushed it right back out to his place.

I don't imagine that's the way it really happened, since Sonny didn't weigh as much as a jack handle. But legends grow from little grains of fact, and I suspect this one sprouted up as an illustration of Sonny's generally contrary approach to life. Sonny was the kind of stubborn man who would push his pickup all the way into town to save a dollar's worth of fuel, and he was the kind who'd steal a long-dead woman's bones and take them home with him—not because he had some perverted designs on the remains, but because he was feeling guilty that she'd been left alone in that cold, dark burrow scratched in the rock over Encampment Creek.

"I suppose we're going to have to drive out to Sonny Toms' before that lunch I promised you," I told Ellen, who listened to my theory with a bemused grin crinkling the corners of her mouth.

"You think this Sonny took the bones?" she asked.

I shrugged, pulled my sunglasses out of my pocket, put them on, and asked a purely rhetorical question. "Who else?"

If there's anything that looks more out of place than a 1955 Airstream trailer parked in the middle of the prairie and watched over by a twenty-five-foot wooden jackalope—a relic of Sonny's abbreviated career as a chain-saw artist—I can't imagine what it is.

Sonny's place, located a quarter of a mile off an unpaved, secondary county road, was a veritable museum of the bizarre and useless, putting even the tourist traps littering the Black Hills of South Dakota to shame. To keep the jackalope company, he had a gigantic wooden Indian brandishing a tomahawk who stood sentry near the door of his shed, an eighteen-foot plaster elk that he picked up at a dude ranch on Togwotee Pass serving as an oversize and out-of-proportion lawn ornament—not that he had a lawn—and a life-size, ceramic grizzly bear holding a sign reading BEARLY GETTIN' BY, lurking on the porch he built to go around the front of his trailer. Just for good measure, his twenty-acre plot was jammed cheek by jowl with every other widget and gilhoolie an ambitious pack rat could find and drag home in thirty-odd years—baby carriages and washing machines, scrap lumber and refrigerators, rusted Studebakers and geriatric John Deeres, bar stools and bed frames.

"It's a good thing Curly Ahearn hasn't seen this lately," I told Ellen as we eased over the metal cattle guard leading up to his hovel. "He'd want to have it declared a toxic-waste dump so he could apply for cleanup money from the Superfund."

Sonny's driveway was storm rutted, with a thick growth of ragweed, tumbleweed, and crabgrass sprouting up in the rocky tracks. The barbed-wire fence around his place, which Frankie and I helped mend two years before, was sagging from the weight of neglect. The wooden planks that made up his front porch needed paint, and so did his old International Harvester. Only the shiny Airstream itself, sparkling in the bright October sunshine, seemed to defy time and decay. Which made it seem even more out of place, surrounded by rubble and otherworldly paraphernalia.

I let the Bronco roll to a stop under a silver aspen and switched off the engine. "Wait just a minute," I told Ellen, who had cracked her door. "Let's give Sonny and T-Bone a minute to figure out they've got company. T-Bone doesn't like anybody walking in unannounced."

They say God looks out for idiots and drunks, but since Sonny Toms isn't a full-time subscriber to either of those denominations, many people in Victory breathed a little sigh of relief when he'd had the good sense to adopt a German shepherd-Doberman–cross pup named T-Bone to fill in for the Creator. The dog, for his part, realized his good fortune immediately upon being introduced to his new home, where the rabbit population was reaching maximum density, where Sonny was always handy with a ten-pound bag of soup bones if he didn't feel like hunting for his supper, and where nobody cared if he slept inside on the worst winter nights. Sonny profited from the confederation because even a beer-swilling lumberjack will think twice about picking on a scrawny half-pint like Sonny, if the scrawny half-pint is accompanied by ninety pounds of snarling, slobbering hound dog that looks mean enough to eat railroad spikes and shit tenpenny nails.

For years, the pair were inseparable, with T-Bone a permanent fixture in the back of Sonny's old Harvester, mouth wide open and snout pointed into the wind. But these days, T-Bone is getting a little long in the tooth and is in semiretirement as a full-time house sitter for Sonny's Airstream. Still, it doesn't pay to surprise him, because so far he's still got his own teeth.

The procedure when visiting Sonny was to park in the driveway with the windows up, and after a while T-Bone would shuffle out to look you over. If he recognized you when he planted his saucer-size paws on your car door and peered in with his rheumy old eyes, he'd sit down and wag his tail until you got out to scratch his flea-infested ears. If he didn't like what he saw, his ears would go back and his lips would curl, baring a couple of ice-pick-size fangs. Nobody was quite sure what he'd do if you ignored his polite request to go away and got out of your vehicle at this point, because it had never been tried. I suspected it wouldn't be pretty.

From where we'd parked, I could see a patch of the dog's dun-colored hide in the shadows at the side of the porch, and his lack of movement suggested that in addition to the other infirmities of old age, he might be getting hard of hearing. I gave the horn a blast to get his attention.

When even that rude wake-up call failed to get the sleeping mutt's notice, I slipped out of the Bronco and cocked my ear to the silence, my nostrils treated to the pungent aroma of sage carried on the breeze. On the other side of the car, I heard Ellen's door close softly. We stood there for a moment, listening to the melodic jangling of some wind chimes hanging in the branches of a willow tree over by the shed and the love song of a magpie, the only sounds breaking the morning stillness.

The tourists who come to Wyoming in summer are often surprised, even frightened, by the quiet that sometimes envelops you on the Western prairie. Used to the background noise of civilization—the trilling of telephones, the insistent voices of radio announcers, the throaty rumble of eighteen-wheelers gearing down for a long climb on a distant freeway—their civilized brains can't adjust to its absence. And while they can't always put a name to their discomfort, the combination of the quiet and the emptiness of the landscape, uncluttered by signs, buildings, and in most cases foliage, is often enough to send them scampering back home, complaining all the way about the godforsaken desert, where it's always a hundred miles between towns and where they drove thirty miles one morning without passing a single car going the opposite direction.

"Hey, T-Bone!" I called, scuffing off in the direction of the porch, the toes of my boots making little mushroom clouds of dust above the cracked and dry ground. "Come say hello, you mangy mongrel. I've got someone here I want you to meet."

Behind me, Ellen followed with short, hesitant steps.

"Will he bite?" she whispered, taking hold of my bicep and digging in.

"Nah," I said, "just stand still and let him look you over. When he's satisfied, we'll go in and roust Sonny out of bed."

By the time we reached the middle of the driveway and T-Bone still hadn't expressed even a passing interest in our unannounced arrival, the first twinges of uneasiness began to poke at the back of my spine. And when I saw that the door of Sonny's trailer was open about six inches, the doorsill coated with a small drift of fine dust from the early-morning wind coming down off the Snowies, the twinges became Klaxons of alarm.

"There's something wrong here," I told Ellen, eyeing the door and the curtained windows of the trailer and bringing my hand down to unsnap the holster of my .357 Ruger Blackhawk. Still facing the doorway, I sidestepped along the porch toward T-Bone, the dog's body completely visible in the shadows now, his tongue hanging out and his legs extended in rigor mortis. Around the animal's snout, a swarm of green bottle flies buzzed, landing on his glassy eyes and frolicking in the pool of thick, blackening blood congealed around his open mouth.

The cause of his death was obvious—a small, crusted bullet hole right above the bridge of his nose.

"Get back in the car!" I whispered to Ellen, who back-stepped her way to the Bronco, edged around to the passenger's side, and slipped in, never taking her eyes off the gruesome tableau. When I heard her door close, I decided it was time to move. Drawing my revolver and thumbing the hammer back, I flattened myself against the side of the trailer next to the ceramic bear and nudged the door open with my foot. It opened easily, and along with the gentle brush of cooler air from the Airstream came an almost metallic, sweet aroma that was all too familiar to me. The coppery smell of blood.

Although I'd never been inside before, Airstream trailers like Sonny's are all laid out in the same fashion. The front door opens on a small sitting room, and a narrow hallway leads through a tiny, partitioned kitchenette to a small bathroom and a bedroom at the back, just large enough for a double bed and a tiny dresser.

Cautiously, I slithered through the open doorway and into the sitting room, squatting on my haunches and sweeping the room with the muzzle of my Blackhawk. As my eyes adjusted to the relative darkness inside the trailer, I was struck by the orderliness and absolute cleanliness of Sonny's immediate living quarters, the eight-by-ten room a striking contrast to the general clutter and chaos that characterized the rest of his life. Spotless white curtains draped every window, and over the backs of an old recliner and a small sofa, he'd thrown colorful afghans, probably prizes picked up at one of the garage sales he haunted in Laramie on Sunday afternoons. On a small, brass stand rested a dust-free sixteen-inch color television, atop which sat a framed black-and-white high school graduation photograph of a much younger Sonny wearing a black high school graduation robe and mortarboard, his arm around the slim waist of a fresh-faced, smiling, and similarly attired young woman. It was the only picture in the room, the last thing he must have looked at as he removed the greasy pair of work boots lined up beside his chair.

Down the hall, I could see the back of a wooden chair, the only piece of furniture visible in the partitioned kitchenette from my vantage point, and beyond that, at the end of the hallway covered with a tidy hooked rug, the foot of his bed and a bit of the blue and white patchwork quilt that covered it.

I saw plenty of carnage in my years as a homicide detective in Denver, and I figured I'd seen just about every nasty thing one human being can think of when trying to inflict pain on another. But I still wasn't prepared for the grisly sight that greeted me when I duck walked around the kitchen partition and got a look at what was behind it. There—his wrists tied to the arms of a maple captain's chair with bent coat hangers, two broken fingers on his left hand pointing upward at right angles to the back of his hand, his face pockmarked with small, ugly round wounds that looked like burns, his throat slashed from ear to ear below his jawline, and worst of all, the skin peeled from his chest and his nipples severed—was the body of Sonny Toms.

I don't know how long I stayed there, acid burning the back of my throat and my head spinning from dizziness, but it must have been quite a while, at least long enough for Ellen to become so worried that she decided to follow me. I heard her yelp as she got close enough to T-Bone to see what had killed him, but even that wasn't enough to bring me back to my senses. I was still sitting there, numb and in a kind of stupor, when she worked up enough courage to follow me inside the trailer and to the kitchenette, where the sight of Sonny's face, hideously contorted in its rictus grin, caused her to scream even louder, a scream filled with loathing and dread.

"My God!" she groaned, and backed away quickly, her hand pressed to her mouth and her stomach heaving, the contents seeping through her clenched fingers.

It was a perfectly normal reaction given the circumstances—and one that echoed my own queasy sentiments exactly.

4

From the police-department's office, where eight surly law enforcement officers—Albany County Sheriff Anthony Baldi, three sheriff's deputies, two officers of the Wyoming Highway Patrol, Frankie, and myself—as well as a still-shaken Ellen Vaughn, had spent the evening trying to make sense of the situation, we could look out through the steamy window and see a growing knot of townies hanging around outside, braving wind, dust, and growing chill in an effort to get the real story a little earlier than their neighbors.

If the discovery of a few old bones was enough to set the hearts of Victory's gossipmongers pounding, the news that an honest-to-God murder had taken place nearly pushed them over the edge. In my time in Victory, nothing had primed their morbid curiosities or their fertile imaginations like Sonny's death, and the knowledge that there might be a killer among them had them quivering with unprecedented fervor.

Across the street at Shapiro's Hardware, Howard Shapiro and Billy Sun could barely keep up with the avalanche of customers who just dropped in to buy a new handgun and enough ammunition to fill a shopping bag. When they ran out of handguns, Howard made a significant dent in his overstocked supply of hunting rifles and shotguns.

And Howard certainly wasn't the only merchant who had a good day on Sonny's tab. The bars were all full of beer-swilling gossipers, and at Ginny Larsen's, the cook ran out of the dinner special—roast pork, fried apples, and mashed potatoes—by 5:30, setting a new record. By 9:30, people were still waiting ten deep for a seat at one of her fifteen booths, the night cook slinging burgers and hot turkey sandwiches as patrons lingered and shared what little information each of them had.

If they were waiting for any of us to give them answers, they were out of luck.

"I still don't get it," said Albany County Sheriff Anthony Baldi, who was in charge of the investigation, the site of Sonny's killing being several miles out of my jurisdiction. A big man whose stocky frame might have been muscular in high school, Baldi had gone to flab. His legs, while muscular enough, looked completely out of proportion to the bulge of his stomach, which stuck out over his belt in a huge pillow of fat. His salt-and-pepper hair was longish, plastered to his head with about a half gallon of Brylcreem. His eyes were small and bloodshot, almost lost behind the reddish bulge of his cheeks, his teeth tobacco stained and yellow behind thin lips, which seemed frozen in a perpetual sneer. His neck looked doughy and dirty around the white collar of his sheriff's department uniform. "You were going out there to see if he swiped some old bones found on the edge of town? Did you think he killed whoever they belonged to?" Baldi asked sarcastically.

"Nah, Anthony," I explained for at least the thousandth time. "I thought he might have taken her home so she wouldn't be lonesome. I don't think Sonny killed anybody."

Anthony gave me a look that said he thought I was some kind of small-town rube who just jumped off the beet topper. I hate it when he does that, which is just about every time I see him. That's maybe the best reason I've got for disliking him as much as I do, the second best being that he's a bully to his men and an arrogant flesh-pressing jerk who personifies everything I can't stand in the practitioners of my profession. Of course the fact that he was my opponent before I'd dropped out of the race for Albany County sheriff the previous year and had said numerous nasty things about me during the primary campaign didn't improve my opinion of him. I hold a grudge with the best of them.

Baldi picked up my patched coffee mug—it would never hold fluid without leaking again—and shook his head in doubt, a maneuver that set the flesh of his thick neck aquiver. "So, do you think whoever killed Sonny killed the bones lady, too?" he asked, his voice dripping sarcasm and condescension.

I fought down the urge to say something derogatory about his mother, maybe punch him in the face. Instead, I grabbed the precious mug out of his paws and slammed it down on the desk top, shattered it beyond redemption. "It's a theory, Anthony," I said between clenched teeth. "And it's one we might have been able to work on if you had gotten one of your deputies out here for a look yesterday afternoon when I called instead of waiting until the evidence grew legs and walked off."

The two Wyoming Highway Patrol officers and Frankie chuckled aloud, because they didn't answer to Anthony, and the deputies bit their lips and knuckles, because they did. Ellen Vaughn, who found no humor anywhere in this investigation, just slumped her shoulders a little further and went back to staring at her feet.

Anthony, meanwhile, looked like a pressure cooker. The little blue veins on his nose stood out like little twisted skeins of garden hose with the water on full and the nozzles closed. His neck and cheeks flushed the color of red long johns.

"All we want is a little cooperation, Starbranch," he growled. As he spoke, he bent toward where I was sitting in my chair, and flecks of spittle sprayed my face. "It's the least you can do, considering that I get the feeling you're not telling me everything you know, considering that you were out of your jurisdiction going out there in the first place, and considering you made such a mess at the scene that we can't tell what's important and what isn't."

I assume he was talking about the fact that Ellen had gotten sick in Sonny's living room, but it's dangerous to make assumptions when it comes to Tony. I didn't like him picking on Ellen in any event; she felt bad enough as it was. I wiped his spittle off my face with the back of my hand, pushed out of my chair, and stuck my face in his. "From what I've seen, Anthony," I said angrily, "you don't need any help when it comes to fucking up a crime scene. Did you get a photographer out there before you moved Sonny? Nope. You moved him yourself, laid him right out on the stretcher. Did you get the fingerprint and forensic technicians in before you let a whole squad of deputies go in there, picking things up and marching around like a herd of buffalo? Nope. The only good fingerprints on anything at Sonny's are going to turn out to be your own. So don't go blaming Ellen or me for fouling up a crime scene."

His little veins were really jumping now, and he was starting to sputter some snappy comeback. I didn't give him a chance. "And did you even think about fingerprinting this office? Well, no, you didn't. You don't know horseshit from hog jowls when it comes to crime-scene investigation, Anthony, so why don't you just cut the crap and admit that none of us knows any more than you about what's going on here."

If I only had a paper bag handy, I would have gladly given it to Anthony, because he looked like he was hyperventilating. "I'm the highest-ranking goddamned law officer in this county," he croaked. He was having a hard time forming the words around his clenched teeth. "I could order you in for a deposition, and hold you in contempt if you didn't do it. I could make your life miserable, Starbranch."

I moved away from him, smiled grandly, and opened the front door. "Well, Anthony," I said, "you've already made me miserable, just by being here. But here's something that may surprise you. I'm the highest-ranking goddamned law officer in this town, and I say it's time for you to get the fuck out of my office."

Anthony looked at me for a minute, measuring my determination, and then took a longer look at Frankie, who—in spite of the silver ear cuffs peeking out from beneath his long braid—looked as deadly as a panther. Then Baldi took a quick look at his smirking deputies, from whom he knew he could count on nothing, and stormed out into the night, blasting his way through the small crowd of onlookers like a boar hog through a flock of geese. "You ain't so smart as you think, Starbranch," he hollered from the door of his brand-new sheriff's department Blazer, paid for with Albany County tax dollars. "There are plenty of things I know about what's going on around here that you don't."

I would have asked him what he meant by that, but in the words of Rhett Butler, a great American, I didn't give a damn.

* * *

Ellen finished the last of her coffee and wiped the cup with a paper towel. When it was clean enough to suit her, she replaced the cup on the rack that hangs above the coffeemaker. She sounded tired and looked worse. "Unless you need me anymore, Harry, I'm going to think about heading home," she said.

I nodded my assent, finished the lukewarm coffee in my own mug, and lit another smoke. "I've got your number if I need anything," I said. "Would you like one of us to follow you?"

A small line creased her forehead. "No, thanks," she said. "I'll be fine. I probably just need a little sleep, and things will look better in the morning. This whole day seems pretty unreal."

While Ellen was shrugging into her jacket, I stood up and pulled the blinds on the front window of the office, locked the door, and started rummaging through the bottom drawer of my desk, where I keep a pint of Jack Daniel's. "I don't know about the two of you," I told Frankie and Ellen as I sloshed three fingers of sour mash into one of the foam cups cluttering my desk, "but I could use a drink." I looked questioningly at Ellen. "Just one before you go?"

She hesitated, then nodded her head yes. "Maybe one, Harry." She said weakly. "I like it neat."

I looked at Frankie, who was walking to the coatrack at the front door, where he had hung his down police jacket and gray cowboy hat. "Frankie?" I asked. "A short one?"

He shook his head no. "You go ahead," he said. "I'll go send the Lookie-Loos packing and make the rounds." He looked dubiously at the whiskey, couldn't resist giving me some advice. "You look like you could use a little rest yourself, Harry."

I rubbed the bridge of my nose and took a deep sip of the bourbon, sighed as the whiskey made a small fire in the pit of my stomach. "I suppose I could at that," I admitted. As the warmth of the bourbon radiated outward, I could feel the muscles in my neck and along my jawline begin to relax.

Frankie checked the charge on his sixteen-inch flashlight and adjusted his holster belt so that it rode a little more comfortably on his muscular stomach. "Hey, Chief?" he said, looking up.

"What is it, Frankie?"

"You have any idea what's going on around here? Who the hell would kill Sonny Toms? And skinning him, for Christ's sake. You have any ideas about that?"

"Not a clue," I said. I had no idea who'd killed Sonny, why they'd tortured him.

"Neither do I," he said sadly. He zipped his coat around his throat and looked through the blinds into the night, which was turning much colder as ten o'clock approached. The first misty drops of rain—rain that could quickly turn to snow—were being driven against the front of the building like grains of blasted sand. "But I've got a feeling it isn't over."

When Frankie had gone—the wind sweeping through the open door and carrying with it the damp smell of winter—Ellen and I sat in meditative silence for several minutes, she sipping her bourbon and me working on a second.

"I've never seen anything like that before," she said finally, searching my face with her dark brown eyes, a bit red around the edges from fatigue and the night's cigarette and cigar smoke in the close office. "It's not at all like the movies, is it?"

"Not many people on the civilian side ever see that," I told her, knowing there was nothing I could say that would really make what she was feeling any better. I pulled my chair forward until I was near enough to put my hands on her shoulders. "Listen, Ellen," I said. "I feel horrible, not only about Sonny, but about dragging you into it. I shouldn't have put you through it, and I'm sorry."

She rested her hand gently on my forearm. "You didn't know he was dead," she said softly. "And you told me to get back in the car. It's not your fault."

But it was and I knew it. One thing that had been bothering me more than a little all day was the disquieting knowledge that my instincts had gotten duller during the years I'd spent in Victory. In the old days, I would never have allowed her to get out of the car in the first place until I'd made sure it was safe. A good cop doesn't allow civilians in his care to get themselves in trouble. After finding Sonny's corpse, I wouldn't have knelt there for God knows how long like some weak-kneed rookie while that same civilian was out of my sight and vulnerable.

I tried to tell myself that my negligence was understandable, since there was no reason to suspect we were walking into a slaughterhouse, but no matter how you prettied it up, the truth was I seemed to have forgotten one of the most basic rules of police work. I wondered how many others I'd forgotten.

As the whiskey continued to work on my nervous system, I knew it was time to make a choice. I could pour myself a third and maybe a fourth, and risk sliding into what could turn into a sucking swamp of maudlin self-pity. Or I could cork the bottle and do something a bit easier on my forty-something body, like eating, which I suddenly remembered I hadn't done all day. "You feel like a steak?" I asked Ellen. "You haven't eaten all day, either, and it's not safe, in my professional opinion, to drive on an empty stomach. I'm buying. . . ."

"Thanks, Harry," she said. She swung her legs off the desk, where she'd been stretching them as she sipped her bourbon, then bent to tighten the laces on her boots. "But I don't think I feel much like eating. Maybe some other time?"

I reached for the bottle and my pack of smokes. "What are you doing tomorrow night?" I asked, hopefully.

She bent down to grace my cheek with a very proper kiss. "I'll give you a call if I get hungry," she said, her face creased in a weak smile. "And Harry," she said, tapping her nail against my pack of Marlboros. "You ought to give these things up. They make you smell like an ashtray."

I peeked through the blinds at the window after we'd finished our good-byes and watched as she started the cold engine on her black Honda Civic, then got out with a scraper and brush to dispatch the blanket of slush that had accumulated on her windshield, a small cloud of exhaust from her idling Honda hovering in the frigid air.

As she bent over from the driver's side to clear the slush on the passenger's side, I looked beyond her and saw something coming down the street that promised to make what was left of the day even worse than it had already been. About a block away Ron Franklin, editor of the *Victory Victor,* Woody Baker, a reporter for the *Boomerang,* and Sally Sheridan, the Laramie correspondent for the *Casper Star-Tribune,* were marching purposefully up the sidewalk in my direction, Franklin and Sheridan clutching white reporter's notebooks and Woody trying to jam a flashbulb—I think he's the only reporter in the world who still has a camera old enough to require them—into his prehistoric Argus.

"No friggin' chance," I said to myself as I pulled my hat and coat from the peg and flicked the light switch off. I bumped through the office toward the back door and reached it just as one of the trio started pounding on the front. There was absolutely no way I was going to hang around to be grilled by those three vultures, me with no real information and plenty of whiskey on my breath. Woody and Sally Sheridan might have been awash in righteous indignation over the fact that I'd been drinking on the job, even if it was late in the evening of a long day, but Franklin would have wanted to share. And since the man can't hold his liquor, before long he'd have been wearing one of my hats backward and wanting to look at my gun.

"I'm doing you a favor, Ron," I muttered as I clicked the door shut behind me and edged into the shadows of the alley, my plan being to wait until they gave up—which I predicted would take about three minutes on account of the growing cold—then sneak back around to where my Bronco was parked at the front of the office and be off before anyone was the wiser.

The plan worked like a charm, incidentally, but the next morning I wished I'd had the good sense to leave the Jack Daniel's at the office instead of carting it home in my pocket so I'd have it in easy reach.

5

I don't know what happens to people between the last snowstorm of the season, which usually comes to the Snowy Range in late May or early June, and the first snowfall of the next season, usually sometime in late October, but it's like most of them forget everything they ever learned about winter driving. On the day of the first bad snowfall, I can count on writing more accident reports and making more phone calls to the tow company in Laramie than I usually make in six months.

"The word *idiots* springs to mind," Frankie grumbled the next morning as we sloshed through ten inches of heavy, wet snow to inspect the first casualty of the day, a collision between the only two vehicles that appeared to have been on Victory's streets at 6:30 A.M. Ray Hladky, a spindly legged scarecrow of a man who owned a driving school in Peoria, Illinois, before he moved to Victory ten years ago, had gotten tired of waiting for the light to turn green at the four-way intersection on Main, and had driven his half-ton Power Wagon right through the red light and smack into the driver's side door of Carrie Wilson's red Yugo. No injuries, thankfully, but threats of lawsuits all around.

That was pretty much how it went for the next two days—one accident after another, including a spectacular crash when a semi carrying a load of sheep missed the turn at the ski area north of town, flipped over, and sent 150 fear-crazed sheep scurrying down the highway and into the path of oncoming traffic. We were busy with both wrecks and terrorized sheep—and looking on the positive side, at least the storm and its attendant traffic disasters temporarily took my mind off my personal troubles, to wit, Karen and my hangover. On the down side, I had no time to do much looking into Sonny's murder.

There were two breaks in the pattern.

One, the manhunt for a life-insurance salesman from Cheyenne who broke one of the cardinal rules of winter survival and walked away from his car after it got stuck in a drift, thinking he could make it the five or six miles back to town before he froze to death. When we found him, he was still alive, but it was up in the air whether he'd lose his nose from frostbite.

Two, a call from Howard Shapiro to complain that someone had snuck into the alley behind his hardware store the night before and spray painted the entire back wall of the building with racist and anti-Semitic graffiti *again*—HITLER WAS RIGHT and BURN THE JEWS in crude, fluorescent red letters six feet high, a few jagged swastikas to round out the effect.

The Shapiro family has been in Victory since the late part of the 1800s, long enough that most of us don't even think about the fact that they're Jewish, except around the traditional Hebrew holidays, when they open the doors of the hardware store and invite everyone to stop in for ethnic treats. They're part of the family around here, and I felt a growing anger that they'd been violated in my town.

"Fucking kids," Shapiro grumbled when I arrived to take some Polaroids of the damage while he painted over the graffiti with a fresh coat of white paint. A tall man with collar-length white hair and work-scarred hands, he was wearing paint-spattered jeans, work boots, and a long khaki hunting jacket. He looked more like a lumberjack than a businessman. "Where do they come up with this shit?"

"We'll find 'em, Howard," I said. I made a mental note to check on the recent whereabouts of a couple of our more notorious teenage reprobates. If they didn't do the artwork at Shapiro's themselves, they might have an idea who did.

Howard jammed his paintbrush in the paint bucket, slashed on a brushful of paint. "You do that, Harry!" he said angrily. "We don't want these little pricks thinking they can pull this crap in our town."

He gave the wall a vicious swipe with his brush. "Or anywhere else, for that matter."

Needless to say, Anthony Baldi made no more progress on the murder investigation during that forty-eight-hour period than I did, although the storm had little to do with his lack of productivity.

The killer hadn't left many clues at Sonny's Airstream, and the few he may have overlooked were, as I suspected, obliterated by Tony's slipshod handling of the crime scene. The fingerprint technicians found plenty of Anthony's prints, and just as many from his deputies, and of course Sonny's were everywhere. But the two partials they found on the top of Sonny's kitchen table and the one they found on the arm of the chair were smudged beyond recognition. The killer had apparently taken the knife he used to kill Sonny and his implements of torture with him when he left, and there wasn't any other physical evidence that was useful, except a couple of spare coat hangers.

When they finally got around to checking around our office, the technicians found no fingerprints that were usable there, either.

The coroner's report, which was released the day after Sonny's autopsy in Laramie, told us pretty much what we already knew. Sonny had been tortured, burned with cigarettes, and had two of his fingers broken before the killer finished him off by slicing his jugular vein and his carotid arteries with a very sharp knife. One stroke, the coroner said.

According to the coroner, Sonny died between 10:00 P.M. and midnight, just about the time Karen and I were thinking about heading for the bedroom in pursuit of multiple orgasms. There was no sign of forced entry at the Airstream, and the coroner found no bruises or abrasions on Sonny's corpse, other than the ones inflicted during the torture.

I learned one other interesting tidbit of information from T. J. Bell, one of Anthony's deputies who had stopped in at Ginny's for coffee in between trips to Sonny's and tours of Highway 130 between Victory and Laramie in search of stranded motorists. Although they'd looked everywhere at the trailer and searched the junkyard thoroughly, the sheriff's investigators hadn't found the bones of the woman Sonny had found in the mine shaft over Encampment Creek.

If Sonny had taken the jawbone of the Mystery Madonna—as she was being called in stories written for the *Boomerang* by Woody Baker—from my office, and the rest of the bones from the shaft, they weren't at his place after he died.

Forty-eight hours after the first snowflakes began falling, the storm had broken, the highway department had cleared the roads from Laramie all the way to Snowy Range Pass, and the residents of Victory were once again driving safely and defensively. It looked like we were in our winter mode and could start looking forward to seven months of relative calm and cabin fever.

Frankie and I had continued looking into the Shapiro vandalism incidents—since the second spray painting, the culprits had also painted their hate-filled diatribes on the walls of the Union Pacific train depot and the side of the grade-school building—and talked to a few local kids we thought might be involved. They all denied everything, and since there were no witnesses and no physical evidence, we took the story to Ron Franklin at the *Victor* and asked him to run a story about the crime and the $500 reward that Howard Shapiro had offered for information. The money might shake something out of the bushes, but for the time being, we'd have to wait.

I left the office at about 6:30, dog tired and hungry, stopped off at Willard Feed & Seed for some grub for Edna's chickens, topped off the tank on the Bronco, and settled in with the warm air from the heater blowing on my legs for the ten-minute ride home.

The farmhouse where I live is on a 160-acre tract of land owned by Edna Cook, the eighty-four-year-old woman whose house sits right next to mine and who rents my two-bedroom place to me for $150 a month. In exchange for free run of the farm and the incredibly cheap rent, I run the odd errand for her and help her feed the two elderly quarter horses and the mangy, ill-tempered Shetland pony she keeps on the place for her obnoxious great-grandkids to ride.

My house is old and in great need of a paint job, but it's warm and comfortable. There's a woodstove in the living room—which I can bank with hardwood on chilly evenings before I go to bed—that fills the house with the pleasant, faint aroma of smoke. There's a big kitchen, a long back room I use as a workshop, a spare bedroom where

I keep my pool table, and a barn off to the side where I park. Right out the back door, I've got a twenty-five-yard target range set up, where I can plink with my .22 or get in a little practice with my handguns, an urge that hits me about twice a year. We share a satellite dish so I can get the Broncos and Edna can graze through the movie channels in search of anything featuring Sylvester Stallone—"If I was just sixty years younger . . ."

All in all, it's a cozy setup for both of us, and I look forward to coming home at the end of the day. The only way she'd get me out of here is with dynamite, but she hasn't expressed any interest in getting me out, and even offered once to lower the rent if I thought it was too steep. I wouldn't let her lower it, because I'd have gladly paid three times as much and still figured I was getting a hell of a deal.

As soon as I got home, I sank my cold, tired feet into my fleece-lined moccasins, started a fire in the stove, and checked the messages on my machine. One from my ex-wife, Nicole, letting me know the child-support check was three days late, one from Mike O'Neal, wanting to know if I wanted to get together and watch football on the weekend. Nothing from Karen.

As the kindling caught in the stove, I threw on some medium-size pine and a little maple, opened an ice-cold Coors, put Van Morrison's *Wavelength* album on the stereo, and sank back into my recliner just as Van was cranking up on "Kingdom Hall." Hungry as I was, I figured dinner might be a bit sketchy—grilled peanut-butter sandwiches and vegetable beef soup perhaps—because I was too lazy to attempt anything more ambitious, like a hamburger. I planned to be in bed by 10:00.

I suppose I must have dozed off around then, because the next time I looked at the clock it was 9:30 and someone was knocking on the front door. For a couple of seconds as I padded over to open up, I entertained the small hope that it might be Karen, stopping by to surprise me with another steak dinner. But as I looked through the frosted glass, I saw Bill Cheney, a rancher who lives about six miles down the county secondary from Sonny's, standing on the front porch, his big hands in the pockets of his blaze-orange down vest and a plaid, billed hunter's cap pulled low on his brow. A typical

Wyoming specimen, Cheney is in his early fifties. Tall—about six-three—his legs are bowed from too much time in the saddle. He keeps his white hair cropped short, and his snowy crown provides stark contrast to a nut-brown face, deeply creased from years of squinting in the sun.

I'd met him several times at Ginny's, where his slender frame belied his reputation as a prodigious eater, and once or twice he'd allowed me to fish on his land. He'd never visited my home before, but I welcomed him in, took his coat, and fetched us both a beer from the refrigerator.

"Sorry to bother you at home," he said when we were settled, "but I stopped at the office as soon as I got back to town and heard the news. You weren't there."

"You could have called, Bill," I said. "You didn't have to drive all the way out here."

He took a healthy drink from his bottle. "It isn't that far, and I did call," he said, "but you didn't answer. I thought you probably took the phone off the hook and unplugged your machine."

He stopped talking, shook his head, a look of disbelief on his weathered face. "Jesus, Harry, is it true Sonny was murdered?"

"I'm afraid so, Bill," I said, "and whatever you might have heard in town, it was fairly gruesome. So far, nobody has any idea who did it."

He pulled a battered box of Ozark Crooks cigars from the inside pocket of his vest and fired one of the hideous things up with a lucifer he ignited with his thumbnail. He sucked in a deep lungful of smoke, blew it out through his nose, nodding as if he'd come to some sort of personal decision. "That's why I came out tonight," he said tentatively. "I saw something unusual that evening." He paused. "It might be important, then again . . ."

Bill Cheney leaned forward on the living-room couch like he was getting ready to tell me a secret, the corded muscles of his big forearms jumpy where they showed beneath the rolled sleeves of his red Pendleton shirt. On his hip, I could see the black scabbard for a buck-skinning knife on one side and the butt of a heavy revolver on the other. There was a good deal of dried blood on the cuffs of his blue jeans. He'd been hunting, I thought, and it looked like he'd filled his license.

"Bill," I began, "it's been my experience that little things often turn out to be big things in a murder investigation, but I've got to tell you this one isn't my show. Anthony Baldi is in charge, and whatever you've got to tell me, he'll have to know about, too."

Cheney grimaced at that, a common reaction among people who have to deal with Anthony Baldi on a personal basis. He ground his barely smoked cigar out in the ashtray. "I don't know about that," he said. "If you think it's important, you can pass it along, but I don't think I'll go out of my way to do it."

"Fair enough," I said. "I can't say as I blame you."

According to Cheney, he'd been on his way into town the night of Sonny's killing at about 10:45 P.M., heading up to Ryan Park in the Snowies, where he planned to set up a camp and start hunting deer and elk at sunup the next morning. But as he came to the turnoff to Sonny's place, he looked left just in time to see a small dark sedan barreling up the drive, taking the sharp left onto the secondary road right in front of Cheney at high speed. "Ran me right off the road and into the pit," Cheney said. He frowned at the recollection. "For a while, I thought I'd catch up with whoever it was and knock the crap out of them, so I gunned it out of the ditch and caught up a couple miles later. By that time, though, I'd cooled down, so I just let it go."

I stood up and poked a hunk of maple into the woodstove, which had burned down to coals while I slept. There was a good chance, I thought, that Bill Cheney had a run-in with Sonny's murderer, unless Sonny had more than one visitor that night, which was highly unlikely. I took a piece of paper off the coffee table and fished around in my pocket for a pen.

"Did you happen to see what make of car it was?" I asked. I was excited that the killer might have left a clear trail after all.

"Nah," said Cheney, "I don't know small cars, but I think it was foreign."

"Could you see who was driving?"

"Too dark." He shrugged.

"Anything else?" I asked, the disappointment apparent in my voice.

A lopsided grin cracked his leathery face. "Yeah, there was," he said, paused for effect. "I got the bastard's license plate . . . 5-167VA."

In Wyoming, license plates are handed out at the county courthouse, and every county identifies its plates with the first number on the license. People in Natrona County, for example, all have a 1 at the start of their license-plate number. People from Laramie County have a 2, and so on. People in Albany County have a 5, which meant that whoever registered the car Bill Cheney had seen was local. It was the best news I'd had all week.

I thanked Cheney profusely for his trouble and, after he was gone, sat alone in the living room, sipping a third beer and considering the knowledge that I faced a professional dilemma. On the one hand, this wasn't my case, and I had information that might be valuable to the person who was in charge of resolving it, namely Anthony Baldi.

My duty as a police officer was to pick up the phone and give it to him at once, even if I had to wake him up to do it.

On the other hand, it would be good to break this case while he was still sitting on his butt. I could keep the license number to myself for a day, have it checked out, and follow it up if it was registered to someone in Victory that looked promising.

If it looked like nothing, I'd pass the number on tomorrow night without mentioning that I was a few hours tardy in doing so.

Hell, it wasn't much of a dilemma after all.

The next morning, I came to the office early and made two phone calls before breakfast—one to Karen's, where there was no answer, and one to Danny King, a friend who works as a detective on the Laramie Police Department.

Too short to make the height requirement on a big-city police force, Danny had left his hometown of Chicago in the early-eighties and wandered west, applying at the police department of every town he stopped in until he found one that would take him. He'd been hired in Laramie as a patrolman and had, through hard work and determination, worked his way up to plainclothes two years before. I met him at a refresher course on rape investigation at the state police academy shortly after Curly hired me as police chief in Victory, and we'd hit it off. Although we didn't see each other as often as either of us would have liked, we traded favors back and forth with some regularity. He tapped in to the police computer for me once in a while, because Victory wasn't wealthy enough to afford one, and I took him fly-fishing two or three times a year at one of my secret spots. It was an arrangement we both approved of.

"Good morning, Hawkeye," King said when he finally picked up my call. He sounded like he'd been polishing his vocal cords with steel wool. "I heard about your most recent hunting expedition. Sure wish I'd been there to see it."

"You've been talking to Frankie, right?" I asked, looking over at the perpetrator of the crime, who was sitting across from me, puzzling over a crossword puzzle in the morning paper, the tip of his tongue sticking out in thought. "I'm going to have to talk with him about this tendency of his to spread lies." The corners of Frankie's eyes curled up a little as he listened to my end of the conversation, but he didn't look up.

At Danny's end of the line, I could hear the background noise of a busy squad room—officers joking with one another as they checked their mail and messages and got themselves ready to face the day. I heard someone calling Danny's name, wondering why he hadn't brought doughnuts. In police work, I thought, some things never change. "Danny, the reason I'm calling, would you turn on your little computer there and check something for me? I need you to run a license plate and tell me who registered the car."

"Why didn't you call the sheriff's department for this?" he asked. "This is a simple enough question, even for them."

"I don't feel like talking to them right now," I explained. "Maybe I won't ever feel like talking to them again."

"So what's the number?" He laughed.

"5-167VA."

I could hear the clicks of his computer keys as he typed the number in. He sighed as I imagined him leaning back for the short wait. I looked out the window as I waited with him, watched the white clouds race across the clear blue sky, their shadows moving along Main Street and sweeping across the cars and trucks parked along the curbs.

"Here we go," said Danny. "That would be a 1986 Honda Civic. Black. Registered to Ellen Vaughn, 856 Garfield Street, Laramie. Phone number 356-8254.

"What'd she do, anyway," he chuckled, "skip on a parking ticket?"

I wished I could tell him it was anything that simple, but I couldn't. Truth is, I was too surprised to speak.

6

Ellen Vaughn lived on Garfield Street, just down the block from the university's Old Main Building and Hoyt Hall, where the literary types spend entire careers arguing over whether Moby Dick was a symbolic representation of God or of Herman Melville's penis.

It's a nice neighborhood, mostly older homes where the kids had outdone themselves getting ready for Halloween, their porches lined with cardboard ghosts, fake tombstones, and spiderwebs from a can.

Down the block, a couple of college-age runners were working in place while they waited for the light to change on Ninth Street, sharing the corner with a serious-looking young man and a more intense young woman, both of them wearing fatigue jackets, berets, and combat boots. Socialists from Jackson Hole, I decided—at least until Mom and Dad got hold of them at Christmas break. Across the street from Ellen's, a young couple was locking lips in the front seat of a Ford Taurus, the windows steamy from their overheated passion.

After speaking with Danny King, it had taken me just under a half hour to make the thirty-mile drive from Victory to Laramie, and I spent the entire ride trying to figure out what to do about Ellen Vaughn and her possible connection to Sonny's murder. I should have turned Bill Cheney's information over to the sheriff's department the minute I got it, and there was no excuse in the world for doing otherwise.

Keeping mum was dereliction of duty at best and a criminal act at worst. I've been known to bend the law before when it suits my purposes, however, so that's what I planned to do—at least for the moment.

I made my decision for what I believed were good reasons. The minute Anthony Baldi learned that Ellen's car had been spotted coming out of Sonny's drive at about the time the coroner's report said he'd been murdered, she would become the number-one suspect, and because there weren't any other suspects, the *only* suspect. But I'd seen her face when we discovered Sonny's corpse, and her horrified reaction couldn't have been faked. No matter what the evidence indicated, I didn't believe she'd killed Sonny, and until I had a better explanation for the fact that her Honda had been spotted at his place, I wasn't going to flap my lips. The only thing I needed was more time to dig up a decent explanation.

I decided to take the simple approach. I'd ask her.

I pulled the Bronco to the curb, killed the engine, and made my way up to the front of the house. The October sun was warm, and there was a smell of hot apple cider coming from the main level of the house where Ellen lived. I pulled off my sunglasses and climbed the steps of the front porch of the tidy brick home. I didn't knock on the front door and disturb Ellen's landlord, because a sign below the mailbox informed me that Ellen lived in the basement apartment, accessible around the back, through the garage, and down a short flight of stairs. As I felt my way through the dark garage, I could see the light at the bottom of her door, could hear the soft sounds of Jimmy Buffett's "Lovely Cruise" coming from behind it.

She opened the door at my knock, barefoot and wearing a raggedy Wyoming Cowboys sweatsuit, her long curly hair tied back in a ponytail and decked out with a new fashion accessory, tortoiseshell glasses. Behind her, scattered across a low coffee table in front of a threadbare couch, was a mountain of textbooks, papers, and the odd bone fragment labeled with identification tags. Ellen Vaughn was still an attractive young woman, but she looked tired. "Harry?" she asked. She opened the door but didn't invite me in. "What brings you out this morning?"

I mumbled a noncommital answer as Ellen looked over her shoulder at her cluttered apartment and then back at me, the same expression Karen had on her face the time she invited dinner guests for Friday night and they showed up on Thursday. "Come on in," she said eventually, "but you'll have to excuse the mess, and me, too. I haven't even had time for a shower today."

In my years as a homicide detective, I'd done plenty of uncomfortable interviews, so I shouldn't have been feeling the tiny flutter of butterfly wings in my gut, but there the little buggers were, just the same. I didn't know quite how to start, so of course I started badly. I pushed by her into the small living room. "This isn't a social call," I said churlishly. "I think you should put on a pot of coffee. We've got a few things to discuss."

One thing you have to say about the Starbranch Command Voice, it ain't pretty, but it usually gets results. With a look of surprise and a touch of annoyance thrown in for good measure, Ellen nodded and pointed me to the couch while she went off to the small kitchenette to make coffee. While it perked, she parked herself on the arm of the sofa, looking uncomfortable, apprehensive, and more than a little irritated. This wasn't the same Ellen Vaughn who'd kissed my cheek on the way out of my office. This Ellen Vaughn was not very glad to see me. I nodded at the pile of textbooks, made a stab at small talk. "Long week?" I asked.

She crossed her arms across her chest. "As a matter of fact, it has been," she said. "For one thing, I haven't been able to sleep. Every time I close my eyes, I see Sonny Toms tied to that kitchen chair and covered in blood. Finally, yesterday, I went to the library and started doing a little research on murders. I don't know, maybe I thought that doing busywork might help by keeping my mind occupied. It didn't, though. Did you know that slitting someone's throat like that is a very common way for Mafia hit men to kill their victims? It's even got a name. They call it a Sicilian Necktie."

She stopped rambling long enough to consider what she'd said, then shook her head to dismiss it. "But I don't suppose there's any reason to believe the Mafia is active in Victory, or that Sonny would be mixed up with them if they were."

"I don't know," I said. "But no, I don't think there's any reason to believe that Sonny ran afoul of anyone like that."

"Then what's up, Harry?" she asked. "I assume you're not here to find out why I haven't called you for dinner, which I would have done if I hadn't gotten so far behind at work. Do you have something to tell me about the murder?"

"Well, yes and no," I began. "There haven't been any arrests and the sheriff's department is at a standstill. But there is something . . ."

Ellen stopped rocking and gave me her full attention, her face drawn and tight, her lips forming a straight, hard line.

"Here's the deal," I said, watching her eyes as I spoke. "I have a witness who says he saw your car out at Sonny's just about the time he was murdered, and I was wondering if you could help me explain it."

For about three seconds after I shared that information with her, Ellen Vaughn looked as if she'd been kicked in the stomach, but then she shook it off. "Not possible, Harry. There must be some mistake."

I shook my head sadly, let her know that I thought it possible, even probable. "The witness had a poor description of your car, Ellen, but he was very specific about the license-plate number. I think your car was out there. The only question in my mind is where you were. Can you remember what you were doing between eight o'clock and midnight the night Sonny was killed?"

"I'm a suspect?" she asked incredulously.

"In my business," I said, "everyone's a suspect until I prove them otherwise. But I'm not in charge of the murder investigation. At this point, I'm asking for my own enlightenment."

"Like hell," she said, her voice laced with righteous indignation. "You think I'm involved. If you didn't, you wouldn't be here."

"I'm just looking for the truth," I said, "and you can either give it to me and let me help you, or you can give it to Anthony Baldi. I'm going to have to let him in on this sooner or later."

Ellen stood up from the arm of the couch and paced the small living room for several moments, her bare feet slapping against the hardwood floor as she walked. Finally, she stopped her stalking and turned to face me, her fists balled and riding on her hips. "I can't believe you think I had anything to do with this," she said tightly. "But I'll tell you where I was . . . and then I want you to leave."

I nodded slightly in agreement, waited for her to go on. I patted my front pocket for a pack of smokes but decided against it when I didn't notice an ashtray handy.

Ellen scowled in disgust. "I had a date that night," she said finally, "and I was with him until almost midnight." She paused for a moment, then continued in a matter-of-fact rush. "I drove out to his house, and then we drove back into Laramie for dinner at the Cavalryman. We got there at seven o'clock, we didn't leave until eleven-thirty, and everyone there will remember us because we had a horrible fight, which ended with us breaking up. I think the last thing I said to him was that he was an untrustworthy, lying, two-timing bastard . . . not much different than most of the men I've met lately."

She stopped to let that one sink in. I felt my face beginning to flush. "I'd tell you to check it out, Harry, but I suspect you're going to do that anyway."

I held my open palms toward her in self-defense. "I'm not saying you killed Sonny," I said. "But I need to know what your car was doing there so I can help you. Tell me who you were with, and I'll confirm your story before I go to the sheriff."

She shook her head in dismissal, and I noticed her eyes starting to tear at the corners. They weren't tears of shame or sorrow, I knew. They were tears of outrage and betrayal. "It's none of your damned business, Harry," she said curtly. "But even though I'm not exactly proud to say I dated the cheating prick for five months, I was out with Tad Bauer that night. If you don't believe me, I suggest you talk to him. I'm sure you know where he lives."

When Ronald Reagan was President, I used to amuse myself trying to imagine him in bed with Nancy.

I could get them in the bedroom together, all right, each of them snuggled up in their own twin beds. But my mind drew a blank when I tried to picture them actually doing the deed. Some couplings are like that, simply too preposterous to understand.

It was the same thing with Tad Bauer and Ellen Vaughn. I could understand what he saw in her well enough. But trying to fathom what might have drawn her to him was an exercise in futility. It certainly couldn't have been an overpowering physical attraction, unless she met him when she wasn't wearing her glasses. About five-ten and close to 200 pounds, the eventual heir to the Bauer beer fortune was not exactly cover material for *Gentleman's Quarterly.* His hair was long and mousy, short on the sides and top, with one of those incomprehensible little ponytails in back, just long enough so it flopped over his collar. His high, tinny voice and his sallow complexion were handicaps, but he compounded his problem by purchasing his entire wardrobe from the L. L. Bean catalog.

In Bar Harbor, a shifty-looking rich kid decked out like he was going to spend the afternoon sipping wine coolers and playing a game of bridge wouldn't be noticed. But in Wyoming, where even our homegrown megamillionaires consider a corduroy jacket with their blue jeans and cowboy boots dressy enough for any occasion, a nerd like Tad Bauer stands out like a bottle of Scotch at a Baptist picnic. One look at the likes of him and we think *Yankee loser*. It's a conditioned response.

I remembered Frankie telling me that he'd seen Tad carousing recently at the Cowboy Bar, which tended to confirm Ellen's accusations about his unfaithfulness. But while I knew that a relatively simpleminded small-town girl from Guernsey, away from home for the first time at the big university, might be impressed by his money and might mistake his poor taste in clothing for sophistication, I hoped someone as smart as Ellen wouldn't be fooled. A woman like her, with her head on her shoulders, ought to see him for what he is, a spoiled, selfish idiot who thinks it's the world's obligation to fulfill his every desire. For guys like Tad Bauer, immediate gratification takes too long, and the only time they actually think about what anyone else wants or needs is when they're trying to suck up to someone they think is richer and more important.

Christ.

But she apparently hadn't seen through him for at least five months, and the mystery of it was enough to keep me occupied all the way home, where I took the puzzle with me into the hottest shower I could stand, the water doing its best to beat a little life into my tired muscles and clear my head. Oh well, I decided—remembering several of the semistrange women I've found in my own bed over the years—there's no way to explain this funny thing called love.

As I toweled myself dry, I decided I'd head into Victory, gird up my loins, and pay Tad Bauer a visit. Then I'd call Anthony Baldi.

And then maybe I'd drink a pint of turpentine to get the taste of those unpleasant obligations out of my mouth.

* * *

I didn't get around to either of those tasks, though, because as I was driving through town on my way to the Bauer place, I noticed a black Ford waiting in front of the police station with a burly, square-headed gent behind the wheel. It was Ken Keegan, an investigator for the state Department of Criminal Investigation and one of the first friends I'd made when I moved to Victory. We'd collaborated on several cases, but I hadn't talked to him for months. I felt a rush of anticipation at the pleasant prospect of catching up over a couple of beers and a chicken-fried steak at Ginny's.

Beside him in the front seat was a man I didn't recognize, a wiry-looking specimen decked out in full Western regalia—jeans, a Western-cut leather jacket, cotton shirt with snap buttons, and a bolo tie with a chunky turquoise slide. He accented his ensemble with a pair of aviator sunglasses and a short-brimmed Stetson like the one Paul Newman wore in *Butch Cassidy and the Sundance Kid.*

He might as well have had the word *cop* stenciled across his forehead. He looked uncomfortable in the clothes, more than a little out of place. I figured him for an out-of-towner who'd been in-state just long enough to drop a week's pay at the Western clothing store and begin to regret his impetuous purchases.

Keegan, meanwhile, looked perfectly comfortable with himself, as usual. A man in his early fifties, six-one, maybe 230 pounds and going to flab around the middle, I'd have wagered he was still wearing the ill-fitting and wrinkled black suit I'd seen him in last. His crew cut could have used a trim, the knot of his tie had been pulled away from the open top button of his collar, and the front of his jacket and white shirt were grimy from the cigarette ashes he constantly dribbled on his clothing.

When they saw me pull into the parking space next to them, Keegan switched off the Ford's engine and got out, his jacket slipping aside to reveal the butt of the .45 he was carrying in his shoulder rig. His pal did the same, but kept the Ford between us and rested his arms on the roof outside the passenger side door.

I reached for Keegan's meaty hand, my face split in a huge grin. "Look what the wind blew in," I said happily. I nodded at his expanded waistline and smiled. "Seems like you've prospered since I saw you last."

"Look who's talkin', Chubby." He laughed. "You've gained a couple of belt notches yourself."

"Just livin' right, podna," I said. "I never saw much point in self-denial."

I nodded at his passenger. "You gonna introduce me to your partner, Ken, or just let us work it out for ourselves?" I reached across the roof and offered my hand, which the man took. His hand was knobby and muscular, his shake firm. "Harry Starbranch," I said. "Chief of police."

"Sorry, Harry," Keegan broke in. "I guess I forgot my manners. This gentleman is Aaron Cohen." He skipped a beat. "He's with the FBI."

It took a couple seconds for that to register. "A feeb?" I asked good-naturedly. Cohen didn't laugh.

"Good morning, Chief Starbranch," he said in a voice that was pure Brooklyn. Maybe five-eleven and 170 pounds, Cohen was a lean man with a blunt nose, a strong jaw, and coal-colored hair that curled out from under the cowboy hat and around his ears. He was wearing tight blue jeans that accented well-muscled thighs. His broad shoulders tapered down to a narrow waist, giving him a solid T-shape. I figured the two-day growth of beard on his face was mostly for effect.

Despite the attempt at localizing his wardrobe, however, Cohen would never be mistaken for a native. I could only imagine what he must have done at the Bureau to get himself sent to Wyoming, where the feds station two agents tops in the whole state, a posting that is regarded, I knew, just a notch above Pahuska, Oklahoma. And why was he in Victory with Ken Keegan, who—like most cops not in the government employ—dislikes federal agents on general principle. I imagined it would be interesting.

They followed me to the office, and I kicked the door open, boosted the heat up a notch, and busied myself at the coffeemaker as Keegan made himself comfortable and Aaron Cohen measured the place. The look on his face said that compared to my office, Pahuska didn't look so bad after all. When everyone was settled, I poured us a round of coffee, sat back in my chair, and lit a smoke. Cohen made a face that let me know he thought my nicotine habit was disgusting. If it hadn't been my office, I had a suspicion he'd have asked me to put my cigarette out. Naturally, I would have declined. Like Keegan, feebs rank pretty low on my scale of desirable companions.

I wasn't sure what brought Keegan and Cohen to Victory, but I could wait until they were ready to talk. When I had finished my smoke, I lit another cigarette off the butt of the last, blew a decent-size cloud of smoke in Cohen's direction, and waited for them to get down to business.

It took only a couple minutes of that uncomfortable silence before Keegan finally came to the point of the visit. He pulled a cop notebook and a cheap ballpoint pen from the pocket of his shirt. There was a little blue stain in the corner of his pocket. The pen leaked. "I hear you had some excitement in town last week," he said. I nodded my assent. "Anything breaking on it?"

I shrugged my shoulders, put my feet on the desk. "It's not my investigation, Ken," I told Keegan matter-of-factly. "I found the body, but Anthony Baldi has taken over from there. You haven't heard anything, have you?"

"Not much," Keegan admitted. "But enough to arouse our interest."

Our interest? I tried not to show my curiosity. The DCI usually serves only as a backup resource for local departments, and the feds usually concern themselves mainly with crime on the state's Indian reservations. For both of them to have taken an interest in the murder of an eccentric junk collector was odd. Very odd. "You're investigating Sonny's death?" I asked as nonchalantly as possible. "I'm sure Anthony could use the help."

"Not really," Keegan chuckled, "unless we find out it's connected to something we are interested in. And frankly, Harry, we thought you might be able to help us fill in the gaps."

I slowly shook my head no, pursed my lips. "There's not a hell of a lot I can tell you," I said. "I included everything I know in the report I gave to Anthony. Have you read it?"

"We've read it," said Cohen, "and you're right, there's not much there."

"It's about all I know," I said. "I haven't been investigating."

Cohen scrutinized his coffee cup for several minutes while Keegan scribbled in his notebook. At length, Cohen looked up and studied me for a ten count. "You were a Denver homicide investigator for a long time," he said. It wasn't a question. "This has got to be a real change for you."

I gave him a grin. "A change for the better," I said.

He nodded like he understood. "But it bothers you to see Anthony Baldi working this case and not you."

What was this? Therapy? "It bothers me to see Anthony Baldi working any case," I said testily.

Cohen noticed the sarcasm, but his face didn't tell me what he thought of it. "You think he's blowing it?"

"I do."

Cohen took off his aviators so I could see the dead-looking brown eyes behind them. He set his cup on the desk and leaned forward. "Is that why you've been working it on your own?" he asked. He used the same tone of voice I imagine he used when he was interrogating bombing suspects. I didn't like it a bit.

"I told you this wasn't my investigation," I said. "What makes you think I'm working it on my own?"

There was a note of challenge in my voice, and Keegan rushed in to defuse it. "It's a guess," he said. "And a good one, considering what I know about you. You were a damned fine homicide detective, Harry—not the kind to toss the ball to someone working your end of the court."

I wasn't mollified by the compliment, even if it did come from a friend. "So what?" I asked. "Maybe I am poking around the edges a little. But even if I am, what does it matter to you?"

Keegan closed his notebook, jammed the leaky pen back in his pocket, and pawed around in the jacket of his coat until he came up with a rumpled pack of Camels. He shook one loose and fired it up with an ancient Zippo, ignoring Cohen's look of distaste. "Maybe it doesn't at that," Keegan said. He drew in smoke, smiled, and let it out in a great, noxious cloud. "And then again, maybe it does. Can you tell us what you were doing this morning at Ellen Vaughn's apartment?"

I felt my breath catch in my throat and a small knot begin to grow in my belly. What the hell was going on here? "You followed me?" I asked incredulously. "Why?"

Keegan rolled his cigarette between his sausage-size fingers, smiled, and stubbed it out in the ashtray. "Nah, Harry, we didn't follow you," he said. "You just showed up. We've had the place under surveillance for the last few months as part of a bigger investigation we're running. And when a cop turns up to visit the object of a stakeout, we usually like to find out why."

He folded his big hands on the desktop and smiled large. "So that's why we're here, Harry. To ask you why."

In the weeks that followed, I had a lot of time to think about what I said next and wonder what made me say it. I had come up with a rationalization I could live with for keeping what I knew about Ellen's connection to the murder from Anthony Baldi, at least temporarily. But there was no good reason in the world for me to lie to Ken Keegan and his feeb buddy, and plenty of reason not to. By lying, I was withholding information in a federal criminal investigation and a local murder, which is a major felony in anybody's book. Nevertheless, that's what I did—and my heart didn't even beat much faster when I did it.

I looked Keegan in the eyes, tried to modulate my voice. "I went to see her because I was worried about her," I said. "She had a bad shock and I just wanted to see how she was holding up."

I couldn't tell whether Cohen bought it, but Keegan nodded his head in understanding. I felt a jolt of relief. "That's reasonable," he said. "How's she coping?"

"As well as can be expected," I said. "She's working—but I don't think she's sleeping all that well."

Now I wanted a little information of my own. Tit for tat. I spoke to Keegan, tried to pretend Aaron Cohen wasn't even in the room. "Can you tell me why you'd have her under surveillance?" I asked nonchalantly. "She doesn't strike me as the criminal type."

Keegan checked the buttons on his coat, stood up, and reached for my hand. "Not now," he said. "But if you'd care to drive over to the DCI office in Cheyenne tomorrow, I think we have a few things you'll be interested in hearing."

"Early morning?"

"Fine," he said. "How about nine-thirty? I think we'll be ready for you then. And Harry . . . two requests . . ."

I nodded skeptically. "Yeah?"

"First, don't do any more on your own until you talk to us tomorrow. You might muddy the waters."

I was noncommital. "What else?"

Cohen stood and put on his sunglasses. "Don't tell anyone where you're going," he said flatly.

I spent the rest of that afternoon puttering around the farmhouse. I tied a dozen caddis nymphs, surfed the satellite for bits and pieces of various football games, and mulled the morning's conversation. I couldn't think of any reason the FBI would be interested in Ellen Vaughn, and as the day went on, my theories became more and more illogical and bizarre.

By eight o'clock, I had worked myself into a funk because it felt like my whole life was going to hell. I had a murder on my hands that I might have been able to solve, if I had the authority to do it right, and at least two other troublesome riddles—involving two women, one dead, one very much alive—for which I had no solutions, and the feds to look forward to in the morning. On top of all that, my ex-wife and I were barely speaking and my girlfriend had gone south.

There's nothing like self-pity to put things in the best possible perspective.

I ended the evening sitting on the front porch in my long underwear, the light from the quarter moon turning the prairie into a depressing shade of gray. I think it was about 12:30 when I rocked back into the house, poured a nightcap, and debated with myself for exactly three seconds before punching Karen's number into the phone.

The man who answered was fairly unhappy about being awakened.

7

For a couple of minutes the next morning, I believed I had actually puked up my pancreas. I'd sat in my living room the night before until almost 3:00 in the morning, when I finally fell asleep in the recliner. I woke with a stiff back, a mouth that tasted like road tar, and the kind of banging headache that always makes me nauseous. After kneeling at the porcelain throne, it took all my strength to shave, shower, dress, and drive myself down to Ginny's for breakfast, my blurry eyes squinting through the windshield and my shaky hands gripping the wheel like talons.

Tell the truth, my self-esteem was at an all-time low, considering the fool I'd made of myself on the telephone with Karen. I wondered if her new English-professor boyfriend ever did anything that pathetic. I doubted it.

I was still feeling sorry for myself when I pulled into a parking space outside the cafe. I killed the engine and groaned my way out of the Bronco, made it across the sidewalk, looking down so I wouldn't trip on the cracks in the sidewalk. Inside, I was greeted by the smell of frying bacon, freshly brewed coffee, and toasted bread. Usually, those are among my favorite aromas in the world, but that morning they only made my stomach churn. I ignored the buzz of excited conversation in the restaurant and made my way to my usual stool at the far end of the counter, hoisted myself up, and took a few deep breaths to stop my head from spinning. That didn't work, so I laid my head down on the cool counter and planted my feet on the floor.

When Ginny came to take my order a couple minutes later, I peered up slowly, noticed her apron was covered in ketchup and coffee stains. It looked revolting. "Mornin', Harry," Ginny said cheerfully. She held her order pad in one hand and pulled a pencil from behind her ear with the other. "You know what?" she asked. "Your eyes look like two tomatoes in a glass of buttermilk."

"You ought to see them from this side," I groaned.

"No, thanks," she said. She studied me curiously. "Hangover?" she asked.

"Nah, just stupidity," I said miserably. "Stayed up half the night. Ended up sleeping in a chair."

She didn't look like she believed me, but I didn't have the energy to argue. "Well, then," she said finally, "if it isn't a hangover, you probably just need something to put a little spring in your step." She grinned mischievously. "How 'bout the morning special—an egg-and-liver shake? Pepto Bismol chaser?"

"Actually," I moaned, "I was hoping that instead of feeding me, you'd show some mercy. Just throw a rope around my neck, hitch it to your bumper, and drag me to death."

She laughed, then poured me a cup of scalding black coffee laced with three aspirin tablets.

While she was off whipping up my breakfast, I tried to read the *Rocky Mountain News,* but even the sixty-point headlines were wiggling like king snakes on August tarmac. I threw the paper down in frustration, growling as I put my fingers against my temples and tried to push my throbbing brain back into shape. Down the counter, Howard Shapiro and Billy Sun were enjoying the spectacle as they sipped coffee and forked up bites of doughnut. "See what you're missing?" I grumbled. I tossed a $5 bill on the counter and started hobbling toward the door. Maybe breakfast wasn't such a hot idea after all.

"Well, I don't know we're missing so much," Howard said. "But *you* did."

"Nah, Howard," I said grimly. "I think I've got it all."

"Not misery, Harry," he said. His weathered, tan face shone with amusement. For such a kind man, he was showing an alarming lack of sympathy for my pain. "Kit Duerr."

I stopped walking, shook my head in confusion. "The football player?" I asked. "Used to be with the Chicago Bears?"

Shapiro nodded eagerly. Billy beamed.

"What the hell are you talking about, Howard?" I asked tartly. "Make sense, will you? My brain's not up to sports trivia."

"He was just here," Howard said. The sun glare off his long white hair was enough to hurt my eyes. "Stopped in for breakfast."

"At Ginny's?" I asked stupidly.

"Yeah, Harry," Shapiro said. "At Ginny's. Said he'd been interested in this area for a while. Said he might even be looking to live here, start a business."

I laughed but stopped when I realized laughing hurt my head. "You've lost your mind, Howard," I said. "You might have thought you were talking to Kit Duerr, but you weren't. You were just talking to somebody said he was Kit Duerr. Don't be such a sucker, podna." With that, I clapped him on the shoulder and turned to leave.

"No, I'm serious," he said as I started to walk away. "It was Kit Duerr. You don't forget somebody looks like that." He waited for me to answer, but I didn't. "Wouldn't it be a pisser if he moved here, Harry?" Howard asked me and the room at large. "That would really put us on the map."

Sure would, I thought uncharitably. If Jackson Hole can have movie stars like Harrison Ford and Christian Slater, the least Victory deserved was a worn-out football player. Pisser indeed.

If Ry Cooder moved to Victory, I thought, *that* would be a pisser.

The Wyoming Department of Criminal Investigation building in Cheyenne was designed by the same guy who did nearly every state building in the capital city. Square and sprawling, it has no personality, but at least it has a big parking lot and a long-legged receptionist at the desk.

While she called up to Keegan's office to announce my arrival, I took a gander at the lobby. It hadn't changed much since the last time I'd visited, and it probably never would—slightly antiseptic smell in the air, white tile floor, marble walls, a few hanging plants, a bank of elevators at the far end. If you didn't know where you were, you might have guessed you were in a building full of CPAs.

What the place needed was something in the stark lobby for visitors to look at while they waited. The receptionist was fine, of course, but one hates to stare. Some Leroy Nieman sports prints on the walls would go nicely, and a decent magazine selection wouldn't hurt either. *Gun Digest* is all right, as far as it goes, but it's not the sort of thing you browse through when you're just killing time.

I'd barely gotten into the first paragraph of an article on the penetration capability of the Casull .454 Magnum when the elevators opened and Keegan came shuffling down the hall to meet me. Keegan was wearing what looked like the same baggy coat over his square body that he'd been wearing in Victory. Same bulge at the shoulder, too. He didn't offer much in the way of a friendly greeting, just stopped when he was fifteen feet away and gestured for me to follow him back to the elevators. When the door closed, Keegan rubbed his eyes like a man who'd had too little sleep the night before and gave me the red-eyed once-over.

We shared a companionable silence while the elevator made its ascent, but Keegan finally broke the quiet as the car came to a stop. "Cohen and I thought it would be best to talk to you here where it's private," he said in his rumbling drawl. He pulled a pack of Camels from his jacket pocket and lit one with his old Zippo. Then he slipped the lighter back in his pocket and adjusted the gold bucking-bronco stickpin in his lapel. "Thanks for coming."

When we stepped out the door on the third floor, Keegan led us down a long, institutional green hallway to a small conference room, where Cohen, dressed in a dark blue suit, white shirt, and red patterned tie, had his nose buried in a thick report. When we came in, Cohen plopped the report on the table and looked up. "I see you found the place?" he said. He made it a question—as if he'd expected a clodhopper like me to have trouble finding a huge building located on a major highway in a metropolis of nearly fifty thousand people—and I caught the edge of sarcasm in his voice.

"I've been here before," I said testily. I noticed that in deference to Cohen, Keegan had crushed his cigarette out. I lit a fresh one and started looking around for coffee. I hadn't waited long before Keegan poured me a cup of the blackest, thickest, most disgusting mud I'd ever seen and tossed down a couple packets of Sweet'n Low. I tasted it and made a face. Keegan grinned sheepishly—in apology, I suspected, for both the foul coffee and Cohen's patronizing attitude.

"Look, Harry," he said, hooking a thumb in Cohen's direction, "you two seem to have gotten off on the wrong foot."

I shrugged in dismissal, took a long sip of coffee, and ignored them.

"Any way we can start this thing over?" Keegan asked hopefully. "Put things back on track?"

I rested my boot against one of the table legs and reared back in the squeaky chair. "Well," I said, "you could start by telling me why I'm here."

"Why do you *think* you're here?" Cohen asked. His voice was as flat as a table.

"If I knew that," I said, "I wouldn't have had to drive seventy miles to find out. I do know this: I'd like you to tell me what interest you have in Ellen Vaughn and in Victory—and I'd like you to do it without a lot of crap." I know there was no real reason for my bad attitude, but I guess I just didn't feel like working well with others. I drummed my fingers on the table and waited while Cohen glared and ground his perfect teeth.

Finally, Keegan sighed and reached for one of the hefty files on the desk, opened it, and thumbed through it until he found what he wanted, his lips moving silently as he read. "I'd like to tell you a story, Harry," he said when he finished. I nodded for him to go on. "But before I start let me ask—how much do you know about the Posse Comitatus?"

His question caught me by surprise, since I'd been nursing the sneaking suspicion this all might involve drugs. Of course I'd heard of the Posse. You can't live in the West or Midwest for long before you start hearing stories about the ultraright-wing neo-Nazis and racists who gravitate to groups like the Posse. I'd read about the paramilitary training camps run by the Ku Klux Klan in Alabama and Georgia, and I'd heard what's come out of the Aryan Nations in Idaho. But as far as I knew, the Posse—while sharing some half-baked social philosophy with their hate-mongering cousins in the Klan—was made up mainly of cash-strapped farmers from the corn states who got together on Saturday nights for bean suppers where the women quilted and the men painted signs demanding that we GET U.S. OUT OF THE UN.

Although I'd heard they frequently made some ineffective symbolic political gestures, like storming the capitol in Illinois on their tractors and refusing to have their driver's licenses renewed because they thought it was their right to drive without one, I'd never considered the Posse a real threat to my safety, or anyone else's. As a matter of fact, it seemed to me that I'd read an article in the not-so-distant past about how they'd pretty much fallen apart since one of their honchos got himself killed in a shoot-out down in Oklahoma, maybe Texas.

Keegan listened patiently as I outlined my understanding of the Posse, nodding his head in the affirmative when I hit on something that was right or that he agreed with. "That's about what most people think," Keegan said when I was done rambling. "And one reason for the lack of concrete knowledge is the Posse's fixation with secrecy. The information flow out of that bunch is tighter than a bull's ass, and everything that's known about them is the result of years' worth of investigation."

He pointed in Cohen's direction to let me know he was talking about the FBI. "They've been working on this for all that time, but even they don't know all that much. What they do know is that the Posse—at least what's left of it—appears to have taken a very militant turn, and that unless they're stopped a lot of innocent people could die. It's a battle the FBI is very interested in winning, and the DCI is cooperating because we agree with what they're doing. Nobody needs another Oklahoma City, Harry."

My mind flashed visions of bodies, stretchers, crying babies. "They need stopping, all right," I said. "But what does it have to do with me?"

"We're going to stop them in Victory," Keegan said quietly, loosening his gravy-stained tie, "and it's likely we'll need your help."

He sounded sincere and friendly. I leaned back in my chair and made myself comfortable, let him know I had all the time in the world. "Tell me your story, Keegan," I said, lighting a smoke, "and be sure to start at the beginning."

Keegan smiled and nodded, took off his rumpled coat, and hung it across the back of an empty chair. Then he sat down, adjusted his shoulder holster to a position that didn't chafe, and scooted his chair up to the table. "I'm going to give you a thumbnail version," he said, "and then I'm going to give you an hour alone with this file. When we've covered all that ground, I'll try to tie it up for you so you can see how it fits."

Down the table, Cohen was taking notes on a legal tablet, making tight, neat letters with an expensive ballpoint. He looked up, broke in on our conversation. "But before we do that," he said, "I want your promise that what you learn here doesn't leave this room."

While I was feeling comfortable with Keegan, I wasn't quite ready to give Cohen anything. Not yet, at least. "What if it involves criminal acts in my jurisdiction?" I asked. "Am I supposed to keep it a secret from my police officer and the mayor? How can I do that?"

"By letting us handle it for the time being," Cohen said, trying to fix me with his empty stare. "And by not trying to cut in on a federal investigation."

In other words, he was saying, don't butt in and don't screw things up. I ground my teeth, balled my fists on my thighs. "So that's the deal," I said. "You're going to let me in on why you've been lurking around my town, as long as I stay out of your way and don't act like a fuckup?"

The look he gave me was close to a sneer. "That's a simple way to put it," Cohen said. He paused. "But yes, that's the deal."

My anger bubbled up before I could stop it. My cheeks burned, my heart raced. I mashed my cigarette out in the ashtray, stood up, and reached for my coat. "Then you can go piss in your hat," I snarled, speaking in a tight rush. "You people can dick around all you want everywhere in the world except in Victory, Wyoming. You start poking around there, and it's my business to know why you're poking, as long as I'm chief of police. If you don't tell me what I came to hear, and do it quick, I'm going to go back out to my car, drive home, and start my own goddamned investigation of the Posse Comitatus—and my first order of business will be to call a press conference. If that doesn't meet your approval, Agent Cohen, then you can call my boss and file a complaint, but I'll just bet he's not gonna swallow a lot of your bullshit, either."

I don't know how Cohen reacted because I spun around and was halfway to the door by the time Keegan caught my elbow in one of his platter-size hands. I pulled my arm loose, but I stopped walking.

He glared at Cohen with a look that warned him to shut up. Then he looked back at me. He looked chagrined and gentle. "I trust you, Harry," he said, a note of apology in his voice. "No conditions."

It was obvious that Aaron Cohen was working up an objection, but he choked it down at the last minute, folded his wiry arms across his chest, and went back to gritting his teeth. Keegan, meanwhile, poured himself a fresh cup of coffee and began telling me about one of the most pathetic band of armed fanatics operating in America.

"In 1983," he began, "an assault team of FBI, U.S. marshals, deputy sheriffs, state troopers, and members of the Arkansas Criminal Investigation Division stormed a little house on the outskirts of Smithville, Arkansas, and shot it out with a heavily armed fugitive named Gordon Kahl, a Posse Comitatus organizer who'd been on the run since shooting a deputy sheriff in North Dakota who'd come to arrest him for violating his probation. A sheriff's deputy was killed in the Arkansas gunfight, but so was Gordon Kahl, and it looked for a while that because of the fallout, the Posse was on the run."

"I heard about that," I said, beginning to relax a little. I sat back down in the chair and nodded for him to go on. In a moment, he obliged.

"Although the Posse had been around since the sixties, spreading the usual racist garbage—that Jews are trying to destroy the country's Constitutional government by taking over the nation's monetary system and then using their financial clout to rob farmers of their land—it didn't really catch on until the farm crisis began in the mid-seventies, when the FBI estimated its members at between twelve thousand and fifty thousand organized into chapters spread across twenty-three states," Keegan said.

"The Posse started booming then, as farmers, most of them from the Midwest, began looking for someone to blame for the avalanche of bankruptcies and foreclosures that were threatening their way of life and the farms their families had worked for generations. Some of them blamed the politicians who'd encouraged them to borrow more money than they could ever hope to pay back and then chopped them off at the knees by cutting price supports and abandoning export agreements to places like Mother Russia. But lots of them started listening closely to what men like Gordon Kahl had been saying for years, that in order to restore a Constitutional government in America, it might be necessary to drive the Jews and other non-Christians out by force. And to make that possible, a lot of Posse chapters started stockpiling weapons and throwing in with the Klan and the Aryan Nations to run camps where members learned guerrilla warfare and practiced shooting pop-up Jews. Some of the leaders even started making plans to attack the government by killing judges, sheriffs, politicians, and anyone else who stood in the way of their revolution.

"The Kahl shoot-out slowed them down, because it exposed the Posse's racism and its ties to lunatic-fringe organizations like the Klan. Some of the money the Posse had been getting from farmers and right-wing businessmen dried up, and membership dropped. While farms were still in trouble, it looked like most farmers were turning away from groups like the Posse, because they were smart enough to see that they were bound to fail. Farmers are good people, by and large, and they want our understanding and our help. They don't want our hate."

Keegan paused and looked questioningly at Cohen, who was staring out the window of the conference room, watching the wind drive three-foot tumbleweeds across the DCI parking lot. Keegan's silence broke his concentration, and he looked at me, his jaw muscles twitching from tension. "I'm a Jew, Chief Starbranch," Cohen said. There was a note of humanity in his voice I hadn't heard before. He was trying to bridge the gap between us. I wasn't sure why. "People like this have been murdering my people for generations. I won't stand by and see it happen today. I've been investigating the Posse since 1975 because I believe their leaders are nothing but storm troopers without the death's-head insignia. And while the organization has lost some of it popular support, the men who guide it are still among us and still as vicious and barbarous as ever, perhaps more so because they've suffered setbacks and are tired of waiting."

I reached into my inside pocket for yet another smoke but thought better of it. I pulled out a pack of gum instead and offered it around the room. Keegan looked thankful, but Cohen turned it down. Pushing away from the table, he stood and began pacing his end of the small room like a panther, talking as he moved. "In the last few years, the Posse has become more like the Irish Republican Army, more secretive, the cells more militant. Now, according to our best information, they've stockpiled enough arms and money to finance their objective, a revolution precipitated by the assassination of numerous symbolic targets—judges, law-enforcement officers, bankers, Jewish leaders. We think they began three months ago by kidnapping a district-court judge in Iowa named Jacob Haines who refused to stop a local bank from foreclosing on a family farm owned by a Posse member, and who had gone on record saying that in his opinion, the Posse was just a bunch of juvenile delinquents playing soldier. Haines hasn't been seen since, and we fear he's dead."

Although I was interested in the story Keegan and Aaron Cohen were telling, you couldn't say I knew where it was going, unless you wanted to lie. The notion that Sonny might have been a member of the Posse Comitatus was ludicrous. And Ellen Vaughn, tucked away in her tiny basement apartment, studying old bones and planning the armed overthrow of the federal government? Well, I suppose anything's possible, but I doubted it.

Cohen must have read the skepticism in my face, because he walked to his end of the conference table and riffled through the stack of folders until he found the one that Keegan had been reading earlier. He gave it a brisk shove in my direction and nodded to Keegan, who stood and leaned against the windowsill.

"That file is a synopsis of what the FBI knows about the Posse," Keegan said. "Why don't you take a good look at it, and then we'll come back and see if we can't answer your questions."

When they were gone, their footsteps receding down the long, sterile hallway, I cracked the thick file, wondering whether it would tell me if Cohen had been on hand when Gordon Kahl suffered his fatal case of lead poisoning. It didn't, but over the long hours that dragged into late afternoon, it told me plenty of other things.

It told me, for starters, that the Posse's goal is to institute a Christian government in this country where the white majority is sovereign and where there's no law higher than the county sheriff. One look at Anthony Baldi and you start to see the problems with this kind of thinking, but they have a solution. If the sheriff abuses his power by imposing a bunch of illegal restrictions on the citizens or letting outside law-enforcement officers operate in his jurisdiction, the Posse can remove him from office simply by dragging him out to the busiest street in town and hanging him by the neck until sundown.

It told me these zealots believe the federal income tax is illegal, desegregation of schools is immoral, and that we should all be allowed to carry flamethrowers and bazookas into the local savings and loan if we feel like it, because the Second Amendment says that kind of behavior is dandy.

It told me, as Cohen and Keegan had before, that the Posse intends to wage a holy war against the American government and that according to information collected by the FBI, they've built a terrible arsenal of weapons to use against their enemies. It told me that some people associated with the Posse had already killed on numerous occasions, and its members should be considered armed and dangerous.

It told me the Posse was just one of many right-wing paramilitary organizations around the country whose members were steamed at the federal government's efforts at gun control and held deadly grievances for the way federal officers handled the Randy Weaver and Waco incidents. These days, those groups were not only preaching their usual dogma, they were laying the groundwork for massive armed resistance and terrorist actions in order to further their goals.

What it didn't tell me was why the FBI and the state were interested in Victory, or how I'd stumbled into one of their stakeouts while visiting Ellen Vaughn. For that, I'd need Ken Keegan and Aaron Cohen, but I had a feeling I wouldn't like their answers. While I waited for them to come back, I thought about my friends and neighbors in Victory, and I couldn't picture a single one of them involved with a bunch of racist maniacs like the Posse.

About three years ago, when Mike O'Neal bought a new shotgun, he had to fill out a card that asked, among other things, whether he'd ever belonged to an organization trying to overthrow the federal government. "Does voting Democrat count?" he asked the clerk, who didn't think his question was nearly as humorous as we did, because voting Democratic is definitely considered subversive behavior in some parts of Wyoming. Still, the occasional Democrat and college socialist is about as subversive the subversive element in Wyoming gets, and even if there were some Posse members among the residents of my town, I thought I'd know about it, because you can't keep something like that a secret. I might have been drunk a little too often in the last few years, but I hadn't been in a coma, had I?

If there was a chapter of the Posse in Victory, I should have known it. I decided that if Keegan and Aaron Cohen believed that Victory was a hotbed of revolutionary activity, then they were wrong, and I planned to tell them so. I eased back in my chair and finished my last cigarette, the smoke drifting up toward the fluorescent light fixtures and hanging under the drop ceiling like a noxious brown cloud. When I looked up, Keegan was standing in the doorway, his hands in his hip pockets and the tails of his coat pushed back far enough to show the scarred butt of his .45.

I waited for him to speak. "Cohen thought I should handle the rest of this by myself," he said.

"So handle it, Ken. All I see are question marks."

Keegan straightened up the pile of files and folders he'd left behind. Then he walked to the windows and adjusted the blinds so the glare from the late afternoon sun wouldn't blind us. When he was finished, he sat down and looked at me across the table. "Are you familiar with Wolfgang Bauer's politics?"

"The beer maker? Or his kid, Tad?"

"Both."

"I haven't made it my business, no."

Keegan stood, poured himself a fresh cup of coffee, and took it to the window. He used his finger to open a small hole in the blinds and spoke to me while he looked out over the windblown parking lot. "Well, then, let me tell you these people think Lyndon LaRouche is too liberal," he said. "They're about as right wing as you can get in America, and they're happy to put their money where their mouths are. Trouble is, they've got lots of money."

A small piece of the puzzle almost snapped into place. "They've been giving money to the Posse?" I asked. "For arms?"

Keegan nodded agreement. "We think so," he said. "At least we think old man Bauer has been writing them plenty of checks. We think Tad's involvement may be of the hands-on variety."

I would have laughed out loud, but it would have been rude. "You're kiddin' me," I said. "Tad might snort a little cocaine or cheat on his income taxes. He's the sort who might commit date rape—and he's definitely the sort you'd want to watch around the churc collection plate. But mixed up with people carrying guns who migh shoot him if he gets out of line? Not Tad Bauer. He doesn't have th balls."

Keegan hesitated, on the edge of impatience. "That may be," h said. "But we know old man Bauer gave Tad a quarter of a millio dollars four months ago, and we know that Tad passed it on to a Poss operative, who used it to buy explosives, automatic weapons, and ove fifty thousand rounds of ammunition. We know Tad was there whe the payment was made."

He turned from the window to face me. There was a hard look i his eyes and his square jaw was set. "What we don't know is what hap pened to the hardware after that, because we lost track of them," h said. "We've been watching the Bauer place in Victory all summe hoping to pick up the trail again."

I couldn't believe what I was hearing. They'd been operating i Victory for months without my knowledge. How was it possible? An what about . . . "Ellen Vaughn?" I asked quietly.

"She's his girlfriend, Harry. We were just watching her to cove the bases."

My heart sank. "Is she involved?"

"We don't know. We haven't seen anything that proves it eithe way."

"And Sonny?"

Keegan poked at something on the floor with the toe of his sho "No idea," he said. "But I've been in this business too long to belie in coincidence."

I didn't believe in coincidence either. No cop does. I nodded m head sadly in agreement.

Keegan crossed the room, put a friendly hand on my shoulder. let it rest there. "Something to take with you, Harry," he said. "A li tle advice. Watch out for these people. They'll slit your throat, watc you bleed to death, and their pulse won't break a hundred. What I hope is that you'd keep a low profile and call us if anything unusu happens. You're a cop, Harry, not a cowboy."

I stood, reached for my coat and hat. "I'll keep it in mind," I sai "but don't worry. So far, I haven't seen or heard anything that indicates a crime's been committed in my jurisdiction. And until I do, I'm nothing but an interested observer."

At that moment, we both knew that definition of my involvement left a lot of wiggle room. I was wiggling before I even got home.

The early evening crowd looked light when I pulled into the neon-drenched parking lot at Gus Alzonakis's. A couple of eighteen-wheelers, their big diesels idling and their running lights lit, sat off to one side waiting for their drivers to finish their prime ribs and coffee. Closer to the entrance, fifteen or twenty family cars and four-by-fours were schooled together, a lonely-looking confederation in Gus's asphalt sea. Among them, however, were several vehicles that I recognized, including the Chevy station wagon belonging to Edna Cook's fifty-two-year-old son, Curly's Isuzu pickup, and near the curving sidewalk leading to the entrance, the brown-and-white Blazer I'd last seen parked in Tad Bauer's barn.

It had been my intention to stop in for a quiet dinner before I headed out to the farmhouse, but the sight of the Blazer gave me other ideas. After restarting the Bronco, I eased it over to the other side of the parking lot to a spot that was hidden by the big trucks but still provided me a decent line of sight to the front entrance of the restaurant. I cut the engine and the lights and reached into the glove box for my binoculars. Call it idle curiosity, but I wanted to see what Bauer was up to. With the glasses focused so that they were sharp at the front door, I laid them on the seat beside me and rolled the windows down to the chilly evening breeze.

In the old days, I sat plenty of stakeouts where nothing happened for weeks on end, and the payoff was a fleeting glimpse of a suspect or a witness scurrying from his car at curbside into the place under surveillance. I was used to waiting, and I filled the time by running what I knew about this case through my mind in a kind of unstructured loop, hoping that my subconscious might spot the connections—between the old bones Sonny had found on Encampment Creek, his murder, Ellen Vaughn, Tad Bauer, and the Posse Comitatus—that my conscious mind was finding it impossible to make. There was a connection, had to be. But with what little I knew, it would have either taken an incredible intuitive leap, or a huge stroke of luck, to divine it.

That evening, my intuition seemed to have taken a powder, but I hoped I could make my own luck. As I sat in the dark, smelling the sweet scent of pine and wood smoke mingled with the delicious aroma of barbecued steaks from inside the restaurant, I watched a few more vehicles arrive and a few customers depart, couples mostly, with their arms around each other's waists as they strolled contentedly down the walkway to their cars. Seeing those happy couples made me think about the miserable state of my own love life, a topic I was still mulling when I looked through the glass doors of the restaurant and recognized Tad Bauer, who had come into the lobby and was dropping coins in a pay phone. I used the glasses to zero in on Bauer's back, watched him shift his weight from foot to foot impatiently until he made his connection.

Tad had dressed up for the evening in his chinos, powder-blue Oxford shirt, red power tie and, God help him, Top-Siders with no socks. I guess he thought there was an outside chance someone might invite him to go sailing on the Charles that evening, and he just wanted to be ready. The man, as I've often noted, was an idiot.

At that moment, though, he looked like an unhappy idiot. I wished I had been a lip-reader so I could have understood what he was saying, but even without a script it looked like young Tad was giving the person on the other end a piece of his mind, a commodity he could scarcely spare. The sort of man who talks with his hands, he punched the air in front of himself with rapid jabs, his cheeks and neck turning bright pink.

He talked for about three minutes and then slammed the receiver down. There was a sour look on his face and he was fumbling with a roll of what looked like antacid tablets, which he popped into his mouth and crushed between his capped molars like peanuts. When he'd choked them down, Tad took a long look down the hall toward the restaurant, as if making sure his conversation hadn't been overheard. Then he stormed out of the restaurant and across the parking lot to his Blazer.

As he was fishing in his pockets for the keys, I started my engine, the noise muffled by the deep rumble of the idling diesels. It was my intention to follow him for a little while, and no harm done. As I'd told Keegan, I was just an interested observer and this is what observers do—they observe.

Even if they have to sneak around to do it.

Tad wasn't a very good driver. He lurched to the edge of the parking lot, then gunned the engine, making the tires squeal and his rear end fishtail like a slalom skier on a treacherous course. It was no trick to follow him, even with the lights off, because his family's estate lies at the end of one of the few paved streets in Victory, and he was obviously headed in that direction. I knew the road so well I could have followed him by closing my eyes and feeling for familiar potholes, but that wasn't necessary. By the time I got to the four-way intersection on Main, I could already see his taillights an eighth of a mile ahead, turning left through the front gates of the estate.

I pulled to the curb and cut the motor. I'd give him a few minutes to get comfortable, and then I'd ease my way through the narrow belt of aspens at the edge of his property and settle in for a spell. My biggest worry was that I'd bump into one of the feds who were also watching his place out there in the dark forest and be mistaken for a bear. Worst case, they might shoot me by mistake. Best case, I'd have to explain what I was doing there, which would be difficult.

When five minutes had passed, I buttoned my coat up around my neck, took a pair of warm wool gloves out of the seat pouch, and started picking my way through the grove of trees that separated me from the Bauer estate. It was tricky out there in the dark, working through the deadfall and undergrowth without a flashlight, but the light from the moon peeping through the overcast was enough to give some definition to the forest shapes. At the edge of the clearing I stopped, sank down with my back against a large pine, and pulled the binoculars from my pocket. They wouldn't pick up much in the dark between me and the house, but I could focus in clearly on the warm light coming from the windows of the estate as Tad turned the fixtures on one by one.

It was twenty minutes later that I began to imagine I could see the dark outline of a large man standing by the side of the barn. I squinted, trying to make him out, but I couldn't be sure where his limbs and body ended and the background began. If it was a man, he was dressed in dark clothing to take advantage of the night, and he was doing the same thing I was—watching Tad Bauer's house. I decided the only way I could find out who he was was by creeping closer, but the risk was too great. For the time being, I'd watch him watching. I have to say one thing, though; he was patient and still, and it wasn't long before I was starting to think I'd been wrong and my eyes had been playing tricks on me.

Across the front lawn of the estate, I could hear the hum of the mercury-vapor yard lights and the occasional cry of a night-hunting bird. I turned my attention back to the house, where the lights were blazing on both the lower and upper floors. From one of the corner rooms, I could see the flickering luminescence of a television set. I wished I had thought to bring a thermos of hot coffee, and I wished I could light a cigarette. I searched my pockets for a substitute, but the best I could do was an old package of cinnamon-flavored toothpicks from the last time I'd tried to quit smoking. I threw those into the bushes at my side and scrunched down into my coat. If I had to sit there in the damp and cold, waiting for who knew what, at least I could make myself warm.

If you've ever sat alone in the forest at night with no fire or flashlight, you know it isn't long before even the most stouthearted outdoorsman begins to imagine that the woods around him are teeming with slobbering, starving meat eaters just waiting for him to drop his guard. Although I was sure they were all around me, I was especially concerned about what I heard sneaking through the undergrowth to my right, the leaves whispering as they were brushed by something furry. I strained my eyes to pierce the shadowy brush, but it was no use.

Finally, a small head appeared at the base of the nearest chokecherry bush, the animal's nose pushing forward cautiously as it sniffed the breeze to see if it could find a clue about who I was and what I was doing there. I had my pistol out of the holster before I realized that I was about to shoot a common house cat, a big gray tom from the looks of him, and none too happy about sharing his space with me. He hissed once before walking stiff-legged to the pack of cinnamon toothpicks I'd tossed in his direction, gave them a good snuffle, and disappeared the way he'd come.

After that, I kept the revolver on my lap. Not that I was afraid of the cat or the dark. I just wanted to be ready in case he came back with some of his friends. I suppose I was a funny sight, sitting out there armed and jumpy, but since there was nobody there to see me, I didn't care.

It was 12:30 A.M. when I saw the yellow headlights of a small car turning in to the estate, its tires crunching gravel as it came to a stop in pitch darkness beneath an aspen at the front of the house. The car door slammed, and I could hear the tap of someone's heels on the concrete of the front walk. I adjusted the binoculars and focused on the doorway, just as Tad's visitor opened the front door, the light streaming out to illuminate her features.

Tad's houseguest was Ellen Vaughn . . .

And she'd used her own key.

8

Later that night, someone snuck into Ernesto Varga's chicken coops and poisoned all his chickens, but I didn't hear about it until 9:15 the next morning when I walked in the front door of the office and saw Ernesto sitting in a chair in front of Frankie Bull's desk with two of the dead birds nestled in his lap.

A small, nervous man with a thick mane of straight black hair he combed back from his high forehead, Ernesto Varga ran the U Gas It station at the edge of Victory's city limits and used the money he made there to feed and clothe his family—his wife, who was in the final stages of multiple sclerosis, six kids, and the mother-in-law he'd brought up from Los Mochis, Mexico, about four years before. He supplemented his meager income by doing odd jobs—landscaping, wood splitting, and the like—and raising chickens. As long as the hens were productive, he sold their eggs. After that, the birds went into his family's stew pot.

Technically, it was against the law to raise chickens within the city limits, but Ernesto needed the income, and frankly, lots of us in Victory wanted the eggs. When we drove by his dilapidated old house—with sheets of corrugated aluminum patching the roof, plywood sealing up the broken windows, and always at least one dead pickup truck leaking on the driveway—Frankie and I just pretended we didn't see the two chicken coops in his yard or the hundred or so chickens that were always pecking around his threadbare plot of ground for scraps.

That morning, Ernesto looked angry, but his anger was tempered by an even more powerful emotion—fear.

According to Frankie and Ernesto, who told me the story as soon as I'd hung up my coat and scoured the office for a black plastic trash bag—which I held open so Ernesto could deposit the corpses of the birds—the Varga clan had called their dog inside around 10:30 the night before, watched a little television, and went to sleep around midnight. None of them heard or saw anything out of the ordinary until the next morning, when Ernesto came out about 5:30 to care for his chickens and saw twenty or thirty of their dead bodies scattered around his yard. He found the rest of them dead inside the coop and came to the reasonable conclusion that the only way someone could have killed them all without waking his family was to creep in and toss enough poisoned feed around the coop and yard to kill his entire stock.

He'd brought a coffee can full of suspect chicken feed to the office and Frankie had already made arrangements to send it to the Department of Criminal Investigation lab in Cheyenne so they could run tests and tell us what agent the chicken killer had used. He'd also made an inspection of Ernesto's yard and chicken coops that had failed to turn up anything that might help us identify the culprit. There were so many people moving around the Vargas' property every day that it was impossible to pick out footprints that didn't belong; none of the neighbors had seen anyone lurking around, the suspect hadn't left anything behind.

A quick call to Shapiro's Hardware—the only place in Victory that sold various poisons for rats, mice, and other pests—confirmed Frankie's suspicion that the poison hadn't been purchased there, at least recently. According to Howard Shapiro's records, the last sale of strong poison they'd made was almost four months previous, and that had been to Curly Ahearn, who needed some arsenic to clean out the tribe of skunks living in the pasture next to his house.

If the DCI could tell us exactly what poison had been used, maybe we could do some legwork and find out where it had been purchased and by whom, but that was about our only hope. I explained that to Ernesto, who was twisting his gimme cap in his hands like a dishrag and whose eyes betrayed his resignation to the fact we'd never catch the perpetrator.

"It's not just the chickens, Chief Starbranch," he said sadly when I'd finished. "I can always get new chickens. It's my family I'm worried about. I can't get a new one of those."

"You think whoever did this is after your family?" I asked. The Varga clan was poor, and the kids—all of whom were under ten years old—always looked like they could use a haircut and a new suit of clothes. But they were a polite, law-abiding clan. They worked hard and they bothered no one. "Why would anyone want to harm your family?"

Ernesto shrugged his slight shoulders and looked down at his knobby knuckles. "Who knows?" he said quietly. "But they say they gonna hurt us."

"Who says?" I asked. I felt my face clouding and a stirring of protective anger in my gut as I imagined what I'd like to do to the kind of bully who would threaten anyone as simple and decent as Ernesto Varga. "Nobody's gonna hurt you if I can help it, Ernesto. That's a promise."

Frankie Bull—who's suffered his share of the brand of Western racism that looks down on Hispanics, Indians, and nearly everyone who isn't a white Protestant—was wearing a dark scowl of his own. He leaned forward at his desk, his hand resting on the hilt of his bowie knife. "You better show him the note, Ernesto. Then he'll know what you mean."

Ernesto nodded in agreement, reached into the inside pocket of his brown canvas work coat, and fished around until he came up with a folded piece of blue-lined notebook paper. He laid the paper on his knee and unfolded it carefully, smoothing it with his rough hands. When he was finished, he handed the paper to me—holding it with the tips of his fingers as if he suspected it was contaminated.

"This was tacked to the door of the chicken coop," he explained, his eyes darting anxiously from the paper to me as I began to read.

The note was written in black ink by someone with a tight, jerky scrawl—but in spite of the bad penmanship, the message was painfully clear. "The chickens was just a warning," the note read. "Better get your lard-assed cactus-nigger wife and your greaser kids out of Victory before we come for *you*!"

I felt like wadding the note in a ball and setting it aflame, but I slipped it inside a manila folder and pushed it to the corner of my desk. "I'm sorry about this, Ernesto," I said, pointing at the folder. I felt like I was apologizing for the whole world, not just the bastards who'd written the note and killed his chickens.

He smiled gently to let me know he didn't think I was personally responsible. "No need for you to be sorry, Chief Starbranch," he said. "You're just tryin' to help."

There wasn't much more we could do for him right then, and we all knew it. "We'll drive by your place as often as we can," I told him. "I wouldn't worry too much if I were you. Chances are this was just a bunch of—"

Ernesto's head popped up like it was controlled by a wire. "Wouldn't worry?" he asked, as if he couldn't believe what he'd heard. "These people used poison on my chickens, Mr. Starbranch." He paused as if his point was proven, then went on in a rush. "I'm gonna go home and get my gun out of the closet—"

"Come on, Ernesto," I broke in, "I don't think that's—"

"Then I'm gonna start loadin' our stuff in the truck."

I felt my shoulders sag as Ernesto stood and jammed his hat on his head. His bushy hair stuck out at the sides like black wings. "We liked livin' in Victory," he simply, "but we don't wanna die here."

When Ernesto Varga had gone, Frankie Bull and I chewed over the poisoning of his chickens and discussed the possibility it was related to the recent vandalism at Shapiro's Hardware. Based on what he'd read about similar examples of racial violence and intimidation in other parts of the country, Frankie thought both incidents were the work of teenagers—and if I hadn't learned about the suspected activities of the Posse Comitatus in Victory just the day before, I might have agreed wholeheartedly. As it was, I had a gut feeling the Posse was somehow connected to the vandalism and the poisonings, as well as Sonny's murder. Since the connections seemed too tenuous in my own mind, though—the paintings and chicken poisonings seemed the work of amateurs, while Sonny's murder was definitely done by someone with a more brutal, active bent—I decided to keep my suspicions to myself for the time being.

Still, Frankie's theory couldn't be discounted entirely. We put our heads together and drew up a list of the town's youthful miscreants, young men and women who might be capable of poisoning helpless birds. Since there are only about twenty people of high-school age in Victory, however, it was a very short list—the same people we'd suspected of spray painting Shapiro's Hardware, at least until their alibis checked out.

"Kenny Sanders and Jared Barnes," Frankie said, writing their names at the top of a fresh page in his notebook. "They're the only ones who come to mind."

High-school seniors, both of them hulking louts who'd been on the wrong side of the law on numerous occasions, Sanders and Barnes were large young men who got a kick out of intimidating the other kids with their imposing size. "It's worth a call," I told Frankie. "Why don't you get hold of their parents? Find out where they were last night."

While Frankie found the right numbers in the Victory phone book and punched out the digits for the Barnes household, I took a few minutes to find out what had happened in Victory while I'd been in Cheyenne the day before—poked through the wire basket where we file our call and arrest reports before moving them to more permanent folders at the end of each week. From the look of things, Frankie had earned his wages while I was away from the office. There were at least eight copies of traffic citations he'd written, plus a half-dozen incident reports, most of them for minor violations—except for the fistfight he'd apparently broken up during the late afternoon at Robbie Moore's steak house.

I knew I owed Frankie some kind of explanation for being gone for all of the previous day, since I hadn't even bothered to call in. It's not very considerate in a two-person shop for one of the two to dump everything on his partner. I wasn't eager to talk about it, though. I needed a little more time to sort out what I'd learned in my own mind before I unloaded it on someone else.

I was still scanning the last of the reports when Frankie slammed the phone down and folded his muscular arms across his chest. "Shit," he grumbled. "Shit, shit, shit."

"Nobody home?" I asked.

"Oh, Mrs. Barnes was home all right." He scowled. "But Jared wasn't, at least not last night."

I smirked skeptically. Mrs. Barnes had provided an alibi for her delinquent son on more than one occasion that later proved untrue. "Where was the young whippersnapper?" I asked. "Out collecting for the American Cancer Society?"

"Nah," he said. "He's in Denver for a concert. Left about three days ago."

"And Kenny Sanders?"

Frankie grimaced. "Mrs. Barnes says they're sharing the same room at the Bonaventure Motel."

"Easy enough to check." Hell, maybe they *were* in Denver.

"Sure," he said, lifting the phone receiver again. "I'll call the motel," he said. He paused, shook his head. "But if they've been there the whole time . . ."

I finished his thought. "Then who killed those damned chickens?"

I listened to Frankie's end of the conversation while he spoke to the owner of the Bonaventure Motel and confirmed the recent whereabouts of Sanders and Barnes. It sounded like the boys had indeed been in Denver for the last few days, which meant they weren't suspects in the slaughter of the Varga hens after all. I felt a stab of disappointment and saw the same emotion written on Frankie's face.

Frankie was still on the phone when my own line jangled. I picked up the receiver and held it between my shoulder and ear while I lit a smoke. It was Mayor Curly Ahearn, my boss, calling from his bar. In the background, I could hear the sound of the jukebox and muted conversation of the early morning crowd at the Silver Dollar.

"Mornin', Harry," he rasped. "Enjoy your vacation?"

I didn't know what he was talking about, and I wasn't in a mood to play games with Curly just then. "What vacation, Curly?" I asked sharply. "You know damned well I've—"

"I called three times yesterday," he broke in. "Twice, I got the answering machine and the third time, I got Frankie. Left a message, which we both know you haven't answered."

I reached across my desk for the short stack of pink phone-message slips waiting there and fanned them out like a deck of cards. Sure enough, Curly's was there, about third from the top. "Sorry," I said.

"I was working out of the office all day. Just got in and haven't had time to make any calls."

"Business?" he asked.

"Of course it was business, Curly," I said testily. "If you'll remember, there was a murder outside of Victory just the other day, and a few other strange things have been going on here as well."

"That's what I'm callin' about," he said. There was an edge of irritation in his own voice now. Time to back off.

"Yeah?" I asked, waited for him to go on.

"Have you learned anything about Sonny's killing yet?" he asked a second later.

"Not much," I admitted. "At least nothing I'm ready to talk about." In the background, one of his customers yelled for the barmaid to bring him another beer and tomato juice.

"Well," he said, "I guess I don't have to tell you that the sooner you wrap this thing up the better."

"No, Curly, you don't have to tell me that," I said. "Believe me, we're working just as fast as we—"

"Because I have a feeling something very wrong is happening in Victory," he interrupted, "and I'd like to put an end to it before somebody does something stupid."

"Stupid?"

"Yeah, stupid," he said. "People in town have heard what's been going on, not only at Sonny's, but at Shapiro's and the Varga place—and they're scared. You might not have noticed it, since you weren't around the office yesterday, but there are more guns on the street than I've seen in years. This town is turnin' into an armed camp, Harry, and scared people sometimes do stupid things."

He paused briefly. "I'd like to put this behind us before that happens."

I didn't bother telling Curly I'd noticed the same thing myself. Almost every pickup on the street had a rifle in the rear window rack, and more than a few people on the street were packing sidearms. Not that it's unusual to see people carrying guns around here, particularly during the fall hunting season. There are no restrictive gun laws in Wyoming, and because of that, it's legal to carry firearms almost anywhere you want, unless your weapon is of the automatic military variety.

Still, it seemed I was seeing even more weapons around town than normal, and I agreed with Curly it was in the town's best interest to calm people down before someone got careless. I promised him I'd do everything in my power to keep the lid on the keg. Maybe, I suggested, Frankie and I could do some extra patrolling, make people feel we were watching out for them. People are more secure when their hometown cops are a visible presence.

That sounded good to Curly. Before he'd let me off the phone, however, he made me promise to call him on a more regular basis.

It did not sound quite as good to Frankie, who groaned when I told him my plan for us to spend the day walking a beat. Like any good horseman, he hates to walk, particularly when he can ride. But even he saw the wisdom in making ourselves more visible. We agreed to meet at Ginny's for lunch, and decided he'd walk the south end of town while I walked the north.

I turned on the answering machine and pulled my coat from the peg as Frankie shrugged into the black leather motorcycle jacket he wears in lieu of a uniform coat. When it was zipped, he adjusted the bowie knife and .44 Magnum on his hip, seated his black Stetson on his head and his mirrored aviator glasses on his nose, gave his long braids a flip, then shuffled off in the direction of Gus Alzonakis's steak house.

Down the block, I could see Anthony Baldi's sheriff's department Blazer pulling to a stop in front of Shapiro's Hardware. Aaron Cohen was in the passenger's seat and Ken Keegan was in back. As I closed the door to the office behind me, I saw them heading my way, so I did the only thing I could think of to avoid talking to Tony Baldi. I turned my collar up against the wind and scurried off in the opposite direction.

By the time I got back to the farmhouse that night, I was in a truly lousy mood. For starters, my feet were swelling from all the walking I'd done that day, and the tickle at the base of my throat was the first sign of a cold coming on. Also, I hadn't had a cigarette since early afternoon, and every nerve in my body felt like it had direct access to a light socket.

I cursed when I discovered that the pack in my coat pocket was empty, and realized I'd forgotten to stop for more before driving home. Before I even knew what I was doing, I was digging through the trash can in search of a butt that wasn't too disgusting to smoke. I found one that was only half-soggy from the coffee grounds it had been buried in, and almost lit it before I was saved by the telephone jangling in the living room. I crushed the butt between my fingers and yanked the receiver from the cradle.

"Harry?" The tentative voice on the other end of the line belonged to Ellen Vaughn.

"Ellen? Is something wrong?"

"I need to talk to you, Harry. Could I come out to your house?"

"Sure, you could do that," I said, looking at the shambles of my place, dirty socks on the floor and plates on most of the end tables. "But I could come to your apartment if you like. Or we could meet somewhere. Do you know the Copper's Corners bar on Third Street in Laramie? I could be there in half an hour."

"There's no sense in your driving in," she said. "I need to get out of here for a while anyway. Is an hour all right?"

"Sure. Have you eaten? If not, I'll throw a couple of chops on while I'm waiting."

"Sounds good. I'll bring the wine."

For the next sixty minutes, I cleaned like a madman, stuffing my dirty clothes into the closet in my bedroom, the dirty dishes in the cabinet under the kitchen sink. I gave the floors a lick and a promise with the broom, and even made sure there was toilet paper in the bathroom. When I was finished, I looked around and decided the house looked presentable enough, as long as she wasn't wearing her glasses.

The chops had just begun sizzling under the broiler when I heard her knocking at the back door. She was wearing blue jeans and a chocolate-brown leather bomber jacket with a fleece collar, her dark hair pulled back and held in place with a lavender ribbon. Her eyes were so bruised and bloodshot it looked like she was wearing goggles, and from its size and puffiness, it looked like her nose might be broken as well. "Thanks for letting me come out," she said. "I didn't know where else to go."

I took her by the arm and led her into the kitchen, where she sank heavily into one of the chairs, her shoulders slumped and her bottom lip quivering. I turned away and poured her a whiskey. "What happened, Ellen?" I asked, handing her the glass, which she took gratefully, draining it in one swallow. I could feel an undirected anger building, feel the blood pounding in my ears and my cheeks starting to burn.

"It was Tad," she said, rubbing the empty glass between her palms. "I really thought he was going to kill me." Her sobs came freely then, and I held her while her tears soaked my shoulder. I patted her back and told her that she was safe now, that I'd look after her. I told her it was all right to be afraid, and all right to be angry about what had happened. I told her the bruises would soon be gone, and I told her that if the son of a bitch ever tried this again, I'd break his neck with my own hands.

When she'd had her cry, she hurried off into the living room to compose herself but was back five minutes later, wiping her swollen, purple nose with a tissue. When she pulled it away from her face, it was flecked with blood, and I felt an anger building in me that I hadn't felt since my oldest son was jumped by a bunch of punks with baseball bats on his way home from junior high school. After he came dragging in to the kitchen, his new jacket ripped at the shoulders and his lips bleeding from where they'd beat him for his pocket change, I tracked them down at the Cherry Creek Mall and arrested them before I had the chance to do what I really wanted, which was to give them an opportunity to feel some of the pain and humiliation they were so eager to inflict on those who were weaker. For me, controlling anger like that takes a supreme effort of will. It's dangerous, and a part of me that's a bit frightening.

Ellen must have sensed what I was feeling, because she took both of my hands in hers and pulled me toward a seat at the table. Then, she poured herself another whiskey, took a second glass from the cupboard, and held the bottle over the glass with a question in her eyes.

"No, thanks," I said. "I'm trying to cut down, and besides, I want to listen to you with a clear head."

"I suppose it was my own fault," she said. "After you left the other night, I stewed for a long time over what you'd told me, and there was no way my car could have been at Sonny's the night he was killed—unless someone took it from Tad's house, where I'd left it while we were out to dinner."

"And you think that's what happened?" I asked.

"I don't know. That's what I went there last night to find out. I'd finally decided that the only way to handle it was to confront him, so that's what I went out there to do."

I didn't tell her that I'd been watching the house when she arrived, because that would have meant explaining more than I was ready to explain. Instead, I watched her as she fought the memory of what must have been a terrifying experience. For a moment, it looked like she might cry again, but she swallowed it and went on. "When I told him that someone must have taken my car, he denied that it was even possible at first, kind of laughing like I was some kind of paranoid or something. But I kept at him for a long time, wouldn't let him off the hook.

"Finally, I told him that you had a witness, and that's when he started acting crazy, banging the walls and swearing. He wasn't worried about me, and he wasn't denying anything anymore. All he wanted to know was if I'd told you who I was with that night, and what you'd said."

"Did you tell him?"

"No, I was getting pretty scared by then. I'd never seen him so violent, and he was swearing, Harry, calling me a lying cunt and a fucking bitch, over and over. Then, he hit me the first time, in the face, and we didn't talk much more after that."

"What did he say exactly, Ellen? Can you remember?"

"How could I forget?" she asked. "He said, 'If you get me involved with the cops, you fucking slut, I'll cut your fucking throat.'

"I think he meant it, Harry. You should have seen his eyes, like an animal's. The only way I could get out of there was to beg."

"And he let you go."

"Yeah," she said, shivering at the memory. "But he kicked me in the stomach first and told me that if I knew what was good for me,

I'd keep my goddamned mouth closed. He said I'd be sorry if I didn't."

"He'd never done anything like that before? He'd never hit you?"

"Jesus, Harry," she said, "I'd finally figured out that he was a bastard, and that's why I broke up with him the night Sonny was killed. But I'd never seen anything in him that suggested he could be so vicious, not in all the time I've known him."

According to Ellen, she'd met Tad Bauer at the start of the summer, and even though he seemed pretty full of himself, he was charming and generous. Once, he picked her up after work and flew her to Denver for a romantic dinner, just because he thought she was looking tired and a little blue.

"He was the kind who'd send flowers to the office for no reason, and ask the radio station to dedicate my favorite song," Ellen said. "I'd just come out of a bad relationship that had lasted for three years, and I suppose the attention was good for my ego. I don't know. At any rate, we dated for the rest of the summer, and I spent a lot of my free time with him."

"Until last week?"

"That's right. I didn't start to suspect that he was seeing other women until late September," she explained. "And it was this month before I knew for sure."

"Ellen," I said, "I have to ask you something, and I want you to be truthful."

"Okay."

"In the time you spent with Tad in the last few months, did it seem to you that he might be involved in something illegal? Something he wanted to hide, besides his other women?"

"You mean business dealings?"

"Whatever."

"No," she said thoughtfully, "he never talked to me about his business, although I assumed he was working for his father's brewing company. He did get calls at home at odd hours, but he took them in his study. I never heard what he was discussing."

"How about visitors? Did anyone come to the house who looked odd or out of place? Anyone you can remember at all?"

"No," she said. "A couple of times, people came to the house while I was there, but Tad didn't invite them into the living quarters where I was. Alex made sure unexpected visitors stayed in the front hall."

"Alex?"

"Tad's bodyguard," she said. "Someone tried to kidnap Tad about fifteen years ago so they could get a ransom from his dad. Ever since then, papa has hired a bodyguard to stay with Tad all the time."

"I've never seen the bodyguard in town, or around the place."

"That's because Tad doesn't believe he's necessary. When they're away from Chicago and his father isn't around to see what's going on, Tad and Alex go their own separate ways. Tad spends every minute that he can carousing and Alex stays at the estate working out and watching X-rated movies on the VCR."

"Do you know his last name?"

"Thibault, I believe. He sounds like he's from the Midwest. Harry, why is any of this important?"

"I don't know," I said. "It may not be important at all. Tell me this: Tad usually goes home with the rest of the summer people after Labor Day, doesn't he? Do you know why he's stayed on?"

"I thought it was because of me," she said quietly. "Now, I don't really know."

"One more thing, Ellen."

"Yes?"

"Can you tell me why you came here this evening?"

"I was afraid to stay at home," she said simply. "And I trust you."

I trusted her, too, and I believed what she'd told me. Ellen Vaughn was a woman who'd gotten herself mixed up in something dark and brutal, but I didn't believe she had blood on her hands. At that moment, I was happy I'd kept Bill Cheney's information to myself. And I intended to keep it to myself until I found some way to get Ellen out of this mess. In the meantime, I'd see if I couldn't make life a bit less comfortable for Tad Bauer.

"If you'll press charges, I'll go out and arrest him for assault in the morning," I said. "He'll be out of jail by noon, but at least you'll have the satisfaction of seeing him in handcuffs."

"No," she said, "I can't do that. After what I saw in Tad's eyes last night, I'd be looking over my shoulder the rest of my life if I was responsible for putting him in jail, even for an afternoon. His ego couldn't handle it and he'd get even, Harry. And you might not be around to stop him."

As much as the cop in me hated to admit it, she had a point. The police, and the justice system in general, have a dismal record when it comes to really protecting the victims of this kind of abuse. We can arrest the abusers, the chickenshit wife beaters, the cowardly kid rapers, the craven losers who thrash the women in their lives to show them who's boss, but we can't watch over the victims twenty-four hours a day afterward. And too many times, as soon as they think we've stopped watching, the abusers are back.

If we're lucky, the victim comes out of that scrape alive. Too often, they don't.

"I understand," I said. "But how about this? How about tomorrow Frankie and I go out there and scare the crap out of him? If Tad's half the man I think he is, that'll be all it takes to convince him to leave you alone."

It was the first thing I'd said all night that made her smile.

"That," she said, "sounds like a fine idea."

Ellen picked at her meat and salad, but she put away most of the bottle of wine she'd brought in her coat pocket. When she finished the wine and I finished my meal, she excused herself from the table while I cleared away the dishes. A few moments later, I heard the shower running. She opened the bathroom door and poked her head around the corner.

"I'm making myself at home," she said. "I hope you don't mind."

"Not at all. There's a bathrobe hanging on the back of the door, and a fresh toothbrush in the medicine cabinet. I hope you like soap on a rope. It's all my youngest son ever gives for presents."

She was laughing gently as she closed the door, and I made my way into the living room, where I pulled Van Morrison's *Moondance* album from the stack and turned the stereo on low. Nothing Ellen had told me put any pieces of the puzzle into place. She wasn't able to tie Tad or any of his cronies to Sonny's murder or to the Posse Comitatus. But the violent way he'd reacted when she pushed him about who might have taken her car said he was worried. I wanted to know exactly what he was worried about.

I closed my eyes and let the good music wash over me. Morrison's raspy melodies, I've found, are appropriate for any situation—contemplation, relaxation, stimulation. He was into the third chorus of "Caravan" when Ellen padded in from the shower, barefoot and bundled into my favorite terry-cloth robe.

"You know," she said, toweling her dark hair, "until last night, no one ever hit me in anger before. At first, I just felt surprised. It took a while for my brain to figure out it was really happening. Then, I got scared, and then the pain started coming on, so bad it made my stomach roll. I can't imagine going through it again."

"Is it still hurting?" I asked. "I could crack some ice and wrap it up in a washrag. That might take some of the swelling down."

"No, thanks," she said, sinking down onto the couch, fluffing one of my raggedy pillows, and tucking her lean, muscular legs up underneath the robe. "I spent all last night with a cold pack on the bridge of my nose. What you see here is a definite improvement."

We listened to Morrison in companionable silence, until the last cut ended and Van's voice trailed off into the Irish ether like a Celtic piper's call.

Without makeup, Ellen looked even younger than her years, and the memory of the vague stirrings of lust I'd felt when I first met her caused a tiny quiver of shame to go scurrying across what's left of my shriveled conscience. I was glad I hadn't acted on my hormonal urges and that I'd behaved myself. I just hoped that nobody found out, since that kind of thing can spoil your reputation.

"I think you should stay here tonight," I said. "You look like you could use a good night's rest, and I'll wake you up in plenty of time for your morning classes."

Ellen leaned forward, holding my robe shut at the neck and searching my face for some hint of my general trustworthiness. It's a look I'd seen before.

"You'll be safe here," I said, smiling what I hoped was my most reassuring, asexual smile. "The bed's comfortable, and I'll be right here on the sofa if you need me."

Ellen got up and walked across the room, where she gave my shoulder a pat and mussed my hair.

"Thanks, Harry," she said. "I could use a friend right now."

When I could hear her snoring softly in the bedroom, I got out my box of fur, feathers, and colored string and tied a half-dozen decent Renegades. I never use the things myself, but they're Curly's favorite fly, and he's always running short. I figured that if I waited for just the right moment—about two seconds after he'd lost his last unraveling Renegade in a bramble bush—I could trade them to him for a six-pack apiece. As I worked, I listened to the north wind hurling itself against the eaves of my sturdy little house, the pine logs crackling cheerfully in the woodstove, and the gurgling of the pot of water I'd put on top of the stove to boil for tea.

I felt good, and it suddenly dawned on me that this was a banner day. For the first time in recent memory, I'd spent an entire evening without taking a drink, not even an after-dinner beer. I looked at my hands to see if they were shaking, but they weren't. My vision was clear, and I didn't have the cold sweats. There weren't any pink elephants marching around the living room, either. All of those, I decided, were good signs.

Even so, it occurred to me that if I continued along this particular path of abstinence for very long, I'd probably have to come up with a couple of new vices to replace my old ones. I'd never really tried clean living before, but I half suspected that my body wouldn't react well to it over the long haul. The only problem would be finding a replacement vice that didn't require me to eat anything made of tofu or take part in any exercise that demanded too much physical exertion. I can't see any point of making myself tired, even if it is good for me.

When the tea had brewed, I turned the lights off and sat for a while in the dancing orange glow from the stove, letting the soothing warmth travel through my sore feet and up my legs. In a few minutes, I thought, I'd drag a wool blanket out of the hall closet and curl up in front of the woodstove. But first, before I could talk myself out of it and feeling more guilt than you can imagine for not doing it sooner, I picked up the phone and punched out a familiar number.

It rang five times before it was answered, the small, nine-year-old voice having a hard time competing with the raucous background noise—his older brother's heavy metal and what sounded like a heated argument over homework between his mother and his middle brother.

"Starbranch residence," he said. "May I help you?"

It was, I knew, his entire repertoire of telephone etiquette, and unless I said something soon, he'd probably hang up.

"Hi, sweetie," I said finally. "This is your daddy. . . ."

9

I had set the alarm for 6:00, but Ellen beat me awake the next morning and had coffee bubbling on the stove and a pound of bacon sizzling in the cast-iron frying pan by the time it went off.

I stayed on the couch for a while with my eyes closed, listening to her rustling around the kitchen and smelling the luscious aroma of coffee. That's one of my favorite ways to wake up in the morning, and it's maybe the worst thing about being a bachelor. There's nobody but you to make the morning coffee, and you can never wake up to the ambrosial scent if you're the one who has to get up and make it.

Even though Ellen was wearing yesterday's clothes, she looked fresh and rested, and she was humming a tune to herself while she puttered. The dark purple of her shiners had mellowed some, and her nose was beginning to look like a regulation nose again. When she saw me standing in the doorway, she gave me a cheerful smile and a wave.

"You look like a man who needs an eye-opener," she said, dragging one of my ceramic mugs from the cupboard. "Do you take it black, or adulterated?"

"As black as Tad Bauer's heart," I said, taking the steaming cup gratefully.

"I don't think I can brew it that black," she said. "I don't know if anyone can, although the river sludge my grandpa called coffee might have come close."

When the bacon was done and I'd fried a half-dozen eggs and browned some toast, we took our breakfast outside and munched happily in the late October sunshine. Across the yard, Edna Cook was coming back from her chicken coop with a couple dozen brown eggs in her wire basket. When she saw Ellen, she hesitated for about a tenth of a second and then headed in our direction when she realized my companion wasn't Karen or my ex-wife, both of whom are occasional visitors to the farm. It's not that my friend Edna is a snoop, it's just that she likes to know who I'm spending time with.

I stood up to relieve Edna of her egg basket. "Mornin', Edna," I said. "Coffee?"

"No, thanks. I already had a pot."

Ellen stood and dusted off the seat of her jeans, then offered Edna her hand. "Ellen Vaughn is my name. How do you do?"

"Well, I do fine, young lady, thanks for asking. If those chickens don't start doing a little better though, they're gonna be soup."

The two of them shot the breeze while I carried our dishes back inside. When I returned, they were old pals.

"I was just telling Ellen that my miserable-acting grandchildren are coming to visit me this weekend, and they're bringing their miserable-acting children with them," Edna said. "So if you call on the phone, Harry, I probably won't answer."

I explained to Ellen that Edna always pretends to be deaf when her extended family is around, even though she can hear better than I do.

"It saves me from having to have a lot of conversations with them about what I should do with the rest of my life." Edna grinned wickedly. "And besides, they're not afraid to talk about me when they think I can't hear 'em. It gives me a leg up on 'em if I know what nasty little plots they're cooking up."

"You're a clever one, Edna," I said. "I was thinking about having my two youngest kids up for the weekend, too. Halloween is Thursday, and I thought that if they came up that afternoon, I could drive them back to Denver on Sunday night. Would you mind if we saddled up the horses and took a ride?"

"Hell no, it would probably do those lazy ponies some good," Edna said. "But don't let them get on the Shetland pony. He's been bucking pretty good lately, and I want to save him for my great-grandkids."

When Edna had gathered up her basket and was on her way home, Ellen pulled her car keys from the front pocket of her tight jeans and gave me a firm hug around the middle. "Thanks, Harry, for everything," she said. "I don't have any family anymore, and I get to feeling pretty alone sometimes. I think you've pulled me through, and I want you to know that I owe you one."

"You owe me nothing but a pack of Doublemint gum," I said. "And I'll take the one you're carrying in your shirt pocket." She handed me the gum. I opened it and folded a stick into my mouth, smacked my lips in appreciation.

"I'll call you," she said, smiling as she scuffed off in the direction of her car. "I still owe my wonderful company at dinner."

"I'd rather have you owe it to me than beat me out of it."

"I never welsh on a debt," she said. "It's one of my better qualities."

To tell you the truth, Ellen wasn't the only one who was feeling alone, except I didn't think a good night's rest and a decent meal would be much help in my case. I felt like the safety of my community was slipping out of my hands and I was having trouble holding on. So when I got to the office that morning I told Frankie everything. I told him about Bill Cheney and confronting Ellen with the information that he'd seen her car at Sonny's the night of the murder; I told him about Aaron Cohen and Ken Keegan; I told him about the Posse Comitatus and the feds' suspicions that elements of the Posse were operating in Victory. I told him of my hunch that those elements might have had something to do with the spray painting at Shapiro's and the business with Ernesto's chickens. Finally, I told him what Tad Bauer had done to Ellen.

He listened quietly to the whole story and nodded his head in agreement when I told him that I didn't think Ellen had been involved. "I knew there was more going on than you were saying," he said when I'd finished. "But I figured you'd get around to telling me in your own good time. So what do you think we should do?"

"There's not a hell of a lot we can do right now," I said. "So far, the only crimes that took place in our jurisdiction were the spray painting at Shapiro's and the killing of those chickens. We're not getting anywhere fast with those. There's also Tad's assault on Ellen, but she won't press charges."

"Too bad. I think I'd enjoy going out there to roust the asshole,"

Frankie said. "I never could figure men who pound on women and kids, but it gives me a certain amount of satisfaction to give them a dose of their own medicine."

"Well, we may get the chance to do that. I told Ellen that even if she wouldn't press charges, there was no reason why I couldn't have a heart-to-heart with Tad. Who knows, maybe he'll try to thump one of us while we're visiting, and we can arrest him for that. And if he doesn't try, maybe I'll just beat the shit out of him and say that he did."

"That's not legal, Harry. I know that because I watch a lot of television shows about lawyers."

"I'm aware that it's not within the letter of the law," I said. "But I'm not opposed to ignoring the letter of the law in the name of justice. Are you?"

"Not in the least," he said.

"Good. In that case, I'll take Tad, and you take the bodyguard. It'll be over before they know what hit them."

"Bodyguard? Who said anything about a bodyguard?"

"I knew there was something I'd forgotten to mention," I said, pulling a spare set of handcuffs from the cabinet and checking the load in my revolver. When I was satisfied, I set the hammer down on an empty cylinder and snapped the weapon into my holster.

Frankie smiled like a man who's just realized he's been conned, muttered a curse under his breath.

"Don't worry, podna," I said. I stood, pulled my hat from the rack. "I hear he's on the small side."

Alex Thibault, who opened the door when we rang, looked like he was big enough to go bear hunting with a stick. Barrel-chested and ham-fisted, his thick legs looked like tree stumps and the muscle shirt he was wearing did justice to the massive bulk of his upper body. The top of his head had been shaved bald, but the bottom half of his face was hidden by a full beard, black and curly. There were jailhouse tattoos on each of his fingers, but they were so blurry I couldn't read what they said.

Thibault merely grunted when I flashed my badge and told him I wanted to speak with his boss, but he let us in, motioning for us to wait in the foyer. He rumbled off in the direction of the living quarters, the muscles in his thick thighs bulging like cantaloupes under the tight fabric of his workout sweats.

"Better living through chemistry," Frankie muttered when Tad's gorilla was out of hearing range. "If he keeps taking those steroids, though, his gums will bleed and his nuts will shrink to the size of chickpeas."

"Maybe you should warn him when he comes back," I said. "I'll bet he'd be grateful to know what's in store for him. Then again, he might break you over his knee like a bad habit."

"He might try," Frankie said, looking in Thibault's direction with a hungry stare.

While we waited, I took a look at what I could see of the interior of the house and decided it was further proof that lots of money won't buy an ounce of class. I suspected that whoever decorated the place had visited every garage sale and auction in a thousand-mile radius to buy as many hay rakes, harnesses, old lanterns, broken-down shotguns, and privy seats as they could find. Then they hauled all that junk back to the Bauer home and nailed it to the walls.

Farm-implement chic.

Among the high-priced refuse and debris, however, there was a little good stuff mixed in. A couple of nice Jim Bama prints were hung on the walls next to a Conrad Schwering painting of the Tetons in autumn. Someone in the family must have a little taste, I decided. I doubted it was Tad.

I had walked over to take a closer look at the Bamas when I heard Tad's voice from somewhere beyond the living room, grumbling about being disturbed during his shower, a diatribe he continued until he and Thibault made their way back to the foyer. Bare chested and wearing a cheap pair of rubber bath thongs, Tad looked doughy and soft, already going to flab around the middle. He wasn't quite thirty years old, I guessed, but he looked every day of forty, especially now, without benefit of his styling gel and his expensive clothes.

While Tad glared at us, Thibault stayed about five feet behind his right shoulder, doing an interesting sort of isometric exercise with his arms that made his biceps quiver like a 747 revving up for takeoff. Neither of them invited us to sit.

"Alex says you want to talk to me," he said. He sounded as tough as an out-of-shape fat guy can sound, I suppose, but I wondered how he'd sound if Thibault wasn't slobbering in the background.

"Alex was right," I said. "You know who I am, Tad, and I think you know why I'm here. You beat a friend of mine up the other night, and what I want to know is . . . did you get a hard-on while you were hitting her?"

Tad's eyes narrowed and his jaw clenched. Thibault watched the three of us like ants on the sidewalk. "The fuck you talking about?" Tad sputtered.

"You heard me," I said. I hooked my thumbs under the leather of my holster belt and smiled. "I asked if hitting her made you horny. It's a simple question, Tad, yes or no."

It's true I'd gone to the Bauer estate that morning with the intention of provoking Tad, but I never dreamed it would be as easy as it was. Of course, he must have known why we'd come, but I don't think he was expecting that we'd dispense with all the niceties of polite conversation and go right for his throat. The direct verbal assault caught him off guard, in large part, I think, because he wasn't used to dealing with people who treated him with no respect. Especially cops.

He didn't fall for it right away, though, because a small voice in his pea brain must have been telling him that even though he wanted, more than anything in the world, to punch this mouthy, no-account cop in the chops, it might not be real smart to do it, on account of he might get punched back. Worse, he might wind up in jail.

Tad Bauer was bright enough to figure out that the entire Victory police force was standing in his living room, one of them openly insulting his masculinity. If he tried to pop me, it would be our word against his and his bodyguard's, and in Wyoming, who would the courts believe?

Three of us standing in the foyer that morning knew the answer to that question. The fourth, Alex Thibault, hadn't figured it out yet and apparently thought he'd deal with us the same way he dealt with other people who acted lippy with his pudgy boss, by cracking their skulls like walnuts. He was edging closer to Tad's shoulder, his flat eyes locked on mine like a barracuda's, when Tad motioned him back with an impatient wave of his hand. "I don't know what the hell you're talking about," Tad said, "but unless you've got a warrant, I think it's time for you to leave."

"I don't need a warrant," I said, shaking my head and moving forward until I was sure I'd invaded his personal space, "because I didn't come here to charge you with any crime or gather any evidence." I smiled even wider. "I just came out to talk to you, give you a little advice."

I emphasized my next point by giving him a sharp poke in the chest with my right index finger. "And what I've come to say is this. . . ." I poked him again. Harder. Kept my finger pointed at him like a knife blade. "I don't tolerate shit like you pulled out here the other night in my town, ever," I growled. "You mind your manners around here, you little bastard, or I'll eat you for fucking lunch."

That last was just a bit too much for Tad, who gave out a fairly good imitation of a howl and lunged at my hand. He grabbed hold and began trying to twist my arm around and down. "Get them the fuck out of here," he screamed at Thibault, who was already moving around Frankie and toward Bauer and myself.

I learned two important lessons in the next few seconds.

First, I learned that one of the things Frankie has taught me about hand-to-hand fighting is true. If you make a little knife of your hand and jab it, stiff fingers first, right into the base of someone's sternum, it knocks the air out of your opponent immediately and makes it difficult for him to keep twisting your arm. When I tried the maneuver on Tad, all the air in his lungs *whooshed* out and he fell on the floor moon-eyed, gagging, moaning, and trying to reinflate his bagpipes, all at the same time.

Second, I learned that even though monsters like Thibault may not have the brain power to remember their own phone number, some of them can move faster than a mongoose. Tad had barely hit the floor before Thibault crashed into my midsection with a linebacker's block that lifted my feet a good six inches off the tile and pitched my body about four feet backward, where its progress was rudely and abruptly halted by a Sheetrock wall.

I lost a little of my own wind in that collision, and was seeing a few pretty, swirling patterns in front of my eyes when I felt his brawny fingers close around my windpipe. I tried a feeble kick in the general direction of his gonads, but there was no power in it and his brain was in such an antediluvian state of development that it would have taken a couple of minutes for the pain signals to reach that far, even if the kick had connected—much too long to do me any good.

Had it been up to me, all I could have done would have been to close my eyes and give my ass a metaphorical kiss good-bye, because there was no way I could have pried his fingers away before he either crushed my larynx or snapped my neckbone like a pencil, either one of which seemed likely to happen in the next three seconds.

Fortunately, Alex Thibault had problems counting as high as two, so he'd forgotten I hadn't come alone. And in forgetting, he was setting himself up to learn an important lesson of his own: Never turn your back on someone like Frankie Bull in a street fight unless you've got a death wish. With a war cry that sounded in the close quarters like a golden eagle swooping down from the gray dawn sky on a prairie jackrabbit, Frankie clapped his hands hard on either side of Thibault's head, right over his ears. From the inside, it must have sounded like about a half pound of dynamite going off right in the middle of his cerebral cortex, because Alex shrieked in agony and shot away from me like a scalded cat, holding his temples as he staggered backward.

Thibault wasn't finished though, not by a long shot. Like a boxer who's caught off guard by an uppercut and momentarily stunned, he found his balance quickly, dropped his hands to fighting position, and began circling to Frankie's left. Frankie tracked his movements with his body at a right angle to Thibault's, his right leg stretched forward and his left backward, knees bent and feet flat on the floor.

Thibault came straight in, going for a bear hug around Frankie's chest, his teeth clenched with determination and rage. But when he was less than three feet away, Frankie drew his right knee up to waist level and lashed out with a short-range side kick that caught Thibault at the base of the throat. The impact knocked him backward, but he had enough juice left to come back with a sloppy overhand right, which Frankie blocked above his head. Pivoting his left wrist, he grabbed the inside of Thibault's arm and twisted it outward and down toward the bodyguard's waist. At the same time, he was following through with a powerful, twisting, right-handed punch to Thibault's nose—a combination that put the beefy musclehead flat on his back and out of commission.

Like most serious fights, it was over in less time than it takes to tell it, and Frankie had the cuffs on Thibault before a referee could have finished an eight count. Thibault's nose was already swelling, and there was plenty of blood coming from his nostrils.

Tad, meanwhile, had wisely played possum while the fists were flying, and didn't resist when I pulled his hands behind his back to fit him with his very own set of stainless-steel bracelets.

"You two cocksuckers are under arrest," I rumbled in his ear, "for felonious assault on a police officer."

They were back on the streets three and a half hours later, of course—the exact amount of time it took for Tad to call his father in Chicago, who called Jackson Simpson, Laramie's own version of F. Lee Bailey, who called Forrest Thomas, the district-court judge in Albany County, who called me, to let me know I was expected to have Tad Bauer and Alex Thibault at the courthouse in Laramie at 1:30. Simpson would enter a plea for Tad and his bodyguard, and Thomas would consider bail.

Neither had said much since we'd brought them to the office, fingerprinted, and booked them that morning, and their sullen moods weren't improved by the thirty-minute ride to Laramie in the back of the police car with their hands still cuffed behind their backs. Not only is a ride like that uncomfortable, but it seemed like everyone in Victory had heard about the arrest and was waiting on Main Street to catch a glimpse of the two reprobates as we marched them from the office to the car and drove them out of town—well under the twenty-mph speed limit. Tad, still wearing his thongs and a ragged Bart Simpson T-shirt we had laying around the office, grumbled that we were putting them on display, but we ignored him. Until the bail hearing, he was my prisoner and I was the boss. If he felt that we were going out of our way to humiliate him, well, that was his opinion and he had a right to it. In the meantime, we'd drive as fast—or as slowly—as we damned well pleased.

If you're familiar with the court system, you know that an arraignment like the one we were on our way to is a simple affair. On our side was Paul McDermot—a nervous-looking, jug-eared assistant with the county prosecutor's office who could never seem to find a suit to fit his bony frame. He'd tell the judge what Bauer and Thibault were charged with and make a bail suggestion. The judge would then take the defendants' not-guilty plea from Simpson and—after talking a little while with the attorneys—decide whether to grant bail and how much it should be.

The only unusual thing about this hearing would be the fact that someone had pulled some strings to make sure Bauer got a little same-day service. Usually, people charged with felonies have to wait in jail at least overnight, but if you've got enough money and the best lawyer it will buy, I suppose you can sometimes even convince a judge to break with his routine.

It was too bad, I thought, that Tad might not have the chance to enjoy our hospitality overnight. The eight-by-ten jail cell in Victory is very cozy, and while the TV has been on the fritz since 1986, there are always plenty of other enjoyable and relaxing ways to pass the time, like counting the number of bricks in the wall and catching up on your reading. When prisoners get bored with our extensive collection of *TV Guide*s and *Watchtower* magazines from the Seventh Day Adventists, Frankie is always willing to let them borrow one of our law books. The Wyoming state-statute books dealing with the maximum penalties for various crimes are always popular loaners.

Frankie and I sat at the prosecution table with McDermot while Tad and Alex took seats at the defense table with Simpson—a tall, ropy man of sharp angles and a mane of flame-red hair—who'd come dressed for the occasion in a suit nobody else in the courtroom could have afforded, a tasteful gray Stetson hat, and soft-looking black cowboy boots.

Simpson, naturally, told the judge his clients were innocent, that the state's accusations were lies and that until the matter came to trial, where the prosecution's case would fall apart faster than a graham cracker in milk, he saw no reason the nice young men he represented shouldn't be let out on their own recognizance. He even hinted that once his clients were cleared, he might bring a civil case against Frankie, myself, and the Town of Victory for all the pain and emotional suffering we'd put them through.

Thomas—140 pounds of agitated jurisprudence who looked like he'd rather be anywhere than our courtroom—listened to both attorneys and set bail for Bauer and Thibault at $25,000, with ten percent surety. It was less than the $50,000 McDermot had suggested, but it was enough to send a message to Simpson and the defendants that the judge took the charges seriously. He set a preliminary hearing date of December tenth.

"But, Your Honor," Simpson argued, "my client has to return to Chicago shortly for business, and it would be very difficult to come back here on that date. Could we possibly expedite the hearing?"

"Sorry, counselor," Thomas said, "but I'm leaving on vacation tomorrow, and I won't be back to work until December ninth. If your client thinks he might have trouble getting back here on the prescribed date, though, I'd be happy to give him the name of a good travel agent."

I'm sure Simpson was itching to launch into one of the blustery, impassioned orations he's known for, but there was no one in the gallery but us chickens and his rhetoric would have been wasted on Forrest Thomas, who'd heard it all before. With a resigned shrug of his shoulders, Simpson packed his yellow legal pad in his briefcase and told his clients they were free to go as soon as they gave the clerk $2,500 apiece. "And yes," he said, answering the question in Tad's eyes, "they'll take a check."

Outside, we shook hands with McDermot, and Frankie and I decided we'd stop off at the Buckhorn Bar for a cheeseburger before heading back to Victory. The Buckhorn is my kind of place—bullet holes in the backbar mirrors and Patsy Cline on the jukebox—and if you go in the afternoon you miss most of the college kids who start streaming in around happy hour. We were just getting in the car when Bauer called down from the top of the courthouse steps.

"Hey, Starbranch," he yelled, his flip-flops slapping a rhythmic tattoo as he bounded toward us, two concrete stairs at a time. "How the hell are we supposed to get home?"

"Good question," I said, flipping him a quarter. "Maybe you could call a cab."

The last cab company in Laramie went out of business in 1963, but I wasn't about to tell him that. It's my job to get defendants to court in one piece.

What happens after that is their own lookout.

10

I don't know. Do *you* think you're a drunk?" The question came from Curly Ahearn, who'd just refilled my highball glass with diet cola for the third time, and was more than a little amused by the question I'd just posed.

I'd stopped by the Silver Dollar late that afternoon to fill my boss in on recent events and let him know he'd likely be getting a call from Jack Simpson in the near future. Business done, our conversation had meandered in a more personal direction—to wit, my sobriety.

As far as Curly is concerned, stopping by the neighborhood bar to knock back a couple of cold beers at the end of a long day is a patriotic act, and anybody who doesn't indulge just can't be trusted. Of course, Curly's definition of a normal level of alcohol consumption is different than most people's. As the owner of the Silver Dollar Saloon, it's his considered opinion that the guy who coined the phrase "Everything in moderation" had probably just looked in his wallet and discovered he didn't have enough cash to pay for the next round of drinks.

Maybe the mayor wasn't the best person to ask.

"Until recently I didn't think I had a problem," I said, though I knew even as the words left my lips they weren't true. Fact was, I'd been drinking fairly heavily for most of the last year—since the resolution of a case that had left Victory littered with corpses, one of them of my own making. At the end of that chain of events, I'd dropped out of the race for Albany County sheriff—a job eventually won by Anthony Baldi—and watched as my latest attempt at reconciliation with my ex-wife, Nicole, had broken up like a wooden schooner on a rocky shoal.

It had been Nicole's contention that if I gave up my aspirations of being sheriff and settled in as Victory's police chief for the duration, I'd grow sedentary and give in to my most unlovable tendencies—lack of ambition and love of booze. The previous year had proven her right. I thought I was happy with my simple life in Victory and didn't think much further than the end of the week. And I drank nearly every day, often to the point of fuzzy-headed intoxication.

I hadn't wanted to admit I had a problem, though it was becoming increasingly apparent to me I did. Time to do something about it, I figured—which explained the diet cola. I'd go sober for a week, see where it led. After that, maybe I'd go for two straight weeks in a row.

I slurped more of my soda, cracked an ice cube between my teeth, and glanced down the bar. About four stools down, Ginny Larsen was skinning some lanky cowboy at liar's poker. Newcomer, I thought. If he'd been around longer, he'd know that Ginny keeps at least four one-dollar bills hidden away in her pocketbook—ringer bucks with poker hands in the serial numbers high enough to win every time she finds some greenhorn to play with her.

"They're playing for drinks," Curly explained needlessly. "You'll notice she has four empty glasses in front of her, and the cowboy only has the one he bought when he came through the door. So what decided you to go on the wagon? You're not starting to take Baldi's bullshit to heart, are you?"

"Nah, it's nothing like that," I said. "I was asking whether you thought I drink too much."

"Cut the crap, Harry," he said. "This is your pal Curly you're talking to. It was that Coburn fella, wasn't it?"

"Cohen," I said. "And yeah, I guess he might have something to do with it."

What Aaron Cohen had said specifically when he called that afternoon was, "I asked you to keep your fucking hands out of this, Starbranch. The last thing I need is some drunk who thinks he's Roy Rogers fucking up a five-year investigation. What the hell did you think you were doing, arresting them for some chickenshit thing like that?"

Granted, Aaron Cohen was very angry when he said it, and he

might not have meant the part about being a drunk, but if he'd heard about my drinking, then somebody must have told him. And if somebody told him, then it was probably all over town—a prospect that bothered me considerably. It's hard to have faith in the cops who are paid to protect you if you think they can't walk a straight line without a safety net.

Curly popped his dishrag against the walnut bar. "Well, fuck him," Curly said. "I'm your boss, and I think the only drinking problem you have is you won't buy a drink. But if you want to lay off for a while to prove to yourself you can do it, I think that's fine. Just see if you can't be finished with this little experiment before the next Monday-night football game, will you? It's your turn to spring for beer."

I nursed my soda while Curly worked his way down the bar, freshening mixed drinks and setting out full long necks to replace the empties. At a couple of stops, he took some extra folding money from a customer and stuffed it through the slit in the lid of the gallon jar resting conspicuously in front of the backbar mirror. The jar, I knew, held donations patrons of the Silver Dollar had made in the last few days in order to buy Sonny Toms a decent funeral. Neither the coroner nor the sheriff's department had been able to locate any of his kin, and unless some of Sonny's friends came forward, the best he could get was a cheap pine box in the county plot. None of us wanted to see that, so Curly had talked Larry Morton, the undertaker, into keeping Sonny on ice until we could raise enough money to send him off properly. From the looks of things, that would only take a few more days.

Considering the grief I'd taken from Aaron Cohen, Ken Keegan, and Anthony Baldi that afternoon as soon as they found out I'd hauled Tad Bauer into court, I was feeling pleased with what Frankie and I had done. I'd told Curly the whole tale, and he agreed there was no reason for the feds and Anthony Baldi to order us around our own town, "Posse Comitatus or no Comi-goddamned-tatus."

"If a son of a bitch assaults a woman and tries to punch a police officer," Curly had said, "he deserves to be arrested. And if the feds and Anthony Baldi don't like it, they can kiss my bony ass."

Still, he'd cautioned me to avoid blowing their investigation completely, and urged me to try getting along with them as much as possible, since they were our only pipeline to information about the progress of the joint federal-state investigation in Victory.

"You know," he said, "it really makes me mad they didn't inform one of us a long time ago about what they're looking into here. If you hadn't told me, I might never've known."

"I guess they're working on a need-to-know basis," I said. "But I thought you needed to know, even if they don't."

"Thanks for that, Harry. I just wish we weren't so helpless. Do you really think Tad is going to sue us? What could he possibly get? Hell, all this town owns are a half-dozen stop signs, one stoplight, and a town hall that's caving in on itself."

"Nah, he won't sue," I said. "I don't think his attention span is long enough for something like that."

To cheer me up, Curly palmed a few quarters from the till and loaded up the jukebox with my favorite bar songs—plenty of George Jones, Ry Cooder, and Dwight Yoakam, with a dose of Little Feat thrown in for good measure. He topped off the selections with his own favorite, "I'm Gonna Hire a Wino to Decorate Our Home," which he sang in the tempo of a Scottish battle march while dancing a clumsy two-step behind the bar.

He was still braying away when I sensed someone climbing onto the stool next to mine and caught a whiff of her cloying perfume, the kind of heavy, flowery stuff you find in scratch-and-sniff advertisements in *Cosmopolitan* and *Vanity Fair.*

"Hi, Harry," said Sally Sheridan. "Fancy meeting you here."

Of the handful of reporters who cover Victory on a regular, or irregular, basis, I have the most respect for Sally, although she's the most demanding of the bunch, and the most unforgiving. A tough, stout woman with flaming red hair and a notorious temper, she works as the Albany County correspondent for the *Casper Star-Tribune,* which bills itself as the state's largest newspaper and tries to keep track of events in its 97,914-square-mile coverage area by means of a small staff of full-time reporters, most of them deskbound at the paper's headquarters in Casper, and a stable of correspondents like Sally who call in daily with tidbits of information from towns like Baggs, Ranchester, Newcastle, Lusk, and Victory.

Since the bigwigs in Casper are mainly interested in stories about the colony of rare black-footed ferrets discovered a few years ago near Meteetsee and the government's decision to reintroduce wolves in Yellowstone Park, it's sometimes difficult for part-timers like Sally to get basic news into the paper, unless it's fairly sensational. To edge out the wolf stories on page one, most correspondents know they've got to come up with something juicy. Corruption, murder, madness, and mayhem are always good candidates, but even that sort of saga doesn't guarantee their story will be played above the fold. Sonny's murder, for example, only rated a six-paragraph story on page five, for which Sally might have earned twenty bucks.

Once in a while though, one of the correspondents hits the jackpot, an exclusive that not only edges the environmental writers' esoteric think pieces off the front cover but might win the long-suffering stringer a permanent job on the paper's full-time staff. It's that possibility that keeps bulldogs like Sally Sheridan in the bushes of the hinterlands for years, although why anyone would aspire to a career as a reporter is beyond me.

It was clear that she was on the scent of a story now, though, and my early-warning radar was jangling. I'm always a little uneasy about talking to reporters, since their job is to blab things I'm usually trying to keep secret, like the names of suspects under investigation and the details of crimes that haven't come to court yet, but I'm especially nervous around Sally. On the one hand, I make it a practice never to tell her lies, because she'd flat rip my ears off in print if she ever caught me. On the other, I seldom want to tell her much of what I know. Finding a way to tell her just enough so we both walk away happy is a circus act worthy of the Flying Walindas, and I've crashed as often as I've walked away unscathed.

She ordered a shot of peppermint schnapps and a beer chaser and came right to the point.

"Has there been any progress on the Toms investigation?" she asked. While she waited for my answer, she pulled a reporter's notebook from the suitcase-size purse she lugs around and drained her schnapps with a satisfied smack of her lips.

"On the record? Or off?"

"Give me a break, Harry," she huffed. "There's no such thing as off the record with me, and you know it. If you don't know the answer, just say so."

"Then I don't know much. I don't think there's been much progress, but then I'm not on the sheriff's department's list of people privy to that sort of information. Maybe you should ask Anthony Baldi."

"Then how about this? Is there any truth to the rumor that Anthony is about to arrest a gang of terrorists who've been holed up in Victory? That they're tied up with Sonny's murder?"

"Jesus Christ, Sally," I stammered. I reached for my glass of cola, wished miserably it was filled with bourbon. "Where did you hear something like that?"

She signalled Curly for a refill on her schnapps. "I've got a good source," she said. "And even though I can't name him, the paper's agreed to go with the story in tomorrow's edition. Right now, I'm just looking for confirmation."

I let what she was telling me sink in as Curly topped off her shooter. He'd heard a little of what she was saying, and even though he was trying to act nonchalant, I knew his ears were trained on our conversation like a bat on a june bug. We both knew that if Sally was telling the truth, and there was no reason to suspect she wasn't, life might get very interesting come 6:15 the next morning, as soon as the delivery trucks dropped the first copies of the paper at local news boxes.

"You say you've heard terrorists are hiding in Victory and Anthony's going to arrest them?" I asked, making quick eye contact with Curly, who gave me a "What now?" look and leaned his elbows on the bar in front of Sally.

"Why do you do that, Harry?" she shot back. "When someone asks you a question you don't want to answer, why do you always ask them the same question back? Do they teach you that in cop school, or what?"

"Cop school," I agreed. "But it looks like we've both got questions on the table here, Sally, and we'd both like to have the answers. Maybe we can work a trade."

"Maybe," she said. "What do you want to know?"

"The name of your source."

"No way," she said, "and you know better than to even ask me."

"Then how about if I guess?" I asked. "You don't have to answer out loud. Just take a nice, long swallow of your beer if I get it right."

"And in return, you'll give me what?"

"I'll give you a first-person exclusive about finding Sonny's body."

"Not enough," she said. "That's old news. In return, you'll either confirm my story, or deny it."

"Sorry," I said. "In the first place, I don't know enough to do either. And in the second . . . well, in the second I don't think I'd tell you even if I did."

"Fair enough," she said. "It looks like we're at a standstill. But the story's going to run, with you or without you."

She heaved herself down from the barstool, collected her purse, and downed what was left of her beer. "I'll give you a call tomorrow," she said. "Maybe then you'll want to explain how something like this could have been going on in Victory without you knowing about it. I'm sure that's something people around here will want to know."

She whirled on her heels and was steaming toward the front door of the saloon when the answer hit me like a bolt of lightning.

"Hey, Sally," I called. "It was Anthony Baldi, wasn't it? He told you all about this? And you believed him?"

She didn't stop to respond, but the slight hesitation in her step told me all I wanted to know. In an effort to grab the credit for busting a Posse Comitatus cell in rural Wyoming, Anthony—who'd known about the investigation all along and feared that after today Tad might get spooked and leave the state—had gone to the press with a version of the story that made him look good. And if I put my mind to it, I could almost imagine his reasoning. Like a good little soldier, Anthony had cooperated with the feds and the DCI for months, the payoff being the understanding that when the bust came down, he'd get part of the glory—as long as the bust was made in Wyoming—and that kind of thing translates into votes come election time. But if Tad left the state, the whole deal was off, even if he was arrested later somewhere else.

Letting Sally Sheridan in on the doings had the potential for disaster, but it was easy to see how Anthony could benefit from the fallout. There was an outside chance that bringing the investigation into the public domain would force Aaron Cohen's hand. He might arrest Tad while he still knew where he was, even if he didn't have enough evidence yet to get a conviction. If that happened, Anthony would get the publicity he craved as desperately as a vampire craves blood. Even if Tad skipped and Aaron was forced to follow him, Anthony could make up any lie he felt like and nobody in the world would contradict him, since the FBI never, and I mean never, comments publicly on a case that is currently under investigation.

The day after Tad hopped a jet back to Chicago, or wherever, and Aaron Cohen caught the next flight in that direction after him, Anthony could hold a press conference and claim sole responsibility for driving the Posse Comitatus out of Wyoming before those terrorists could wreak mayhem and murder among the citizenry. And because of its "no comment" policy, instituted by J. Edgar Hoover himself, Aaron would be forced to bite his tongue and let him get away with it.

Although it was beginning to look like I might have underestimated Anthony Baldi—a mistake I've been known to make with people I don't particularly care for—I had a reasonable suspicion that at approximately 6:30 A.M. the next morning, two very unpleasant things would happen as a result of Sally's story.

First, Aaron Cohen would go ballistic.

Second, he'd blame me for everything.

As you might have guessed, there wasn't a single wolf story the next morning on page one of the state's largest newspaper. Two of the five columns above the fold were devoted to a color photograph of a couple of young boys in baseball caps performing reconstructive surgery on the jack-o-lantern they were going to set out on their front porch that evening to scare the trick-or-treaters.

Under the headline, "Right-wing Extremists Under Investigation in Victory," Sally's story took up the other three columns. Ginny's was as quiet as a library as patrons at every stool and booth nervously sipped their coffee and tried to come to grips with the ramifications of the bizarre tale they'd been served with breakfast. For my part, the opening salvo of a force-ten migraine was banging away behind my peepers before I'd even finished the first paragraph.

BY SALLY SHERIDAN
Special to the Star-Tribune

VICTORY—Members of the Posse Comitatus, the right-wing paramilitary group responsible for several violent deaths around the nation in recent years and suspected of the recent kidnapping of a district court judge in Des Moines, Iowa, have reportedly been under investigation in this small community for the last several months.

According to reliable sources in law enforcement, the investigation has been a joint effort of the Albany County Sheriff's Department, the state Department of Criminal Investigation, and agents of the Federal Bureau of Investigation. While specifics of the investigation are scarce, sources said that the law-enforcement agencies are generally interested in violations of federal law regarding the possession and interstate transportation of fully automatic weapons and military explosives. They have also been investigating a possible link to the Posse's known efforts to overthrow the United States government, and to the kidnapping last July of District Court Judge Jacob Haines, who was taken at gunpoint from his home in Des Moines by suspected Posse members.

Donald Noyes, special agent in charge of the FBI's Rocky Mountain Region in Denver, yesterday refused to confirm or deny that the investigation is ongoing, or that the federal bureau is involved.

Cecil Carnie, director of the Wyoming Department of Criminal Investigation, also refused comment.

And Harry Starbranch, chief of police in Victory, said that he could not confirm or deny that the investigation was underway, because "I don't know enough to do either, and I don't think I'd tell you even if I did."

Other law-enforcement sources, however, speculated that the Posse's activities in Victory might be connected to the recent torture-murder in this town of Sonny Toms, a junk collector whose mutilated body was discovered at his home by Starbranch and a woman identified as Ellen Vaughn, a graduate assistant at the University of Wyoming.

There have been no arrests in that murder, and while Albany County Sheriff Anthony Baldi says his department has several leads, there are no leading suspects. Still, Baldi agreed that Toms may have been connected to the Posse Comitatus.

"It's possible," Baldi said. "It would explain a lot."

While the law-enforcement sources, who agreed to comment for this story on condition that they not be named, refused to identify the individuals in Victory who are under investigation for illegal activities within the Posse Comitatus, they speculated that the investigation will be completed and arrests made in the near future.

The Posse Comitatus, which was founded in 1969 by Henry L. Beach, is a white supremacist organization dedicated to the institution—by force if necessary—of a "Christian" government in America . . .

The story went on for another fifteen inches, but I didn't finish it because I could feel every pair of eyes in the room burning holes in my hunched back. It was Carrie Wilson who finally worked up the gumption to ask the question that was on everyone's minds. "So tell us, Harry," she said, fanning the air with her rumpled copy of the *Star-Tribune.* "Is this all bullshit, or what?"

Despite the general fogginess I suffer every morning until the caffeine balance in my bloodstream is restored to the proper level, the robust pain that was now marching around the back of my head with the enthusiasm of a Marine Corps recruit, and the fact that my imagination was busily trying to envision all of the bad things that could happen as a result of Sally's ill-timed scoop, I carefully folded my own copy of the paper, tucked it away in my jacket pocket, and swiveled around on my stool to lay their collective fears to rest. I knew I'd have to choose my words carefully, because what I said in the next couple of minutes would travel through Victory at the speed of light.

"I've heard the same rumors," I said, "but to be honest, I only heard them a little while ago myself, and I don't know much more than anyone else. I do know a few things for certain, and here they are. One: there's no reason to believe that anyone in Victory is in danger. Two: there's no evidence linking the Posse Comitatus to Sonny's murder, no matter what Anthony Baldi might have said to the contrary. And three: there's no reason for any of you to start looking sideways at your friends and neighbors. People around here are as safe as they ever were."

Ginny wiped her hands on her apron and searched my face with her soft brown eyes. "I've read about these people," she said. "Didn't they kill that disc jockey in Denver a few years ago?"

"Alan Berg," I said, "but that may not have been the Posse. They suspect Berg was killed by neo-Nazis, although I suppose there's not much difference when you come down to it."

Ginny nodded at the information, but the worry lines on her forehead told me she wasn't particularly comforted by it. Terrorists of any persuasion aren't the sort of people you want to rub noses with, whether they're "Christian" terrorists with a Bible and an Uzi, American Nazis with bald heads and black leather jackets, Klansmen with white hoods and burning crosses, or Arabs with a snootful of hashish, a pound of gelignite, and a desire to visit the garden of Allah.

"Well, it don't matter, there ain't any disc jockeys around here anyway," said Randall Horsch, a bulky former engineer for the Union Pacific Railroad who'd been stopping in at Ginny's for a short stack of buckwheat pancakes every morning since he retired in 1971.

"So what are they after?" Carrie demanded, indignation creeping up her face like mercury in a thermometer. "What would they want with any of us?"

I shrugged my shoulders, but Ginny had an idea.

"Converts?" she asked. "Maybe they're looking for converts."

"Well, if that's the case," huffed Horsch, "I wish they'd try to convert me. The last person who tried convertin' me was a strikebreaker tryin' to convert me from a union man into a filthy scab."

"I take it he didn't make a lot of progress," I said.

"Nah." Randall grinned. "I ran him over with a forklift."

When I got to the office, I thought about answering some of the messages waiting on my desk—two from Aaron Cohen, two from Curly, one from Ken Keegan, one each from Ron Franklin and Sally Sheridan, one from the *Denver Post,* and one from Ellen Vaughn—but first I punched out the number of the Laramie Police Department and asked for Danny King. I already owed him so many favors that we'd lost count, but he'd still been willing to help out when I'd called him the evening before to see if he'd run Tad Bauer and Alex Thibault's names through the national crime computer. I wasn't expecting to learn anything earth shattering, so I wasn't disappointed.

"It looks like Tad Bauer is clean," he said around bites of his obligatory morning doughnut. "The NCIC didn't give us any hits."

In the old days, there was no way for a cop who arrested a suspect in one part of the country to find out in a hurry whether the perp had been arrested anywhere else. He could send copies of the suspect's mug shot, his name and birthdate, through the mail, hoping that someone would recognize the offender and take the time out of his busy day to write back with the information he needed, but that was a hit-and-miss proposition, usually a miss. With the advent of the National Crime Information Center a little over twenty years ago, however, all a policeman had to do was send the suspect's name and date of birth into the NCIC, a big computerized database run by the FBI in Washington, D.C., and within minutes their computer would spit out everything he needed to know about the suspect.

Like everything else in life, though, there are a couple of flaws in the system. First, if your town isn't wealthy enough to afford a computer linkup to the NCIC, you can either try getting the information by phone, which can take longer than most of us have to spend, or you can rely on the kindness of strangers, as long as those strangers have the right kind of computer. In my case, that means that if I want criminal information in a hurry—and I seldom do—I either have to go through Anthony Baldi—an unpleasant prospect—or through someone like Danny King, which works all right as long as I can afford to keep bribing him with fishing trips. Second, only twenty-one states belong to the network, feeding the criminal histories of everyone they arrest into the database. If you're lucky, the suspect you're checking out was arrested previously in one of those states, and you get a hit. If you don't get a hit, all it means is that the crook has never been nicked in a state that belongs to the NCIC.

"Well, it's always worth a shot," I told Danny. "How about the other one, Thibault?"

"Better luck there," he said. "Alex Thibault was arrested once, in Pekin, Illinois, five years ago for aggravated assault and battery."

"He do time?"

"Nope, the DA dropped the charges when the victim suddenly decided not to testify."

"Was there a written incident report?"

"No," said Danny, "all I have here is a summary. According to that, though, he was arrested for attacking someone who'd come to visit the home of his employer. Crushed the guy's voice box and broke half a dozen ribs."

"Thanks for the trouble, Danny. I appreciate it."

"No problem," he said. "Does it tell you anything useful?"

"A little," I said. "It tells me Alex Thibault is a creature of habit."

I tossed the messages from reporters in the wastebasket and spent the next half hour tracking Ellen Vaughn. There was no answer at her apartment or office, but a secretary finally helped me find her in the anthropology lab, where she explained that she'd been working on a computerized facial reconstruction from the skull of a young man from the Clovis period who'd probably hunted the huge, prehistoric bison that roamed these high plains eleven thousand years ago. He was a nice-looking fellow, she said, if your taste runs to short, hairy men with lantern jaws and heavy brow ridges. "Imagine," she said, "this guy could have been the John Travolta of his generation."

She'd gone to the lab, she explained, to get away from the telephone, which had been ringing constantly in her office since she arrived at a little after 8:00. A couple of reporters had called, wanting to interview her about discovering Sonny, but most of the calls were from heavy breathers who hung up after a few seconds.

"I've got to tell you, Harry. If this is what happens when you get your name in the paper, I don't think I want to be famous."

"Did any of them say anything? Have a voice you could recognize if you heard it again?"

"No," she said, "but I could feel something on the other end, something bad, and it was enough to make the hair stand up on the back of my neck."

"How many calls are you talking about, Ellen?"

"Fifteen or twenty. I finally quit answering and came down here to the lab."

While it was possible that the calls had been made by a crank who simply saw Ellen's name in the paper and decided that harassing her might be an enjoyable way to spend the morning, they might also have been part of a scare campaign to keep her quiet while the heat was on Tad Bauer. Either way, we couldn't wait for the phone company to trace her incoming calls, because they usually won't get involved until the customer has been bothered for at least ten days. I asked if there was someone she could stay with for a little while, just until the publicity blew over.

"Why, Harry?" she asked tentatively. "Do you think these are more than prank calls?"

"I don't know," I said truthfully. "But I'd feel better knowing you weren't home alone at night for the time being."

"Well," she said, "the Starbranch Hotel seemed fairly accommodating."

"It's accommodating," I agreed, "but it might be a bit crowded. Two of my sons are coming for a visit this afternoon, and they'll be there for the weekend."

"I'm sorry, Harry," she said quickly. "I didn't mean to impose—"

"It's no imposition," I assured her, "but I have a better idea anyway. I'll call my friend Mike O'Neal, and see if he'd mind letting you use his guest room for a little while. His wife works at the university prep school right there on campus, and you could ride back and forth with her."

Ellen was hesitant at first, but I think she must have been truly frightened by the calls, because she agreed to let me discuss the idea with Mike. He agreed, of course, and said he'd call Katie to arrange Ellen's transportation.

With that settled, I called Curly to discuss strategy but was informed that he was in a meeting with Anthony Baldi and couldn't be disturbed.

Aaron Cohen, on the other hand, was more than eager to take my call. "I'd just like you to know," he said, "that if you've screwed up my investigation with your little stunt at the Bauers', I'll find some way to bust you for it if I have to break every rule in the motherfucking book."

Say what you want about Aaron Cohen, but at least you know where the guy stands.

11

I bought a couple of twenty-pound pumpkins on the way home for the boys to carve, but when I got there the kids—up to their elbows in pumpkin gore—were already using a couple of steak knives to hack the half-dozen pumpkins they'd brought with them into free-form goblins and ghouls.

The boys mobbed me before I even got in the door, passing out giant hugs that left gobs of seeds and slimy orange pumpkin innards stuck to my pants legs and babbling a mile a minute about the drive up from Denver and what they had planned for the weekend.

I gave Sam, my eight-year-old, a wet kiss on the cheek and put my arm around eleven-year-old Tommy's shoulder as I gazed at their handiwork. I noticed with a start that Tommy had grown at least an inch since I'd seen him last—the top of his head came to my armpit. His straight brown hair was cut in a sort of modified bowl cut—long on top and cut short on the sides. His front teeth are a little crooked, which was kind of cute when he was small. Now, however, it was time for braces. I tousled his hair and knelt down for a closer look at the pumpkins.

"Nice monster," I told Sam. All joints and long bones, Sam has a head topped with hair so red it's orange and his ears come to sort of a point, like an elf's. When he smiles, which is most of the time, his nose crinkles and the thousands of freckles on his face begin to dance. He was smiling as he squatted down beside me for a better look at the creature's two-inch fangs and insane-looking eye slits. "It's the scariest looking thing I've ever seen," I told him. "We'll put it on the porch and nobody will dare come near it."

"It's a kitty, Dad," he said in that tone kids take when they think their parents are acting like total morons. "Mom says it looks just like Garfield."

"Well," I laughed, "now that you mention it, it does look a little bit like Garfield."

I picked one of them up in each arm and carted them in from the porch, their wiry arms clinging to my neck with all the strength they could muster. They smelled good, that little-boy smell that's a pleasant mixture of sweat and the soap from last night's bath. It was so good to see them that I wanted to keep hugging them and never let go.

When you come right down to it, I've been a lousy excuse for a father, something Sam and Tommy haven't figured out yet. Their nineteen-year-old brother, Robert—conspicuous in his absence—caught on several years ago, and that's why he hadn't come along. He doesn't like me much these days, and I can't really say that I blame him. I just wish he understood that when I left his mom, I didn't do it with the specific intention of ruining his life.

Judging from my own experience, I imagine he'll forgive me sooner or later, as soon as he has enough living under his belt to have learned, firsthand, that love affairs and marriages sometimes fall apart, even if the partners are basically good people. It wasn't until my marriage to Nicole fell apart the first time that I was able to forgive my own father for letting his marriage to my mother crumble. By the time I knew enough to tell him I understood, though, he was already dead. I hope Robert and I are working on a better timetable.

The boys' mother was leaning against the kitchen counter, still wearing her car coat over a peach-colored pullover sweater, black, form-fitting stirrup pants, and high-heeled boots. A tall woman with long, wavy auburn hair and dancing blue eyes, Nicole looks much better as she nears forty than she did at twenty-five. She never believes me when I tell her that, but it's true. She works hard on her figure and the years have been kind to her face, with its marble white skin and high cheekbones.

The smile she gave me when I breezed in with the boys tucked under my arms like footballs was strained. Even so, it made me forget the thousands of reasons we're bad for each other and remember the first years of our marriage, when we'd meet each other in the kitchen come evening and share our day's experiences over wine and a long supper before tumbling happily into bed. We hadn't started to fall short of each other's expectations yet, and those nights were filled with promise and wonder.

"I hope you don't mind us making ourselves at home," she said tentatively, "but the boys were so anxious to get here that they made me leave two hours earlier than I'd planned so they'd be here in plenty of time to work on their pumpkins and costumes."

"Costumes? I haven't given that a lot of thought."

"No problem," she said, "they brought everything they need with them. Sam wants to be the King of the Zombies and Tommy thinks he'll go as a cannibal chef. The Galloping Gourmet with a twist."

"A cannibal?" I groaned. "Whatever happened to Ewoks? Whatever happened to Oscar the Grouch?"

A genuine smile cracked Nicole's face. It broke my heart. "Get out of your time capsule, dude. Those costumes are for babies." She laughed. "Now, the operative phrase in costume selection is gross-a-rama. As in 'Gross-a-ramaaa! That costume is wicked ugly!' "

"Yeah, Dad," Sam chirped. "That means it's cool."

While Sam filled me in on how he was going to turn himself into a deformed creature of the night by dousing his body with gelatinous fake blood, smearing his face with white makeup and black eyeliner, and adorning his limbs with an awful assortment of oozing lacerations and cancerous-looking growths, Nicole browsed through the refrigerator until she found a bottle of Chablis.

"I suppose I've got time for a glass if you don't mind," she said, pulling a corkscrew from the drawer. I noticed she didn't bother to remove her coat. "Then, I'll leave you men to your mischief and head back to Denver. Do you know what time you're planning to bring the boys home Sunday?"

"About suppertime," I said. "I was thinking of taking them to the football game tomorrow and out to shoot black-powder rifles with Curly on Sunday morning. If we have time, Edna said we could sneak in a horseback ride."

"Judging from what I read about you in the *Denver Post* this morning, it sounds like you could use some fun," she said. "Are you okay, Harry?"

I told her about the Posse and our little run-in with Tad Bauer while she filled a couple of glasses and carried hers to the kitchen table, where she sank down on one of the chairs. There was a painful tension between us, and it was making me nervous, almost too nervous to speak. I took a small slurp of the astringent wine and left the rest on the counter. What I really wanted to do was grab the whole bottle off the table, tip it to my mouth, and drain that sucker dry.

I settled for a cigarette, which I smoked while I finished filling her in on recent events in my life and Nicole caught me up on hers. A stenographer in federal court, Nicole hasn't remarried, but that isn't because there are no applicants. She's doing just fine, she says, without a full-time night man hanging around to leave his boxer shorts on the floor and his boots where she can trip over them. She says living with me spoiled her for anyone else, and like lots of things she says, you can take that just about any way you want.

While Nicole sipped her wine and told me about a murder trial she'd been working on for the past ten days, I smeared Sam's face with white makeup, outlined his lips and eye sockets with black, and dipped red goo all over his cheeks and hands. When he was convinced that he looked sufficiently zombielike, I helped with the rest of his outfit—a black shirt, black pants, black velvet cape, and a black top hat. He thought he looked truly hideous, but Nicole and I could only look at each other and grin because no matter how much white goop you plaster on the poor kid's face, his bright red eyebrows still poke through.

Tommy was a little easier. All he needed was a chef's hat made out of white cardboard, a white shirt, white apron, a meat cleaver, bloody red handprints from the top of his hat to the cuffs of his trousers, and a precancerous-looking stick-on mole for his nose. Nicole pawed through her purse until she found a black marker and topped his ensemble off by putting a catchy advertising slogan on his apron: HAVE A FRIEND FOR DINNER AT CANNIBAL TOM'S FINE EATS.

By the time we were finished, the boys were hopping around the kitchen like they had bees in their britches, eager to hit the streets and start scaring people. I offered to fix them a sandwich beforehand, but they wouldn't hear of it on account of their plan to dine exclusively on candy for the next couple of days, providing I'd get off my lazy duff and take them trick-or-treating before everyone in Victory ran out of goodies.

"Well," Nicole said, reaching for her keys, "it looks like you have places to go and people to see. I'd better get a move on."

As I watched her kneel down to hug the kids, I realized, much to my surprise, that I'd missed her in the last few months. In many respects, I had the life I'd always wanted in Victory, a life that hadn't been possible when I was married to Nicole because our definitions of success are so incompatible and she could never understand my desire to jump off the fast track, even if it meant a life of semipoverty and isolation. But that didn't change the fact that my kids were growing up without me and I'd caused a lot of pain for a woman who was not only my wife but my friend.

"I've got an idea," I said hesitantly, exhaling the last of my smoke. "It's already dark out there. Why don't you stay till morning? We'll take the boys out trick-or-treating, stop off at Robbie Moore's for some dinner, and have a visit. It'd be nice."

She didn't answer right away, just shook her head no and gave me a sad smile. "We've been down that road before, Harry," she said. "No, thanks."

I don't think I sounded desperate, but maybe I did. "Look, all I want to do is talk. Drink a little wine. Have a dance. Spend a little time with the boys. Smear your firm, luscious body with warm honey—"

"Harry!" she said, sneaking a look at the boys to see if they'd picked up on my incomplete pass. They hadn't, but that didn't mollify Nicole. She clucked her tongue and fixed me in a mock glare while she pulled her car keys from her pocket and flipped through them for the one that fit her ignition.

"Come on, it was just a joke," I said placatingly. "Tell you the truth, I've sort of missed having you around."

"Me, too," she said softly, then went on before I could answer. "But I haven't missed fighting, and I haven't missed feeling like you resent it when I tell you I need more from life than—"

"Nicole," I interrupted. "I'm not asking you to sleep with me. All I want is a few hours of your time. If you're not comfortable with that, I guess I understand. . . ."

Nicole sighed and jangled her keys nervously as she watched the boys, who were now so restless they were trying to jam their trick-or-treat bags over each other's heads.

"Come on, Dad," Sam groaned, "it's already dark."

"Yeah, Dad," Tommy chimed in. "It's been dark for ages already. Let's go!"

"Oh, shit," Nicole said, drawing her coat closed at the throat. "I'll stay on two conditions."

"Name 'em," I said, giving her my zillion-watt smile.

"One, you make coffee in the morning. No self-respecting woman makes coffee for a man in this day and age."

"All right," I whined. "What's number two?"

"If these boys get sick from too much candy in the night, you get up with them. I plan to be sleeping like a baby."

Trick-or-treating was judged to be an unqualified success, and so was dinner afterward. The boys didn't touch their burgers, on account of the fact that they'd been gobbling bite-size candy bars, chocolate-covered raisins, and jawbreakers by the double handful. But they held their grubby hands out like gentlemen when I introduced them around and didn't pass gas or belch within hearing range of strangers.

With the boys off in the kids' corner of the restaurant, where we'd bribed them with quarters for video games, Nicole finished her second glass of wine and with a mischievous wink dropped a coin in the jukebox. She'd found "our song," Judy Collins singing "Someday Soon."

"Dance, cowboy?" she asked. She pulled me onto the small dance floor, where we polished our buckles in two-step time while most of the other customers watched from the sidelines. I've never been much of a dancer, but Nicole compensates for my clumsiness with a grace that even makes me look skillful as a partner. I don't think she could help me fake it through a polka, but on a slow buckle polisher, we do all right.

I'm not going to tell you I had the faintest idea what we were up to emotionally, though, and maybe she didn't either—but it felt good and comfortable to have her in my arms while the song took us back to a time when we truly thought that love is strong enough to survive anything, even growing older and apart.

Back at the farmhouse, Nicole scrubbed the boys' faces and got them ready for bed while I lit the jack-o'-lanterns and the woodstove and heated some apple cider on the stove. The idea was to make ourselves comfortable and then gather round the fire for the telling of my favorite ghost story, Mark Twain's "The Golden Arm." I usually botch the dialect, but I do a passable imitation of a wailing banshee. It's a great tale for scaring the girl next to you right into your arms, if you've got a girl who needs scaring in that direction. Which I did.

And when the boys were finally asleep, we stayed that way, sipping hot, spiced cider with our shoes off and our legs stretched out together on the ottoman. With her back nestled across my chest, I could smell the clean scent of her hair, mingled with the cinnamon of our drinks. I might have fallen asleep that way, too, if she hadn't casually draped her leg across mine and started rubbing the inside of my foot with her toes. The electricity from that touch traveled north like lightning, frying my inhibitions like a rasher of cheap bacon. When I found her lips, they tasted like peach brandy, and I drank until I got a woody that made it uncomfortable to sit still.

"Oh, Jesus," she whispered, dragging her fingernails across my crotch, an act that made my legs twitch like a hound dog getting his belly scratched. "Here we go again."

"Let me see if I've got this straight," Curly said, pouring an eighty-grain measure of black powder down the muzzle of his .54 caliber buffalo rifle and thoughtfully patching a ball. "You've quit drinking. You're thinking about turning your whole life upside down—and now you're sleeping with your ex-wife again? No, Harry, I don't think you're crazy at all."

To escape the hordes of people who'd been after us for one reason or another since Sally Sheridan's Halloween surprise—the reporters who began calling my house at 8:00 A.M. Saturday morning, the agents from the FBI and the state, who'd left a half-dozen messages on my machine, and the constituents who'd been phoning Curly at home at the rate of about three an hour—we'd bundled the boys into their coats right after breakfast Sunday morning, sent Nicole shopping in Laramie, loaded our black-powder shooting gear into the Bronco, and sneaked off to the sagebrush plains north of Lake Hattie to slaughter some coffee cans and enjoy the smell of burning sulfur in our nostrils.

The boys stuck around for a half hour or so and shot a couple of times before they got bored and took off to explore a little beaver pond on the stream leading into the lake.

Shooting a muzzle-loading black-powder rifle, the kind they quit making around 1840, is certainly an esoteric sort of pastime, but Curly and I have been shooting them once a month since I moved to Victory, when we had the first round of what had undoubtedly become the world's longest-running challenge match. We shoot for steak dinners, with the loser buying, and it's cutthroat competition at its best. In my personal opinion, there's no food quite as delicious as a steak that someone else pays for, and I'll stop at nothing in order to win. Sometimes, I sing while Curly's trying to aim. Sometimes, I tell him dirty jokes and leave out the punchlines, purely for the aggravation factor. Sometimes, I stand right behind him when he's trying to aim and blow in his ear.

Sometimes it works.

But it wasn't working that day.

So far, he'd hit nineteen straight shots. I'd hit fifteen and missed four. Since we were only going to twenty, it looked like I'd be buying dinner. With the pressure off, Curly was waxing philosophic about his perception of my sanity or lack of same.

"Look, Curly," I said, "that was kind of a rhetorical question. I don't think I'm crazy. What I meant was, am I acting foolish?"

"I don't know. Do you feel foolish?"

"I suppose not," I said truthfully. "Just a bit confused."

"Then unless she wants you to marry her again and move back to Denver—which I absolutely forbid on account of I couldn't hire another police chief for what I pay you—I say don't worry about it," he said. He squinted downrange against the sharp breeze and brought the long rifle to his shoulder. "I know plenty of men who date their ex-wives, and some of them get along better than they did when they were married."

With an almost imperceptible twitch of his finger, he released his muzzle loader's hair trigger, and the big gun spewed out a heavy cloud of noxious gray smoke. When it cleared, the coffee can he'd been aiming at was still bouncing through the sagebrush.

"I don't know about you," he grinned, "but I think I smell the aroma of mesquite-grilled rib eye."

"I hate it when you gloat," I grumbled. "And this time, you have nothing to gloat about. I told you when we started this morning that I thought someone had knocked my sights out of line. That being the case, fifteen out of nineteen isn't bad. And besides, payday isn't till next week, so you'll just have to wait a while to collect."

"You know," he laughed, "you're sounding more and more like the Boston Red Sox. You always choke in the clinch, and you've got a million excuses."

We cased the rifles and rounded up the boys, who'd both had plenty of time to fall in the pond. It had been Sam's contention that they ought to strip out of their wet clothes, swim out to the beaver dam, and convince the beaver to come out and play. His older brother had thankfully talked him out of that notion. Instead, they'd lured the beaver out with bits of apple, and he'd apparently thanked them by putting on quite a show, racing around his little pool, and slapping the water happily with his broad, flat tail.

It was a performance city boys seldom have the chance to enjoy, and on the way home, Curly rounded out their experience by telling them everything he knew about beavers in general, and the role the homely animals played in the exploration and settlement of this very valley.

I'd heard the story before, so while he rambled, I drove, keeping my eyes on the sides of the road for deer and letting my mind sift through the bewildering events of the last forty-eight hours. The day before had been nearly perfect. Nicole and I had taken the boys to the football game—where the Pokes flat annihilated Air Force, their archrivals—and we'd lingered over a friendly dinner afterward, all of us laughing and joking and acting for all the world like a normal family. And late at night, with the kids asleep, we'd crawled under the covers and relived some of my fondest memories.

This morning, though, we'd both been quiet and self-conscious, each of us waiting, I think, for the other to do or say something that would shatter the little dream we were dreaming and send us packing back to the reality we'd been living for better than five years. A friend of mine once defined mixed emotions as watching your mother-in-law drive over a cliff in your new Cadillac, and while I can't speak for Nicole, that's what I was feeling, mixed emotions. On the one hand, there was no question that I still loved her, had never really stopped. On the other, there was a lot of emotional baggage traveling with our relationship, and there was no way we could ignore it and just start over. The things that drove us apart in the first place were still unresolved, and we'd each built lives since the divorce that didn't include a place for the other.

Should I do the right thing and let her get on with life, unencumbered by a cord of deadwood in the form of a middle-aged small-town cop with commitment psychosis, no financial future, and no ambition to be anything else? Or should I go with my heart, ask her to marry me once for old-times' sake and move into my little bungalow in Victory? Was it possible to find a compromise that would make us both happy? Would we wind up hurting each other even worse than before?

Should I just take a vow of celibacy and save everyone, including me, a lot of trouble?

I didn't know. All I knew for sure was that it made my palms sweat thinking about it.

Luckily, I didn't have to make a decision right away, because Nicole had the boys' bags packed and was waiting for us at the front door when we pulled up in the driveway after dropping Curly off at his house.

When I cut the headlights, she glanced back over her shoulder to see if she'd left anything behind and walked purposefully out to the car, her hands in her pockets and the same uneasy expression on her face she gets whenever she's on her way to the dentist, which I know from experience is something she likes only a little better than a gynecologist with cold hands.

I stepped out of the car and listened politely while the boys anxiously told her all they'd learned about beavers and black-powder rifles, and when they were finished and racing off in the direction of the horse pasture for one last adventure, I tried to gather her in my arms for a kiss. She pushed me away, a melancholy look in her blue eyes, biting her lower lip. We stood there for a while, scuffing the gravel with our shoes and glancing toward the corral, where the boys were scratching Edna's irascible pony between the ears and feeding him bits of some treat they'd tucked away in their pockets.

"We didn't have time to go for a pony ride this weekend," I said, watching the gentle wind ruffle her hair. "Maybe next time?"

"Sure, Harry," she said. "I'm sure they'll look forward to it."

Nicole shivered and pushed her hands deeper in her pockets, drawing her coat around her body like armor. I had the sudden urge to take her face in my hands and kiss away the tears that I suspected were forming in the corners of her eyes, to tell her I'd never hurt her again. Instead, I just swallowed and listened to the howl of a coyote calling from the prairie beyond the barn. And then it was quiet again, and Nicole raised her face toward mine. Her mouth looked full and plum red in the twilight. "Do you think it's too late for us?" she asked.

"I don't know," I said, turning my face away. "But I think I'd like to try again."

When I looked back, she was brushing the first tear away with the heel of her hand. "That's not good enough, Harry," she said. "You can't *think* you want to try again, you have to know it, really know it."

She smiled, reached out for my cheek with her gloved hand. I accepted her caress, felt the moisture of her tear on the leather, but I didn't answer. "You're a mess," she said. I couldn't argue with her observation, so I waited for her to go on. "I've got an idea," she said finally. "Let's just pretend these last nights never happened. That way you won't have to worry about what it means."

I reached up to hold her hand against my face. "I don't want to pretend it didn't happen," I told her truthfully. "I love you, Nicole. I'll never stop."

She pulled her hand away from my face and jammed it in her pocket. "I'll never stop loving you either," she said. Her tears were leaking freely now. "And if it was just me . . . I'd chance it. But the boys . . . I can't let them hope."

I felt a lump growing in my throat and knew pretty soon I'd be crying myself. I took a deep breath to force the emotion down. "You're right," I said. "We've all been through enough—but damn it—"

"You're right about that, Harry," she broke in. There was heartbreak in her voice. "We've all been through enough."

When they were gone, I sat in the quiet living room, listening morosely to the echoes of their voices filling my house and watching a "Wheel of Fortune" rerun with the sound off, which is the only way a thinking human can actually watch that program without risking permanent brain damage. As I watched, I wrestled with a couple of competing and equally compelling desires. Instead of sitting there like a toad, it seemed that if I truly wanted to put my family back together, I ought to jump in the Bronco, drive like hell, and catch them before they crossed the Colorado line. I could bring them, forcibly if necessary, back to Victory with me, and we'd plan out a new life together. I'd do whatever it took to make it work, even if it meant leaving Victory and moving back to Denver.

Failing that, I wanted to slither out to the kitchen and guzzle down enough bourbon to knock me senseless.

I settled for a beer—my first in days—and a bowl of nuked chili from the stash of Ten Alarm Serrano Special I keep in the freezer, packed away in little single-serving containers, perfect for the guy who never has to feed anyone but himself.

Okay, so I was feeling sorry for myself again, sorry for the years of pain I'd brought on people who love me most. But at least this time, for maybe the first time in the last year, I was dealing with it unaided by Jack Daniel's, Johnny Walker, Old Grand-Dad, or any of the other Southern rogues I usually turn to in times of need.

Instead, I picked up an Elmore Leonard novel I'd been saving for a special occasion, wrapped up on the couch in my wool blanket, and read until I finally drifted off to sleep about 3:00 A.M.

I dreamed of Canada geese, flying in a high wedge over the Tetons, their honking clear and plaintive as they passed the ice-rimmed waters of Ditch Creek, turning to sorrowful whispers as they headed south across the Gros Ventre.

The Indians used to believe those birds carried the souls of old warriors to a happier place, a place where they were always young and strong and sure.

I'd like to think they were right.

12

When Esmerelda Ruiz let herself into Tad Bauer's house the next morning at around 8:00, she told Frankie and me her first thought was the sloppy *pendejo* she worked for had killed a deer in the hills behind his place and dragged it in across the living-room rug, where she'd have to clean it up.

But as the Bauers' housekeeper left the foyer and made her way cautiously into the living room, the less it looked like Tad had been stocking up on venison and the more the room looked like the set for one of those *Friday the 13th* movies her husband was always making her watch on cable.

For one thing, Alex Thibault, in one of the form-fitting T-shirts he wore to show off his muscles, was lying facedown on the floor, one arm tucked underneath his torso at an uncomfortable-looking angle and the other stretched out in front of him like a swimmer taking a long forward stroke. The back of his powder-blue shirt was caked with drying blood and there was a lot more of the stuff that had soaked into the white wool carpet around his head.

As she sidestepped away from Thibault and headed toward the telephone in the kitchen, she said she was dimly aware of another wide trail of blood leading out of the living room in that direction. She literally stumbled over the second corpse as she backed her way through the dining room, keeping her eyes on the weight lifter, who wasn't going anywhere fast. She landed on her rump with her hands behind her and her legs in a wide V. And there, right between her tennis shoes, was Tad Bauer's face, or what was left of it, at least, staring right back at her with its one remaining eye.

He was still wearing his deck shoes and an expensive-looking cream-colored cashmere sweater, and for a couple of seconds, she thought there was some kind of long snake working its way out of the bloody stain on his belly. It didn't take her long to realize the snake was in fact a six-foot section of Tad's intestine, which—judging from the fact that his hands were still gripping it like a jumbo Polish sausage—he'd apparently been trying to stuff back in when the killer finished him off.

Esmerelda didn't hang around to see if there were any more surprises, and I think it must have taken her about three minutes to run from the Bauer estate to the Victory police station, an impressive little sprint considering she lost one of her sneakers along the way.

Esmerelda—a tough-looking, thirty-something Chicana dressed in skintight black jeans and a Hard Rock Cafe sweatshirt, her thick black hair pulled back in a long braid and her ruddy face flushed—was so upset, she was almost babbling. But between us, Frankie and I were able to make sense of the tale she gabbled out in a whirlwind rush of profanity and shock. "When I see the bastards, I scream," Esmerelda said breathlessly at the end of her story of discovering the corpses. "I see those fucking bodies and I just keep screaming."

She seemed to notice for the first time she'd lost a shoe, and stared curiously at the horny big toe poking through her heavy wool sock. *"Hijo de puta,"* she grumbled, wiggling the digit. She stretched her sock out and folded it over so the toe was covered, but the effort of that mundane task seemed to push her into some kind of post-traumatic breakdown. She leaned forward with her head between her legs, took a dozen deep breaths, and vomited. After that, she didn't say much of anything, just sort of crumpled to the floor.

I rushed forward to pick her up and help her back to her seat, but she was limp and kept slipping out of my arms. I looked almost helplessly in Frankie's direction.

He shrugged. "Why don't I take her back and lay her down on that cot in the cell?" he suggested. "You do what you need to do in here."

I nodded gratefully, and while Frankie cared for Esmerelda, I rang Ginny's to see if she'd come over and stay with the housekeeper while we went to investigate at the Bauer estate. Next, I dialed Ivinson Memorial Hospital in Laramie and asked them to send an ambulance to the crime scene. I also called Curly and got him out of bed. I didn't want him at the Bauer place, but I imagined that as soon as this news got around, I'd need him to run interference with the media and our constituents.

On the way out the door, I grabbed a Polaroid camera and pulled my .357 from the holster a quarter inch to check the draw. I didn't know who killed Tad Bauer and Alex Thibault—yet—but I wanted to be ready when I caught up with him. And catch up with him I would. Whoever had pulled the trigger on Bauer and Thibault had pulled it in my jurisdiction, maybe the worst mistake of his life.

I'd spent too much time watching from the sidelines, but now I finally had a case. I reminded myself there are more than a few killers serving out their lifetimes in the Canyon State Pen who know how that can turn out.

Tad Bauer and his bodyguard had died violently and painfully, but a quick look around the house told me the struggle hadn't lasted long. They'd apparently been watching a movie in the den when the killer arrived, because the television and the VCR were still on, and a couple plates of nachos and chili were still sitting, half-eaten, on the TV trays they'd pulled up in front of their favorite chairs. I guessed the four empty Budweiser cans had belonged to Alex and that Tad had been sipping from the bottle of French wine on the coffee table. While I took a quick tour of the den, Frankie popped the tape they'd been watching—a piece of garbage titled *Back Door Girls.*

We worked our way into the living room and found nothing out of place, nothing that indicated they'd been ready for trouble or expecting it. We'd tear the house apart from top to bottom later, and we might learn something different, but my initial impression was that Tad had known the killer and let him in.

I snapped a dozen pictures of each corpse in situ and shot a couple more after Frankie rolled Alex Thibault onto his back. The weight lifter's face and neck were purple from livor mortis, and his limbs had stiffened in death to such a degree that it took both of us to pull his arm away from his belly in order to pull up his shirt. There were two entrance wounds on his abdomen, either one of which would have done serious damage, either one of which would likely have proven fatal. The bullet the killer put in his brain had just been insurance.

Later on, the coroner would stick a thermometer in his innards and—judging by his internal body temperature and the temperature of the room—make some estimate of the time of death. I had no scientific way of fixing the moment when Alex died, but experience told me he'd died around midnight. Rigor mortis, the stiffening of the joints after death, is a temporary phenomenon that begins about three hours after death. Within twelve hours, it's really rolling and the corpse is virtually rigid. If a body's been dead more than thirty-six hours, the joints become flexible again, but that hadn't happened yet.

Tad had gotten the same treatment, except the blood trail leading from the living room said he'd taken his two abdominal wounds there and had time to crawl thirty feet into the dining room before the killer ended his escape attempt with a slug above the left eyebrow. The concussion had destroyed the upper half of his face on that side and taken the back of his skull completely off. When we lifted him to turn him over, what little was left of his brain plopped out on the dining room floor and on our feet.

It looked to me like a contact wound, the kind made by jamming the muzzle of a firearm right up against human flesh and pulling the trigger. Contact wounds, especially to the head, are more destructive because the hot gases rushing out the bore follow the projectile in, build up inside the skull, and literally blow it apart trying to get out. Tad Bauer saw it coming, lying on his back and clutching his intestine as the killer stood over him, pressed the muzzle against his forehead, and squeezed the trigger.

It takes a special kind of person to do something like that, to look right into the eyes of a man who's lying gut shot and bleeding, listen to his pitiful cries as you bend down, close, touch him with the hot muzzle, and watch his eyes as you send him to eternity.

"This is one cruel bastard," I said as Frankie wiped some of the gray goo that was Tad Bauer's brain from the instep of his boot.

Frankie nodded in agreement. His sharp features registered revulsion but also anger at the level of carnage. He watched, grim faced, as I ran my hands down Bauer's pants legs and walked back into the living room to do the same to Thibault. Neither one of them was armed, and while it was possible the killer had taken their weapons with him when he left, I doubted they'd been armed at the time of their deaths. I'd ask the lab to run tests to see if there was any powder residue on their hands, but I didn't think they'd find any.

These men had been executed by someone who knew his business, a tactical shooter who'd taken the advice his teacher had undoubtedly given him to heart: Two in the belly, one in the head—guaranteed to leave 'em dead.

Aaron Cohen, Ken Keegan, and Anthony Baldi stormed in as we were finishing our initial inspection, followed by a half-dozen of Anthony's deputies and three EMTs from the ambulance.

Anthony—dressed in a sharply creased khaki sheriff's department uniform, Sam Browne belt, and black combat boots with his trouser legs tucked in the tops—had probably intercepted the radio call to the ambulance crew and followed them over from Laramie. His first stop was Alex Thibault's corpse, which he prodded with the toe of his boot as if trying to wake him up.

Cohen, meanwhile—the tails of his beige trench coat flapping behind him like wings—gave me an unfriendly shove as he pushed by on his way to the dining room. He took one look at the corpse and whirled around with a look on his face that can only be described as mad-dog rage. "What the fuck happened here?" he snarled, his hands balling up into fists and his lips stretched so tightly against his mouth that I could almost see his canines.

He took a couple of steps toward me, and the set of his jaw said he'd like to shake an answer out of me. I took a deep breath, narrowed my eyes in my most determined glare, and shook my head no. He got the message, but I could tell he was working himself up to a verbal assault in lieu of the physical one that had been his first choice.

I spoiled his momentum before he had the chance to get warmed up. "I don't know, hotshot," I growled menacingly. "Why don't you tell me? Am I mistaken, or haven't you been watching this place all summer? If you were doing your job, you'd have seen who came in here last night and they wouldn't have walked away from this quite so easily."

"I took a night off," he rumbled. Before he went on, he looked over at Anthony Baldi, whose expressions said he realized if it came to a fight, they'd have to go through Frankie to get me. It was not a prospect Tony Baldi looked forward to. "Ken and I are the only ones who've been watching out here and we needed a rest. I went home a little after eight last night." It obviously galled him to be giving me an explanation for his behavior, because he was almost spitting words. I wasn't quite ready to back off.

"Well, it looks like you went home too early," I said. "And I'll tell you something else while I've got your attention. This murder took place in my jurisdiction, and that makes it my case. Those being the facts of the matter, I'd appreciate it if you'd get the hell out of here until I finish what I have to do."

I left Cohen fuming while I focused my radar on Tony Baldi, who was standing slightly in the background with his thumbs hooked in his belt and a stormy look crinkling his high forehead. At least he'd stopped wearing the hairpiece he'd worn during his election campaign, which raised him in my estimation. Not much, but a little. I gave him my biggest fake smile. "Anthony," I said, pointing at the sheriff's department officers who'd come with him, "you get those deputies out of here before they start destroying evidence like they did at Sonny's."

I didn't wait for him to answer. "And Ken," I said, looking at my big friend, who was trying to hide the tiny smile that was growing at one side of his mouth, "if you want to be helpful, you could call a decent team of evidence technicians over here from the DCI. I want this place gone over with a microscope, and I don't think Anthony's the man to do it. While you're at it, how about calling the coroner?"

Keegan stifled a chuckle and nodded, then went outside to make the calls on his cellular phone. Unfortunately, Cohen wasn't ready to back off either. When I turned away to make sure the deputies were on their way out, he grabbed my elbow and pulled me back around to face him. At six-one, I'm a couple of inches taller than he is, and I'm a good thirty pounds heavier, not that much of it fat. What he saw in my eyes convinced him to drop the physical crap, but it didn't dull his tongue.

"This is a federal matter," he said, "and I'll take it from here. Don't get in my way, Starbranch, or I'll have the Bureau hit you so hard you'll be looking out your asshole when you shit. I'm warning you, listen to me or—"

"Nah, you listen," I said. I put the palm of my hand on his chest and gave a push. He backed up a step, a startled look in his eyes that quickly grew cold. "You may have been looking into Tad Bauer's activities as they relate to federal crimes, but his murder took place in the city limits of Victory, Wyoming. That makes it my case, and there isn't a law on the books that says otherwise.

"And don't get in my way," I said, shoving him again, "or I'll arrest you for obstructing a murder investigation. Now, get the fuck out of here while I'm still in a good mood."

"I'm not going anywhere," he said, pushing his trench coat aside so I could see the butt of his automatic.

I couldn't back down—not in front of Frankie, Ken Keegan, and Anthony Baldi. Especially Anthony Baldi. "You've got five seconds," I said. I let my hand drift down to the butt of my own weapon. "Then I'm gonna have Officer Bull take you down and lead you out of here in handcuffs."

I don't know how I expected Cohen to respond to that threat, but as I watched his face harden, I had the distinct impression he was wrestling the urge to draw his weapon. He might have done it, too, if Tony Baldi hadn't pushed himself between us and grabbed Cohen's biceps in his hands. "Let's go, Aaron," Baldi said, watching Frankie and me like rattlesnakes. "This crazy son of a bitch means what he's saying. We'll get this straightened out, but this isn't the time or place."

When Cohen realized he was on his own, he let his hands drop to his sides, but his eyes had the same flat look I've seen on all those television documentaries about boa constrictors. It was the look of a predator regarding his meat. "You're going to be very sorry," he said softly—but at least he was leaving as he said it.

When the coroner officially pronounced the victims dead and Frankie and I gave the okay, the EMTs hauled Tad Bauer and Alex Thibault away in body bags to the coroner's lab in Laramie. It took all three of them, plus four of Anthony's deputies, to get the stretcher bearing Thibault's corpse out of the house and into the meat wagon, on account of his great bulk.

The aluminum gurney carrying the earthly remains of Tad Bauer had been much easier to navigate, although it had taken the EMTs a bit longer to collect all the bits and pieces of him that were scattered around the dining room.

The technicians from the DCI arrived as the ambulance was pulling out, a somber team of five men with a vanload of equipment, high-powered vacuum cleaners to suck evidence from the walls and carpets, fingerprint gear, cameras, tools for digging spent bullets out of walls and floors, you name it.

While they worked, Frankie and I waited outside with the mob of lawmen and curious townspeople who had gathered in the driveway. The deputies had set up a yellow-tape barricade to keep the civilians and the reporters at bay, but on our side of the boundary, Aaron Cohen was deep in conversation with Anthony Baldi, waving his arms and occasionally gesturing angrily in my direction when he made an important point.

They were still talking when Ken Keegan lowered his square self onto the front-porch steps next to Frankie and me and lit maybe his fifteenth cigarette of the morning. I liked Keegan, but frankly, he smelled pretty rancid from all that smoke. I turned my nose upwind and sucked in a lungful of fresh mountain air, perfumed with pungent lodgepole pine and the tangy smell of aspen. He drew deeply on his cigarette, blowing it back out in a long stream from his mouth and nostrils. "Are you sure you know what you're doing, Harry?" he asked, gesturing toward Cohen with his cigarette. "We're all on the same side here."

"The last time I heard, Ken, murder wasn't the kind of crime the FBI gets involved in unless the locals ask for help. I haven't asked yet, but I'll be happy to share anything I learn, which is more than I can say for some people."

Keegan sighed sadly. "It's not as simple as that, and you know it," he said. "It looks like this may be part of some organized criminal activity, and that gives Cohen every right in the world to be directly involved in the investigation. If he wants to make trouble for you, I think he can probably make a case that you're the one obstructing the investigation of a murder. It'd turn out to be an ugly pissing contest, and one that wouldn't do any of us a bit of good."

What he was saying was true, of course, and in the best of all possible worlds, the good guys should work together without allowing their petty personal differences to get in the way. But this wasn't the best of all possible worlds, and I was tired of Aaron Cohen's arrogance, tired of being treated like a puppy who's thrown a few bones to chew on while the big dogs work the banquet.

I stood up and looked down at Keegan, so squat he looked like a keg of beer. "Listen, Ken, I've got no objection to working with you, or the FBI, if I have to—but from now on, it's got to be an equal partnership. We share everything, or nothing. No more covert surveillance in Victory without telling me. And the next time Aaron Cohen pushes me, pokes me, speaks to me in anything but a courteous tone, or even hints that he's gonna pull a weapon, I'm gonna to clean his clock."

Frankie was listening to my tirade with a thoughtful expression on his face, imagining, no doubt, what entertainment value he'd find in a fistfight between Cohen and me.

"That might be interesting for both of you." Keegan chuckled. "But I'm sure he'll agree to your demands. If we're gonna to be partners, though, maybe we should divide up the investigatory work so we're not duplicating efforts. Any suggestions?"

"Well," I said, "since you two know what you're looking for, why don't you toss the house after the evidence team leaves? Frankie and I will start looking for witnesses, follow up at the morgue, and make a call to Bauer's father in Chicago. If you have any idea how I can make contact with Thibault's family, I'll call them, too."

"Sounds reasonable," he said, "but don't worry about calling Thibault's next of kin. To our knowledge, he didn't have any."

While Keegan shuffled off to explain the deal to Cohen, Frankie and I walked back to Bauer's living room to check the progress of the evidence team. The fingerprint expert had coated every surface with fine, white powder and another technician was on his hands and knees, worrying the carpet where Thibault had fallen with his vacuum and a pair of tweezers. The others had loaded a dozen bags and satchels stuffed with evidence to be examined at the lab in Cheyenne. At the rate they were going, they wouldn't be finished until late afternoon, which meant Keegan and Aaron Cohen would be tied up for most of the day.

It was going to be a long afternoon for Frankie and me as well, but before I began the legwork, I had to get in touch with Ellen Vaughn. I didn't believe she had anything to do with the murders, but I still wanted to know where she'd been when they happened.

The secretary in the anthropology department at the university said Ellen had called in sick, so I dialed out to Mike O'Neal's, where the phone rang about thirty times before his wife Katie picked up, sounding like her mouth had a fleece lining and she'd popped a handful of tranquilizers for breakfast. I could imagine her standing in the kitchen in her fuzzy house slippers and the tattered blue bathrobe she wears for most of the day on weekends. I'd suggested to Mike on more than one occasion that he buy her a new robe, but so far he'd ignored my advice.

"What's going on out there, Katie?" I asked. "You sound like hell."

"I'm sure I sound better than I feel," she said. "But compared to everyone else around here, I'm the picture of health. That's why I'm up waiting on them, and they're all lying around feeling sorry for themselves."

"Is it anything serious?"

"Depends on how you define serious," she said. "If you ask Mike, I'm sure he'd tell you he's dying, but I think it's just the flu. I'd look for most of us to make a remarkable recovery in a couple of days."

"Is Ellen around by any chance?"

"In bed," Katie said. "Do you want me to wake her up? I don't think she feels much better than anyone else, but she's a woman so she tends to handle discomfort better than this bunch of men I have around here."

"Yeah, yeah, I've heard that routine before." I chuckled. "That's why God made the flu, you know, so women could nurse us men and feel useful for a change. I'll let you get back to your duties, Florence."

"Harry?"

"Yes?"

"Screw you."

"Nice talk for a school marm. Next, you'll be using the F word. How long have you been cabinbound anyway? I think the strain is showing."

"Since the night before last," she sighed. "That's when we all started getting sick, and I started putting people to bed. It's only been two days, Harry, but it seems like a month. Know what I mean?"

"Well," I said, "let me know if there's anything I can do. And have Ellen call me when she's up and around."

"Okay," she said. "Harry?"

"What is it?"

"She's a nice girl. I hope she's not in trouble."

When I put the phone back on the hook, Frankie looked up from the stack of Polaroids on the desk and reached for his coffee mug. He sipped noisily then reached up to massage the bridge of his nose with his calloused fingers. There were worry lines on his forehead, and he was biting his lower lip in concentration. "You'd better tell me how you want to handle this," he said. "We haven't gotten much practice on murder investigations around here lately."

I pushed my revolver forward on my belt so I could lean back comfortably and ran my fingers along the sides of my scalp. Outside, a bank of dark clouds was rolling in from the north. Snow clouds, thick and heavy with moisture. By evening, we'd be slogging through a few inches of slush on the sidewalks and black ice on the roadways.

"We won't get the autopsy results until late tomorrow," I said. "And we might not hear anything from the DCI evidence lab until the day after. What we've got to do in the meantime is try to find a witness, anyone who saw anything unusual around the Bauer place last night. I've got a feeling we're not going to come up with much, but that's where we start . . . where you start, I should say. I'm going to stay here for a while and get in touch with Wolfgang Bauer, find out what he wants to do once the coroner releases the body."

He shook his head and pulled an orange from his brown-paper lunch bag. "Damned if I know where to start on witnesses," he said.

"I was here last night until after one o'clock working on a piece of sculpture, and when I got through, I was still keyed up, so I drove and walked around town until after two-thirty.

"There was absolutely nobody on the streets, Harry. This place was a vault, and the only person who might have seen anything was me."

"No traffic on the streets?"

"I don't remember a single car going through after about ten forty-five, when the steak houses closed."

"No traffic from the bars?"

"Nah," he said, working on the orange. "Hell, even the gas station closed early."

"Well, you may have missed something. Start on the north end of town, the houses nearest the Bauer estate, and go door to door if you have to. Maybe somebody saw something useful. I'll make these calls and then hit the bars, the steak houses, anything else that was open. Maybe one of the waiters or barmaids saw something."

Frankie looked doubtful, but he pulled his coat down from the peg, jammed his big black hat around his ears and took off down Main on foot, crashing through the piles of fallen silver leaves cluttering the walk like an icebreaker on its way through the Bering Strait. I thought he was probably wasting his time, but I've got to tell you that at that moment, I'd gladly have traded jobs with him. I'd only met old Wolfgang Bauer briefly a couple of summers before when he came to the office to complain about trout fishermen trespassing on his property, and I hadn't particularly liked him. Like him or not, though, the man was about to get the worst news of his life, and I was the messenger. I've delivered this kind of horrible news more times than I care to count, and it's never gotten easier. The best thing to do is get it over quickly, cleanly, and professionally, then get out before it gets messy.

Wolfgang's home number was unlisted, but Chicago information had the number of the brewery's business office on Lake Shore Drive. I got as far as his personal secretary, but that icy-sounding woman wasn't about to disturb the boss unless there was a damned good reason. When I identified myself as the chief of police in Victory and told her the call was an emergency relating to Tad, she grudgingly patched me through to the old man, whose creaky voice was laced with the annoying nasal twang peculiar to the Great Lakes region.

I could picture him, a handsome man with a mane of wavy white hair and impeccably tailored suits, and remembered what an unpleasant surprise that voice had been the first time I heard it. He answered on his speakerphone, one of those monstrosities that makes people sound like they're talking to you from the bottom of Carlsbad Cavern but allows busy executives to continue whatever important business they were conducting before you interrupted them with your call. "Bauer here," he said, all business.

"Mr. Bauer," I said, taking a deep breath and jumping in with both feet, "this is Harry Starbranch. We met once before. I'm the chief of police in Victory."

He didn't answer for a beat, and when he did, he answered cautiously. "Yes, I remember," he said. "What can I do for you?"

"Well, it's not what you can do for me. I'm afraid I have some very bad news regarding your son."

There was a five-second silence on the other end of the line, and when he responded, he was obviously much closer to the mouthpiece.

"He's hurt?" Bauer sounded almost hopeful. Hurt he could deal with. That's what hospitals and doctors are for.

"No, he's not hurt, Mr. Bauer. I'm sorry to tell you that he was murdered. Last night, at your home in Victory. He and Alex Thibault were both shot to death."

Bauer's gasp was audible, and there was another loud noise from his end, like he'd knocked something breakable off his desk. When he spoke again, his voice was soft and quivering, filled with the kind of shock and great sadness that other parents can only imagine in their worst nightmares. "Where is my son now?"

"He's at the Albany County coroner's office. They'll be doing an autopsy this afternoon, but they should be ready to release the body tomorrow or the next day. I'll need to know what kind of arrangements you want to make."

"They're cutting him?" he asked, horrified.

"Yes, Mr. Bauer, it's the law in deaths where the cause is suspicious. We'll need the information for the investigation and perhaps for the trial."

"Have you arrested someone?" He sounded wary, as if he was reluctant to hear the answer. If what I'd learned about him at the DCI was true, I could understand his hesitation. It was just starting to sink in that his politics might have gotten his son killed. Not only that, but he could be in trouble himself.

"Not yet, but we're working on it," I said. "I should tell you the state Department of Criminal Investigation is also working on the case, as is the FBI. I'm sure we'll catch whoever did it sooner or later."

"Tell them to get the body ready for me," he said. There was tangible relief in his voice, and he was back in charge of his emotions. "I'll be there tomorrow."

His tone told me I was being dismissed, but I wasn't quite ready to hang up. "Mr. Bauer?"

"What is it?" he asked gruffly.

"I'd plan on spending some time here if I were you. We've got plenty of questions about this case, and we think you have some of the answers."

He didn't answer, and I listened to the crackle of the long-distance connection for a full five seconds before he hung up in my ear.

I spent the rest of the afternoon talking to every waiter, waitress, busboy, barmaid, and gas-station attendant in Victory who might have been on the streets after 11:00 P.M. Sunday and seen anything out of the ordinary, but the answer was always the same. It had been a typical Sabbath evening in Victory, the kind of dead-quiet, nothing-shaking, roll-up-the-sidewalks-at-dusk evening that drives kids like my oldest son absolutely wacko.

If you've ever walked the streets of a small town like Victory late at night, you know the kind of eerie quiet I'm talking about. With the houses dark and the only sound on the night air the winter wind rustling through the pines, you'd swear you were in the middle of an honest-to-God ghost town if you didn't know for a fact that there are people behind those shadowy windows, curled up under their down comforters like old bears tucked away for a long winter's sleep.

On a night like that, a fresh murderer running into town from the direction of the Bauer estate with a gun in his hand, or roaring out the driveway in a getaway car would be the sort of thing you'd tend to remember. But nobody saw anything like that, and the closest

Frankie and I came to a clue all afternoon was provided by Carrie Wilson. Carrie—a frail and nervous-looking spinster who shared her Social Security income with her two small French poodles—had called the office around 5:30 to tell us she'd heard about the double murder and thought she'd seen the killer skulking through her backyard a little after 2:00 A.M. wearing a black outfit and heavy work boots.

"I turned the porch light on, and recognized him right away," she said.

"And who was it, Carrie?" I asked, rolling my eyes at Frankie, who had his boots off and was rubbing the soles of his tired feet.

"Harrison Ford," she said. "I didn't believe it either, but it's true."

A little after 6:00, I looked out the front window to see the first heavy flakes of snow filtering through the yellow light from the mercury-vapor lamps on Main. Already, the storm was starting to sock us in, cutting visibility to about fifty yards and softening the hard edges of the buildings across the street.

The headlights of the convoy of cop cars and evidence vans broke through the soup heading south toward Laramie like tramp steamers picking their way through a treacherous reef in heavy fog, their low beams barely picking out the track twenty feet in front of the vehicles, then diffusing in a swirling miasma of gray. Ken Keegan's car was following the pack and broke off in front of the office, pulling to a snow-crunching stop next to my Bronco.

Keegan is so big it seems to take him ten minutes to finish getting out of a car, but as he stood beside his sedan, stretching his broad shoulders and looking up at the sky to let the wet snow fall on his blocky face, he looked smaller—just tired, maybe, but not the picture of robust self-confidence I'd come to expect. I pulled a half-pint of bourbon from the drawer and poured him three fingers in a heavy mug. The man looked like he could use a jolt.

Inside, he shook the snow from his topcoat like a Labrador retriever and ran his fingers through his buzz cut to get rid of the snow that was rapidly melting on the top of his head. He took the mug of whiskey in both hands gratefully and drained it before he'd even unbuttoned his coat. "Shit," he said, shivering as the sour mash worked its way down his throat and began warming his stomach, "I could really come to dislike Anthony Baldi. When you spend time with that man, an hour seems like a week."

Frankie grinned and reached for the whiskey bottle to pour another dollop in Keegan's mug. "I take it Anthony was his usual helpful self?" Frankie asked.

Keegan pursed his mouth in disgust. "He was fine as long as he stayed outside ordering his deputies around and schmoozing with the reporters," he said. "But every time I'd turn around, he'd be back inside grabbing evidence and groping through the technicians' stuff like an old lady at a rummage sale. I spent half the day baby-sitting him and the other half worrying what he'd pull next. What kind of cop is he, anyway?"

"I don't know, Ken," I said. "He used to be with the Laramie Police Department before he ran for sheriff. In those days I hear he was pretty good, but maybe he's finally reached the level of his own incompetence."

Keegan cracked a smile, tossed his coat in the corner, and sighed deeply as he creaked his bones into one of the metal chairs. The bottoms of his trouser legs were soaked from the snow, and his wing tips looked like they might dry out in a month.

"Where's Wonder Cop now?" I asked. "Is it too much to hope he's gone home for the day, or can we look forward to him dropping in here to ruin what's left of the evening?"

"I sent him back to Laramie with Cohen," Keegan said. "I volunteered to come by here and fill you guys in on our day." His eyes crinkled as he held up his mug in toast. "And you know what?" he asked. "They think I got the short end of the stick."

While Keegan sipped the rest of his bourbon, I told him what we'd learned since leaving the Bauer estate that morning, which was nothing, unless we wanted to give Harrison Ford some serious consideration as a suspect.

Unfortunately, nothing is what he and his team had come up with as well. "The evidence geeks didn't look very happy," he said, "and we didn't find anything at the house that sheds light on what happened—no records or documents that might be helpful. Nothing that ties the Posse to any of this, or Tad to the Posse."

Keegan took a deep sip of his whiskey, screwed his face up in the obligatory grimace, and cleared his throat. "Right now, it looks like we've got the bullets that killed them, but no murder weapon, no decent fingerprints that didn't belong to Bauer or Thibault and no other physical evidence that would help us identify the killer," he said hoarsely. "They might find something at the lab, of course, but at this point I'm not holding my breath."

I stood up and walked to the window, which was rapidly steaming over with condensation as the storm picked up and the temperature dropped. I heard the clink of the whiskey bottle as Keegan poured yet another bracer, then the scratch of his lighter as he lit a smoke.

"I've got a hunch the killer is still somewhere nearby," I said, "and I think he or she is someone who knew Bauer well. Problem is, I can't think of anyone in town he was close to. Did you and Cohen see him with anyone we might be interested in?"

"No," Keegan said. "It's been pretty unproductive. Of course, we didn't have a very big team, just Cohen and me, and we split our time. There's a chance we missed something, but the only people we saw at his house all summer besides Ellen Vaughn, Thibault, and the housekeeper were a few women, who may or may not have been hookers. They didn't stay long."

I rolled my eyes in frustration. "Listen, Ken," I said. "I hate to say this, but it sounds to me like this was a low-budget deal, considering how important Cohen made the investigation sound when I came to see you in Cheyenne."

Keegan nodded his head in agreement. "It's an important investigation to the FBI," he said, "but there was apparently a lot of disagreement over the wisdom of tracking the arms shipment through Bauer."

I nodded for him to go on.

"The feeling at the Bureau was that Bauer was a dilettante who the Posse counted on for money, but who wasn't enough a believer to be trusted with anything important," he said. "Most of the other agents involved in this have been concentrating elsewhere."

"Cohen disagreed, I take it?"

"Yeah, he had a suspicion Bauer was playing a more active role than anyone thought. At least he figured Tad would eventually lead us back to the guns. Because he's been on the case so long, the Bureau let him go with his instincts, but they apparently weren't convinced enough to support him with any manpower."

"And what does he think now?"

"He thinks he was right all along. He thinks Bauer and Thibault were killed by the Posse as a way of tidying up loose ends. And naturally, he's furious at you. He thinks your meddling somehow brought this to a head before he was ready. When the Bureau lost track of the weapons after the purchase went down, Tad became—at least in Cohen's mind—the only link to them. Now, unless we can find a way of making Tad talk from the grave, that link is broken. He thinks that with Bauer dead, he may not find those weapons until they're used on innocent people."

"What do you think, Ken?"

"Overall? Overall, I think he may be right. My gut tells me that for one reason or another, Tad and Alex were murdered by the Posse. I don't know why, and I may never know, but I believe that's the truth. I think that even though we haven't been able to pick them out, there are other Posse operatives working in this area—and I think that with Bauer dead, the trail will start getting cold fast."

Frankie and I ended the evening at the Silver Dollar, watching the Oilers and the Eagles duke it out on the big screen and shooting a little eight ball while Curly sat on a wobbly stool at the side of the pool table, drinking boilermakers and grousing about how slow business was on account of the murders. It's his theory that people don't drink as much when they're scared, and a double murder is real scary.

Across the room, Lou McGrew, his thrice-married, thrice-divorced bartender, was leaning across the bar, deep in conversation with a weathered specimen in a bright purple Western-cut shirt with shiny pearl buttons, a carefully waxed handlebar mustache, and the faded outline of a Skoal chewing-tobacco can in the right rear pocket of his jeans. It looked to me like Lou had undone the top two buttons of her tight blouse since the last time I'd talked to her, undoubtedly in order to give the middle-aged cowpoke a better look at her more than ample bosom. She was trolling, the old devil, and it looked like she'd gotten herself a nibble. When she caught me looking, she tossed her mane of curly blond hair, gave me a wink, and went back to her tryst. Since we were the only five people in the place, she could afford to reel her catch in at leisure.

While Frankie ran the table, having perhaps his best game in his miserable life, I sent Curly off to make himself useful by grilling us a couple of cheeseburgers. By the time Curly got back to the table with our meal, the hot grease was already soaking through the paper plates. I grabbed one of the things and bit deeply, wiping the juice that trickled down my chin with a paper napkin.

"Listen, not to throw a pall over the festivities," Curly said, resting a tall bourbon and a fresh beer on his knee, "but we've got enough money in the kitty now. What would you two think about burying Sonny two days from now?"

"Here in Victory?" Frankie asked.

"Nah," Curly said, "we only collected about four hundred bucks, enough to buy him a cheap coffin, but not enough to get a plot in the cemetery. I talked to Bill Cheney, though, and he thought we ought to plant Sonny on his property. He says he's got a little creek running through the north end of his land that Sonny used to fancy and we can bury him there. Said Sonny was a good neighbor when he was alive, there was no reason to expect he'd be a bad one dead."

"Bill Cheney's a good man," I said, feeling a little twinge of guilt for not having told a soul about what he'd seen the night Sonny was murdered. I was more convinced than ever that Ellen hadn't been involved, but there was a voice inside me saying it was unprofessional to withhold information from Ken Keegan and the others.

"Yes, he is," Curly said. "When you come down to it, I suppose he's the closest thing Sonny came to having a relative around here. Cheney won't come right out and say it, but I think he misses him."

According to Curly, Jeffrey Burnside—a minister in the Universal Life Church who got his credentials through the mail and officiates the occasional nondenominational wedding in Victory, as long as there's an open bar—had agreed to say a few words and lead the mourners in a chorus of "Amazing Grace." After that, a few of us would load Sonny in a van for the ride to his final resting place, where

Cheney would use his backhoe to cover him up. The whole thing, Curly said, would be over by 10:00 in the morning.

"I don't know," he said, "it doesn't sound like much. Maybe we should do more."

"It's probably more than Sonny would have wanted," Frankie said. He'd finished his burger in about five bites and was chalking his cue for another game of pool. In his black jeans, white long-sleeved shirt, silver armbands, and black leather motorcycle vest—his huge bowie knife sheathed in a beaded scabbard on his hip—he looked more like an outlaw biker than an officer of the law. He hunched over the table and lined up his break. "If you ask me, the best thing we could do for him now is find out who killed him."

"Any news on that front?" Curly asked.

"Not a bit," I said, "but I'm sure Anthony expects to make an arrest any day now."

"You betcha," Frankie said. He broke the rack violently, but only one ball—a solid—dropped in a side pocket. "Just as soon as the killer marches in to his office begging to confess."

He was lining up his next shot when the bar phone started jangling and broke his concentration. He shook his head in disgust and stood up from the table, rested the cue against the table as Lou grabbed the phone irritably. "Silver Dollar," she snapped, jamming the receiver between her jaw and her shoulder as she shook a cigarette from her pack and fired it up with a kitchen match. "Yeah, hold on."

"Harry!" she yelled, waving the phone in my direction. "For you."

A man usually takes a few long walks in his lifetime. When he gets married, for example, the walk down the aisle is about a thousand miles long. But there's no walk as long as the one a man makes when he's called to the phone at a bar, because the outcome is seldom good. It's usually someone he doesn't want to talk to—the people he wants to talk to are already with him at the bar—or somebody who's going to spoil his party with bad news. I approached the phone warily, lifted the receiver like it might burn. "Harry Starbranch," I said.

"I'm glad I finally found you," Karen said. "I've been calling all over."

If you've ever been on a big roller coaster, you know the sensation you get when you tip over the edge of the highest run, like the bottom of the world just dropped out and you'll keep on falling through eternity. That's the feeling I had the second I recognized her voice. The blood seemed to gush right out of my head, and I grabbed the railing of the bar to keep myself on my hind legs. "It's been a busy day," I croaked. "I haven't been home yet."

"I heard about it on the radio," she said. "Are you okay?"

"Yeah, I'm fine. A little tired."

"You sound it. Look, I'm sorry to bother you at Curly's, but I needed to talk to you. Can you talk now, or would you like to call me back later?"

"No, now's fine," I said, looking down the bar at Lou and the cowboy, who were obviously listening to my end of the conversation. When I caught them at it, they turned away and started trading sweet nothings again. There might have been some embarrassment showing on Lou's cheeks. Then again, that faint red blush might have come from the red neon Budweiser sign blinking in the window.

"I've been thinking about you a lot the last couple of days," she said softly.

"Yeah? And what have you been thinking?"

"I've been thinking that I miss you, and that I might have made a mistake."

"With the professor?"

"No, with you. Maybe I was pushing too hard. Maybe I shouldn't have been mad because you didn't give me something you never said you'd give in the first place. Hell, maybe I'm just a bitch. Who knows?"

"You're not a bitch, Karen. And I've missed you, too."

"That's nice."

"Nice?"

"Well, maybe not nice. But it's better than not missing me at all."

I laughed self-consciously and mumbled some idiotic response, but I was fresh out of small talk. It's pretty tough to make friendly chitchat with someone when your emotional response to that someone is as raw as a fresh burn. She sensed my discomfort and came to the point of her call. "Do you have plans later this evening?"

"No, not really. I'm going to go home in a half hour or so and crawl into bed. I have a feeling it'll be another long day tomorrow."

"Feel like some company?"

"Pardon?"

"You heard me, Harry. I said, do you feel like some company? If it's okay with you, I thought I might throw a quart of lotion in my purse and drive out to give you a back rub. At least I could start on your back . . ."

"That sounds good," I said lamely, and without, I'm sure, the enthusiasm she wanted to hear. "But are you sure you want to make the drive? It's real nasty out there, with the roads—"

"Harry," she said, "I've driven in snow before. It doesn't sound like you're in the mood for visitors. Or is it just this visitor?"

"I don't know, Karen," I said. "Maybe we need a little more time."

She paused for several long seconds to consider what my words really meant. "How much time are we talking here, Harry?" she asked finally. "Until this case is over? The end of the week? A month? The rest of our lives?"

I told the truth, though it hurt me to do it. "I wish I could say, Karen. I just know it isn't now."

"All right," she said, her voice cracking just a little as it traveled the icy wires between Laramie and the Silver Dollar. "Will you call?"

"Sure, I'll call. Soon."

If I closed my eyes, I could imagine her lying naked in my bedroom, the silver-blue light of the moon tracing her long legs, the outline of her bottom, the hollow of her spine. I could almost feel her warm breath on my throat, smell her musky perfume, hear the soft, staccato gasps of her orgasm.

"No, Harry," she said sadly, drawing me back. "I don't think you will."

Back at the pool table, I chalked my cue and missed an easy shot on the six, leaving Frankie in good shape for his last two solids. As he banged them in the pockets and lined up for a straight shot on the eight, it occurred to me that Karen was probably right. Almost without knowing I'd done it, I'd made some sort of irrevocable decision about our love affair. And while I was having trouble seeing beyond my feelings of uncertainty and loss, an optimist might have pointed out that making such a difficult choice represented a not-so-insignificant victory of sorts.

I just didn't know what I'd won.

13

That night's storm cloaked Victory in a white shroud of snow, the early slush giving way to twenty-three inches of downy powder the ski bums were going to love.

As I stood at my office window at midmorning watching the first of them crawl through town in their four-wheel-drive station wagons, their roofs burdened by aluminum ski racks bearing thousands of dollars worth of foreign-built, foreign-engineered, parti-colored instruments of death, I wondered for perhaps the millionth time why anyone in his right mind would strap a couple of fancy-looking, glorified barrel staves on his feet and go careening down a two-thousand-foot mountain slope at velocities equaling or exceeding that achieved by a projectile fired from your average cannon. I tried it twice and nearly killed myself.

Still, the skiers seem to like it, and as Curly is quick to point out, they contribute a lot of money to the local economy, especially if the ski area gets to open earlier than normal on account of a November storm. That being the case, I try to keep my opinions about their general mental stability to myself, and never act smug when one of them stumbles in after an accident looking for a doctor.

An hour earlier, Frankie had tromped through the front door swearing because he'd been caught by an eighty mph crosswind on the sagebrush flats between here and Laramie—where I'd sent him at a little after 6:30 that morning to pick up the autopsy reports on Tad Bauer and Alex Thibault—that pushed his cruiser right across the oncoming traffic lane and into a shallow ditch, where his left front tire exploded on impact.

He'd changed the tire without major injury and had convinced the driver of a county snowplow to pull him out within fifteen minutes, but the incident had disrupted the continuity of his life and as a result, his mood was dark and brooding. I'd taken the report from him without much comment and left him to stew over the injustices of chance and public service while I read its contents.

According to Albany County Coroner James Bowen—a lanky scarecrow of a man who'd won the job four years before in a runoff election against a geriatric mortician who campaigned on the cost-containment platform—I'd read the situation at the Bauer estate fairly accurately. Judging by the level of rigor mortis, livor, and the body temperatures of the victims, he fixed the time of death at between 11:30 P.M. Sunday night and 1:30 A.M. Monday.

Each of the men, he said, suffered three wounds from what he believed—and what ballistics would probably confirm—was a .45-caliber weapon loaded with the kind of hollow-point bullets that expand to roughly twice their size once they make contact with something relatively pliable, like human flesh. The .45 is a round that was originally designed to stop people who are attacking you at close range and kill them, and it does the job nicely, particularly at distances under twenty-five yards, when the heavy slug is still traveling at peak velocity and has enough oomph to rip through a body and open an exit wound the size of a softball.

People have been known to keep coming after being hit in the gut by a .45, but even a monster like Alex Thibault had found two of them in the breadbasket and another one in the head too much lead to carry. Bowen said the first round, which entered about an inch above his belly button, had ruptured his transverse colon, exploded his duodenum, knocked a sizable chunk out of his pancreas, and blown away a half-pound hunk of back muscle as it exited a little to the right of his spine. The second round, about an inch higher and a couple of inches to the left, had popped his beer-filled stomach like a water balloon and poked a hole to the left of his backbone that was nearly an identical twin to the first.

While either of those wounds would have eventually killed him, Bowen said the shooter came back within a couple of minutes to finish the job. With Thibault lying on his stomach, the murderer fired a round point-blank into the back of his head that roared through his parietal lobe and traveled at a downward angle through the rest of his brain, turning it to something that resembled Jell-O in a blender as it moved. It exited right beneath his chin.

The shooter was really mean to Tad.

According to Bowen's report, Tad had taken the first round low in the stomach, and the slug, fired at him from a forty-five degree angle, had opened his belly like a mackerel, spilling several feet of large intestine from the gaping wound. The second blast, high in his mid-section, had pretty much destroyed his liver and clipped his spine, a shock that probably paralyzed him from the waist down, at least temporarily.

It didn't kill him, though, because he had time to drag himself into the dining room, gut shot and spewing blood like a fountain, before the killer had finally kicked him over on his back, placed the muzzle directly on the skin above his left brow ridge, and squeezed the trigger, charring the flesh around the wound with powder burns and opening the entire top of his head to daylight.

Death from that wound, the coroner noted, was instantaneous, and the only relatively comforting information in the rest of the report was the blood-alcohol levels of the victims, which were high enough to indicate they may have been so drunk at the time of the shooting that the booze acted like an anesthetic.

Shutting my eyes and fixing the layout of the Bauer home in my mind, I tried to picture how it all might have come down, and while I still didn't know the who or the why, I could make an educated guess about the how. The way I saw it, Tad and Alex had been home alone, drinking and watching skin flicks, when they had an unexpected visitor. I remembered Ellen telling me that Alex made guests wait in the foyer unless Tad knew them pretty well, so the fact that the shootings took place in the living room suggested the visitor had at least made it past the initial checkpoint.

I could imagine them standing in the living room with the killer—a man as I saw him—arguing loudly when someone made a threatening move. Thibault, the muscle-headed linebacker, moves in to protect his boss and catches a couple in the stomach for his trouble. The killer, turning, fires two at Tad, and while young Bauer moans and drags himself off toward the kitchen trying to escape, turns back to the prone Thibault and drills a third round through the back of his head.

After that, he follows Tad out to the next room, executes him, holsters his weapon, picks up the spent shell casings from what I was sure ballistics would tell me was a semiautomatic pistol, checks to make sure he hasn't left bloody footprints all over the place, makes a quick but thorough circuit of the room to catch anything else he may have left behind, and disappears into the night.

When I let my senses roam, I could almost smell the acrid, sulfur stink of cordite in the room, feel the punch of the automatic as it jumped in my hand, hear the dull, flat thud of the bullets slapping home. I could see the victims dying through the killer's eyes and feel the rush of adrenaline that comes with taking a human life.

But try as I might in that little mind game that all homicide detectives play, the one where they try to put themselves inside the killer's head, I couldn't imagine a face to go with the hand that pulled the trigger, couldn't imagine exactly why he thought he needed to kill those men. I've worked with detectives who are a lot better at that particular part of the hunt than I am, guys who excel at what they do because, at some psychic level, they're almost able to become the crook they're stalking. With his scent firmly in their noses, it isn't long before they start thinking like he thinks, feeling what he feels, fearing what he fears. And because they're on precisely the same wavelength, they're often able to make an arrest because they know what the killer is going to do next, almost before he knows it himself.

Not me. I've always relied on old-fashioned, boring police work, finding a fact here, a fact there, laying them end to end like paving stones until I've built a road to the murderer's door. A little luck doesn't hurt, either. The Starbranch method takes more time, but it usually gets me to my destination.

Still, I was impatient to push the investigation forward. For one thing, I was worried about the mood of Victory's citizenry, the fact that so many of them were toting weapons. It was important to solve the murders of Sonny, Tad, and Alex before someone got hurt accidentally, or worse yet, gave in to the Western penchant for vigilantism and shot an innocent person. Also, I was angry, not just the anger most cops feel when they're challenged on their own turf, but the raw, violent anger that cries out for justice. There was a mad dog loose in Victory. I wanted to bring him down, the sooner the better.

Before he'd left the office the day before, Ken Keegan had promised to call me as soon as he heard anything from the DCI lab, but I was in no mood to sit on my hands all day waiting for the phone to ring. I jammed the autopsy reports in a folder and stowed them in a file cabinet and dialed his office. He picked up on the second ring, sounding tired, grouchy, and more than a little hung-over.

"You sound chipper," I said. "Well rested, vigorous, ready to face the day. . . ." I was trying to sound nonchalant, but he picked up the slightly accusatory edge in my voice.

"I told you I'd call. . . ."

Sometimes, I just don't know when to quit. "I know you did," I said, "but I thought I'd beat you to it, catch you before you got busy, while you're still reading your morning paper. . . ."

"I've been here since 6:00, wiseass," he rumbled. I waited for him to go on, but the only sound in my ear was an annoying snap and pop coming through the phone lines, a phenomenon that begins around here within minutes after serious snow starts falling and keeps getting worse the longer the storm continues.

I had the feeling I'd be waiting all day unless I made the first move. "I don't suppose you have those lab reports yet," I said tentatively. "I know they're not due till tomorrow, but I thought—"

"You thought wrong," Keegan snapped. "Have you ever known a bureaucrat who got a job done early, Harry? I think that violates our contract or something. The lab chief said no formal report until tomorrow, at the earliest, and that's what he meant."

He didn't fool me for a second. I laughed a little at his bureaucrat joke and then pushed on. "Then how about informal?" I asked. "I presume you didn't go out in this storm at the crack of dawn just so you could catch up on your filing? I know you've been down there looking in on them. I can feel it . . . so share."

"If I don't, you're gonna keep pestering me, aren't you, Harry?" he asked dejectedly.

"Yeah, Ken," I said brightly. "I guess I am."

Keegan sighed audibly. "All right," he said, "but this is preliminary—"

"I know the drill," I said impatiently. "Of course it's preliminary."

I could imagine my long-suffering friend shaking his square head in frustration. "They pulled six bullets from the walls, floor, and furniture," he said, "all of them from what looks like a .45 auto—"

"Did they find casings?"

"One, under the sofa. It looks like he picked the others up." I waited for him to go on. "No fingerprints on the casing, and none in the house that can't be accounted for. . . ."

"Damn . . ." I muttered.

Keegan was on a roll. It sounded like he was reading the bad news from a list. "No hair, clothing fragments, or blood that didn't come from one of the victims . . ."

I felt a wave of disappointment. "I suppose it's too much to hope the shithead dropped his wallet," I said bitterly.

"Yep, it sure is. He didn't drop his business card, either, and he didn't leave us a scrap of paper with his phone number—"

"What about a struggle? Did they find any bruises? Any tissue under their nails?"

"No bruises, except some old ones I think you might know something about, and nothing under their nails except a little coke residue under Tad's right pinkie."

"So what do you figure?"

"Well," he paused, "I don't think we have enough to say it was a professional hit, but they were definitely hit by a professional. Know what I mean?"

"I'm afraid so," I said, looking over at Frankie, who was listening and watching me over the page of the newspaper he was pretending to read. "You're telling me we have nothing but a bullet casing, which is useless until we find the gun it came from."

"No," he said, his voice brightening, "I didn't say we have nothing. We have something . . ."

"What?"

"Footprints, Harry, at least a couple of partials. You just can't walk around in a slaughterhouse without stepping in something once in a while, no matter how careful you are. Nobody is ready to go out on a limb yet and say for certain, but if I were a betting man, I'd say our killer was wearing a brand-new pair of waffle-soled work boots yesterday morning. Size twelve."

"That's wonderful," I groused.

"Sure it is," he said brightly. "It's the break you're looking for, Harry."

"Huh?"

He chuckled. It sounded like rock chunks in a crusher. "All you have to do is look around town until you find somebody with great big bloody feet."

Around noon, I got out our industrial-size broom, located the Bronco under a snowdrift in front of the office, and skidded north on Main in the direction of the Bauer estate. Another phone call, this one to Brees Field in Laramie, the only decent airport in the county, had confirmed that Wolfgang Bauer and his wife had been aboard the 9:45 United Express commuter flight from Denver, a thirty-minute carnival ride over the Medicine Bow Mountains known affectionately in these parts as the "Vomit Comet."

In good weather, at least half of the dozen or so passengers packed into the tiny, cigar-shaped Beechcraft can be expected to toss their tuna as the plane bounces through the Rocky Mountain turbulence like a yo-yo. In really ugly conditions, like the ones we were suffering that morning, the number of paying customers making use of their complimentary barf bags would hit at least eleven before the plane cleared Berthoud Pass in northern Colorado, and number twelve would usually chime in before Tie Siding south of Laramie, if not from airsickness then simply out of sympathy.

Factoring in the time I allowed for their stomachs to settle after the airplane ride from hell, fifteen minutes at the Avis counter, where a gum-snapping woman told me they rented a new Cadillac Eldorado, and an hour or so on the snow-packed two-lane between the airport and Victory, I reasoned they ought to be arriving at their summer home at any time. I wanted to be the first person in town to greet them and tell them on behalf of everyone in Victory how sorry we all are that their son had met such a tragic end. I also hoped that if I caught the old man while his defenses were still down, he might tell me something useful.

It occurred to me as I was bumping along the rutted snow trail on Main, my windshield wipers fighting a losing battle with the dime-size flakes and my heater barely pumping out enough warm air to keep the moisture on my eyeballs from freezing, that I probably ought to have called Aaron Cohen and Ken Keegan to see if they wanted to come along. But since we hadn't decided who'd be responsible for this part of the investigation, hadn't even discussed it in fact, they might be grateful that I'd taken the initiative and saved them a perilous drive. They might be mad as hell, too, but I guessed I could handle it.

At the edge of town, I turned off the main road and into the Bauers' long drive, crunching through the axle-deep snow, the back wheels fighting for traction. A single set of tire tracks marked the way, zigzagging back and forth across the narrow road. Someone had broken a lane through the virgin blanket of snow on the way in, and because there was only one set of tracks, it looked like they were still there.

I reached down to the lever at the right of the stick shift and kicked the vehicle into four-wheel drive. The bite and pull of the front wheels was more than enough to straighten the nose of the Bronco and keep me pointed in the right direction. If the storm kept up for another day, though, I imagined I'd need to drag a set of tire chains out of the toolbox and put them on at least two of the four wheels if I wanted to get back and forth to the farmhouse until spring.

The rented Caddie was parked under the aspens at the front of the house, but it didn't look like it had been there for long. The snow filtering down through the bare branches of the trees had covered the windshield in a mushy film of white, but the heat coming off the big Detroit engine was keeping the hood clear and sending tendrils of steam upward like the morning mist off a freshwater marsh. I pulled in behind it and cut the motor, just in time to see a huge man clumping out the front door in his shirtsleeves.

About six-four and a good 260 pounds, the goon's biceps were as big around as my waist and his neck was so thick it was actually wider than his head. And if his size wasn't intimidating enough, he was carrying what looked like a .44 Magnum in his right hand, although his hairy paw was so big the horse pistol looked like a derringer. I rolled down the window with my left hand and reached under my coat to unsnap my .357 with my right, not that I thought it would be much protection. To protect yourself from a man who's as big as your average economy car, you need something more along the lines of a bazooka.

Although he was carrying the weapon loosely at the end of his arm with the muzzle pointed down, when he'd come within fifteen feet of the car, I could see that it was cocked and ready for business. At eight feet, he stopped and took a two-handed shooter's grip on the weapon, still pointing the business end at the ground at his feet, but eminently ready if I tried anything funny, which I had no intention of doing.

I held my hands up to show him they were empty, then reached slowly into the inside pocket of my coat to retrieve my badge, which I passed out the window for his inspection. He took it and studied it, but he didn't seem to believe it.

"I seen one of these for sale once at the war surplus," he said, pitching the badge back through the open window.

I picked the badge up from the seat and put it back in my pocket. "Yeah, well, the difference is, that one's the real thing," I said. "My name's Harry Starbranch, and I'm the chief of police around here. I'm the one who called Mr. Bauer in Chicago the other day."

He gave me a thin smile. I wasn't telling him anything new. "I heard you also arrested his son last week on some cooked-up charge," he said, working the heavy Magnum into the waistband of his trousers and sticking his balled fists on his hips. Even at rest, he looked like a stunt double for the lead ape in *Gorillas in the Mist.*

"I arrested him and his bodyguard for assaulting a couple of police officers," I explained.

He shook his blocky head in disbelief. "And kicked the shit out of both of them in the bargain," he said. "I can't see Alex Thibault letting you take him. Tad, okay, but not Alex. What was he, stoned?"

"Not stoned, just careless. He turned his back on the wrong person."

"You?"

"No, Frankie Bull. He's a police officer on the force."

"Sounds to me like he is the force." He chuckled. "Remind me not to tangle with him. I hate a man who fights dirty."

"Me, too," I said, "unless he's on my side."

The thug grinned at that, something the man should never do if he happens to be in the company of small children, since his smile looked a little like an alligator's when it's biting into a bloody leg of mutton. A good orthodontist would have suggested getting a few of those sharp snaggleteeth capped, maybe recommended a nice bridge to plug the black hole in his mouth where his two front teeth used to be. "Listen, Chief," he said, "I'd love to stand out here in the freezing cold all day shooting the shit, but my employer might start wondering where I am. Is there something I can do for you?"

"For starters, you could tell me your name."

He hesitated for a second as if trying to make a difficult decision. "Max Kellog," he said finally. He did not offer to shake. "Mr. Bauer's bodyguard.

"Anything else?" he added.

I put my hands on the steering wheel, felt the warm air coming from the heater on my knuckles. "I'd like to talk to Wolfgang," I said simply.

Kellog shook his head no. "Not that. I don't think he's in the mood for visitors." He grinned again. "As a matter of fact, I know he isn't, since he told me so himself not five minutes ago when he saw you drive up."

My hands weren't warm yet, but I shut off the motor anyway, grabbed the door handle and popped the driver's side door open a hair. "Well, Max," I said, "he's going to have to talk to me sooner or later, surely he knows that. I just thought he might like to get it out of the way before he goes over to Laramie to claim the body and make arrangements for his son."

"He ain't goin' to claim the body," Kellog said. "He called his attorney from Chicago yesterday and had him make the arrangements."

"So where's Tad?"

"Already gone, man." Kellog shrugged. "Flown home first thing this morning."

"And Alex?"

"Same deal. Who the fuck knows, maybe he got a two-for-one special on the coffins."

"Then why," I asked, struggling to make sense of what I was hearing, "is he here? What was the point of flying two thousand miles in a damned blizzard if he wasn't even going to look after his own son's body? Christ, if he was going to get it done by proxy, he might as well have stayed home."

"You got me," Kellog said. He turned back toward the house and yelled over his shoulder, "Maybe he wanted to get out of the city for a couple days. I just work for the man, I don't ask questions."

I kicked the door open and jumped out, the snow swallowing my boots and a few inches of my calf. I started to follow him up the walk, but my coat was caught on the door handle. By the time I had it free, he was almost at the front door.

"Kellog!" I hollered, my voice muted by the frigid wind starting to blow down from the peaks. He stopped with one hand on the door handle and looked back toward the Bronco. "He has to talk to me because this is a murder investigation. I'm going to wait out here for five minutes while he makes up his mind. If he won't cooperate, I'll come in and get him and we'll talk at the station. . . ."

Kellog smiled again, but there was no humor in it. "Wait right there, Chief," he said, pointing to the spot where he wanted me to stay with an index finger the size of a cucumber. "I'll go talk to the boss."

When Kellog had gone inside, I stood beside the Bronco, stomping my feet in the snow to keep them warm and tightening my wool scarf around my throat to keep the icy flakes from drifting down the back of my shirt.

In the foothills behind the estate, the black patches of lodgepole pine stood in stark relief to the smooth coverlet of white on the meadows. At the edge of one of the small clearings about 250 yards away, a fork-horned mule deer buck and a heavy doe picked their way slowly along the tree line, heading downhill toward the grounds of the estate, where they knew they'd find enough dry grass beneath the powder snow to fill their hungry bellies. The doe was in the lead, stopping every three or four steps to cock her ears and scan the feed ground with her sharp eyes for predators. Deer are a common sight on the outskirts of Victory year round, as are small herds of pronghorn antelope. But in a few weeks, these same foothills would also become home to hundreds of elk, which migrated every winter from the high country around Ryan Park to the lower elevations closer to the Little Laramie River. By late February or March, the huge animals would be so bold and hungry that some of them would be cruising the backyards of Victory to nibble bushes and the occasional sprig of buffalo grass peeping through the snow.

I watched the deer until they reached the end of the meadow and disappeared into a small gully where they'd likely wait until evening before creeping out onto the open grounds of the estate to feed. When I looked back toward the house, Kellog was standing in the open doorway, gesturing impatiently for me to come inside. The lord of the manor had apparently granted me an audience, and his head leg breaker didn't want to keep him waiting.

Ken Keegan's evidence boys had done a good job of cleaning up after themselves, with the exception of the white carpets, which were probably beyond salvation. There were towels thrown over the worst of the bloodstains, and as we made our way through the living room toward the den, Kellog and I stepped around them as carefully as if they were land mines. My nose tingled with the aroma of Pine Sol, furniture polish, and some kind of air freshener, but it wasn't enough to completely cover the faint copper-penny odor of blood. It's a smell that some especially sensitive people swear they can detect in a place where violent death occurred years after the fact, but I thought that in this case, the unpleasant scent could probably be cured by a new rug.

Wolfgang and his wife, Magda, were in the den, nursing cups of hot chocolate and listening to some classical music on the CD player. Even at midday, the den was dark because the heavy, navy-blue curtains were pulled closed, and the fire flickering in the fireplace did little to dispel the gloom.

Bauer, looking tired and disheveled, sat in one of the overstuffed black leather recliners, the weak yellow light from a table lamp illuminating half his wrinkled face and leaving the other in shadow.

Magda, her shoes off and her stockinged feet resting on a chunky footstool, had wrapped a knitted afghan around her shoulders and was skimming a copy of the *Laramie Boomerang,* the one with a four-column photo of the ambulance crew wheeling her son's body out of this very house the morning before. Her face had the taut, pinched look of someone whose emotions are strained almost to the breaking point, and is maintaining control only through a superhuman effort of will or the aid of mood-altering drugs.

When I trailed Kellog into the room, Magda looked up from her reading, but her eyes were so vacant that her brain may not have been registering my presence. With hair the kind of deep brown color you seldom find in nature and pancake makeup so thick it looked like she'd put it on with a trowel, she looked more like a mannequin in the old ladies' department at Jordan Marsh than a living human being. She was probably about her husband's age, in her early sixties, but she looked that afternoon like she was a hundred years old.

Wolfgang, on the other hand, looked like he had a little spark left, in spite of all he'd been through in the last twenty-four hours. His silk rep tie was loosened at the collar and his white hair had the rumpled look of someone who'd been running his fingers through it all day, but his cold blue eyes skewered me as soon as I came through the door, and he left me standing there self-consciously as he took my measure. When his gaze finally traveled as far south as my boots, which were dripping all over the floor, he shook his head in disgust and leaned forward in his chair, clasping his big-knuckled hands together on his knees.

"I understand that unless I agree to speak with you now—less than an hour after I've arrived in the place where my son was murdered, before my wife and I even have time to unpack our bags—you're going to take me in for questioning. Is that correct, Chief Starbranch?"

He spoke to me in a tone I'm sure he uses on all the yes-men who work for him at the brewery when they screw up, the sort of well-modulated, tightly controlled manner of speaking that suggests he's just barely restraining the urge to bite your head off. Behind me, I could hear Kellog as he leaned up against the door frame, the wood creaking painfully as it took his weight. On the mantel above the fireplace, a brass ship's clock chimed the half hour.

He obviously wasn't going to invite me himself, so I took a seat in one of the chairs across the room from Wolfgang, laying my Stetson crown down on the maple end table. I pulled a notebook from my jacket pocket and uncapped a felt-tipped pen. "I'm sorry if it seems insensitive," I said. "But I'm investigating your son's murder, and my first priority is catching the person who killed him. So yes, I did tell your friend there that if you wouldn't talk to me, I'd take you to the station. I don't want to intrude on your privacy or grief, and I wouldn't if I didn't think it was extremely important."

Bauer didn't respond but took a long sip from his mug of cocoa, let the aromatic steam play around his nostrils. When he was finished, he placed the cup on a ceramic coaster and looked at his gold Rolex. "You've got three minutes," he said. "My wife and I have a great deal to do this afternoon."

I didn't let him intimidate me, plunged into my list of questions. "Mr. Bauer, can you tell me when you last spoke to your son?"

Bauer cast a sideways glance at his wife, who was still absorbed in her reading. "I don't know exactly when I talked to him last," he said. "He didn't call often, but the last time I talked to him was probably three weeks ago."

"And how did he sound? Was anything bothering him? Was anything out of the ordinary?"

"He sounded fine," Bauer said. "Why wouldn't he? He was enjoying a hard-earned vacation and recharging his batteries. His biggest gripe was that he couldn't find a decent clothing store. So big deal. Other than that, he was fine."

I already knew the answer, but I asked the next question anyway. "He worked for you at the brewery?"

Bauer nodded in the affirmative. "For the last ten years," Bauer said. "Management. He's going to replace me when I retire."

We both caught his reference to Tad in the present tense, as did Magda. He corrected himself quickly. "He was going to replace me," Bauer said. "Now, I don't know what's going to happen. He was our only child."

Magda's face flushed and she looked up from her newspaper, the muscles on the right side of her cheek twitching and her lips compressed in a tight line. Bauer reached over to give her hand a couple of perfunctory pats, but she pulled away before he could finish. She acted like his touch might scald.

I looked back at Bauer, who was obviously surprised by his wife's reaction. "I know Tad came to Victory every summer," I said, "but he's never stayed this late into the fall before. Do you know why he extended his visit?"

"I told you," Bauer snapped, "he was taking an extra-long vacation. He stayed because he liked it here, that's all. He wanted to get in a little skiing before coming back to work the first of next month."

"And his bodyguard? What can you tell me about him?"

Bauer shook his head. "Nothing much. He was recommended by a security agency in Chicago, and Tad seemed to like him. He'd never been in any trouble, as far as I know."

Although Bauer had a calm, blank look on his face, I figured he was lying. It had been easy for me to find out about Thibault's previous brushes with the law, and I had to believe that a man of Wolfgang's stature ought to have a few connections in law enforcement who were at least as familiar with the NCIC as I was. I tucked my suspicion away for further contemplation. "Did Tad have any friends out here that you knew about? Besides Thibault?" I asked. "Anyone who visited him at the house?"

"I assume that like most men his age, he had girlfriends and friends whose company he enjoyed," Bauer said. "But I couldn't tell you who they are, because I try to stay out of my son's personal life. I don't think he had a steady girlfriend, though, if that's what you're asking. If he had, he would have said something."

I turned from Bauer and looked at his wife. "How about you, Mrs. Bauer?" I asked. "Did Tad say anything to you about friends here in Victory? Can you tell me anything that might add to what your husband's been saying?"

If she understood my question, she gave no indication, but she was staring at Wolfgang with the same kind of single-minded hostility you sometimes see on the faces of the criminally insane. Most strong men would flinch from a look like that, but Bauer was doing a good job of not noticing. He answered for her, his voice taking on a harder edge of impatience. "He said nothing to either of us," he said. "As a matter of fact, he said nothing in any of our conversations that could have a bearing on his murder."

"Mr. Bauer," I said. "I could use some cooperation here. You may not think anything your son said was important, but it might have been very important. Why don't you tell me as much as you remember and I'll—"

Bauer waved me off dismissively. "I want you to find out who killed him, but his mother and I can't do your job for you," he said. "If we think of anything that might be of assistance, we'll be sure to call. . . ."

He stood up from his recliner and caught Kellog's attention with a slight wave of his fingers in my direction. Kellog straightened his bulk upright in the doorway, where he was still waiting, and nodded that he understood. "Now, if you'll excuse us," Bauer said, "Mr. Kellog will see you out."

This was, without doubt, the strangest conversation with a victim's next of kin I'd ever had. When I'd spoken to Wolfgang on the phone the day before, there'd been some human emotion in his voice, but if there was any there now, I couldn't detect it. Neither he nor his wife had asked about the crime, the investigation, or possible suspects. They hadn't asked about how their son died, and they hadn't even shown a pretense of wanting to help. Not only that, but I had the feeling they were hiding plenty, and that Mrs. Bauer wasn't happy about it. I wondered if I'd have a chance to talk to her alone before they went home to Chicago. I doubted that I would.

"Just a minute," I said, leaning back in my chair and crossing my legs at the knee. "I have a couple more questions before I go."

Kellog had begun ambling in my direction, but Wolfgang called him off with a hand signal and looked back in my direction, an ominous expression on his weathered face. He waited for me to go on, and I let him fume for thirty seconds before I obliged.

"Do you think," I said finally, "that your family's politics could have had anything to do with your son's death? Something you know he was involved in that might have backfired?"

Bauer stiffened. "What are you suggesting?" he asked.

"I'm not suggesting anything," I said. "It was just a question."

He answered, but his tone let me know he was only doing it to humor me. He sounded like he was talking to an idiot. "Chief Starbranch, my support of conservative political causes and candidates is well-known, and over the years I've given money to a good many organizations that needed and deserved my support, including, I'm sure you know, the John Birch Society and the Heritage Foundation," he said. "But to my knowledge, neither of those groups is known for killing those people with whom they have a falling out. I fail to see how the two could be connected, and I frankly think that's one of the most asinine questions I've ever—"

I closed my notebook with a snap and stood to face him. "How about the Posse Comitatus?" I asked abruptly. I was tall enough to look down at the top of his silver head, but Wolfgang wasn't intimidated. He met my eyes and held them while I continued. "That's a group known for settling its differences with a gun. Did you support them with money, Mr. Bauer? Did your son? Did your involvement with them go deeper than your checkbook?"

Wolfgang took a deep breath, fighting to control his anger. Beside him, his wife's knuckles were turning white as she dug her long fingers into the leather of the armrest. When he answered, his voice was terse, clipped, his patience at an end. "If you're accusing me of something, Mr. Starbranch," he spat, "you'd better think twice. And from now on, if you want to speak with me, do it through my attorney. I want you out of here."

With that, Wolfgang whirled on his heels and rumbled past Kellog on his way out of the den and into the living room, where I quickly lost sight of him. When the sound of his footsteps faded, I glared at Kellog and turned to Magda. "I'm very sorry about your son," I told her, handing her one of my business cards. "If you think of anything, I'd appreciate a call."

Magda nodded her head in agreement and took the card, her hand shaking a bit from nerves or from the strain of trying to gouge a hunk out of her La-Z-Boy, I couldn't be sure which. I tucked my notebook away in my pocket, buttoned my coat, and was halfway to the door when I stopped and turned back in her direction.

"Mrs. Bauer," I said gently, "I know you and Mr. Bauer didn't come to Wyoming to make arrangements for your son, since your husband did that by phone yesterday. Can you tell me why you're here?"

She looked away from me toward the closed window, the yellow light from the fireplace and the lamps making her look even more sallow and worn out. "We came here," she said quietly, "because my husband wanted to check the condition of the house and collect a few of his belongings. We're putting the estate on the market."

I got back to the office around 2:30 and found a note from Frankie saying he'd gone out to help the highway patrol on an accident call south of town. In addition to his note, there were phone messages on my desk from Curly, confirming that Sonny's funeral service was set for 9:00 A.M. Wednesday, and from Sally Sheridan, who'd told Frankie she had a tip about Tad's murder and wanted my comments for a story she was writing. There were other messages on the answering machine from Ron Franklin, who wanted to know if he'd be allowed to take pictures at Sonny's funeral, and from Edna Cook, who wanted to know if I'd mind picking up five pounds of rock salt and a half gallon of red wine on my way home from work.

I made myself a note as a reminder to pick up Edna's supplies, pulled the blinds on the front window, and turned my desk lamp on. Then, I pulled a legal pad out of the desk and began making a list of everything I knew about this case.

At the top of the first sheet, I wrote the word *crimes.* At the top of the second, I wrote *evidence.* At the top of the third, I wrote the word *suspects,* and at the top of the fourth, the word *conclusions. Guesses* would have been a better phrase, I suppose, but it doesn't sound very professional, and if I was going to sit there all afternoon spinning my wheels, I at least wanted to look good while I was doing it.

I made several entries on the first page—the murder of the Mystery Madonna and the theft of her bones, Sonny's murder, and the double murder of Tad Bauer and Alex Thibault. As an afterthought, I added weapons shipment and kidnapping to the list. Even though there was no proof of a strong local tie to either of those, I put them down because I suspected they were part of the fabric. I also noted the spray-painting vandalism at Shapiro's hardware and the slaughter of Ernesto Varga's chickens.

Under evidence, I included everything I'd learned from the coroner about Sonny's murder and the killings at the Bauer estate, as well as an accounting of the physical evidence we'd gathered so far—a handful of spent slugs and a bloody footprint made by someone wearing new work boots. I also included the fact that Ellen Vaughn's car had been seen at Sonny's the night he was killed, and the FBI's suspicions that Tad had been involved with the Posse Comitatus, had played a role in the purchase and shipment of illegal automatic weapons and explosives, and may have known something about the kidnapping of a district court judge in Iowa.

Under suspects, I had three names—Ellen Vaughn, Alex Thibault, and Tad Bauer. I drew a line through Ellen's name and beside it wrote the word *alibi,* because she had a good one, at least for the night of Tad's murder, and I truly believed she hadn't been involved in Sonny's death. I crossed out Tad's name as well as Thibault's, because they were both dead. I'll admit that for a while there, Tad was on my list of suspects in the Sonny Toms killing, and it was still possible that he'd done it, or at least watched while someone else did. But he hadn't killed himself or Thibault, which meant that at least one killer was still running free, and I had no idea who he was.

Which left me with the sheet labeled CONCLUSIONS, across which I drew a giant question mark. It was a reasonable assumption that the Posse was the connection between most of the disparate events of the last dozen days, but I didn't know enough to fill in the gaps. Did Wolfgang know the name of Tad's Posse contact in Victory, and if he did, how could I make him tell me? What was going on with Wolfgang and Magda Bauer? What were they hiding? Was Magda's apparent dislike for her husband the result of anger, or fear? Why had they really come back to Victory? Beyond that, Tad's killer must have known Victory well enough to make it out of town without being noticed, which suggested he'd been here before. Had anyone seen him? Was he still in the area? Why had he come to the Bauer estate the evening of Tad's murder? Did he come when Cohen wasn't around to see him because he was aware of the surveillance and knew when the FBI agent and Ken Keegan were taking a breather? What had he hoped to gain by killing Tad and Alex? What had Sonny's killer hoped to gain? And where, for Christ's sake, were the bones of the Madonna?

I was still chewing on that one as I picked up the phone and dialed Mike O'Neal's, where Ellen answered on the second ring, sounding a little out of breath, but otherwise healthy and alert. In the background, I could hear the sound of a vacuum cleaner running and Katie yelling over the top of the ruckus for the boys to pull their snow boots off before they came in the house.

"You're sounding better," I said. "The last report I got, the head nurse out there wasn't sure you'd pull through."

"That was yesterday." She giggled. "Forty-eight-hour bug. Today, we're all home on account of the snow, so of course the kids dragged me outside first thing this morning, where we just finished building a snow fort strong enough to repel the Huns."

"You're getting along?"

"They're good people, Harry, and they've made me feel at home. You're lucky to have them as friends. . . ."

"I know, except watch out for Mike. He lies all the time."

"Like about you and the deer?" she asked mischievously.

"Yeah," I laughed, "like that. It didn't happen at all like he said."

"Did you miss all those times?"

"Well, yes, I did, but I meant to."

"I'll bet," she said skeptically. "At any rate, it's a good story. Mike says he tells it all over town."

"I imagine he does," I said, doodling as I talked. "He's made a career of it, as a matter of fact."

"Harry," she said, her voice turning quieter and more serious, "we heard yesterday about what happened to Tad. It's awful. Do you have any idea . . . ?"

"Not yet," I said. "To tell the truth, I don't quite know which way to go."

"You know," she said, "a part of me almost felt relieved when I heard about it, but another part of me wasn't. It's hard to know that someone you were close to is dead, even if it's . . ."

"Someone like Tad?"

"Yeah," she said. "He was a prick, but he didn't deserve that. If there's anything I can do . . ."

"There's not much," I said. "But one thing . . ."

"Whatever you need."

"Okay, then think back. I know you said Tad never introduced you to visitors if they came to the house, but do you remember even getting a glimpse of anyone? I need to find out who his associates were, and I'm hitting a brick wall."

"Of course," she said, then considered her answer for a good thirty seconds. "I'm sorry, Harry, but I never saw a face."

"How about conversations, then?" I asked. "Ever hear him talking on the phone?"

She looked dubious. "There was once," she said. "We were watching TV when he got a call. He took it in the living room and closed the door. I couldn't make out much of what he was saying, but he was angry, talking loud. At the end he was yelling—something about threats. I think whoever he was talking to had threatened him, and he didn't like it."

"Was he like that when he came back?" I asked. "Still angry?"

"Not really mad anymore," she said. "But he was acting sort of strange, like he couldn't get comfortable. He sent Alex out on some errand or other, then we closed the door to the den and stayed up most of the night watching movies. He was drinking a lot, not that there was anything unusual about that."

"Do you think that he might have been afraid of something? Afraid of someone?"

"Now that you mention it," she said finally, "I think he might have been."

"When was that, Ellen? When did this happen?"

"I remember exactly when it happened," she said. "Four days before Sonny was killed."

14

The Reverend "Red Eye" Burnside got his nickname in the early 1970s, shortly after he wrote away to the Universal Life Church and bought himself a set of minister's credentials through the mail for five bucks. For twelve bucks, they would have sent him the stuff to be a cardinal, but he was on a tight budget in those days, and most of the hippies who were willing to pay him $25 and all the pot he could smoke to officiate their offbeat weddings around Victory didn't give a damn if he was a minister or a bishop, as long as he'd read the wacky ceremony they'd dreamed up and sign the marriage license afterward.

He'd agreed to officiate at Sonny's memorial service—being held in the Silver Dollar on account of the fact that Toms declined membership in either of the two local churches—because Curly had given him an open tab at the bar and because he'd liked Sonny, who'd once done such a fine job of temporarily repairing an old Jeep owned by Burnside that the reluctant minister was able to sell it for $1500 to a Kentucky Fried Chicken franchise operator from Cheyenne, who drove it as far as Buford before the vehicle's jury-rigged motor blew apart and started blasting cylinders through the engine block.

Burnside—a barrel-shaped, friendly faced man in his early forties—had started the service in the Irish fashion, asking Curly to pass around shot glasses filled with whiskey to the twenty-five or so mourners in attendance. Glasses in hand, he asked us to join in a solemn toast to our departed friend, a man Burnside noted always minded his own business and treated his fellow townspeople with courtesy. After that, we all gathered around the coffin for a reading of Sonny's favorite poem, "In Flanders Fields," by John McCrae, a piece Sonny must have liked since it was marked by a red ribbon in a well-thumbed poetry anthology on his bookshelf.

"In Flanders Fields the poppies blow," Burnside began in his deep, melodic voice, "Between the crosses, row on row . . ."

As he read, the mourners bowed their heads in contemplative silence—most of us, I'm sure, thankful the reverend was keeping things simple. None of us had known Sonny Toms that well, but all of us knew him well enough to know that he'd have boycotted his own funeral if he thought it would involve a lot of fabricated sentimentality.

When the poem was finished, we punched up Willie Nelson on the jukebox and listened while he sang "Amazing Grace," his beautiful country voice lingering on the high notes as we hummed along. Then, we carefully folded the American flag draped over the coffin, said a silent prayer, and wheeled Sonny's remains out the front door into the bright morning sunlight, where Bill Cheney's van was waiting to carry Sonny to his final resting place on Beaver Creek.

The whole thing was over in less than thirty minutes, and as we gathered on the icy sidewalk to watch Cheney's van as the funeral procession of one rolled slowly down Main, it occurred to me that it hadn't been such a bad send-off after all. There's a lot of comfort in knowing that in a town like Victory, the sense of communal responsibility runs so deep that the townspeople will pull together to make sure that even an eccentric loner like Sonny Toms is sent on his final ride with dignity and honor.

"I suppose it would have made him happy to know that his last act was to stiff me for twenty-seven drinks," Curly said, holding his hand over his eyes to cut the glare. He's never one to indulge in cheap sentimentality, at least the public kind.

"Twenty-six," I said, putting an arm around his shoulders. "I didn't finish mine, so you can pour it back in the bottle when nobody's looking."

It started snowing again early that afternoon. The thick, fluffy flakes buried the few cars parked on Main and piled up in calf-high drifts between the sidewalks and the streets. Down the block, Howard Shapiro and Billy Sun fired up one of the hardware store's new snowblowers and were battling to keep the hundred feet of walkway in front of the store clear of anything a customer could slip on, the blower shooting a plume of powdery snow a good twenty feet in the air like a geyser.

It was coming down, I noticed, right on top of Ray Hladky's Power Wagon, which had been parked in front of the store since Sonny's service that morning. I imagined Ray had stayed on at the Silver Dollar after the funeral, as had most of the other mourners, who'd understandably decided that the warm cheeriness of the saloon was preferable to going back to work before lunch or fighting the blizzard that hit shortly thereafter. There've been a lot of nights when Curly simply passed out blankets at closing time during a bad storm so his patrons wouldn't kill themselves trying to get home, and I figured this would probably be one of those nights.

At that point, the road between Victory and Laramie was closed because of the storm, and the road north into the Snowies wasn't even worth thinking about. For the time being at least, Victory and all of her residents were cut off from the rest of the world, and there was nothing we could do about it until the county plows were able to break through the mess, which likely wouldn't happen until the wee hours of morning.

Around 2:00 in the afternoon, I'd sent Frankie out in the Bronco to run the five-mile stretch of highway between town and the ski area to make sure none of the early-season snow bunnies had gotten themselves stranded. Since none of them had, and since there was no good reason for both of us to sit around the office, I'd given him the rest of the afternoon off. Like almost everyone else in town, he'd headed straight to the Silver Dollar, where I planned to join him when I closed the office.

With the Mr. Coffee happily brewing a fresh pot of sludge and the vintage radiator banging away like an old Studebaker as it desperately tried to keep the office temperature at a barely livable sixty-eight degrees, I turned on KOWB to catch the hourly weather report and learned that the storm was expected to blow itself out within the next twelve hours, but it would be followed by subzero temperatures, which might last well into the next week.

During my first winter in Victory, there was a forty-day stretch when the thermometer never rose higher than twenty below, and it was my first real taste of the awesome brutality that characterizes a Rocky Mountain winter. When it's that cold, a breeze of fifteen mph—which is below average around here—can crank the windchill factor to sixty below, and any exposed part of the human body can freeze in the time it takes to walk fifty yards. Cattle and horses freeze solid in their pastures, and whole herds of sheep, which huddle together to share what warmth their woolly bodies generate, are covered over by drifting snow. After the storm, their owners find them by looking across the plain for the biggest lump and digging down to retrieve the bodies of the frozen animals so they can at least sell the hides.

We've had cold snaps like that nearly every winter since, although none of them lasted forty days, and I've almost come to enjoy them. For one thing, weather like that almost guarantees that Victory will never grow much bigger than it already is, since there are few people foolhardy enough to live here year-round.

For another, there's a weird feeling of accomplishment that comes from going about the business of everyday life while the elements are conspiring to kill you. It's one thing to hop in your car and drive a few blocks to the Laundromat when you live in Phoenix and the only thing you have to worry about on the road are retired couples who creep along in their big sedans at ten miles an hour and never signal before they change lanes. It's another thing to dust the snow off your car in Victory and drive thirty miles to the nearest Laundromat in Laramie when the black ice on the highway is two inches thick and the wind-driven snow has cut visibility to under twenty yards. Doing your laundry on a day like that makes you feel downright heroic, and you can imagine how good you feel after doing something really difficult, like making it to work on time on a morning when the cold has turned your motor oil into something that resembles chocolate fudge.

In the face of such harsh conditions, people tend to develop self-reliance in a hurry, and with that self-reliance comes the fierce independence of thought and action that's characterized Wyoming since it became the first state to give women the vote.

If nothing else, a good cold snap usually tends to keep people indoors and out of mischief, as long as it warms up before they start getting cabin fever and going after each other with chain saws. I hoped this one would break long before that happened—the mood in Victory was tense enough as it was.

The phone rang as I was pouring coffee, and I was tempted to let it go. Sally Sheridan had been dogging my trail for days, and even though I'd escaped talking to her at Sonny's funeral by promising to call her at her office that afternoon—a promise I'd cheerfully broken—I figured she wouldn't let me slide for long. If it was her on the phone, I didn't want to answer, but because I'd forgotten to turn the answering machine on, I didn't really have a choice. I picked it up on the third ring and let enough irritation slip into my voice to let Sally know—if it was Sally calling—that she'd caught me at a bad time.

"Something wrong, Harry?" Ken Keegan asked, his voice alternately strong and crackly as it navigated the ancient phone lines.

"Nothing that a long vacation wouldn't cure," I said, relieved that it was Keegan and not Sally Sheridan. "We buried Sonny Toms this morning. I thought I might see you there."

"Couldn't make it," he said. "I been tied up at the office all day."

I got a mental image of my square friend tied up that made me smile. They'd have to use a lot of rope. "Anything interesting going on?"

"Well, I guess that depends on how you define interesting," he said. He cleared his throat. "I got the lab reports back on that chicken feed you sent in," he added.

I sat forward eagerly. "Yeah? What was it?"

"Compound 1080," Keegan said. "You remember that stuff?"

I did indeed, and it made my heart sink. From the 1950s to the early seventies, 1080 had been used all over the West as a coyote poison, but the feds had banned it because the poison snuffed everything in the food chain, including eagles. It hadn't been available to anyone in the area for more than two decades—except in very limited circumstances—but the poison used on Varga's chickens could have come from any one of a hundred area ranchers or trappers who'd used the stuff while it was legal and kept a little of it around. "Goddamn it," I grumbled. "Why can't it ever be simple, Ken?"

Keegan recognized my problem. If any records of who'd purchased and used Compound 1080 in its heyday were still available—which was exceedingly doubtful—it would take months to track down the people who bought some in our area and find out what happened to their supplies in the intervening years. I didn't have that much time, and certainly not the manpower, to do the job.

"If it was simple," he said sympathetically, "why would anyone need us?" It was a rhetorical question aimed at making me feel better, so I didn't answer. I didn't feel better, either. I was still stewing when he changed the subject. "Speaking of need," he said, "do you remember last summer when those two bodies were found outside the Wind River Indian reservation, and speculation was they were poachers?"

I was still thinking about coyote poison, so his question took me by surprise. "Yeah, it rings a bell," I said, scrambling mentally. "There was some feeling up that way they had it coming, so the locals didn't push the investigation very hard."

"That's about right," he said, "but the state sees it different. The attorney general wants an arrest, and says he needs me as his lead investigator."

"Good for you," I said halfheartedly. "Give you some time to get in a little skiing, maybe a winter trip through Yellowstone."

Suddenly, I realized what he was telling me, and the sinking feeling got worse. "Does that mean you've been . . ."

"Reassigned?" he asked helpfully. I hate it when he finishes my sentences like that.

"Yeah, reassigned. What happens to your investigation over this way?"

"For me it's as good as over," Keegan explained. "The only reason the DCI was involved was as a courtesy, to hold the feds' hands. If they're not interested in Wyoming anymore, we've got more important things to do, too."

"And Cohen," I asked. "What happened to him?"

"Cohen's shifting focus," Keegan said. "The federal boys figure with Tad and Alex dead, there's not much chance the killer'll stick around your neck of the woods. In fact, they got some kinda tip he's already grabbed the guns—if they were ever in Victory—and left the state. That being the case, they've ordered Cohen over to Idaho because they think the weapons will turn up there." Keegan paused to light a cigarette, the click of his lighter barely audible over the wires. "He ain't happy about it, but what's he gonna do? He's a government hound, Harry . . . he's gotta trail the best scent."

"When's he leaving?"

"As far as I know, he's already gone," Keegan said. "Last I talked to Cohen—early this morning—he was on his way to Twin Falls. He wanted to stick around long enough to talk to Wolfgang Bauer while he's in Victory, but I guess the FBI is gonna have somebody else talk to the old man when he gets back to Chicago."

"Good luck with that," I said. "I think the old bastard knows what's going on, but you'd have to work on him for a couple hours with brass knuckles before he'd open up."

The fact that the investigation of the murders at the Bauer estate—and, in a roundabout way, Sonny's—was down to me and Tony Baldi—at least for the time being—stiffened my resolve to solve it before the sheriff did.

Strictly as a matter of professional pride, I was damned if I'd let Anthony Baldi come in and take over the investigation of Tad Bauer and Alex Thibault's deaths, but the technicalities of jurisdiction would only keep him away for so long. In Wyoming, the sheriff is the highest-ranking law-enforcement officer in the county, and I'd have to let Baldi take responsibility for the case if I didn't arrest someone quickly. I figured he was already poking around the edges of the murders, but I didn't think at that point he knew any more than I did. It galled me, but he had every right to involve himself in the action, and if he needed any other reason—besides the fact it's not a good idea to have killers on the loose—he could always say he decided to horn in before people in Victory got so scared they started shooting each other.

On a personal level, it was more complicated, but no less urgent. I know it wasn't exactly logical, but there was a part of me that viewed the murders in Victory as a personal affront. I didn't care for Tad and Alex much, but while they were within the city limits, they were under my protection. Murder always makes me angry, but it makes me especially angry if it happens on my turf. It's the killer thinking so little of me and my abilities he believes he can rub my nose in gore and walk away laughing.

The prick who'd shot Tad Bauer and Alex Thibault had rubbed my nose in their lifeblood, and I could hardly wait to get even. Call it selfish, macho crap if you want, but there it is. I wanted the killer caught—and I wanted the satisfaction of letting him know who brought him down.

Trouble was, the storm was making it impossible to do anything but hunker down and try to stay dry. I'd have to wait it out and make the best of things, at least until the next morning.

Around 5:30, I turned on the answering machine, locked up, and started breaking trail down Main toward the Silver Dollar, where the blinking neon beer sign in the frosty window was about the cheeriest thing on the street. Judging from the number of lonely-looking cars parked in front of the saloon and those being buried by the snow in the parking lot, almost all of Curly's regulars had decided to take shelter from the storm in the mayor's port. From half a block away, I could hear country music blaring from the jukebox and the sound of friendly laughter. Through the window, I could see four or five couples on the small dance floor and a knot of people gathered at the bar, long-necked beer bottles in hand, listening with rapt attention to the story one of their companions was telling.

I followed a couple of lumberjacks through the double doors, the woodcutters stopping just inside to stomp the snow from their feet and unzip their heavy jackets. The smoke from around a thousand cigarettes hung in a smelly cloud about eighteen inches below the ceiling, and Curly's ineffectual smoke eater was clacking away in its losing battle to keep up.

While I waited for my eyes to adjust to the light, I took a deep breath to savor my favorite aroma in the world—essence of barroom—a delightful mixture of bourbon, cheeseburgers, cigarette smoke, cheap perfume, and the atomic residue of every beer that's ever been poured and pissed away since the place opened for business.

As I was edging through the crowd toward the bar, I passed a small table where Lou McGrew was handing out a round of fresh drinks to the four or five cowboys who were gathered around, their eyes gleaming, either from anticipation of a frosty brew or appreciation of

Lou's new miniskirt, I couldn't tell which. She'd frosted her hair since I'd seen her last, and in the near-darkness of the barroom, she looked exactly like Dolly Parton. When one of them reached up with a gnarly paw to pat her on the rump, she balanced her tray of empties with one hand and slapped his mitt away with the other. She caught my eye as she was dancing away and stopped to point an accusatory finger in her would-be suitor's direction. "Mind your manners, hoss," she said. "The law's here."

While the cowboys at the table laughed and enjoyed their friend's embarrassment, Lou sat her tray down on the next table and motioned me over. I obliged, scanning the crowd as I negotiated the room. At the bar, I saw Frankie among the group of men and women gathered there, as well as Mike O'Neal and Billy Sun. Curly was behind the bar listening to their conversation, mixing a half-dozen Seven and Sevens lined up in front of him like soldiers and puffing on one of the huge cigars he breaks out when he's feeling especially festive. I couldn't see the person telling the story they were so intent on, but from the admiring looks on their faces, I thought he must be stringing a hell of a windy.

Lou pushed a runaway strand of hair from her forehead. "Evenin', Harry," she said, a friendly smile on her face. "Welcome to the cultural hub of the universe."

I unbuttoned my sheepskin coat and folded it over my arm. The room was so packed with people it was too warm, almost humid. "Is everybody in town here?" I asked. "Or did three or four of them have the good sense to stay home?"

"Nobody's gone home tonight except Ginny Larsen," she said. She nodded toward a couple of Styrofoam boxes stacked next to the microwave. "But she sent some dinner over for Curly before she left, and there's plenty to spare if you're hungry. It'd only take a couple of minutes to heat it up."

"Sounds lovely," I said. She looked beyond me briefly, flashing a cheery grin at one of the lumberjacks at the pool table. There was a pink stain on her front teeth from where her lipstick had rubbed off. "What's the special of the day?"

"Something brown," she shrugged, "with gravy."

I pointed in Curly's direction, where the mayor was so engrossed in the story he was listening to that he seemed to have forgotten he was in the process of mixing a trayful of drinks, his leaky bar gun dribbling soda on his boots. "Has His Honor eaten?" I asked.

"Yeah." She laughed. "But he specifically said to ask you if you wanted to eat when you came in. Said you already owed him so many dinners one more wouldn't matter."

The idea of warmed-up meat and heavy cream gravy didn't sound very appealing. I'd wait until I got home later, maybe fry up some lean ham and scrambled eggs. "Think I'll pass," I said. "Give my poor arteries a break."

When Lou had turned away to take drink orders and flirt with the men at the next table, I edged up to the cluster of merrymakers standing at the bar, clapped my hand on Mike's shoulder by way of hello. "I see you've gotten healthy enough to sit up and take nourishment," I said, motioning toward the half-full beer bottle he was holding.

Mike grinned hugely and threw his arm around my shoulders. "You're not going to believe who we're talking to," he said, grabbing my elbow and dragging me further into the gabble of conversationalists. "Come on, I'll introduce ya."

The object of his enthusiasm was leaning against the bar of the Silver Dollar, a tall highball in his hand and at least three replacements within easy reach. When he saw me, he broke off the tale he was telling and stood himself up to his full height.

I recognized him immediately. Not that I knew him personally, of course, but it's hard for us die-hard football fans to forget the faces of the greats, and Christian "Kit" Duerr, once known as the meanest man in pro football, had definitely been one of the greats.

A 260-pound nose tackle for Mike Ditka's Chicago Bears, he'd been responsible for thirteen quarterback sacks the year the Monsters of the Midway chewed up the NFL on their way to the Super Bowl against the New England Patriots—although he'd missed that game because he was on suspension for biting a linebacker's leg in the last regular game of the season.

When he saw me approaching with Mike, Duerr flashed a hearty smile and reached through the gaggle of admirers for my hand. "Well, hello," he rumbled. His sandpaper voice held a trace of Midwestern accent. "You must be the Harry Starbranch I've been hearin' so much about."

I nodded to acknowledge that I was indeed Harry Starbranch and wondered what stories my friends could have told him he'd possibly find interesting. Then I realized his shake was crushing the bones in my hand. I winced through my thin smile and pulled my hand away, hooked the thumb of my injured paw in my belt loop.

Duerr's grin told me the pain he'd just inflicted hadn't been unintentional. The man was sizing me up, taking my measure. When he had it fixed in his mind, he wrapped his huge hand around his glass and tipped back another swallow.

Mike, meanwhile, was gushing. "Kit was just tellin' us about the time Refrigerator Perry bet a sportswriter he could eat a whole baby pig at a sitting, then griped because they didn't bring enough applesauce," Mike said almost breathlessly. Rubbing shoulders with Duerr had apparently turned my buddy into an idiot.

The ex-football star was dressed a little uptown for this crowd, with a huge diamond ring on his right hand, about thirteen pounds of gold chain around his stump-size neck, and a calf-length coyote coat that probably set him back a couple grand. Still, he acted right at home, and it seemed the local rednecks felt pretty comfortable with him, too. A couple of young women in the bunch were making goo-goo eyes every time he looked in their direction, and even Frankie—who would have arrested anyone else walking around Victory dressed in such an outrageous costume out of general principle—looked impressed.

"Guess what?" Mike continued, his beery-red face positively glowing with excitement. "Kit says he's thinking of moving out here and buying a bar. Can you imagine?"

"Well, that's the rumor floating around," I said flatly. "Guess we can always use another bar. Lord knows, we hardly have enough to keep this town in booze as it is." I looked at the mayor, who was eyeing me curiously. He knew from my tone Duerr had made a poor first impression. "How many bars do we have for our 650 residents now, Curly?" I asked. "Six? That's hardly enough to go around."

Curly, anxious to avoid unpleasantness, broke out in a goofy grin.

"Yeah," he said. "We got enough churches already, we can always use another saloon."

With that, Duerr dismissed me with a nod, picked up a fresh drink, and launched into a story about the time he and a couple of offensive linesmen from the Bears had gotten into a brawl at a Chicago blues club called the Kingston Mines. He followed that with a tale about a postseason game during which a 290-pound tackle had kicked him so hard in the groin that the team doctor had suggested putting his Johnson in a cast.

"I told him no, so of course it healed funny." Duerr laughed. "I'm the only guy I know can piss around a corner."

15

I stayed at the Silver Dollar until around 2:00, listening to Duerr tell one outrageous story after another. His was not the kind of personality that grows on me—aggressive and almost compulsively profane—so I was fairly glad when he finally called it a night and went off in search of a bed.

Someone said they thought Duerr was staying at a local motel—maybe the Plainsman, a decent place behind Gus Alzonakis's steak house. From what I'd read about him, Duerr was not married, and I wondered if he'd had time to cultivate any female companionship from among the local talent pool. Ask me, it was a mighty cold night to sleep alone.

As Curly was passing out the blankets to his snowbound patrons, I drove back to the farmhouse and crawled into bed. The next morning, I woke feeling tired and queasy. I crawled out from under the covers at a little after 12:00 and fixed myself a brunch of black coffee, scrambled eggs, and a stack of toast made from Edna's bread. I drank the coffee, nibbled on the toast, and ignored the eggs. I lit a cigarette and the taste almost made me nauseous. I stubbed it out and rubbed my temples with my fingers.

From the kitchen window, I could see Edna out in the corral, breaking through the ice on the horse trough with a ballpeen hammer. I've offered to feed and water her horses for her on a number of occasions, since it makes me feel a little guilty to watch the old woman forking hay and shoveling manure, but she always turns me down, her logic being that if you can't provide for your own animals, you don't deserve to have them.

The mangy Shetland rubbed up against her as she worked, trying to stick his drippy nose into her coat pocket, where she always keeps an apple or two for treats. She whacked him on the snout, and he hopped away, looking mightily offended, but it wasn't long before he was back again, and this time he hit pay dirt, a nice Jonathan, which he gulped down in a single bite. The other two hay burners, having better manners, stood around stamping their big hooves and snuffling until she rewarded them, too.

When I could see that she was almost finished, I pulled a second mug from the cupboard and filled it with steaming coffee.

I walked to the kitchen window and pushed it open. The blast of cold air was heaven. "Have you had enough caffeine today?" I yelled out the window. "Or could you stand another cup?"

"Sounds fantastic!" she hollered back cheerfully, giving her horses a final pat and latching the squeaky gate behind her on the way out. The snow in the yard came above her knees, but she blasted through it with the determination of a mule and was at the back door pulling off her boots and a couple of the many coats she wears before I could find the sugar and make a quick circuit of the kitchen to make sure there wasn't any underwear or dirty socks on the floor. "You sick, Harry?" she asked with concern.

"Nah," I said, pulling the belt on my bathrobe a little tighter and pouring her a cup of coffee. "I didn't get home until very early this morning, and I needed to catch a few hours of sleep before I head back to town."

"Do you have any idea," she said, her eyes twinkling, "how long it's been since I've had a reason to stay out all night? It was 1963, Harry, almost thirty years. He was a surveyor, if I remember correctly."

"You've got a dirty mind, Edna," I said. "That wasn't why I was out all night. I was out all night because I was working."

While she sipped her coffee and buttered a piece of toast, I told her about Kit Duerr and the problems the storm had caused in town. I also told her as much as I could about the murders of Tad and Alex, and the fact that with the FBI temporarily out of the picture, the case was left to Tony Baldi and me.

"It's funny," she said when I'd finished, "the newspaper said the bad element had left town. Just goes to show you shouldn't believe everything you read."

"The newspaper?"

"Yeah, this morning's *Tribune.* Didn't you see it?"

"No, I didn't. Did Sally do another big story?"

"Front page," Edna said between robust bites.

"What'd it say?"

"Well, here," she said, reaching into the pocket of one of the coats she'd parked on the back of her chair and pulling out a dog-eared copy of the paper. "See for yourself."

It's a good thing I'd already finished my breakfast, because the three-column photo of Anthony Baldi on the front page would have spoiled my appetite. But as queasy as looking at Tony's oily face made me feel, the story itself was worse.

This time, Sally and Tony had really outdone themselves. Under a huge headline that read, "Sheriff says Posse Comitatus Responsible for Double Murder in Victory," Sally's story made Tony look like Elliot Ness and the rest of us look like Keystone Kops. If they'd been in my kitchen at that moment, I'd have happily strangled the pair of them.

I spread the paper on the table and began to read.

BY SALLY SHERIDAN

Special to the Star-Tribune

VICTORY—Albany County law-enforcement officials say a grisly double homicide in this small mountain community last week may have been connected to right-wing extremists whose goal is to overthrow the American government and who have been stockpiling weapons here, unhindered by local police.

Albany County Sheriff Anthony "Tony" Baldi said yesterday that Wolfgang "Tad" Bauer and Alex Thibault, whose corpses were discovered by a cleaning woman at the Bauer family's opulent estate, may have been shot to death by members or associates of the militant Posse Comitatus, with whom the victims were linked, and with whom they appear to have had a falling out.

"According to evidence I have, it seems most likely that Bauer and Thibault were gunned down for political reasons by the Posse Comitatus," Baldi said. "Bauer had been the focus of a joint investigation by the Albany County Sheriff's Department, the Federal Bureau of Investigation, and local investigatory agencies for several months, and we were nearing the point when we could have begun making arrests. Unfortunately, Bauer and Thibault were killed before that happened, but we still have enough information to be confident that the murderer will be apprehended in the very near future.

"While local police are conducting an investigation in Victory, an investigation that has turned up no leads so far, my information indicates the killer, or killers, are still in the area. We intend to see that they don't get away with this," he said.

Baldi said that the FBI, which conducted a low-manpower investigation in Victory during the late summer and fall, has since concentrated its efforts in another Western state. "But the sheriff's department is still carrying the ball for them in the Wyoming end of their investigation," Baldi said. "If anything is turned up by myself or my deputies, we'll naturally turn it over to the federal agents. We've established a very close working relationship with them."

Baldi said he believes the members of the Posse who were operating in Victory for the last months chose the small community as a base of operations because they felt safe there. "Victory is served by a tiny police force that seldom has to deal with anything more serious than a parking ticket," he said. "The Posse believed they could do whatever they wanted there, and to a certain extent, they were right. For example, we think they may have moved a large number of automatic weapons and explosives out of Victory after the murders, and they did it right under the noses of the local police."

Baldi said that according to his information, up to $250,000 worth of automatic weapons, explosives, and ammunition may have been stored in Victory by Posse operatives for the last several months. And while he believes those weapons have since been moved to another location, perhaps one of the Posse's military-style training camps in Idaho, he said there are still some loose ends to tie up in Wyoming.

"For one thing, we haven't closed the books on the recent murder of Sonny Toms in Victory, although it looks like he was killed because of his ties to the Posse," Baldi said. "For another, we need to take a closer look at the trail the Posse left as it moved through Wyoming, including the slayings of Bauer and Thibault."

While Baldi would not comment on many of his plans for continuing the investigation, other law-enforcement sources say that Baldi will likely apply for a warrant to search the Bauer estate.

The estate, on the northern boundary of Victory, is owned by Chicago brewer Wolfgang Bauer, who was reportedly in Victory last . . .

That's where Sally's story jumped to page sixteen, and when I'd finally thumbed angrily through to the back section, I was treated to Tony's assertions that the money used to purchase the weapons actually came from Wolfgang; that Sonny "was likely working for the Posse in some capacity"; and that Tony was "prepared to exert his authority as the county's highest-ranking law-enforcement officer to see that the books on these horrible murders are closed."

Toward that end, he said he planned to haul everyone even vaguely connected to any of the murders in for questioning, including the people who had been present when the bodies were discovered. By that, I assumed he meant Esmerelda Ruiz and Ellen Vaughn, although I wouldn't have been surprised to hear that he wanted me in the hot seat as well.

At the end of her story, Sally noted that, as usual, I'd been unavailable for comment on any of the nine occasions she'd tried to catch me at the office on personal visits, visits during which she noted that the office was closed and locked during business hours.

"You look like a man who's just discovered Bondo on his new sports car," Edna said as my eyes ran through the final paragraphs of the story for the third time, my chest getting a little tighter with each reading.

I crumpled the paper closed. "Huh?"

"I said you look madder than a constipated badger," she said.

"I am mad, goddamn it," I snapped. "And I'd appreciate it if you'd spare me your humor. You'll notice I'm not laughing."

She slammed her mug on the table so hard it sloshed lukewarm coffee over the paper. "Well, excuse me," she huffed. "I thought you'd already read the damn thing, and that's why you were hiding out here at noon on a workday. I was just trying to make you feel better."

With that, she grabbed a handful of coats off the back of her chair and marched out of the kitchen. She slammed the door extra loud, and I could hear her cussing me all the way across the driveway to her own back gate.

"Way to go, you idiot," I grumbled to myself as she stomped up her snow-covered walk, her wrinkled face crimson with anger and her tiny, birdlike hands gesturing madly in punctuation to her anti-Starbranch invective. I ran out on the porch in my bathrobe and bare feet and called out a whiny-sounding apology just as she turned the corner, heading full steam toward her own back porch, but she didn't acknowledge it because she was pretending to be deaf.

"I know you can hear me, Edna," I hollered. "I know you can hear me because I know you well enough to know that you're standing there where I can't see you, listening to everything I say."

There was no answer, but I knew she was listening. "I'm sorry! I didn't mean to be rude," I yelled. "If you'll forgive me, just this once, I'll buy you that Tom Selleck western the next time I'm in Laramie, and you can watch it all day long."

Nothing. It was like talking to the wind. "Come on, Edna," I begged. Beneath my robe, the hair on my legs was standing up in puny defense against the cold and my testicles had retracted at the speed of light. "I said I'm sorry!"

When her hand finally snaked around the corner, her gnarly old fingers pinched together in an okay sign, I felt a little better, although I figured I'd have to spend at least an hour in a hot bath before my balls noticed it was safe to come out again.

I scrambled back inside, soaked in a bath hot enough to make my legs red as boiled lobster and restore my manly organs to some sort f equilibrium. Then, I slipped my old bones into a soft red union ıit, a pair of jeans, and a Grand Targhee Ski Area sweatshirt with ıe sleeves cut off. I got a good fire going in the woodstove and called rankie at the office to let him know where I was. Next, I called Ken eegan in Cheyenne to ask if I could drive over that afternoon and o through his files on the Posse. He said that would be fine, as long s I'd spring for dinner and maybe a couple of cocktails at the Hitch-ıg Post afterward.

After that, I hunted up the phone book and started calling every eal-estate office in Albany County. That sounds like a much bigger ob than it is, since there are only about ten real-estate companies oing business in the whole county, and only four of them do much vork in the Victory area.

I wasn't surprised by what I learned—that none of them had rented ny homes or cabins near Victory since September first, and only a ouple had rented units during the summer, all of them to families vhose vacations had long since ended. Still, unless the killer had left he state or gone to hide out in Laramie, he had to be staying some-vhere. That meant motels or seasonal rentals. Due to the public ıature of motel living in these parts, I suspected the shooter had cho-en a rental.

When I finished with the real-estate companies, I called Esther Campbell at the Victory branch of the Albany County Library and ıad her pull five months' worth of *Laramie Boomerangs* and weekly *Victors*. Naturally, she grumbled at my request that she look through he classified sections of those papers and write down the names and ıumbers of any private citizens who had advertised rental properties ince the first of June, but she agreed to do it on condition that I re-urn copies of Robert Crais's Elvis Cole detective mysteries I'd bor-owed around the middle of September. "I don't even care about the ines," she said, "but there are other people who might like a chance o read those books. You're not the only person in town who likes Elvis Cole, you know."

Esther said she'd have the job done by a little after 2:00, so I spent he sixty-minute interim calling ranchers and landowners north of own to see if any of them had rented line shacks, cabins, or hired ıands' housing in the last few months. Rod Colby, who owns a little six hundred-acre place south of the ski area, said he'd rented one of the cabins on his property to a retiree from Yuba City who'd come for the fishing in September and left around October tenth. Other than that, and the deer hunters who stayed at his place for a few days around the middle of October, he said it had been a pretty slow season.

The other ranchers said variations of the same thing, although Wally Pike said he'd rented one of his smaller places . . . to his mother-in-law. "And I'd appreciate it if you'd come out here and throw her out," he carped.

Carl Bonner and Jim O'Meara, who have places further up the mountain, said they hadn't rented any of their buildings or cabins since spring, though both of them said they had parties coming in the next couple of weeks for elk season.

Tom Clay said he hadn't rented to anyone all year, although he was thinking of trying to beef up his outfitting business, what with the cattle market so lousy. "Why don't you think about coming up here to hunt?" he asked. "I've got so many elk on this place that anybody can get one—even you. And if you can get an elk, I figure it'll be great advertising."

Brenda Rogers said her husband, Gary, was out trying to save a heifer that had fallen through the thin ice on the irrigation pond, but no, they hadn't rented out either of the two smaller houses on their property. "I've got eight kids living out here," she said wearily. "Who the hell would want to live around that, unless they had to?"

At 2:15, Esther called back with five telephone numbers and a dire warning to get my overdue books in by close of business the next day. Three of the numbers belonged to landowners I'd already talked to, one was a Cheyenne exchange, and one had a Colorado area code.

The Colorado number turned out to be a real-estate management company, and the property they'd been advertising was an eight-bedroom "lodge," complete with sauna, Jacuzzi, and a small rodeo arena. Although the place was a "steal" at $900 a week, the agent said it had only been rented for one week in September to a group of Wang computer executives who'd come west to play golf at Old Baldy and try to figure a way of getting their company's finances out of the dumper. The Cheyenne number belonged to a gruff-sounding old geezer who said he'd been thinking about renting his summer cabin, because his wife never wanted to go there with him anymore on account of the fact that he refused to install indoor plumbing. Unfortunately, he said none of the three people who'd called to inquire had been willing to put up the $1,200 deposit he requested.

All right, so I really hadn't expected the person, or persons, I was looking for to march up and sign a lease under their own names. But by God, it was too cold to be sleeping outdoors.

Maybe they hadn't rented a place at all. Maybe they'd just found a vacant cabin, broken a window, and helped themselves. Since the owners of a lot of the properties around Victory only fly in for a few weeks a year, a transient can make himself at home for a long time before anyone shows up to complain.

I tracked Frankie down at Ginny's, where a spirited debate was raging in the background over whether Vanna White, whose game show they were watching on the color set behind the counter, is an actress or an airhead. "She's both, goddamn it!" Frankie yelled before he'd even said hello. "Now, will you all be quiet? I've got a phone call here."

I told him what I wanted him to do after he finished coffee—go back to the office and pull the list of houses and cabins in the area owned by summer people. Most of them are outside town limits, but since Frankie and I freelance security services to many of the summer people who own them, it's our job to check on the buildings periodically throughout the winter months anyway. I wanted him to start making the circuit that afternoon, and since he'd have to cover about ninety miles of bad road, I suggested he start as soon as possible.

"You really think this guy is hanging around Victory?" he asked.

I was going on gut hunch, but it was a strong one. "I do," I said. "I've got this feeling his business in Victory isn't finished yet. He's around here, Frankie. I can feel him."

"And if I find one of the summer houses occupied?" he asked. "Where'll you be?"

"I'm going over to Cheyenne," I said. "So, if you find something unusual, don't do anything. Give me a call at the DCI and wait until I get back. Don't go in alone."

"You got it, Chief," he said. "Listen, it's Frieda's birthday and we've got reservations at the Cavalryman in Laramie for supper at seven, so I'll look around until six. If you don't hear from me, that means I didn't see anything out of place. I'll catch the rest of the houses in the morning."

"Fine," I said. "I'll make the rounds of town tonight when I get back from Cheyenne."

"Bye, Harry. Watch your topknot."

"Frankie?"

"Yeah?"

"Give her a birthday kiss from me."

"I will." He chuckled. "But not on the lips."

It was late afternoon when I pulled into the parking lot of the state Department of Criminal Investigation in Cheyenne. The asphalt lot was covered with a hard sheet of ice and dirty snow, which reflected the bright afternoon sun like a mirror. Even with a good pair of sunglasses, I'd been squinting so tightly against the glare that my whole face hurt. My hands were sore from gripping the steering wheel, and for the first time in several days, I wanted a drink to calm my nerves.

I don't like driving in winter much, and the trip over the mountain from Laramie had been hairy, the kind of ride where you take a deep seat, a short rein, and hope for the best. It had been especially nasty around Buford, where an eighteen-wheeler carrying a load of drilling pipe had jackknifed on the icy road and tipped over on its side, sending a hundred tons of pipe clattering down the highway like giant, metallic pick-up sticks. The driver had escaped with his life, but a young woman who'd been behind the rig in an old VW Beetle was seriously injured when she crashed into a section of runaway pipe. The demolished VW, the pipe, and the rig were still on the interstate when I'd driven through, guided past the obstacles by a couple of tough-looking highway patrolmen.

Keegan met me at the front desk, looking tired and rumpled, his tie loosened around his thick neck and his dress pants sagging beneath the slab of his belly. He had a cigarette hanging in the corner of his mouth and a pencil jammed behind his ear. He wasn't wearing his suit coat, and even his shoulder holster seemed to droop. Not even the sight of the receptionist, her long legs encased in sheer black nylons and crossed high enough to reveal a shocking amount of thigh, was enough to perk him up.

"You look like fifty miles of dirt road," I told him charitably. "If this is what happens when you work for the state, remind me not to apply."

"It isn't the job," he said as he led me toward the bank of elevators, "although I've got plenty of paperwork to catch up on before I head up to Meteetsee."

"Then what's the problem?"

"My daughter," he said as the elevator door *whoosh*ed open and he lumbered in. "She got in a fight with her husband and moved back in with us for a while. She ain't so bad, but my five-month-old grandson was up screaming all night."

"I remember that," I said, thinking back to the many nights when Nicole or I would walk the floor all night with one of our boys, who'd fall asleep scant moments before I was scheduled to start my shift. "I always found that a little bourbon works."

"Jesus, Harry," he said, a look of righteous indignation on his square face. "You can't give a kid whiskey, even if he is keeping you up all night."

"Not the kid, Ken. The bourbon is for you. After a lot of experimentation, I found that about five fingers of Jack Daniel's will drown the noise of a houseful of squalling kids. Of course, a decent pair of earplugs doesn't hurt, either."

"Thanks for the advice," he said as we stopped at his floor. "I'll keep it in mind tonight."

There wasn't much activity in the institutional green hallway: a file clerk pushing a cart loaded with books and reports and a couple of secretaries leaning against the wall, smoking cigarettes and gabbing in subdued voices. At the door of the conference room where I'd had my first look at the Posse files, Keegan flipped the lights on and pointed to a stack of documents on the long table. "I had the clerk bring these in for you," he said. "You're welcome to take all the time you want with them, make copies . . ."

I tossed my coat on one of the metal-and-plastic chairs and pulled a thick file folder off the top of the stack. "Thanks," I said. "I'll come and let you know when I'm finished. We still on for dinner?"

"If you don't mind," he said, "I'm gonna take a rain check. The way I feel, a big dinner and a couple of beers and I'd be facedown on my plate. You don't mind, do you?"

"Nah," I said, "I know just how you feel. Go home and get some sleep."

He watched me poke through the first pages of the top file—the heavy synopsis of the Posse's activities I'd read on my first visit to the DCI—leaning against the department's copying machine to take some of the weight off his legs. Overhead, the fluorescent lights buzzed softly, bathing his lined and weary face in their unnatural yellow light. "You have any idea what you're looking for?" he asked.

"None whatsoever," I said. "But I've still got too many questions and not enough answers. Some of them are probably in here. I've just got to be smart enough to pick them out."

He nodded his understanding and left me to my chore—about sixty folders filled with interview notes, forensic reports, reports from field operatives, surveillance notes, analytical profiles, historical profiles, and tax records. It was nearly everything of real importance the FBI had put together on the Posse since 1976, all of it the legacy of Aaron Cohen, who'd brought the documents when he came to Wyoming and left them behind for inclusion in the DCI's case files.

One huge folder contained nothing but the names and addresses of people who had contributed to the political campaigns of right-wing Posse candidates for local office in the Midwest. Another bulging folder was crammed with copies of the hysterically venomous letters members of the Posse had sent to judges, local officials, national politicians, and newspapers in their effort to spread their campaign of religious intolerance and racial hatred.

There were also two thick files of photos, grainy black-and-white glossies, of various Posse members and hangers-on. Tags were stuck to the backs of the photos identifying the subjects who were known to the FBI and speculating on the identities of others.

Still more folders were filled with historical information, psychoanalytical profiles of the Posse's leadership, lists of sympathizers, hierarchical organizational charts, and evidence detailing the Posse's connections to other white supremacist hate groups like the Aryan Nations, the Liberty Lobby, various local militias like the one suspected of having ties to the men who blew up the federal building in Oklahoma City, and everyone's favorite pointy-headed idiots, the Ku Klux Klan.

One folder contained nothing but a copy of an internal memo outlining the Posse's plan to insinuate a sympathetic candidate into the American political mainstream in a bid for high elective office—the U.S. Senate at minimum and perhaps even the Oval Office. Another folder was a report by the Anti-Defamation League about the national upsurge in right-wing paramilitary activity.

It was heady stuff, and certainly more than I could have assimilated in several weeks of close study. That day I only had a few hours, and before long I found myself skimming, reacting to the information on a visceral level, hoping that something would trip my internal alarm system and provide me the lever I needed to pry the case off center.

While I wasn't blinded by any flashes of insight, I did, after a while, begin to get a better feeling for the kind of men and women who are attracted to the Posse in general and its more militant wings in particular. And while it would be easy to write them off as nothing more than the modern-day equivalent of Adolf Hitler's SS or Joseph Stalin's NKVD, the American version of Pol Pot's butchers or the trigger men in a Salvadoran death squad—as the sort of ignorant, disenfranchised fanatics who have carried out mankind's dirty work since the dawn of time—that oversimplification doesn't take America's responsibility for the movement into account.

While its leaders were formed in the same bloodthirsty mold that gave birth to men like Adolf Hitler, the Posse's membership, for the most part, is drawn from American bedrock, from the landscape of our heartland, from the most basic and previously stable elements of our society, the farm family. When a farmer is told one year that he needs to produce more than he can sell, when he's encouraged to borrow more money than he can ever hope to repay, when he's beaten down when the crops come in by embargoes, ever-higher interest rates and taxes, the fear of bankruptcy, and the threat of foreclosure—he naturally feels anger because he's no longer in control of his own destiny.

And when his elected officials, the men and women he has entrusted with the safekeeping of his way of life, turn a deaf ear to his misery, when they tell him, in fact, that his poor management of the land and his finances are to blame for his troubles—there are always men like Gordon Kahl waiting in the wings to fill the void. Men who offer him a scapegoat for his suffering—the Jews, the blacks, the Hispanics. Men who have a ready explanation for his circumstances. He may not want to believe what they say, but he does because theirs is the only explanation being offered that doesn't blame him.

If you ask me, we have nobody but ourselves to blame for the growth of organizations like the Posse Comitatus. We've crushed the hand that feeds us, sown our rich earth with salt.

But then, nobody asked me.

Guys like me are just paid to clean up the mess.

When my eyes finally began to blur from reading in the harsh light, I turned to the heavy photo files, packed with well-thumbed pictures of the Posse's leaders, as well as its heavily armed rank and file. There were at least fifty photos of Kahl and other Posse bigwigs like his friend William Rhinehart, who died in a federal prison in Arizona. There were pastoral photos of Posse members and sympathizers taken at their family farms, photos taken at forced farm auctions, and photos taken during the arrest and trials of various Posse operatives and organizers. There were lots of poor-quality photos, obviously taken from a great distance, of military-style training camps in Idaho, Missouri, Georgia. There were grisly photos from Kahl's autopsy. There were several photos of the Posse's victims—men like deputies Robert Cheshire and Ken Muir—whose lives were snuffed out because they stood, however briefly, in the way of the Cause.

There were photos of Wolfgang Bauer, Tad Bauer, Alex Thibault. There was a formal portrait of Judge Jacob Haines of Des Moines, whom the FBI believed was yet another victim of the Posse's holy war.

Toward the end of the file were a half-dozen eight-by-tens taken at Kahl's funeral services in Heaton, North Dakota, the killer's coffin draped with an American flag. What initially drew my attention to the last of these pictures was the honor guard from the local chapter of the American Legion who had turned up to shoot off their World War II vintage carbines in farewell to a fellow veteran. All aging and overweight, one of them dressed inappropriately in a gaudy

Hawaiian shirt, the honor guard was ringed by a large crowd of mourners, a few of them standing stiffly at attention as the Legionnaires fired their last salute.

Even though Kahl had served in the armed forces and was by tradition entitled to be buried with military honors, it seemed ironic that this man, who had killed at least three lawmen and died in a desperate attempt to overthrow his own government, had been given what amounted to a hero's send-off.

I took the photo from the file and checked the ID tag on the back. Only Kahl's immediate family were positively identified. I flattened the picture on the table and studied it more closely, looked beyond the honor guard in the foreground to the faces in the crowd. It was early June 1983, the cottonwoods and maples were in full leaf, and most of the mourners were dressed in comfortable summer clothes, the men in shirtsleeves and the women in cotton dresses and light jackets.

To the side, under the temporary canvas pavilion erected by the funeral home where the family sat, a few women wiped their eyes. Behind their row of metal folding chairs stood a phalanx of burly young men, most with their hands folded at their belt lines, a few with heads bent in silent prayer, the others looking intently at the honor guard from the American Legion. They looked uncomfortable in their Western-cut, polyester blazers, but fresh scrubbed and earnest, their cheeks still plump with the vestiges of baby fat. Compared to the hard cases in the photos taken at the paramilitary training camps, these men looked almost achingly normal, the kind you'd see at every 4-H show and county fair in rural America.

The longer I looked at it, though, the more something in the photo began to nag at me. There was something in it that was wrong, something out of place, something that was making me uncomfortable.

I studied the photo for several minutes, my eyes stopping briefly on each member of the crowd, but they kept returning to the mourners in the funeral pavilion in general and one of the men positioned behind the seated family members in particular, his large hand resting on an old woman's shoulder as if to give her comfort from the shocking reports of the Legionnaire's guns. A big man who stood a good head taller than the rest of the men in the group, the bottom half of his face was hidden by a full beard and the edges of his face were blurred by the grain in the photo. His coat was tight across his deep chest, his nose was long and straight, his features finely chiseled. His eyes were light colored, blue or sea green; it was impossible to tell in the black-and-white photo. His high forehead led to a thatch of wavy hair, possibly dirty blond or light brown.

At the office next to the conference room, I borrowed a magnifying glass from one of the typists and used it to bring his face closer. Under magnification, the grain of the photo was more apparent, the fine detail even less clear than before. The photo had been taken in 1983, more than ten years ago, so if I'd seen this man recently, he would have aged considerably. I tried to imagine his face with another decade of living on it, a few lines around the corners of his eyes, a more modern haircut, maybe a pair of glasses, thinning hair.

It didn't do any good. If I'd seen him before, I couldn't remember where, and I couldn't remember when.

On impulse, I slipped the photo into my jacket, straightened the junk on the table, and turned off the lights.

I was pretty sure Keegan wouldn't mind.

Victory was quiet when I got back to town around 9:30, my stomach pleasantly full of the rare prime rib that the Hitching Post is famous for and my nerve ends buzzing from the three cups of strong black coffee I'd used to wash it down. I made a quick pass through town, stopping at a few of the businesses to make sure the doors were locked and at the office to check the messages. There was a hurriedly scrawled note from Frankie saying he'd come up empty at the seasonal homes he'd had time to check that afternoon, but that he'd take a swing by the rest of the places on the list before he came in to the office the next morning. There were also messages from Curly, Ellen Vaughn, and Ron Franklin. I threw Franklin's message in the trash and dialed the Silver Dollar, but Lou said the mayor had gone home an hour earlier. Then, I dialed Mike O'Neal's number.

"Hi, Harry," Katie said when she picked up. "Mike says it's your fault he stayed out drinking beer the other night and missed his daughter's school play. He says he only stopped by for a quick one, but every time he'd try and leave, you and this Kip Dirt would pull him back in and make him order another round. Is that true?"

"Duerr." I chuckled. "Kit Duerr. And no, Katie, it isn't true that I forced your bum of a husband to screw up his family obligations. The man, as we both know, is a pathological liar."

"I figured he was fibbing." She sighed. "Did you want to speak with the lying scum, or did you call to talk to me?"

"I dearly love talking to you," I said, "but I actually called to return a message from Ellen. Is she around?"

"She left an hour and a half ago," Katie said. "Told me not to wait up. Can I tell her anything when she comes in?"

"Yeah," I said, "tell her to give me a ring in the morning."

Which was unnecessary, as it turned out, since Ellen was waiting in my kitchen when I pulled in at the farmhouse twenty minutes later, sipping a glass of red wine and looking better than I'd ever seen her before. With her dark hair swept high on her head and her milky face accented with big, gold hoop earrings, she was wearing an expensive, soft-looking sweater that didn't hide her curves and black stretch pants so tight they probably came out of a spray can. She was barefoot, with her legs stretched out in front of her on one of the kitchen chairs.

"I'm glad you leave your door unlocked," she said, toasting me with her half-filled glass. "It could have been a cold wait otherwise."

"It's an old Wyoming tradition," I said, stomping the snow from my feet and peeling out of my coat. "In the backwoods, we rustics always leave our doors unlocked in winter, just in case some poor, unfortunate traveler gets lost or stuck and needs somewhere warm to come in and drink wine. We figure it's the least we can do for our fellow man . . . especially if our fellow man is a woman."

"Thanks, Harry," she said, a blush beginning to highlight her cheeks. "Have you had a long day?"

"Seems long."

"Well, I know you're probably too tired for company, and I wouldn't have just barged in like this, but I've been trying to get you on the phone all day and I haven't had any luck. I finally figured I'd just come out here and park myself until you got home."

"That's fine," I said. "Is something wrong?"

"No, not really," she said, "but I didn't think it would be right to leave without saying good-bye."

"You're going back to Laramie?"

"No," she said. "As a matter of fact, I've decided not to go back there. I'm leaving for California the first part of next week."

"California?" I stuttered. "What about school?"

"Tell the truth," she said, standing to lean against the counter, her arms cradled beneath her breasts, "I can't concentrate. I keep thinking about Tad alive, and asking myself how I ever let myself fall for such a loser. Then I think about Tad dead . . . and I just feel sad. I need to do something."

"That's understandable."

"If it were just Tad and Sonny and the murders, I think I'd probably take a few weeks off and call it good. But I can't seem to shake this horrible feeling I've had since Tad's murder. I feel like someone is watching me all the time. Maybe it's irrational, I don't know, but I don't feel very safe, Harry. The only time I've felt safe recently . . . is when I've been with you."

"So you're going to California to get away?"

She nodded almost sadly, then hiked herself up so that she was sitting on the counter, filled my wineglass, and raised her own. "A toast," she said.

I raised my own glass. "To what?"

"To better tomorrows," she said, clinking the rim of her glass against mine. "I'll miss you, Harry."

We sipped, and when we were finished, she set her glass down on the counter. She took mine and placed it beside hers. Then, she put her arms around my neck and pulled my face down, kissing me tentatively at first, then more insistently, the tip of her tongue darting across my upper lip. I felt her warm breath on my cheeks, felt her hook a leg around my waist and draw me even closer. As we kissed, she took my hand and guided it toward a breast, gasping softly when I found it.

I don't know why, but I'm pretty sure I started seeing stars about then, and I figured if we kept this up for long, the sky would surely fall. That's when she reached for my zipper, and while part of me wanted her to find it more than I wanted air, another part of me was coherent enough to realize that I couldn't let it happen. I broke the kiss and gently took her hand away from my crotch. "What are we doing here?" I asked, the words catching in my throat.

"I don't know about you, Harry," she said, pulling me toward her again. "But I was hoping we were going to make love."

"Why?" I stammered.

For a split second, she looked surprised, then confused, then hurt. And then she started to laugh. "Because it would feel good . . . because we find each other attractive . . . because I haven't made real love to anyone in a long time . . . because it beats the shit out of a handshake. Why do people ever screw around, Harry?"

"No," I said idiotically. "I know why. I mean why? Why me?"

She took my face in her hands, a soft, understanding smile playing at the corners of her mouth. "Because all I've been doing for the last few days is listening to Katie O'Neal talk about what a great guy you are, and how any woman would be lucky to have you, in spite of what I understand are your myriad faults. Because I think you're sexy, Harry, and decent. Because I think it might be cozy to wake up in your bed with you beside me. Because I want a good memory to take away from Wyoming. Because my goddamned car is stuck in your driveway, and I couldn't go home if I wanted to. Is that enough, or should I go on?"

I shrugged helplessly, starting to laugh myself. Fact is, I didn't want her to go home. I wanted to finish our bottle of wine, enjoy her company, put some music on the stereo, and dance, maybe kiss and tickle a little more. And then I wanted to tuck her into my bed . . . alone. As much as I agreed that making love would be about the most pleasant thing I could imagine right then, I also knew it was the last thing either of us really needed. I'd like to tell you that my own reluctance was based on my desire to protect Ellen from doing something she might regret later. She'd just gotten out of one bad relationship and she didn't need to take a chance on another, although I didn't think I'd be as bad for her as Tad Bauer. But while that really was a part of it, I also understood that making love to Ellen would break the compact I'd made with myself regarding Nicole. If I wanted to give my marriage another chance, and I believed I did, I just couldn't be sleeping with college girls, no matter how persuasively my libido argued that I ought to quit worrying and oblige the lady's request.

I explained all that to Ellen, and she listened without comment.

When I was finished, she hopped down from the counter, refilled her wineglass, walked out of the kitchen and into the living room, shaking her head as she went. "That's the first time I've ever tried to seduce a man and been turned down," she said as I stood in the kitchen, staring into my burgundy and trying to figure out what the hell I'd just done. "Usually, it's the other way around. Now, at least, I know how all those horny, unrequited bastards felt."

As I listened to the first whiskey-soaked strains of the Tom Waits album she put on the stereo, I certainly knew how I felt, and it had nothing to do with sexual frustration. I just felt ancient. Precambrian.

Older than dirt.

16

Anthony Baldi arrested Ellen Vaughn on suspicion of murder a little after 10:00 the next morning—about four hours after she and I had finished breakfast, shoveled her car out of the snowbank in the front yard, and I sent her home.

As I pieced it together later from Ellen and Baldi, Tony had gotten a call the night before from Bill Cheney, the man who'd seen Ellen's car at Sonny's the night of his murder. Although Cheney hadn't been anxious to go to Baldi with that information in the first place, he'd apparently gotten tired of waiting for me to act on his tip and picked up the phone to share what he knew with the sheriff.

The information was enough for Baldi to bring Ellen in for questioning as soon as she got back to her apartment after spending a chaste night in my bed. When he found she'd ended an abusive relationship with Tad Bauer only days before he was murdered and that she was planning to leave town, he figured he'd better arrest her and fill in the details later. He had opportunity in one of the three killings and motive in one of the others, and that was enough for the time being.

I guess I didn't really blame him. From a certain perspective it looked bad.

Ellen's car had been witnessed coming out of Sonny's property the night he was murdered, and the only person who could provide an alibi was Tad Bauer. The employees of the supper club where Tad and Ellen had dinner the night Sonny was murdered could only account for her whereabouts for part of the evening. There was no one to vouch for them after they left the club.

And when it came to Tad, Ellen wouldn't have been the first

woman to kill the man who'd been punching her around. She might have gone to his house with the express purpose of settling the score, murdered him in cold blood, and killed Alex simply because he was there.

It *could* have happened that way, although I knew it didn't.

Apparently, Tony Baldi hadn't gotten around to checking Ellen's alibi on the night Tad and Alex Thibault were murdered. As soon as he did, he'd learn she'd been at Mike and Katie O'Neal's home, sick and in bed. That would eventually get her off the hook for those murders, and in the final analysis I didn't think there was much evidence to tie her to Sonny's killing, either.

For the time being, though, Ellen Vaughn looked good as far as suspects go—certainly good enough for the arrest. After that, he had forty-eight hours before he had to charge and arraign her or let her go, two days to check her story and search for new evidence.

She phoned me at the office before Tony locked her up. "Please come, Harry," she asked plaintively after she'd told me about her arrest. Her voice was small and afraid. In the background, I could hear the routine noises of the jail—prisoners yelling at each other through the bars, the drone of television sets and radios, the clanging of cell doors. "I don't know who else to call."

I followed a county snowplow for the entire thirty-mile drive from the office to the sheriff's department in Laramie, the rear end of the Bronco sliding dangerously on the black ice every time I pressed the accelerator or touched the brakes. The thirty-mile-an-hour wind that was blasting down the slopes of the Snowies took the windchill factor down to about forty below, and my poor heater could barely keep up. I peered through the small window of frost-free glass on the windshield and tried to keep my eyes on the road, what I could see of it beneath the tendrils of powdery, wind-driven snow that whipped across the treacherous asphalt.

By the time I reached the outskirts of Laramie, my hands, face, and toes were numb from cold. When I pulled into the parking lot at the sheriff's office, I got out, buttoned my sheepskin coat to the collar, and stamped my feet to get the circulation going before I tried to navigate the icy walk leading to the building.

The Albany County Sheriff's Department occupies the basement f the four-floor county courthouse building, an imposing granite ructure built in the 1930s that also houses the county court, county ssessor, county clerk, district court, and on the top floor, the county il, which is run by the sheriff's department. The building is hot in e summer and frigid in the winter, and the prisoners of the jail have led numerous complaints with the American Civil Liberties Union oncerning the inhuman conditions they have to endure as the ounty's guests. There's a new jail building under construction across e street, but it won't be finished for another year. In the meantime, risoners wear minimal clothing in the summer and lots of extra lay-rs in winter. On some winter mornings on the fourth floor, it's cold nough to see your breath.

I stopped by the front desk of the sheriff's department, but the dis-atcher said Tony Baldi was out on a call and not expected in for an-ther half hour. I told her I'd be back and took the elevator to the ourth floor, where I waved through the glass partition at the jailer, ho buzzed me through the locked door to his office.

The rotund jailer was Mackay Smith, a former patrolman from the asper Police Department who lost his job on account of his weight roblem. I'd hired him on the rebound almost two years before dur-ng my brief tenure as Albany County sheriff, and he'd been grateful or the opportunity. When I came through the door to his office, he eaved his bulk up from the desk and reached for my hand. "Nice to e you, Harry," he said. His breath smelled like garlic and onions. It hasn't been the same around here since you left."

I didn't know if he meant that things were better in my absence, r worse, but I was in a hurry and didn't ask him to elaborate. I hung y jacket and hat on his office rack, unbuckled my Blackhawk, and id the weapon and holster on his desk. "Ellen Vaughn," I said with-ut preamble. "I need to talk to her."

Smith studied my face for a minute, working out some internal onflict. "Does the sheriff know you're here?" he asked finally.

I shrugged my shoulders and smiled. "Tony's not here," I said, "but he was, I'm sure he wouldn't mind me seeing her. Professional cour-sy, you know, Mackay?"

Smith hesitated for a long moment then nodded agreement.

"Yeah," he said in a voice edged with sarcasm. "Tony's a real professional. I'm sure he wouldn't object at all." With that he pushed the button that released the electronic lock on the door separating his office from the jail proper. The jarring buzz that signaled the electronic lock was disengaged continued until I turned the knob and opened the door. I stood in the doorway and looked back over my shoulder at Mackay Smith, who was already sitting at his desk again, opening a sandwich of some sort wrapped in aluminum foil. "She's down there," Smith said, pointing to the far end of the row of cells. "Last one on the right."

I closed the door behind me and walked toward the far end of the jail. The air reeked of prison smells, the astringent scent of disinfectant, the odor of vomit, musky sweat, and cigarettes. The afternoon sunlight coming through the barred windows at the end of the corridor dappled the walls with yellow light but did little to display the lingering gloom. A trusty was pushing a cart filled with books down the corridor, and in most of the cells, prisoners were either sleeping or watching talk shows on their small, black-and-white television sets.

There was no television playing in Ellen Vaughn's cell, and in the murky shadows I could see her small body curled up on the metal bunk suspended from chains anchored to the wall. She was on her side facing the wall, her knees drawn almost to her chest. She was trembling but apparently not from the cold, since her woolen blanket was still folded neatly at the foot of the bunk. When she heard my footsteps stop at the front of her cell, she looked over her shoulder, rolled over, and sat up. Her feet barely touched the floor. "Harry?" she asked, as if she mistrusted her own eyes.

"Yeah, kiddo," I said. "How you holdin' up?"

She stood shakily and walked to the bars at the front of her cell, reached through with her small hand. I took it in my own. It felt dry and feverish. Her face was flushed, eyes red from crying. Her hair was mussed and her clothes—the same ones she'd been wearing when she left the farmhouse that morning—were wrinkled and wilting.

She gave me a weak but relieved smile. "I've been better," she admitted. When I didn't answer immediately, she went on. "He's not exactly a nice man," she said, meaning Anthony Baldi.

"He's not paid to be nice," I said, surprised at myself for defending him, even to that extent. "He's paid to solve crimes." I gave her hand a reassuring squeeze. "But the important thing is, the worst is over."

She gave me an incredulous look, pulled her hand free, made a gesture that covered most of her cell. "I suppose you mean the interrogation," she said tightly, "but this is no picnic either. How long do you think I'll have to stay here?"

"That depends on whether Tony Baldi has enough evidence to convince the district attorney to charge you," I explained. "If he doesn't have it now and doesn't get it soon, they can only hold you for forty-eight hours." I paused momentarily. "If he and the DA think they have enough to bring charges, you'll be arraigned and the judge will decide on bail. If you make bail, you could get out then."

She thought about that for a while before I continued. "My guess," I said, "they don't have enough to charge you. I think you'll be here forty-eight hours, tops."

She looked down at the floor, and I could barely hear her when she spoke. "I didn't do it, Harry," she said. "I didn't do any of it."

I put my hands on the bars, leaned close to her. I could smell the lingering traces of her perfume. It smelled like apples. "I believe that," I told her. "So you've got nothing to worry about. They can't prove you killed Sonny—there's no motive, no weapon, no way to prove you were driving the car Bill Cheney saw the night Sonny was murdered. And you've got an alibi for Tad and Alex. The little evidence they have for his killing is so circumstantial, I think they'll have to let you go."

Her whole body seemed to frown. "They can't prove I *didn't* kill Sonny, either," she said.

It was not a question, but I answered anyway. "Not yet," I admitted, "but it doesn't matter. What matters is—"

Sudden anger flashed on Ellen's face. She reached through the bars and grabbed my forearm, dug her nails into the flesh. "It matters," she whispered. "Don't you understand that?"

"Why?" I asked. "You'll be out of jail. You can go home and—"

She pressed her fingernails deeper into my skin. It stung, but I didn't pull away. "To what, Harry?" she asked. "This arrest will poison my whole life. You think the university will keep someone around who's a suspect in multiple murders, even if the evidence is scanty? You think the folks in California are going to want someone like that around students? You think this won't hurt my chances for a job after graduate school, even if I'm never charged?"

"Well, I don't know about that, but—" I stammered.

"It'll ruin me," she said bluntly. Her bottom lip began to tremble and she bit hard to make it stop. A tear appeared at the corner of a reddened eye. She let go of my arms and brushed it away with the heel of her hand. "I've only got one chance . . ."

I was washed by a wave of paternal protectiveness. "I know a couple of lawyers who'll work cheap. I'll call them, have them get in touch with you today. After that, I'll do whatever I can to help."

"Get me out of this, Harry," she said simply. She looked into my eyes, held my gaze forcefully with her own. "Find out who really killed them, so you can prove it wasn't me."

Tony Baldi was waiting for me in his office when I finished talking with Ellen Vaughn, his feet up on his desk and a cigar in the corner of his mouth. A cloud of gray smoke hung near the ceiling, so thick and noxious it burned my eyes. He didn't offer me a seat, so I took one without being invited on the old railroad bench I'd brought to the office during my brief tenure as sheriff a little over a year before. I felt a pang of regret at not having taken the bench with me when I left—it would look nice at the police station in Victory—but when I resigned as sheriff I'd been in too big a hurry to worry about anything as trivial as antique furniture.

Baldi blew a smoke ring above his head and waited until it had drifted upward about a foot before he destroyed it with a forceful breath. I felt a wave of revulsion at being in the same room with him with the door closed. For one thing, he looked vaguely disgusting, with his oily hair, food stains on his pants, and a shirt so tight it couldn't quite cover the flab of his belly. For another thing, even beneath the smell of his cigar I could smell his bitter sweat. The man needed a shower, and a bigger shirt. "I'm disappointed in you, Harry," he said, still not looking in my direction. "Real disappointed."

I didn't answer right away. Not that I cared a damn what Anthony

Baldi thought about me. Before I'd dropped out of the sheriff's race a little over a year before, Tony Baldi had been my primary opponent and he hadn't fought fair. Instead of talking about issues, Baldi had smeared my reputation with off-the-record stories about my drinking and womanizing, most of them lies and the rest gross exaggerations. I didn't mind not being sheriff anymore—it was my own choice—but I had a deep and abiding dislike for Baldi as a result of his attempted assassination of my character.

Still, I'd come to his office, so the least I could do was keep the conversational ball rolling. "That hurts me, Tony," I said with all the mock sincerity I could muster. "It really does. Would you like to tell me what I've done to cause this fall from grace?"

Baldi took his feet off the desk and stabbed the air between us with his cigar. "How about withholding evidence in a capital murder investigation?" he sneered. The doughy flesh around his collar was growing red, and pink splotches bloomed on his cheeks. "How about obstruction of justice? I could charge you with both of those crimes, Starbranch. How would you like that?"

I knew exactly what he was talking about, but I played dumb anyway. "Come on, Tony," I said. "The Bauer and Thibault murders happened in my jurisdiction. Even if I knew something you don't—which I doubt is the case—there's nothing in the law books that obligates me to share it with you. We're independent investigators, Tony, not partners."

He stood up from his desk and crushed his half-smoked cigar out in a glass ashtray, where it continued to smolder. I noticed the tail of his shirt was hanging out the back of his pants. "That's not what I'm talking about, and you know it," he spat. When I didn't answer, he went on. "Bill Cheney came to see me this morning."

I looked at him blankly, as if I couldn't place the name. My feigned innocence only served to anger him more.

"He tells me you've been sitting on information that places Ellen Vaughn's car at Sonny Toms's house the night of his killing," Baldi said. He sat on the edge of his desk, dangled his fat legs. "You want to tell me why, Harry? Why you've been protecting a murderess?"

I shrugged nonchalantly, took my time snagging a cigarette from the pack in my coat pocket and lighting it up. When it was going satisfactorily, I took two or three deep puffs and made a point of knocking a bit of ash on the carpet. "She didn't kill Tad and Alex, Tony," I told him. "She's got an alibi. Have you checked that out?"

Baldi glowered and waved dismissively. "Maybe she does," he said grudgingly. "But that still doesn't clear her for Sonny Toms. She was there, Starbranch, and I'm gonna prove it. Then I'm gonna charge her with murder in the first."

I took another drag of my smoke, stood, and walked to Tony's desk, where I ground it out in his ashtray. At close range, his body odor hung like fog. "I think you've got dick," I told him. "I think you jumped the gun."

He stood and brought his face close to mine, so close I could see the deep pores on his nose, smell the coffee and tobacco on his breath. "We found some small bloodstains in the upholstery of her car, Starbranch," he said. "Did you know that?"

I shook my head dumbly. It would take awhile for DNA testing to be completed, but if the blood matched Sonny's, it was bad news for Ellen—more circumstantial evidence, but another link in the chain.

"I didn't think so," he said, smiling thinly. "But here's what I do think. I think your little college bimbo got herself all caught up with these fuckin' Nazis from the Posse Comitatus and went over the edge, just like that stupid Patty Hearst. I think she's been helping them for months, even when they killed Sonny Toms. Who knows, maybe the guns and violence got her wet." He was really rolling now. "I think she knows who killed Bauer and Thibault, even if she didn't do it herself. I think she's up to her neck in this shit and I'm gonna hold her head under until she drowns."

He smiled wickedly. "But here's the best part, Harry. I think she's been squeezing your ignorant pecker so hard you've had to close your eyes." His smile grew wider, crazier. "You've been hosing a goddamned terrorist, Starbranch! Protecting her!" He made a shame-on-you gesture with his index finger. "What do you think that's gonna do to your precious reputation when it gets out, Harry?"

Tony Baldi laughed out loud. "Hells bells, podna," he said happily, "this is a *whole* lot worse than bein' a pukin' drunk!"

* * *

Around 1:00 that afternoon, Ken Keegan and I stopped for comfort food at a little Mexican restaurant in West Laramie.

After my blowout with Baldi, I'd arranged for an attorney friend to meet Ellen at the jail. Then I called Keegan from the county commissioner's office and asked him to drive over from Cheyenne for lunch. He'd agreed, and I spent the hour until his arrival pacing the halls of the courthouse, thinking about the case against Ellen Vaughn. I was angry, but also worried. There was no way I could protect her from the bad things coming her way as a suspect in Sonny's murder, unless I could do as she suggested and find the real killer. Trouble was, I didn't think I was very close. As the hour dragged on, my funk deepened and my stomach bubbled with frustration. I wasn't ready to give in and have a few beers, but I figured some spicy food would burn the bad spirits away.

The restaurant we chose when Keegan arrived only had four tables and a dozen ratty stools, but it's always packed, a favorite of the Union Pacific crews who work the railroad's Laramie-to-Rawlins run. In addition to an inexpensive menu of entrees that'll make your taste buds bark, the owner makes the meanest green chili north of Juarez. We each ordered an extra-large bowl of it to go with our enchiladas.

I'd filled Keegan in on Ellen Vaughn's arrest, and we moved from there to the murders of Bauer and Thibalt. I restated my feeling their killer was still around Victory and had to be staying *somewhere.* I told him about the preliminary checking Frankie Bull and I had been doing on area rentals, with no success. I told him I was beginning to feel hamstrung and impotent to deal with a major murder investigation with only two policemen, Frankie and myself.

I wasn't truly worried that Baldi would charge me with obstruction of justice or withholding evidence, but I also told Keegan I wanted to solve the case in a hurry and remove the temptation. Keegan listened attentively, and when I was finished, he leaned back in his chair and unbuttoned his wrinkled suit coat. "You know, Harry," he said when the pretty Chicana waitress had taken our orders, "I'm supposed to leave for Meteetsee in the morning, but I'm going to tell them I won't be up there for a few more days. I don't feel right about leaving now."

I dipped a tortilla chip in a bowl of chunky salsa and popped it in my mouth. The salsa was so hot it stung my sinuses. "I appreciate that, Ken, I really do," I said when I could breathe again. "I'm beginning to think I might need some help on this."

At the back of the small diner, a young Hispanic man wearing a long white apron was filling sugar bottles and watching us closely, unable to take his eyes off the butt of Keegan's revolver, which was sticking out from under the lapel of his suit coat. I mouthed the word *police,* and he nodded his head, turned away, and dropped a handful of quarters in the jukebox. In a few seconds, Flaco Jimenez was wailing away on his accordion, the Union Pacific guys at the tables were tapping their toes, and I could barely hear myself think. I motioned the young man to turn the damned thing down, and he did, a move that drew me a few ugly looks from the railroad crew.

Keegan crumbled a handful of chips into his mouth and absentmindedly wiped the crumbs from the lapels of his suit coat. "I think you're right, Harry," he said. "But I'm afraid that even you and I and your patrolman might not be enough."

"Why's that, Ken?"

"Because I talked to Aaron Cohen this morning, and he scared the shit out of me."

"Why didn't you mention that earlier?"

He shrugged his shoulders and smiled. "Because I've been listening to you."

"Okay . . ." I smiled. I *had* been running off at the mouth. "Why don't I shut up and let you bring me up to speed?"

Keegan leaned forward with his elbows on the table, talked over the music. "You remember me telling you Cohen was on his way to Idaho when he left Victory?" he asked.

I nodded that I did. "To the Posse's training camp," I said.

"Yeah," he agreed, "they're running a couple of informants out of there—and he heard some rumblings about Victory that have him worried."

"Such as?"

"Such as the fact that the big shots in the Posse didn't want Tad Bauer killed, and they're furious he was. Such as the fact they wanted to let the heat cool down in Victory, and are truly pissed that instead of cooling down, the murders have heated things up."

"Does the Posse know who killed Tad and Alex?" I asked cautiously.

Keegan nodded grimly. "The top officers know," he said. "Apparently, whoever Tad and Alex were working with in the arms deal went rogue and did the murders. What Cohen hears, this guy is operating beyond the Posse's control and they want him almost as bad as we do."

I felt a surge of hope. Maybe this wouldn't be difficult after all. "Do Cohen's sources know who we're looking for?" I asked.

Keegan shook his head. "Nope," he said. "Cohen says they're not placed highly enough for that."

I mulled over what he'd told me. "So, we're looking for one man, acting alone," I said, thinking out loud. "It might not be as bad as we thought."

"Oh, it's plenty bad, Harry," Keegan said. He looked around the room to see if anyone was listening, but the busboy was at the end of the counter and the railroad crew was engaged in a spirited discussion. Still, he leaned forward even further and spoke softly enough that his voice wouldn't carry. "Here's the thing. Cohen says the weapons Old Man Bauer paid for never turned up in Idaho. He thinks they're still in this area . . . so he's coming back tomorrow to find them . . . and he's bringing backups."

I blew through my teeth and scowled. "And in the meantime, let me guess," I said sharply. "He wants us to sit tight and not stir the pot any more." I paused, still frowning. "Where have I heard that before, Ken?"

Keegan smiled as the waitress arrived with our heaping platters of tacos, enchiladas, and bowls of fragrant chili. "Come on, Harry," he said when she'd gone back to the kitchen. "We're talking about a lunatic who's probably sitting on a quarter-million dollars worth of weapons and explosives, and knows how to use them. I don't think sitting tight is such a bad idea. Do you?"

I left Keegan around 2:00 with the promise I'd stay out of trouble, at least until noon the next day, when he and Aaron Cohen would meet me at the office in Victory. And looking back, I think that's what I had every intention of doing. At the intersection of Third Street and

Highway 130, I nosed the Bronco out of town toward Victory, a frosty drive that took longer than usual because I stopped for almost ten minutes in the middle of the Big Hollow oil field to watch a young bald eagle feeding on the frozen carcass of a jackrabbit that had gotten itself run over on the highway.

Back at the office, I found Frankie sticking colored pins into a huge sportsman's topographical map of the mountains and foothills in a fifteen- or twenty-mile radius of Victory. The map covered twelve square feet of wall space and was dotted with thirty or forty red, white, and green pushpins, none of them within the boundaries of the town proper. Frankie was standing in front of the map with our list of properties owned by summer people in one hand and a can of cola in the other. His face was drawn, and it looked like he hadn't gotten much sleep. The office radio was turned on to KOWB's top-of-the-hour newscast, and of course, Ellen's arrest was the lead story.

"I guess we can rest easy now," he said wryly, nodding at the radio. "Tony has the terrorist behind bars."

I threw my coat in the corner and took a closer look at the detailed map. The green pins marked summer homes, and the red pins marked cabins that are rented out to tourists, fishermen, and hunters. The three white pins on the map were clustered on Gold Run Creek at the site of an old mining camp that hasn't been used since the 1930s. You can get to them in the summer if you've got an afternoon and a good four-wheel-drive, but there's no way you can reach them after the first snowfall, and they're uninhabitable anyway.

"You check 'em all?" I asked, squinting to read the fine print on the map. Jesus, what next? Glasses?

"All but three on Libby Creek," he said. "I thought I'd run up there this afternoon after I talked to you."

"Find anything worth mentioning?"

"Nope," he said. "They were all buttoned up tight."

"Then why the map?"

"I don't know for sure," he said, rubbing his temples. "It's just this feeling I have that we're forgetting something. It's too cold to be sleeping outdoors, and I've got all the vacant buildings marked. So, if our man hasn't broken into one of the remaining cabins on Libby, then he's got to be staying somewhere else, right? That is, if he's staying around here at all."

"Yeah . . ."

"Well, I thought the map might help me figure out where that'd be."

"And?"

"No help." He shrugged. "He could be staying someplace that isn't on the map."

"Give me ten minutes," I said, "and I'll ride along with you up to Libby. Then, we'll start over at the beginning."

"And check them all?" he asked, nodding at the map.

"Every last one," I said.

If you forget the fact that we were looking for a brutal killer who could have been anywhere, it was a beautiful afternoon for a drive. The road up to Libby Creek had been plowed, so we were able to sit back and enjoy the scenery. The river bottoms were full of animal tracks, and in one open meadow, we saw a small herd of elk lying out in the open to soak up what was left of the day's heat. To the east, the sun caught the faces of Bald Mountain and Corner Mountain, causing their sheer granite walls to shimmer in sharp relief against the ice-blue sky. The hillsides were a complex patchwork of white and green, the pine forests dark and still. To the west, the sun was hiding behind the ridgeline of the Snowies, its cold light forming a soft band of pink beneath the few clouds scuttling overhead. We passed a couple of other cars before we passed the Snowy Range Ski Area, but after that, we were the only people on the road. When I rolled my window down, I could hear the creek that runs alongside the road gurgling beneath the ice, the sound of the gentle breeze working its way through the frozen willows.

The first two cabins we checked on Libby Creek were secure, their drives unmarked by vehicles. At the third, we found fresh tire tracks in the snow and gouge marks around the lock of the back door. With our revolvers drawn and one of us on either side of the entrance, I eased the door open with my foot and came through the doorway in a crouch, waving hello to whoever was inside with the barrel of my

Blackhawk. The kitchen was littered with crushed beer cans, cardboard pizza boxes, and an empty pint of cherry vodka. There were used condoms beside the couch and more of them in the bedroom beside the rumpled bed. Kids, we decided, looking for an out-of-the-way place to party. We tidied up the beer cans and rubbers, and locked the door on our way out.

"The little bottom feeders may be guilty of underage drinking, statutory rape, breaking and entering, trespassing, and malicious destruction of property," Frankie said, tossing the bag we'd filled with trash from the cabin into the backseat of the Bronco, "but at least they're practicing safe sex."

We got back to the office about 7:30, and I looked through the mail, returned a couple of phone calls, and we headed over to Ginny Larsen's for dinner, where the special of the day was liver and fried onions smothered in brown gravy. Aside from the little adrenaline rush we'd enjoyed on Libby Creek, the afternoon had been spectacularly uneventful. There were no signs of habitation or use at any of the houses or rental cabins on our list, nothing to suggest any of them had been opened since their owners locked the places up for the season. Which meant that if our man was staying near Victory, he'd found an out-of-the-way place to hang his hat.

I tried to remember places we might have missed, tried to think of where I'd stay if I was trying to stay close to Victory but keep a low profile while I was doing it. The exercise was fruitless. The fact is that this bit of Wyoming has more than six hundred square miles of land, most of it national forest and public land where nobody checks to see who's coming and going. There are a limited number of modern homes and cabins but dozens of old line shacks, outbuildings, caves, and out-of-the-way campgrounds where you can stay for weeks without seeing another living human being. If you want to search an area like this and have a reasonable hope of finding the person you're looking for—a person who has good reason to avoid being found—you need more than two people to do the looking. To do it right, you need an army, and even an army isn't always enough if the person or persons being hunted have a reasonable degree of woodcraft, which I imagined described our Posse operative fairly well.

I hate to say it, but I was almost looking forward to seeing Aaron Cohen the next day. I was feeling a real sense of urgency, and like Cohen or not, he had the juice to get us all the help we needed with a single phone call. If Aaron found evidence that the killer and the guns were still in the vicinity, he could get the governor to call out the National Guard to search the whole area by plane and helicopter if the thousands of his colleagues in the FBI were too busy to do the job themselves. Hell, I'm not sure I even know the governor's first name, although it might be Bob. As I'd told Keegan, I needed help, and I was no longer feeling particularly choosy about where it came from.

When our dinners arrived, Frankie ate while reading the box scores in the *Rocky Mountain News*. I chewed mine but didn't taste it, letting my mind roam while I absentmindedly watched the restaurant's ebb and flow. Ginny, wearing running shoes and a white apron over her faded jeans and flannel shirt, an order pad sticking out her back pocket and her curly hair damp from sweat, was at the other end of the counter talking Ellen's arrest over with Harley Coyne and his wife, Bernice, who had moved to Victory two years before when they'd retired.

Whenever I saw the Coynes, I thought of that poem about Jack Sprat and his wife, since it could have been written about them.

Bernice, who loved dirty jokes and cherry pie, was a woman of substance, with thick ankles and folds of flesh that seemed to drip down her arms like melted wax. I figured she'd go at least two hundred pounds, which on her five-four frame made her look like a beach ball.

Harley, on the other hand, was as tall as me and so skinny the joints of his knees stood out like huge knots on a lodgepole pine. He had sad, hound-dog eyes and a long face creased by a perpetual frown. That night, I noticed he was carrying what looked like a .45 automatic in the pocket of his corduroy sport coat. An army-issue Colt, he'd probably brought it home as a souvenir after World War II, and I'd have given ten-to-one odds he hadn't fired it since. Now, here the old codger was, carrying the thing around in his coat pocket to protect himself and Bernice, who outweighed him by sixty pounds and looked like she could bench press a Third World country.

Curly was right: things in Victory had definitely gotten out of hand.

With no appetite left to speak of, I pushed my half-eaten platter of liver and onions to the back of the counter and looked out the steamy window of the restaurant onto Main, where the few cars on the street were crawling along, each of them trailing a wispy cloud of gray exhaust, which did not dissipate immediately but hugged the ground as tenaciously as seacoast fog. I imagined I could actually see the cold out there, and even though Ginny's was uncomfortably warm and stuffy, I pulled myself deeper into my heavy shirt and down vest.

When I was a kid, I remember walking home from wrestling practice on nights like this, my hooded parka tied around my chin and my hands bundled into thick woolen mittens, my breath freezing on the down of my upper lip. Once in a while, I'd stop in front of some house along the way to look in through the warm yellow window at the families gathering for dinner inside. They might be passing heaping bowls of spaghetti, maybe a steaming pot roast cooked with mountains of colorful vegetables. At one end of the table, the old man might be sitting in his shirtsleeves, drinking a beer and listening to the kids talk about their day at school. Mom might be there, too, laughing a little at something one of them had to say. There's something about standing outside on a cold night looking in that always made me more envious than usual of any family that could do something as normal as enjoy a meal in each other's company at the end of a long winter day. It wasn't like that at my house, where Mom started drinking with the first soap opera in the morning and Pop came home around two nights out of seven, usually when he felt like beating the crap out of someone. Give my family a nice meal like that, and we'd end up throwing it at one another.

I was still thinking about families when Ginny tapped me lightly on the shoulder, a frown wrinkling her freckled forehead and a note of apology in her husky voice.

"Sorry to disturb your dinner, Harry," she said, handing me the phone receiver, "but it's Carrie Wilson. Says she's been looking all over for you."

It took me a couple of seconds to get my brain unstuck from where had been visiting—LaJunta, Colorado, circa 1963—and back to e present, but I thanked Ginny with a faint smile, gave the long hone cord a couple of yanks to undo the kinks, and took the call.

"This is Harry," I said. In the background, I could hear Carrie's int-size dog yapping at something, probably one of Carrie's stuffed ears.

"I saw him again, Harry," she said breathlessly. I could hardly hear er over the noise of the damned dog.

"What? Saw who again? I can barely make you out, Carrie."

"Shut up, goddammit!" she yelled.

"What?"

"Not you, Harry, The dog. I said I saw him again."

"Who, Carrie? Who did you see again?"

"Harrison Ford," she said triumphantly. "You remember. I saw im in my backyard the night Tad was murdered. I told you about ."

"Yeah?"

"Yeah! I was just walking the dog along the road by the Bauer house nd I saw him pulling in on his snowmobile. But you know what?"

"What?" I asked, reaching over to yank Frankie's sleeve. He looked p from his newspaper, made a face at the phone, and went back to eading.

"I was wrong," she said. "At first, I thought it was Harrison Ford, ut now I see it isn't. It's Tom Berenger. They look a lot alike, you now."

"Is he still there, Carrie?"

"As far as I know," she said. "You want to go with me to talk to im?"

"No, Carrie, I don't," I said, pushing myself off the stool and grabing my coat. "I'm going to go talk to him myself."

"Well," she said, the disappointment evident in her voice. "I don't ee what it would hurt."

"Carrie," I said impatiently, fumbling through my pockets for the eys to the Bronco, "you did the right thing by calling, but you've ot to listen to me. Get off the phone and lock your doors . . . and tay right there. I'm on my way to the Bauer place now."

On the way out the door, with Frankie only a half step behind, I reached down and grabbed the .45 out of Harley's pocket because I didn't want him shooting himself in the leg on the way home.

Sometimes, I thought, a cop has to do more than protect the innocents from bad guys. Sometimes, he's got to protect them from themselves.

17

I doubted we were looking for Harrison Ford, but *someone* on a snowmobile had recently used the road leading to the Bauer es-
ate. The tank-tread tracks of a snow machine stuck out in the fresh
now, marking a clear trail that even an idiot could follow. And when
rankie and I arrived a few minutes after Carrie's call, we followed
hat inviting trail down the long driveway of the Bauer estate, past
he dark and empty main house and the vacant corrals, the Bronco
ithering sideways in the bumper-deep snow.

At the barn, I pumped the cold brakes and brought us to a crunch-
ng stop. In the headlights, we could see the clear trail cut by the snow
achine, heading north away from the estate and toward Encamp-
nent Creek. It looked like the driver was following the same chewed-
p Jeep trail we'd used to get to the cave where Sonny Toms found
he bones of the Mystery Madonna, but there was no way I could drive
: now without chaining up.

I cut the motor and got out, listened for the tinny sound of the
now machine's engine, heard nothing but the pinging of the engine
s it began to cool and the muffled noises Frankie made as he eased
is door shut and buttoned himself into several layers of clothing. The
ain house was dark and silent, and I recalled that Wolfgang and
Magda Bauer had returned to Chicago the day before. I blew into my
ands to warm them, then slipped on a pair of insulated gloves. Over-
ead, a billion stars twinkled in the black November sky and the full
oon threw a wild and impressionistic pattern from the naked aspen
ranches onto the snow at our feet.

"Someone's out there," Frankie said, his breath hanging in great,
eamy clouds around his face.

"Yeah," I said, trying to peer into the darkness beyond the barn. "The question is, where? You think you can chain up while I take a look around? Make sure he didn't double back?"

"No problem," Frankie said, pushing his hands into a pair of heavy elk-hide gloves. "You want just the front wheels? Or chain all four?"

"Better chain 'em all," I said. I pulled a black, heavy-duty flashlight from under the seat and rummaged around until I came up with a woolen watch cap, which I jammed down over my ears. Then I reached under my coat and unfastened the safety strap on my holster.

As I pushed through the snow toward the barn, I could smell the comforting aroma of cut hay and animals, although there was no livestock in either the corrals or the barn. The Bauers usually keep a couple of leased saddle horses around during the summer months, but they send them back to their owner when they close the place for the season.

The double sliding doors of the barn were about ten feet high, big enough to get a haying tractor or a one-ton dump truck through, and held shut by a heavy-duty combination padlock. I gave the padlock a pull anyway, just to make sure the place was secure, and it snapped open in my hands. Whoever was there last had already run the combination to the last number to save effort the next time he wanted in.

I saw what I was looking for near the screws that held the interlocking halves of the big metal hasp to the wooden doors. At the edges of the metal, there were several indentations in the paint and one scratch mark a quarter of an inch long that cut through several layers of red paint entirely, revealing fresh wood beneath. The barn had been broken into all right, by someone who just removed the old hasp and lock and replaced it with his own hardware. He could have accomplished that after Wolfgang and Magda left, but it could have happened before, for all I knew. Wolfgang certainly wouldn't have realized the switch unless he'd had a use for the barn during his brief visit, and he might not have thought anything about it if he had.

The snow kept the doors from opening easily, but by using the hasp as a handle I was able to push them far enough apart to slip my hand through the opening. Then, I put my weight behind my hand and pushed. The metal wheels of the door screeched against the icy metal railing as the left-hand door began to move, but even with every one of my 195 pounds applied to the task, I could only budge it eight inches before it bogged again in the drifted snow.

It was more than enough.

With the Blackhawk ready in my right hand and the clublike flashlight in my left, I slipped through the opening sideways and dodged to the right into the inky blackness of the barn, coming to rest in a crouch about five feet from the opened door. To my left, a shaft of incandescent bluish light from the moon streamed through the crack in the doors, bisecting the floor of the barn like the blade of a knife, but playing out before it could illuminate anything at the rear of the building. The draft from outside had kicked up a small blizzard of dust, which danced through the yellow beam of my flash like flakes of powdered snow tumbling through the late-afternoon sun.

While I waited for my eyes to adjust to the change in light conditions, I tried to open my other senses to danger. Along with the stronger smell of hay, manure, and cut grass were other familiar aromas—the slight odors of gasoline and diesel, old leather, saddle soap and motor oil, the faint stench of a mouse left in a trap.

Above me, I could hear the light tapping of a power line against the side of the building, the creaking of the roof joists settling in the breeze. From somewhere toward the back of the barn came the skittering of tiny claws on wood. More mice, I figured. Maybe rats. Through the opening in the doorway, I could hear the clanking of tire chains and Frankie's curses as he wanged his knuckles for about the tenth time in the last two minutes.

Laying the flashlight on the ground at my feet but keeping the muzzle of the revolver trained on the interior of the barn, I reached slowly around behind me and ran the tips of my fingers along the rough wood of the walls in search of a light switch or a power box. I was rewarded, first by a splinter, which pierced the tip of my index finger like a lance, and then by the cold metal of the power box. With a deep breath, I closed my hand around the lever, brought the Blackhawk up to eye level, snapped the lever to the on position, and flooded the barn with light from a half-dozen overhead fixtures.

The beast that came screaming down from the rafters looked, at first glance, like a hideous apparition from the jaws of hell.

With its huge, dead-looking black eyes reflecting the light, the gray banshee swooped down out of the air toward me, its great wings *whoof*ing like a starched sheet in a stiff breeze, its razor-sharp talons outstretched, aiming for the spot right between my eyes. I pitched myself back against the door, threw my arms across my face to ward off the bloody attack I was powerless to prevent.

The old barn owl changed course at the last second, his wings beating the air around my head in a furious tattoo as it dawned on him that I was more rodent than he could carry away. With a disgusted screech, he flapped his way back up to the rafters in the middle of the barn, swiveling his round head like Linda Blair in *The Exorcist* to look at me over his backbone.

With so much adrenaline pumping through my system I thought I could feel it leaking out my ears, I eased my revolver off full cock so my trembling fingers wouldn't jerk the trigger and ventilate an innocent piece of barn wood by accident. Then I squatted down against the cold wall of the barn, closed my eyes, and concentrated on the hundred or so deep breaths it took to bring my heart rate back under redline. When I opened my eyes again, the old owl had disappeared into the shadows of the building, but I could still feel him watching my every move.

Christ, no wonder mice are so nervous.

"You all right in here, Chief?" Frankie asked, his head and shoulders poking through the opening in the doors and a bemused expression on his face.

"Yeah, sure," I said around my last deep lungful of air. "Why wouldn't I be?"

"I don't know," he said. "I thought I heard a woman scream, and then you cussing. Sounded like 'godfuckingdamcocksuckerpiss.' You've got to admit, it's a little out of the ordinary."

I told him about the kamikaze owl and my brush with death, but I'm not sure he believed me, since the king-size subject of the tale had already gone into hiding. "I think he was just screwin' around with you, Harry," he said finally. "If he'd really wanted you for dinner, he wouldn't have waited until you turned the lights on. He just wanted you to see what he could have done if it suited him."

"Next time I run into him," I grumbled, "I hope I have my shotgun along so I can return the favor."

"Sure, Harry." He laughed. "The only difference would be that he missed you on purpose."

With his brown eyes crinkling at the edges in merriment, Frankie sidestepped back out the door to finish chaining the Bronco, leaving me to lick the wounds to my mangled pride and complete my business in the barn. After taking one last look in the direction of the shadowy rafters to make sure the feathered terrorist up there wasn't planning another sneak attack, I holstered my revolver and began working my way down the row of stalls.

Wolfgang Bauer's barn was sparklingly clean, testament to the compulsive tidiness of the part-time groundskeeper who works for the Bauers during the summer months. The dirt floors of the stalls had been mucked out and raked at the end of the season, although they still smelled faintly of horse dung and sweat, aromas that soak into the very wood fibers after a few years and never leave.

At the back of the barn, I could see an open area with a concrete floor that served as a combination workshop, garage, and equipment-storage area. There was a neat workbench and a long Peg-Board full of shiny new tools, a table saw, and a drill press. Off to one side, a riding lawn mower was covered with a clear plastic tarp, and beside it was a snowmobile encased in a black storage cover with a white Yamaha logo on the front.

Beside the snowmobile, I found another cover and the dirty outlines made by the tracks of another snow machine as it was being moved from its parking place. The snow machine still in the barn had been half of a pair, and I thought I knew where the other one had gone.

If the Posse's operative was using Bauer's equipment as his own, it certainly explained the new lock. What it didn't explain was why he was still lurking around now that the Bauers were gone. Unless, of course, Aaron Cohen had been right all along.

The increasing likelihood of that proposition gave me a shiver that started at the nape of my neck and quickly worked its way down through the bunched muscles of my shoulders. If Cohen was right and there was an exceedingly well-armed rogue killer on the loose in Victory, everyone in my little town was in danger. You don't just smile at a meat eater like that and ask him to give himself up and come on down to the corner jail for a home-cooked dinner of boiled antelope and potatoes, not when he's itching to take a shot—or several thousand shots—at a designated representative of the new world order.

With any luck, I reasoned, Frankie and I might be able to stop him before some innocent bystanders, some of my friends and neighbors, got caught in the cross fire. And a dark night in the snowy foothills behind the estate was as good a time and place to catch him as we were going to find.

I was on my way back to the front door when I noticed out of the corner of my eye that the heavy wooden door to the tack room was unlatched. Call me obsessive, but I ignored my growing sense of urgency long enough to ease the door open and fumble around the inside of the tack room for a light switch. When I found none, I pulled the flashlight out of my pocket and ran its beam across the floor of the room, lighting briefly the five well-used riding saddles, four western and one lonely-looking English, that had been stored there on stands made from two-by-fours. The walls on the right side of the room were cluttered with hanging bits, hackamores, bridles, panniers, and saddlebags, enough gear to outfit a small remuda. On the left wall, hanging from four-inch wooden pegs and coiled to uniform perfection, were three old lariats tied with leather thongs, waiting to be put to use on the pommel of a cowboy's saddle.

Beneath that was a long wooden workbench littered with leather working tools and a bank of deep drawers for accumulated paraphernalia. I pulled the top drawer open and found nothing interesting—pliers, glue, a couple of hammers, artificial sinew for stitching leather, half-used rolls of tape. The second drawer held leather scraps—thongs, hunks of thick leather for patching chaps, saddles, and the like. The third drawer appeared to hold paint—cans of aerosol spray paint, quart-size containers of paint that looked from the dried spills on the sides of the cans like they matched sections of the barn.

I pawed through the paint drawer quickly, the beam of the flashlight dancing off the metal cans.

At first, the black skull-and-crossbones warning on a small can at the back of the drawer barely registered, since most paints are toxic. But when I picked the can up and turned it around in my hand to read the label, my heart began to race.

I was holding a container of Compound 1080, the same poison used on Ernesto Varga's chickens.

The snowmobile trail followed the unpaved county road leading toward Encampment Creek for over a quarter mile, and even though the snow in the little basin was as deep as the wheels of the Bronco were high, with drifts that buried the front bumper, we made good time, the heavy chains on all four wheels cutting through the snowpack like a buzz saw through soft pine. Still, I drove cautiously in second gear, testing some of the deeper drifts by easing into them a few feet, backing up, then powering through to the other side. It's pretty tough to get yourself stuck when you're driving a good four-wheel drive with every available inch of rubber chained, but it is possible. And if you get mired with chains on, you'd best have a good shovel and a strong back, because it's going to take both to get you rolling again.

We drove without headlights, and I avoided using the brakes because I didn't want the brake lights to give our position away. I realized that those precautions were virtually worthless, though, because the metallic thumping of the chains against the undercarriage of the vehicle would carry for miles, and the moon was so bright that only a blind man could have failed to notice our progress. Visibility was at least two hundred yards, and while there wasn't enough light to distinguish detail, there was more than enough to pick up shape and movement across the open spaces in the black-and-white landscape.

As we crossed a small sagebrush flat, I caught a blur of motion from the corner of my eye, downshifted quickly into first, and let the engine drag bring us to a stop. Three doe antelope and a fawn, bounding through the snow like wraiths, cut across the road in front of us and disappeared over the lip of a narrow arroyo to our right, the winter earth seeming to swallow them whole.

Thirty seconds later, a huge pronghorn buck came leaping through the shadows in the tracks of his harem. His black horns, not really horns at all but tightly compressed hair, were thick and heavy, at least sixteen inches long and jutting forward like forked spears. Not Boone and Crockett material, I thought, but certainly a trophy. He plunged in front of the Bronco, his muscular haunches driving his rapid forward motion like pistons, his front legs stiff as he crashed through the snow, which exploded upward, washing away from his deep chest like frothy waves breaking against the bow of a schooner. At the edge of the arroyo, he hesitated for a few seconds, looking back to see if we'd follow, the white moon hanging gracefully over his shoulder, his body broadside in full silhouette. The next instant, he was gone.

At the edge of the basin, the county road makes a sharp turn to the right, following the edge of the tree line as it winds its way through a glacial boulder field, skirting springs, bogs, and a small, unnamed tributary that empties into Encampment Creek a mile beyond. It was here that the snowmobile tracks veered off the main roadway to the left, following a Jeep trail upslope for a hundred yards until the track was gobbled up by the black pine forest. I'd driven up that trail before and knew that it climbs gradually up the face of the mountain for about three miles until the first flat bench, where it opens up in a small, grassy park popular with picnickers in the summer and hunters in the early fall. From the park, you can look out over the whole of the Laramie River Valley to the east. Behind you, the peaks of the Snowies rise up like the continent's vertebrae, treacherous and forbidding, their tips capped year-round by glacial ice, their flanks slippery with skree. Beyond the clearing, the track continues for another two miles until it forks, the right fork ending two and a half miles later at Jim Creek, the left fork continuing for about five miles until it crosses Douglas Creek, where it turns south toward the Bear Creek Campground and Rob Roy Reservoir.

In the driest months of summer, it's a bone-jarring ride as your vehicle bounces in and out of the horrendous ruts and over massive slabs of sharp granite exposed by erosion and wind. You can rip a hole in your oil pan on that road without even thinking, and more than one sightseer has wound up spending an uncomfortable night camped beside his disabled vehicle in the vain hope that another motorist will happen along, thereby saving him the long walk back down the mountain. Wet or snow covered, the trail is vicious, never wide enough to turn around and always ready to send you careening off the narrow shoulder.

I paused at the turnoff, the Ford idling happily while Frankie hummed a tune and adjusted his seat belt, pulling it tightly across his lap and chest.

"What do you think?" I asked, nodding in the direction of the snowmobile tracks, my fingers tightening involuntarily on the steering wheel.

"I think we have to try it." He shrugged. "I don't feel like walking up there after him, do you?"

"Not tonight," I said, popping the gearshift lever into first and flicking on the headlights. There was no way I was going up that mountain blind, even if it meant our man could see us coming for twenty miles. As I let out the clutch, the front and rear wheels bit simultaneously, propelling us up the mountain at a ground-gaining four miles an hour. It took almost five minutes to reach the tree line, and then the tall lodgepole pines blocked out the moon, enclosing us in a forest womb so dark and velvety that even the high beams could penetrate it for less than twenty yards.

I drove with my head sticking out the window, which gave me a better view of our position on the shoulder, but it also made my head swirl with vertigo and my eyes tear, the little rivulets freezing as they streaked across my cheeks. To my left, I knew the side of the mountain dropped away precipitously, the steepness of the slope indicated by the fact that less than thirty feet away, I could see the tops of the tall pine trees growing on the hillside, their tips almost at eye level, the snow dusting their upper branches like powdered sugar.

Occasionally, the rear wheels slipped into the icy ruts and the back end of the Bronco would swing a few inches closer to the edge of the abyss. Each time, I'd turn the front wheels into the hill, grit my teeth, and hold on until the front wheels dug in and straightened us out. The path looked wide enough for us to pass, but there wasn't much margin for error. I just hoped that the deep snow cover didn't conceal places where gobs of the roadway had been washed away in the late summer rains. If our front wheels dipped into an unstable wash, we'd slip over the edge and wouldn't stop rolling for a week.

I couldn't take my eyes off the road for long, but when I glanced over at Frankie, I saw his hand clasped on the door handle, ready to open it and bail out at the first hint of disaster. With my window open, it was chilly in the cab, but even so, there was a sheen of sweat on his forehead.

"If we start sliding backward, reach out and grab a tree, will you?" I asked. "I don't think the brakes will do us much good."

"Screw you, Harry," he said through clenched jaws. "This thing starts to go over, I'm outta here. You want to hang around, that's up to you."

"How far you figure to the clearing?"

"Quarter of a mile," he said. "But if I remember right, the worst part is right around this bend, where the road crosses a little gully with a stream running through the bottom. That stream'll be frozen by now, and slicker than butter. If we make it through that, we're golden."

"Sure we are," I said. "Then, all we have to worry about is coming back down."

I drove very slowly, performing a kind of tightrope act as I tried to keep the wheels from dropping off into the ruts. Not only was I afraid that sliding into them might rob me of the little control I had over our vehicular destiny, they were deep enough that I could easily have broken an axle or become high-centered, an unappealing proposition on a night when the windchill could reach forty or fifty below. At the side of the road, some joker had tacked a purloined Wyoming Highway Department traffic-control sign on a dead tree informing us that the speed limit on this particular stretch of highway was fifty-five mph.

Pretty funny, considering the fact that we were forced to abandon the Bronco as soon as we came to the stream, which was passable on foot, by snowmobile, or by Sherman tank. The last person through the greasy streambed before freeze-up had bottomed out in the muck and gorged great serrated ruts in the pathway through the embankment as they muscled their way out. Since then, the jagged gashes they cut making their escape—some of them over two feet deep—had frozen, and the edges were as sharp as butcher knives. It would take a bulldozer to get the Jeep trail back in shape for vehicle traffic, but that wouldn't happen until spring. Until then, access to the first clearing and the rest of the mountain would be by means other than automobile.

The man driving the snowmobile we were following, whose machine wasn't heavy enough to crack through the frosty morass, had simply skated over the horrendous scored furrows and continued up the mountain.

We had to walk.

I set the emergency brake, pocketed the keys, and moving single file with Frankie in the lead, we began working our way up the darkened roadway, the beams from our flashlights illuminating the narrow pathway immediately in front of us, but blinding us to almost everything in the ebony forest at our sides. My feet were already beginning to chill in my boots, and I slipped constantly on the slick leather soles. Frankie, who'd worn his ugly mukluks to work that morning, made better time.

He walked quietly, on the balls of his feet like a cat, the last in an age-old line of hunters, scanning the tree line for signs of ambush.

Trudging along behind Frankie, my free hand resting nervously on the butt of my revolver and my heart pounding so loudly I swore I could hear it thumping through my sheepskin coat, I saw faces in the shadows of every bush, the gnarled limb of every scrub pine became an arm, the movement of every branch the ghostly outline of a man.

It took almost half an hour to reach the clearing. It was a clear-cut area, the old growth pines harvested for paper pulp several years before. The saplings that had been planted at five-foot intervals to replace them had grown little, and their lonely-looking tips barely cleared the snowpack. By spring, these infant pines would be covered by five or more feet of snow, and many of them would not survive.

We crouched down in the heavy timber at the edge of the moonlit clearing, our flashlights dark as we looked out over the open area and along the tree line for signs of movement. Although he was less than three feet away, I could barely make out the edges of Frankie's broad back as his eyes followed the snowmobile trail through the deep powder. The snow machine's track followed the road for about fifty yards and then broke away heading east, back into the timber. If he followed that course, he could go right back down the mountain to the road, where he'd likely come out behind the Bronco. If he opened it up, he could be back in Victory before we even had time to back our way down the Jeep trail to a turnaround.

"Shit," Frankie muttered. "He outfoxed us."

"Do you think he knew we were following him?"

"Yeah, he knew. And I think he's still playing with us."

"Why do you think that?"

"What do you hear, Harry?"

"Nothing," I said.

"Exactly. We don't hear his snow machine, which means he's shut it down for some reason. He's still on the mountain, but he knows we can't go after him cross-country."

It took us longer to skulk back to the Bronco than it had taken to get to the clearing because we walked in the dark, stopping every dozen or so steps to listen to the night noises in the forest. To my relief, the vehicle was just as we'd left it, perched at the margin of the streambed, its nose pointing uphill. There was no place to turn around, though, so I backed it down the mountain at a snail's pace, one hand on the steering wheel and my body twisted at an uncomfortable angle so I could look out the back window to see where I was going. Frankie had chosen not to ride, and because I was going backward without use of the headlights, was walking a dozen feet in the lead so he could warn me of danger areas. The best plan, we'd decided, was to simply park at the bottom of the mountain and wait until we heard our man coming down.

We were almost to the county road and the western edge of the Bauer property line when Frankie ran his hand across his throat, signaling me to stop.

I killed the engine, set the brake, and joined him at the side of the Jeep trail, where he was leaning against one of the glacial boulders, looking thoughtfully at what appeared to be a heavily used game path leading uphill through a tunnel in the forest. We hadn't noticed it on the way up the mountain, because we were concentrating on the fresh snowmobile tracks in the roadway, but it was clear the pathway had been traveled by someone on a snow machine within the last week. It wasn't a fresh trail, because a few inches of snow had fallen since it had been cut, rounding out the unique, angular impression cut by the treads of the machine. But it had been made recently enough to arouse our curiosity.

"What do you think?" I asked, squinting my eyes and stomping my cold feet.

"I don't know," Frankie said. "Maybe this is where he comes out."

"So if we walk up this path for a quarter mile or so and hide, we might be able to surprise him coming down?" I said, finishing his thought.

"It's as good a plan as any." Frankie shrugged. "We'll be able to hear him a long time before he'll be able to see us, which will give us plenty of warning. And we just might fool him. I think he'll expect us to stay on the road."

While the prospect of a long stakeout in the dark, in the forest, in the snow, was much less appealing than the thought of a long stakeout in the Bronco with the heater blowing a ninety-degree cascade of air across my numbing toes, I was more than eager to make the sacrifice. I had the gnawing feeling that for the past hour, we'd been doing exactly what our man wanted us to do, bumbling along like a couple of slaphappy buffoons while he took us closer to the trap. It was time to turn the tables.

I took the lead as we plowed our way up the game trail, the traveling fairly easy even though the snow came almost to our knees. Here, in the shadows of the tall pines, the sun never became warm enough to melt the upper layer of the snowpack in the daytime, so no tough crust formed as soon as the sun went down. And since the snowmobile rider had already broken a decent trail, most of the hard work had been done for me. With every step, though, a little more snow worked its way up my pant leg and down the top of my boot, where it quickly melted. Before long, my feet would be soaked and then I'd be in trouble. It's one thing to be cold in the mountains, but you're usually safe as long as you stay dry. Once you get wet, all bets are off.

At most, I figured I had an hour before I'd be in serious danger of frostbite.

I leaned forward, pressing the weight of my body against the resistance of the snow, trying to lengthen my stride and bull my way along. In the still air, the only noise was my own labored breathing and the *shush*ing sound of our legs moving through powder. At our backs, the moon shone over our shoulders, our shadows falling long and ghostly on the pathway at our feet.

At the tree line, we lost the moonlight and had to break out our flashlights, but the slope eased and we still made good time, moving rapidly down the tunnel of the game trail, our noses filled with the smell of pine and willow.

I guess I saw the graves first—two rude crosses cut from boards, the edges of the small burial ground marked with rotting buckrail fencing. In the light of the flash, they looked old and weary, the markers leaning at crazy angles, as if they were only standing through sheer force of will. Carefully, I lifted my legs over the railing and tried to read the faded lettering on the markers.

EZRA JENKINS, the first one read. BORN JANUARY 20, 1890. DIED JANUARY 21, 1890. The other grave held the body of Ezra's twin brother, Ezekial, whose birth and death dates were the same.

"I wonder who they were?" Frankie said, the beam of his flashlight working its way along the boundary of the little graveyard.

"I don't know," I said. "Maybe their parents were homesteaders. Maybe gold miners. There were a lot of placer miners working the streams around here in the '90s, and some of them must have had their families along."

A few yards from the graves, we found the ruins of a cabin, the log walls long since tumbled, but the north wall marked by the remains of a stone fireplace. It had been a small dwelling, one room, maybe twelve by twelve. If the man of the family had been industrious, it might have had a small loft. If he'd been lucky, perhaps a single window, since glass was a decided luxury on the frontier.

While I poked through the remains of the cabin, Frankie investigated the little springhouse cut into the hillside about fifty feet away. Since there was no refrigeration at the time the homesteaders and minrs first came to live in this part of the country, they made do with he materials at hand, digging small caverns into the cool earth near heir simple houses where they could store vegetables, salted meat, and ce cut from the river bottoms in February. With any luck, the ice vould keep well into the summer, making it possible for part of the ear to store fresh meat and poultry. Although their primitive cabins nd sod huts have long since crumbled, the Wyoming countryside is till sprinkled with these old springhouses, and they can hold plenty of treasure for historians, antique collectors, and bottle hunters. In he warmest months of summer, they're also favored hangouts for the ocal rattlesnake population, so I tend to avoid them, even in the winer when the snakes have long since left for Florida or St. Tropez, or vherever it is that vipers go when it gets too cold to terrorize innocent humans in the Rocky Mountains.

"Hey, Harry," Frankie yelled from the springhouse. "Look at this."

From the cabin, I couldn't make out the shape of his body, but he yellow beam of his flash was trained on the door of the springhouse. He hadn't yet gone in to explore.

"What'd you find, Frankie? A hundred-year-old bottle of red-eye? f you did, you'd better let me test it to make sure it hasn't gone bad. need something to light a fire in this old carcass."

"Nah," he said. "I didn't find any hooch. I don't even think I can open this door."

"Just give it a good kick."

"Won't work, Harry," he said. "It's brand new oak, and this padlock isn't gonna give up without a hell of a fight."

"Padlock?" I asked, losing every bit of interest I had in poking through the debris of the old cabin. "Why would anyone put a new loor and a padlock on a springhouse in the middle of nowhere?"

"To keep people out," he said simply, which was of course the truth. The only question was, why?

With Frankie guarding the springhouse, it took me less than ten minutes to retrace our path back to the Bronco, where I pulled a sturdy tire iron from the spare-tire well. I hurried on the way back, feeling alone and exposed. I couldn't shake the feeling that I was being watched, maybe even followed, although every time I turned around to look behind me, my back trail was empty. It was the same feeling I get every time I walk through a graveyard or past a dark and abandoned building, and I don't like it a bit. At least the fear kept me from thinking about my freezing feet.

I found Frankie right where I'd left him, sitting with his back against a fallen log, his head tilted back so he could look through the tops of the trees and watch the stars.

"Give me a hand with this, Galileo," I said, jamming the flat end of the iron under the thick metal hasp. Together, we put all of our weight on the lever and pushed down. The long screws holding the hasp in place broke free from the oak with a loud pop, and we banged our knuckles against the door when the tension was released.

Throwing the iron into the snow at the side of the doorway, I pulled the heavy door open and shone my light into the dry, dusty springhouse. The air smelled of cosmoline, and there were long, wispy spiderwebs hanging from the ceiling, their lacy tendrils swaying in the cold draft coming through the opened door.

"Holy shit," Frankie whispered when my light finally found the far wall. There, stacked from floor to ceiling, was the Posse's fabled cache of deadly hardware—M16s, M14s, Uzis, Mac 10s and Swedish AK 5s packed in long wooden crates, at least fifty Beretta 9mm handguns, Mini Uzis, Heckler & Koch MP 5s, and 9mm Colt submachine guns, concussion grenades in boxes of twenty-four, plastique explosive in two-pound blocks, and dozens of green, military-style cases filled with ammunition.

Frankie whistled through his teeth as the light came to rest on one of several long boxes standing upright against the wall. The stenciled lettering painted on one side said the container held one LAW rocket launcher, a shoulder-held weapon that fires a single rocket and can't be reloaded. Although it's a relatively inexpensive and disposable weapon, it's amazingly accurate and destructive enough to turn an armored personnel carrier into bits of pulverized scrap no bigger than your thumbnail.

"Goddamn," I swore. "This is gonna make Aaron Cohen's day."

If you're wondering why no country has invaded Sweden in recent memory, it just might be because of the Swedish AK 5, a lightweight,

.56mm submachine gun that is handed out to everyone in the wedish army and the national guard. It's a legendary weapon among ın nuts, and I was tempted to crack open one of the boxes and pull ne out, just so I could make Curly jealous by describing how it felt my hands.

But I didn't have time for that, because we had to get off the ountain and call in the troops. I thought briefly about leaving rankie to guard the cache but decided against it. In the first place, was possible there was still a killer on the mountain with us, and e had no idea where he was. I didn't want either of us rambling round alone, and the guns weren't going anywhere. It would be posble to drive a heavy truck up the game path leading to the springouse in dry weather, and I imagine that's how the weapons were ansported there in the first place. But with this much snow on the round, you'd have to either bring in a Sno-Cat or take them out on ıowmobile one crate at a time.

Our man might have time to move a few boxes before we could et back with the FBI, the DCI, the sheriff's department and the amned army if necessary, but there was no way he could move the hole stash in the middle of the night.

By dawn, I imagined I could have the place crawling with lawnforcement officers, who'd all be delighted because the bad guys ouldn't be getting their hands on this much high-tech firepower fter all—and one of them might just stumble across the man we were fter in the process.

We closed the door to the springhouse and used pine boughs to veep away as many of our footprints as possible on the way back to ıe car. If our man tried the door of the springhouse, he'd know we'd und his stockpile, because the lock and hasp had been ripped away. till, there was no reason to advertise the fact that our snooping had aid off.

I've got to tell you, I was pretty proud of myself as we walked backard on the way to the Bronco, hurriedly flailing away at our tracks. here's no telling how the Posse would have used the weaponry, given ıe chance, but it's a good bet they'd have shed a lot of innocent ood. Although I hadn't been able to arrest the man I suspected in ıe murders of Tad Bauer, Alex Thibault, and perhaps even Sonny

Toms, Frankie and I had probably saved more lives in the last few hours than most cops hope to save in ten lifetimes. Sure, the Posse is resourceful and determined, and they'd eventually find a way to replace the hardware we'd found, but we'd thrown an industrial-size spanner in their racist works.

Not bad for a couple of small-town hayseeds who spend most of their time writing speeding tickets.

The Bronco's engine caught on the first try, and there was just enough room where the game path left the road to turn around, so with Frankie fumbling with his seat belt, I threw the stick into reverse and craned my neck around so I could look out the back window and see where we were going. I was concentrating on the small patch of ground illuminated by the back-up lights as I began to ease the rear of the vehicle into the turnaround, so I didn't see the tall man who stepped out from behind a thick pine a few yards in front of us and leveled his Mac 10 machine pistol at the windshield.

Frankie saw him, though, and screamed for me to duck, his fingers tearing frantically at the buckle he'd just latched. I spun around just in time to see the smile crack the edges of the gunman's mouth and the first long, blue flames belch from the muzzle of his stocky weapon. Then, the windshield imploded as the heavy .45 slugs crashed into the cab, ripping great hunks of stuffing from the seat between us, snapping the plastic steering wheel like a dry twig, turning the rear window to dust.

I threw myself out the door and landed on my hands and knees at the very edge of the steep slope. With the open door between me and the shooter, I could no longer see him, but as I struggled with the safety catch of my holster, I looked back into the Bronco in time to see Frankie, his face contorted in a hideous grimace, tumble out the passenger-side door, his hand already wrapped around the butt of his .44 Magnum. Before he'd found his footing, though, another fusillade of slugs traced a straight pattern across the passenger-side door, the impact of the bullets tossing him backward like a toy doll.

I could hear Frankie bellowing in pain and rage as I stood, my feet unsteady on the slick embankment, and brought the muzzle of the Blackhawk down to kill the bastard who was standing squarely in the headlights less than a dozen feet away, dressed in black and screaming now in lunatic joy as the machine pistol bucked in his hands, the deadly spray of bullets beginning a rapid arc across the front of the vehicle as he swung the weapon in my direction.

I was too late.

My finger had barely begun to tighten around the trigger when the first slugs from the deadly Mac 10 slammed into the opened door, sending it crashing into my torso, driving my body backward toward the edge of the slope. In the confusion, I jerked the trigger and my shot went wild. Then, in slow motion, I watched the Blackhawk spin out of my hand as I struggled to regain my balance, my arms waving madly as I grabbed handfuls of air. As the soft shoulder at the side of the trail began to crumble beneath my feet, I made one last desperate leap to catch the revolver.

And then I was falling.

I could have sworn that I fell forever, but in reality I think I must have landed on my back about ten feet down the slope, and then I slid for more than twenty yards like a toboggan run amok, bashing into boulders, shrubs, and tree trunks before I finally collided with a granite slab. The crash knocked the air from my lungs in an explosive gasp, and I couldn't seem to draw in enough air to refill them.

I was alive—a fact which came as no small surprise—because the boulder had stopped me from tumbling all the way to the bottom of the mountain. I almost wished I was dead, though, because I seemed to hurt everywhere, even places I didn't know I had places. My face stung from scraping across the ice and snow; my ribs and back felt as if I'd been kicked by a bull. I'd twisted my knee and split my lip. Lying on my back, I could taste the blood, salty and warm, as it filled my mouth. I was nauseous, but I couldn't move yet, so I simply turned my head to the side and spit.

Above me, the firing had stopped, and I could see the gunman's silhouette at the edge of the trail, his body backlit by the Bronco's headlights. He was looking for me down there in the darkness of the slope, searching with both his eyes and his other senses. I could almost feel the evil inside him reach out to touch me as the barrel of the Mac 10 swept my position and continued searching.

He knew the direction I'd fallen, but I'd traveled far enough that I didn't think he could see where I'd come to rest. Still, there was no reason for him to believe that he'd missed me, and every reason for him to believe I was dead. Just to make sure, he calmly snapped a fresh clip into his pistol and raked the slope around me with fire, the bullets kicking up feathery puffs of snow, smacking into the granite boulder, peppering the side of my face with tiny shards of rock. Although the part of my brain most concerned with survival shrieked at me to move, to roll away to safety, I fought the instinct and held my ground until he was satisfied, until the last rumbling echo of the reports had tumbled down the valley. Without thinking, I'd clenched every muscle in my body as he fired, squeezed my eyes closed, trying, like an ostrich that buries its head in the desert sand, to hide myself from the groping fingers of destruction.

When I opened my eyes again, he was gone.

While it would have almost been comfortable to pull my coat up around my neck, burrow into it, curl up like a newborn, and hide until dawn, I knew I had no time to lose. Although I'd realized by then that I hadn't been shot, I was certain that Frankie hadn't been so lucky. I'd seen him going down, and if he was still alive, it was critical that I reach him, get him to a hospital. I didn't have a weapon to protect myself if the killer was still around, so I fumbled around in the snow until I found a stone the size of a grapefruit, jammed it in my coat pocket, and started to crawl.

It took more than ten minutes to claw my way back to the road, pulling myself up an inch at a time by grabbing hold of branches and roots, the palms of my hands tearing on the frozen wood, the leather soles of my boots useless on the icy slope. Even if I could have stood, my left knee was certainly sprained, maybe broken, and I could put no weight on it. My throbbing ribs prevented me from drawing a normal breath, so I sucked the frigid air across my bleeding lips in shallow gasps. The gore on my face was freezing quickly, and when I ran my fingers across my cheeks, I could feel the prickly splinters of granite embedded there. For every agonizing foot I gained, I slipped backward six inches, digging the toe of my right foot into the bank to brake my descent.

I'd gone less than fifteen feet when I heard the killer's snow machine cough to life, the engine tinny sounding and loud as he revved it in warm-up, receding gradually as he cruised back down the mountain, in no particular hurry now that his work was done.

He'd set the ambush, and we'd stumbled into it like a couple of green recruits. And like too many green recruits on the field of combat, we'd paid for our errors in blood.

Creeping forward up the side of the hill on my hands and one good knee, sometimes on my belly, I finally pulled myself over the lip of the roadway. To my left, the Bronco was spouting steam from the holes in its radiator, its one remaining headlight doing battle with the gloom. The tire on the driver's side was flat and the hood was sprung because one of the bullets had smashed the latch.

I dragged myself through the ruts to the far side of the vehicle, where I found Frankie, face down in the snow, moaning softly. I winced in pain as I grabbed the collar of his coat and rolled him over onto his back, used my thumbs to wipe the snow from his eyes. He'd lost his Stetson and one of his ear cuffs. His thick black hair was disheveled. His eyes were squinted closed and his lips were drawn in a tight line from the overwhelming pain of his wounds. There was black blood pooling in the snow where his chest had been and more running from the corner of his mouth, a small ribbon trickling down the side of his face, making a dark stain on the snow behind his ear.

I pulled his coat open and felt the warm, sticky wounds in his ruined chest. Frantically, I ripped his shirt open, but I had nothing to stop the bleeding, no way to stop his life from seeping out into my hands. He'd been shot—I didn't know how many times—and had lost a lot of blood. At each halting breath, more of it bubbled from the gaping wounds.

With the Bronco apparently disabled, I thought in panic there was nothing I could do, no way to get him the emergency care that might save his life. And even if the vehicle had been operational, I realized I might not be able to do anything that would help him in time.

I closed his coat again, stripped off my own coat, and wrapped it snugly around his upper body. Then, with hot tears burning the corners of my eyes, I cradled my friend's head in my arms, rocking him gently for a few short moments until he opened his eyes and looked up at the stars. I bent my ear to his mouth, felt the warmth of his ragged breath. I thought he wanted to say good-bye.

"You've got cold fucking hands, Harry," he whispered hoarsely. "Either you oughta put on some gloves, or figure a way to get me off this mountain before I freeze my red ass."

18

The doc said I might lose a couple of toes, thanks to the frostbite I suffered during my night on the mountain. That was the bad news. The good news was that the wounds to my face and hands were superficial, and although my knee was swollen to the size of a cantaloupe, it was only sprained. At least I could still hobble around, so if you forget the fact that the doctor had to cut a decent pair of jeans to check the damage, my own injuries were minimal.

The best news was that Frankie Bull would live.

It hadn't been easy, but I'd dragged him to the Bronco, tucked him in the backseat, and radioed ahead to have an ambulance from Laramie waiting for us at the entrance to the Bauer estate. Then, using a shovel handle as a crutch, I'd managed to change the flat tire and drive off the mountain with one headlight, my radiator blowing steam like a geyser and the heat gauge creeping steadily into the danger zone. The Bronco finally overheated and died a hundred yards before the Bauer's barn, but by that time we were close enough for the ambulance crew to haul Frankie the rest of the way.

I rode in the ambulance with him to Laramie and—after placing calls to Keegan, Baldi, and Curly Ahearn—I paced the halls at Ivinson Memorial Hospital with his wife, Frieda, for the five hours he was in surgery. When the surgeon found us around 6:00 in the morning, I was so wired on coffee I didn't think I'd sleep for a year, but I still got an emotional boost from his news. Frankie had taken three bullets in the chest and shoulder, and although he'd lost a considerable amount of blood, none of the rounds had hit anything that couldn't be fixed. One had clipped a lung, others had broken ribs and his collarbone and shattered his shoulder blade. He'd be laid up for several weeks, the doctor said, but he'd mend as good as new.

Before the doctor left, he told us Frankie would be in recovery for several hours and might not be able to talk until almost noon—so Frieda and I found ourselves an empty waiting-room couch and sat down, both of us too nervous to relax. A full-blooded Shoshone, Frieda Tall Bull is a beautiful young woman with finely sculpted cheekbones, an aristocratic nose, and a mane of rich black hair that hangs to her waist. At one time, Frieda was a contestant in the Miss Indian America pageant, and she'd met Frankie while he was working as a tribal policeman on the Pine Ridge Reservation in South Dakota and had taken the weekend off to attend the pageant and concurrent festivities. They'd hit it off immediately, but it had taken a while for her family to warm up to Frankie Bull, since the Sioux and Shoshone tribes have been enemies for generations.

They'd married and lived for a couple of years on the Wind River Reservation in Wyoming, until they both started going stir-crazy and lit out for greener pastures. During the two years that Frankie had worked as a police officer in Victory and part-time sculptor, Frieda had been attending the University of Wyoming in Laramie to earn her teacher's certificate. When she finished, she planned to move back to the reservation and work with Shoshone students, although I hoped she'd find something in Victory. Call me selfish, but even though I wished the best for her, I didn't want to lose Frankie Bull as a cop.

Frieda kicked her shoes off, curled her legs under her, and used her coat as a blanket as we sat in companionable silence and watched the bustle of the hospital. I was amazed at how young she seemed, how small and frail. At five-three and less than a hundred pounds, she looked about fifteen years old sitting there, her eyes puffy and red from lack of sleep, biting her lower lip as she worried about her husband. When she saw me staring at her, she smiled. "You look like hell, Harry," she said. "Why don't you go home and get some rest?"

I imagined I did look a sight. My face was a mass of bruises, my hair was a mess, my eyes were red, I hadn't shaved or showered, and I was wearing the huge sweat suit and hospital slippers I'd borrowed after the emergency-room doctors cut off my own garments. Still, I guess I looked worse than I felt. I tried to smile back, but my lips hurt. I nodded down the hall in the direction of recovery. "He might need—"

She waved her hand to cut me off. "You heard the doctor. He'll be in recovery for several hours and there isn't a thing either one of us can do for him."

I shook my head no. "But if he wakes up—" I began.

"If he wakes up," she broke in, "I'll be right here."

I felt a sense of helplessness and frustration, dug around in my shirt pocket for a cigarette but caught myself when I remembered—for about the one thousandth time in the last hours—that I was in a hospital where smoking isn't allowed. I sighed audibly and began drumming my fingers on my legs. "I know you'll be here, Frieda," I said plaintively. "It's just that I feel like I need to—"

"Do something to help?" she asked. Her face softened. "Because you feel like it's your fault?"

I nodded glumly, closed my eyes, and rubbed my forehead with my tired and battered fingers. "It *is* my fault," I told her quietly. "I took him—"

"You're responsible, all right," Frieda said forcefully. She threw aside the coat that was covering her legs and scooted next to me on the couch, took my large hands in her small ones, and looked into my eyes. A part of me was afraid of what she'd say next, but I shouldn't have been. "You're responsible for saving my husband's life," she said. "It's a debt I'll never be able to repay."

I looked down, didn't answer. There was a lump in my throat and it was hard to swallow.

"Now, why don't you do me the favor of going home to get some rest," she said. She leaned forward and kissed my cheek. "You gotta keep your strength up, Harry. I'm a hell of a woman, but not woman enough to care for both you lunkheads."

I promised Frieda I'd check in every couple of hours by phone, then I called the Wyoming Highway Patrol and hitched a ride back to my office in Victory with the officer who regularly cruises the stretch of Highway 130 between Laramie and my adopted hometown. I got back to Victory around eight that morning and, as I'd suspected, the whole place had gone loony.

The first gaggle of lawmen, from the sheriff's department in Laramie, had apparently blown into town a little after 6:00 with their sirens blazing. Every officer and lowly deputy wore a bulletproof vest and had his own riot gun. So far, the department had secured the weapons cache and begun a fruitless ground-and-helicopter search for the gunman.

Ken Keegan showed up with a vanful of DCI heavies about an hour later, all of them carrying M16s and wearing black commando fatigues. In spite of everything, I had to laugh at the way Keegan looked in his commando getup. Imagine a crew-cut Karl Malden dressed up as Rambo and you get the picture.

He didn't act silly, though. I heard later that within five minutes of his arrival, he'd knocked Tony Baldi down a peg and taken charge, dispatching his agents to take responsibility for the weaponry before Baldi could do anything stupid.

Aaron Cohen, who Keegan assured me was "so happy he'd like to shit" over our discovery, had chartered a plane and was expected to land at Brees Field in a little over an hour, accompanied by two or three other feebs from the Idaho contingent. There were a half-dozen or more agents on their way up from the big office in Denver, but none of them would be on-site until noon or later.

So far, none of the sheriff's deputies or DCI agents scouring the mountain around the weapons cache had seen sign of anyone who didn't belong there, with the exception of Wally Pike, who'd been on his way up to Jim Creek to do a little elk scouting around 9:00 A.M. and found his way blocked by an army of cops, all pointing their weapons at him and wondering, not very nicely I imagine, why he was carrying a .30-06 in his rifle rack.

With my knee wrapped in an athletic bandage, my toes soaking in a pan of warm water, and my face taking comfort under a hot, medicated towel, I leaned back with my head against the wall behind my desk and closed my eyes, listening to the hubbub and trying to find my center before I faced the rest of the day. I opened my eyes just in time to see a sheriff's department four-wheel-drive roll by the office on Main, its blue lights flashing. The deputies inside looked stern and very self-important.

"Can I get you anything, Harry?" Keegan asked as the vehicle passed Ginny Larsen's, where a half-dozen patrons had come outside to the sidewalk to watch the commotion.

"Yeah," I said, pointing to his vest pocket. "A cigarette."

Keegan tapped a butt out of his crumbling pack and offered me a light from his Zippo. I drew the smoke into my lungs and coughed it right back out. When I took the butt away from my lips, I noticed that my fingers and hands were covered with dried blood. Frankie's blood mixed with my own—black and flaking from the smooth places on the backs of my hands, embedded in the creases around my knuckles, rimming my cuticles.

I stared at the blood, shaking my head sadly, wrestling with the thought that I could have—should have—done more to keep him from harm. If only I hadn't slipped. If only my shot hadn't gone wild. If only we'd been more careful. If only . . .

Keegan knew what I was thinking. "It's not your fault," he said.

"Of course it is," I growled. "I'm the chief of police around here."

"You're right, you're the boss, and it's your job to protect your people," he said patiently. "But being a cop carries plenty of risk, even in a place like Victory. Christ, you know that. You've been in this business long enough."

I wasn't comforted. "I could have done something. . . ."

Keegan scowled like I was acting ridiculous. "What could you have done?" he asked. "Drawn the killer's fire? Taken the bullets yourself? It sounds like you tried all that."

I turned my head away, dismissing him.

"You were ambushed, Harry," he said, almost angrily. "And it's a damned wonder you're not dead, too."

I searched his voice for the faintest note of accusation. I didn't hear it, although I half expected to. Keegan had warned me to be careful, not to be a cowboy, and I'd ignored every word. "Yeah, Ken," I said miserably. "I'm a lucky son of a bitch."

"You *are* lucky," he said. "You might not believe this, but you did good work out there. You saved lives, Harry, and I'll tell you something else. You're gonna live to see this bastard pay."

"I'll get him, Ken," I said. I felt cold fury growing in my gut. I remembered the fear I felt, crouched on the face of the mountain as the gunman sprayed bullets in my direction, and that memory was humiliating and painful. In my mind's eye, I could see his laughing face as he shot Frankie. He wouldn't be laughing long, not if I could help it.

I'd made my decision at the hospital in Laramie. The gunman had made this the most personal of battles, and I wanted to settle it myself, without the aid of Keegan, Aaron Cohen, the sheriff's department, or anyone else. At that moment, revenge, pure and scorching, was all I cared about. "Bet on it," I said tautly.

"That's a bet I'm not gonna take," he said. "I know he's goin' down. We'll find out who he is and—"

I sat forward, looked into my friend's square, kind face. I stubbed out the cigarette and motioned for him to pass me another. "I saw him," I said quietly.

At first, Keegan didn't understand what I'd told him. Then, as it registered, his brow wrinkled in confusion. "The shooter?" he asked.

I nodded yes.

"You were close to him?" he asked.

"Very," I said, remembering the look of ecstasy on the gunman's face as he sprayed bullets from the barrel of his Mac 10. "He was laughing, Ken. The cocksucker was enjoying himself."

"Then you can describe him."

"Sure." I shrugged. "Six-three, two-hundred-sixty pounds, sandy-haired Caucasian, mid to late thirties. Neck like a tree stump and arms to match."

Keegan was already punching numbers into the phone. "I'll get an artist over here right away," he said. "You can draw him while his face is still fresh in your mind."

I pushed myself to my feet. "Won't be necessary," I said. The ribbon of pain running upward from my knee and foot almost took my breath away. I hopped over to the filing cabinet, opened it, and pulled the photo of the Kahl funeral I'd lifted from his files. "The guy with his hand on that woman's shoulder," I said, sailing the photo toward his desk. "Give him a few years, take away the beard, and he's your man."

Keegan stared at the photo, turned it over, and saw the man wasn't identified on the FBI tag. When he looked up, there was a question on his square face.

"I took the photo from your office after you left," I explained. "There was something about it that bothered me, but I couldn't put my finger on what it was. Now, I realize I was reacting to the fact I'd seen this guy before. Lots of times, as it turns out."

Keegan looked puzzled. "Here? In Victory?"

I nodded in the affirmative. "Victory," I agreed. "Movies, magazines, newspapers, television . . ."

Keegan shook his head as if to clear it. "I guess I don't get what you're tellin' me, Harry," he said. "Why don't you back up a little and—"

I sat back down heavily. "Kit Duerr," I told him simply. "Our big football hero's a stone killer."

Ken Keegan and I sat across from each other in the small police-department office, me behind my desk with my leg stretched out and elevated to the desktop so my knee wouldn't throb, Keegan with his own big feet up on the other side of the desk with his bulletproof vest and heavy jacket off, leaning back in the cheap office chair so far I feared it would break. Keegan had been chain-smoking ever since I'd given him the news about Kit Duerr, which he wasn't ready to believe at first. Gradually, though, he'd had to accept that I was right. The photo of Duerr with the Kahl family was strong evidence, but eyewitness testimony was better. I'd seen Duerr's face as he shot at us, and it wasn't a face I'd ever forget.

Keegan squinted through the smoke and the bright morning sunlight coming through the office window to watch the activity on the street outside. "The thing I don't understand, Harry," he said, "is why you didn't tell me about Duerr last night. If you knew who he was, we'd have had a jump on things if you'd only spoken up. We might even have him by now. Didn't you trust me? Didn't you think I'd believe you?"

There was reproach in Keegan's voice, and more than a hint of anger. When I didn't answer him he went on. "I'll tell you what I think," he said. "I think you didn't say anything because you want to go after this bastard yourself. You've forgotten you're a cop, a part of a team. Instead, you think you're some kinda damned vigilante, not worried about anything but your own selfish revenge." He paused. "Am I warm here, Harry?"

I shrugged because there was no good answer to his question, and I knew it. He was right; I am selfish. I wanted Duerr for myself and I had no excuse for keeping his identity to myself, even for the hours I was waiting in the hospital with Frankie and Frieda.

Keegan scowled. "You're my friend, but I'm beginning to understand why so many people are pissed off at you," he said. "Sometimes, you act like a real asshole and you oughta know better—this Lone Ranger crap has gotten you in trouble before." Then he stood and stomped to the window, looked out at the street with his hands clasped behind his back while I stewed in hopes a little silence would help him mellow.

It worked, because when he finally spoke again, his tone was gentler. Most, if not all, was forgiven. We'd have to discuss our problem again, but we both knew then wasn't the right time. "So how do you figure it, Harry?" he asked, turning back toward me. I felt a rush of relief we were still apparently friends. "You know who the guy is now, I'm sure you've got a theory."

Of course I had a theory, but it still had plenty of holes. I took a few seconds to gather my thoughts. "Duerr did them all, Ken," I said. "I don't know why he killed Sonny, but I've got a pretty good idea why he killed Tad and Alex."

Keegan looked dubious but nodded for me to go on.

"I think Alex and Tad were a couple of fuckups," I said. "Duerr might have tolerated them when Tad was handing out money and financing the Posse's holy war, but he didn't find them quite so amusing once he had the hardware. I'm not sure what caused it exactly, but I think they had a falling out. I think their whole operation was starting to come unraveled and it was making them all edgy."

"And when things got bad enough . . ." Keegan said.

"He killed Tad and Alex," I said, finishing the thought.

"But why did he stay around here after that?" Keegan asked. "Does that make sense to you?"

"Maybe," I said. "It's possible the reason he killed Tad and Alex was that they were getting nervous about having the guns so close to the estate with the place under surveillance. I think they wanted to move them out, but I don't think Duerr wanted to take the chance. I think they argued and he killed them, figuring he'd just wait until things calmed down a little to move the weapons. They were well hidden, so there wasn't much chance we'd find them by accident. The hitch in the plan was the early snowstorm, which pinned the weapons down on the mountain. Once the place got snowed in, he couldn't take the chance of moving the guns out a box at a time on his snow machine, so he's been staying nearby, keeping an eye on things until he had a chance to move them safely."

"That makes sense," he said. "But at least we don't have to worry about his arsenal anymore. Without that, and without the Posse's support, he's isolated and alone."

"He's still dangerous . . ."

"Very," Keegan said, studying the photograph of the Kahl funeral, "but now we know who he is, and with Cohen's help, we ought to be able to bring him in quickly. Kit Duerr's days are numbered."

"Have you sealed the area off?"

"Yeah. The road over the mountain to Saratoga is closed, but we've got a team watching at the top of the pass anyway. His only real options are the highway to Laramie and the dirt road to Woods Landing, and we've got those covered. He's not getting out of here unless he can grow wings and fly."

While I riffled through the bills, year-old bank statements, and credit-card receipts in my desk for some aspirins and a couple of Darvon tablets I had left over from my last root canal, Keegan looked at the photograph and used a red grease pencil to draw a circle around Duerr's face. "Son of a bitch," he said, holding the glossy up to the window for better light. "The man has everything he ever could have wanted. I wonder how he got hooked up with a bunch of lunatics like the Posse."

I started to formulate an answer but didn't finish because there were four pain-relieving capsules clinging to the back of my throat like cockleburs on wool socks. The medication was bantam-weight stuff, but I needed to blunt the pain without putting myself to sleep. When he saw that I was having trouble swallowing, Keegan handed me his lukewarm coffee to wash everything down. The combination of the bitter-tasting pills and Keegan's caffeinated swill was enough to make me gag. I finally choked the medicine down and wiped my lips with a tissue. When I took it away from my mouth, it was pink with blood.

"You really ought to go home and get some rest," he said sympathetically. "You're a wreck."

"That's not the first time I've heard that today," I said sarcastically. "I'll just turn Victory over to you and the rest of your out-of-town flatfeet and tuck myself into my cozy bed while you hunt down the man who tried to kill me and the only police officer on my force. No chance, pal. I'm staying."

Keegan groaned and swung his legs off the desktop. He stood and shrugged into his heavy bulletproof vest, made sure it was fastened securely around his wide middle. "Well, there won't be a lot you'll have to do, but I suppose I can understand why you'd want to stick around," he said. "At least you could go home and get a bath, some grub, and maybe a little nap. Come back after lunch and meet with Cohen. I don't imagine things will really start popping until then anyway."

"And what will you be doing in the meantime?"

He waved the photograph in my direction. "I want to get about a thousand copies of this made and pass 'em out," he said. "And then I think I'll drive up the mountain and take a look around. See if the evidence team has come up with anything we can use."

"All right," I said. "I'll talk to you again a little after noon."

"Can you drive?"

"Breathing is hard," I said, "but driving is a cinch. I'll take the cruiser. It's got an automatic."

"What about your Bronco?"

"If you're feeling generous, you could have someone tow it in. Maybe I can get it fixed. Send Curly the bill."

He jammed a black baseball cap emblazoned with the DCI logo on his blocky skull. "Anything else I can do?" he asked.

"Yeah," I said. "When you get up the mountain, see if you can find my gun."

When Keegan left, I pulled the shades in the office, rested my head on my forearms, and tried to work up the energy to drive to my house. When the phone rang, it sounded fuzzy and far away, like it was ringing in the next room instead of six inches from my ear. The Darvons were kicking in, and the throbbing in my knee was a bit more manageable. I felt warm for the first time in hours and a little drowsy. I finally answered on the fifth ring.

"Just thought I'd check in," Curly said, his voice low and full of worry. "How're you doing?"

"They tell me I look like shit," I said. "But that's not important. The important thing is Frankie will be okay."

"Thank God," he said. "Does he need anything?"

"Nah, Frieda's there," I told him. "He's in good hands." I paused. "She was a little worried about his insurance coverage, though. There shouldn't be a problem with it, should there?"

"The family doesn't worry about a thing," Curly broke in. "It's all taken care of."

"I'm sure that'll ease her mind," I said, tugging at the collar of my shirt. In my mind, I could see Frankie lying naked on the operating table. I could see his dark red blood flowing from his wounds. I could see the doctor's scalpel, the thick needle in his hand as he took stitches in Frankie's chest. Suddenly, the room was too hot, too close. I needed air.

"Harry, are you there?"

"Yeah," I said, licking the salty perspiration from my upper lip. "I guess I'm just not tracking very well."

"Listen, Harry . . . why don't you go home and get some rest? I'll call Frieda and—"

"Thanks, Curly, but there are a few things I need to do first."

"Okay," he said reluctantly. "But then go home. Take a couple of days . . ."

"I don't need a couple of days," I said irritably. "I'll be fine just as soon as I—"

Suddenly, he was angry, his voice forceful and curt. "I mean it, Harry!" he said. "You're hurt and you're tired, and with Keegan and his bunch around, there's no reason to push it. Just do me a favor and go home—"

"Oh, for Christ's sake, Curly," I snapped. "You've never told me how to do my job before, so don't start telling me now. I'll have plenty of time to rest when this is over."

"You're right, Harry," he said, his voice rising. "I haven't told you how to do your job before, because I haven't needed to. But I've already got one critically injured policeman in Victory and I don't want another one. Men who are exhausted make mistakes. Even you, Harry. Go home. It's an order."

"Yeah, sure, Curly. Whatever you say."

"Goddamn it, Harry. I'm serious. Are you going home?"

"No, Curly. I don't think I will. I think I'm going to stay right here and find the bastard who shot my friend."

Curly didn't answer for several seconds, and I filled the silence by wiggling my toes in the cooling pan of water. "Then you're suspended," he said finally.

I pulled my foot out of the basin and sat forward, gripped the phone receiver tightly. "What?" I asked incredulously.

"I said you're suspended," he shouted. "For forty-eight hours, with pay—but you're still suspended."

"I can't believe what I'm hearing," I said. "In the first place, I don't think you know what you're asking. In the second, you couldn't suspend me if you wanted. Read the damned town charter, Curly. You can suspend me for suspected malfeasance, embezzlement, or neglecting to do my job. You can't suspend me because I won't go to bed."

"All right. Maybe I can't suspend you."

"Thanks."

He chuckled. "Don't thank me, Harry. You're *fired.*"

"Oh, Jesus! What are you talking—"

"Town charter, Harry," he said. "The chief of police serves at the mayor's pleasure. I may not be able to suspend you on a whim, but

I can fire you any damned time I want, for any reason I want, including I don't like your tie. You got a problem with that, see a lawyer."

"Fuck you, Curly!" I said through my teeth. "And fuck your—"

"Don't say anything you're gonna regret," he said. "A couple of days from now, you might want to reapply for your job."

I started to tell him where he could stick his lousy job, but his end of the line was already dead.

The farmhouse was as cold as a meat locker when I got there at a little after 11:00, but I soon had a fire going in the woodstove and a breakfast of scrambled eggs, sausage, and coffee working in the kitchen. It's not particularly easy to cook a meal when you're hopping around on one leg, but the domestic chore kept my mind off my troubles, at least for a little while. When my meal was ready, I bobbed it into the living room and flipped on the television to keep myself company while I ate. Needless to say, I was surprised to see my own face on the screen when the picture came in focus—the ID mug shot I'd used in my homicide days—and a Denver cable announcer doing a voice-over report on last night's shooting and our discovery of the Posse's weapons cache. According to the newscaster, the FBI in Denver was giving us credit for capturing the largest stockpile of "terrorist" arms in the region's history and citing our small department for "extreme heroism" as we "faced an overwhelming and brutal assault by forces of this barbaric, racist, and un-American organization." The announcer did not identify Kit Duerr as the suspect, but I didn't think it would be long before that tidbit got out. Then, we'd have more reporters in Victory than residents.

The phone in the kitchen was jangling before he had time to move on to the next story. The voice on the other end belonged to Nicole, and she was obviously frightened.

"My God, Harry! We were on break, and had the TV on and there was your face and—"

"It's all right, honey. I'm okay," I assured her. "A little shaken up, but no permanent damage."

"But the television said—"

"I know. I know. But Frankie's gonna pull through and what happened to me is no big deal. Scratches. Scrapes. A wrenched knee . . ."

"I'm coming up," she said firmly. "If I leave now, I can be there by—"

"Don't do that," I said. "I'm leaving in just a few minutes and I won't be around anyway. You get in touch with the kids before they hear something from someone else. I don't want them to think—"

"I was so scared, Harry," she said, her voice cracking, breaking into muffled sobs. "I was afraid you were . . . I didn't know . . ."

"It's all right, sweetheart, really. I've hurt myself worse working in the yard. . . ."

"I'm so sorry, Harry," she said. "And so very happy you're alive."

"Thanks," I answered, because I didn't know what else to say.

For a few moments, we simply listened to each other breathe, taking emotional sustenance from our long-distance connection. For the time being, we knew it would have to be enough.

"I've got to go," I said finally. "I just came home to change clothes and bathe. I'm meeting the FBI in—"

"That man, Harry? The person who shot at you? Is he still—"

"It's like a cop convention up here," I assured her. "There's nothing to worry about. I'll call you and the boys later tonight and we'll talk it out."

"Promise?"

"Promise," I said. "It may be late, ten or eleven."

"We'll be up," she said.

"Nicole?"

"Yes?"

"It means a lot that you called. I appreciate it."

"I'm proud of you, Harry," she said. "And I want you to remember that I love you."

I love her, too, and I told her so.

When I got off the phone with Nicole, I ran myself a bath hot enough to poach eggs and soaked my leg and foot for twenty minutes. My frostbitten toes were fish-belly white and beginning to blister, but they didn't hurt any worse than if I'd dropped a grand piano on them. My knee was another story. Splashed with vivid reds and purples, it looked like a tie-dyed T-shirt. It was also swollen so grotesquely it looked as if the skin might split, which made it impossible to bend my leg more than three or four inches. I knew I should stay off it until it mended, but I didn't have time for that. Instead, I dried myself gingerly and slathered my knee with pungent purple horse liniment. Then I rebandaged it so tightly I was afraid I might cut off the circulation.

The result wasn't very satisfactory, but it was enough to get me in a pair of jeans and moving under my own steam, as long as I rested most of my weight on the blackthorn walking stick I'd kept handy since the last time I hurt my knee—in a skiing accident the year before.

I pulled on a thick sweater, a pair of loose-fitting, down-filled mukluks, and a Dux Back hunting coat, then I limped into the spare bedroom where I keep my gun safe. The sawed-off ten-gauge shotgun I store in there is illegal in all fifty states, and it's a mean, nasty, ugly-looking piece of work. But at close range, loaded with double-aught buck, it'll knock an elephant to its knees. I held the shotgun under my arm and jammed a dozen shells in the left-hand pocket of my coat.

About ten years before, when I was doing a lot of hiking in grizzly country, I'd purchased a Ruger .44 Magnum for protection from the big bears. It's the same gun Frankie Bull carries as a duty weapon, but it was too much gun for me, so it spent most of its time locked up.

I loaded it, grabbed an extra box of cartridges, and stuck the revolver in the other pocket.

So far in my dealings with Kit Duerr, I'd been outtracked, outsmarted, and outgunned. The next time I saw him, I thought grimly, at least I wouldn't be outgunned.

I buried the speedometer on the way to Laramie, which isn't saying quite what it used to since the damned things only go to eighty-five mph in these newer cars. Still, I blew by everything on the highway and made the trip in under thirty minutes. When I came to a stop in front of the courthouse building with the blue lights flashing, people on all three floors poked their startled heads out windows to see what the hell was going on. I let them gawk as I limped up the stairs to the front door and hopped up to the Albany County assessor's office on the second floor. I guess I was in a bit of a hurry.

When I get an idea in my head, I'm like an old hound with a bone—I don't like to let it go. Despite the fact that Frankie and I had come up puny, I still had it in my mind that if Duerr was staying near Victory, he was holed up somewhere warm and cozy, somewhere off the beaten path, somewhere that offered decent access to town. I knew he wasn't in any of the homes owned by summer people. I knew he hadn't rented a place from any of the locals.

But it struck me while I was talking to Nicole that if there was a home or cabin that didn't fit either of those categories and wasn't on my list of area dwellings, then the county assessor, my old friend Larry Calhoun—who makes the county's living by taxing everything that's nailed down and a lot of what isn't—would be the one to know about it.

I limped into the office but didn't see Calhoun at his desk, nor was he at any of the tall filing cabinets lining the work space. Maybe he was at lunch. His stubby daughter Tina, who serves as his secretary, took one bored look at me as I walked in and went back to her phone conversation. I waited a grand total of four seconds, then regained her attention by whapping the blackthorn walking stick on the tiled counter. In the small office, it sounded like a jackhammer.

Tina Calhoun was so unsettled by the racket that the baseball-size pink bubble she was blowing splattered all over her nose and she dropped the phone when she reached up to pick the stringy Double Bubble away. "Whaaa . . . ?" she stammered, clawing at the sticky ropes of gum with one hand and plucking at the dangling phone with the other. Through the earpiece, I could hear a shrill female voice hollering for Tina to get back on the line. I crow-hopped to her desk and slammed the phone in its cradle, breaking the connection.

"Sorry, Tina, but I need some information," I told her crossly. "Emergency."

"Emergency, Mr. Starbranch?" she asked incredulously, her heavily shadowed eyes opening as wide as they could go without actually popping out of her skull. "You have a *tax* emergency?"

"No, I do not have a tax emergency," I said. "I need to see the property rolls for a five-mile radius around Victory, and I need to see them right now . . . if it's no trouble."

"Yeah, and then what?" she asked, her gaze darting between me and the door as if she were trying to figure out if she could escape before I caught her.

I yanked the police-department roster of rental and vacation properties around Victory from my back pocket and waved it importantly. "And then I want to check 'em against this list," I said. "If your dad is taxing any buildings in that radius that don't show up on this list, I want to know where they are."

"I don't think I can—" she said, her voice growing tighter, riding the ragged edge of panic.

"Listen, Tina," I said, bending down until my eyes were about two inches away from hers, my fists gripping the padded arms of her chair, "not only can you do it, you're going to do it. I need this information for a murder investigation, and I don't have time to—"

"No!" she said, pushing away from me, her hand fluttering as she pointed toward the bank of file cabinets. "You don't understand. I can't do it because he's never taught me the filing system! All I ever do is answer the phone!"

"Oh," I said stupidly. The arms of her chair were suddenly hot pokers in my hands. I let go and stood away, wishing I could simply turn to smoke and disappear. When some people get embarrassed, their cheeks turn bright red. With me, it's the ears, and I'm sure mine were the unnatural color of maraschino cherries.

To her credit, Tina recognized her tactical advantage and milked it for all it was worth. I'd scared her, and now I was gonna pay.

"I don't know what your problem is," she said righteously, "but you've got no right to—"

A loud voice from the doorway behind us interrupted Tina's tirade. "Would someone like to tell me what the hell is going on around here?"

At the sound of Larry Calhoun's brawling baritone, I turned around quickly and saw my friend standing in the doorway with his arms full of manila folders, atop which sat a carryout bag from Mc-

Donald's and a couple of precariously balanced soft drinks. A squat, stern-looking character, he's maybe fifty-five years old, and was a career drill instructor in the Marine Corps before he retired ten years ago and ran for Albany County Assessor. As the official who sets the property valuations upon which taxes are based, the assessor is universally hated around these parts, and it takes someone who's tough and thick-skinned to seek the job in the first place. To keep it, you've got to be meaner than a peach-orchard bear at pickin' time. Calhoun fits the bill on both counts.

"Oh, it's nothin', Daddy," Tina huffed, hurrying to the door to relieve Calhoun of the food but not the paperwork. "Some kinda emergency. You mind if I go on break?"

Calhoun shook his head no and moved to the side as she squeezed through the doorway, already stuffing a couple of greasy fries in her mouth. When she and her lunch were gone, he set the folders on the counter and took a thoughtful sip of his drink. "That your car out front with the flashers on?" he asked.

"Yep," I said. "Guess I was in a hurry."

"For what?" he asked, casting a dubious look around his cramped office. "You got some kinda beef with your tax bill?"

"No," I said. "I rent."

"So what's with the—"

"It's these murders, Larry," I said. "I've got an idea, and I thought you could help."

"Yeah?" he asked, his face wrinkling with uncertainty. "I don't know what I can do for you, Harry. I haven't been in Victory since I did the valuation last spring."

I pointed at his filing cabinets. "I just need your help with some information."

"Okay, but—"

"Here," I said, handing him my list of vacation and rental properties. "I think my suspect is hiding near Victory, but those are all the places I know of where he could be staying. I need you to check this list against your tax rolls and give me the location of every habitable dwelling in a five- or six-mile radius of Victory that doesn't show up on my list."

"You want buildings in the city proper?"

"No, just outside of town."

"Family homes?"

I shook my head no. "Just rentals and seasonals," I said.

"That shouldn't be much of a problem," he said, running his finger down the first page of my roster. "But it may take a while."

"I know you're busy," I said, "but do you have any idea how long . . . ?"

"Give me an hour," he said, pointing to Tina's desk. "You can wait there if you want."

"Mind if I use the phone?"

"Nah," he said, "we're both working on the taxpayers' dime."

When Calhoun had stashed his coat and was ransacking the contents of a tall filing cabinet in the corner of his office, I used my walking stick as a brace to lower myself gratefully into the swivel chair at Tina's standard-issue metal desk. The Darvons and the aspirins had nearly worn off, and the pain in my knee was beginning to demand attention. It couldn't have it though, because it had to contend with the dozens of other bruises, scrapes, and lacerations sprinkled over the rest of my body. I considered asking whether Tina had any aspirin or Midol I could borrow but decided against it because I didn't want to interrupt Calhoun.

Instead, I pulled Ken Keegan's car-phone number from my wallet and waited anxiously while the phone company beamed my call up to a satellite in outer space and back down to Keegan's car, or however it is these calls are completed. Ken answered on the second ring, sounding like he was speaking from downtown Nairobi instead of a mere thirty miles away. "Keegan here," he said. At least that's what I think he said. I could barely hear him.

"Ken, this is Harry!" I yelled. Across the room, Calhoun jumped a little at the noise and turned around to see what was up.

"Cellular phone," I explained. He nodded his understanding and turned back to his files.

"What?" Keegan hollered. "What did you say?"

"Never mind," I said. "I'm calling to see if you had any luck finding Duerr."

"Nothing yet," he shouted. "Where are you, Harry? I'll come talk to you in person."

"I'm in Laramie."

"Laramie? What are you doing there? I've been calling your house—"

"I'm not at my house, Ken. Like I said, I'm in Laramie."

"What are you doing in Lar—"

"Never mind," I said. "I'll talk to you later when—"

"Hold on," he broke in. "Cohen called me about a half hour ago with some information on Duerr he picked up from the feeb office in Bismark, North Dakota, after you identified him as the shooter. You interested in hearing it?"

"Of course," I said.

"You're gonna love this," Keegan said. "The FBI office in North Dakota says Duerr was raised in Kansas farm country. Family went bankrupt in 1973 when Kit was thirteen. Father killed himself the next year."

"Jesus."

"That's not all," he said. "His mother died right after that. Cancer. They couldn't afford chemo. When she was gone, Kit left Kansas, drifted up north to Dakota, and some friends of Gordon Kahl's took him in."

"He lived with them?"

"Yeah, he didn't have any other family left, so these friends of Kahl's sort of adopted him, at least till Kit finished high school and went off to college on a football scholarship. Cohen figures Duerr heard so much about Gordon Kahl and the Posse, he came to idolize the guy. After college, the pros picked Duerr up and nobody in law enforcement remembered his connection to that bunch in Dakota."

"But Duerr kept in touch with them," I said. It wasn't a question.

"Apparently," Keegan said. "If he was sympathetic to the cause, though, he definitely didn't advertise it."

"Until now," I said.

"Yeah," Keegan agreed. "Now the cat's out of the bag, and the Posse apparently wants him as badly as we do."

"Well, they're not gonna get him."

"What was that, Harry? This connection sucks."

"Nothin', Ken. I'll talk to you later."

"Fine," he said. "Call when you get back to your office. And Harry?"

"Yeah?"

"Curly Ahearn's looking for you. I told him I'd have you give him a buzz."

"Sure thing," I said. "I'll do it right now."

When I hung up, Calhoun was straightening up from the file cabinet, shaking his head unhappily. It didn't look like he had much good news.

"Well?" I asked. "What'd you find?"

"Not much," he said. "Your list has everything mine does, with the exception of a couple of nonprofits."

"Nonprofits?"

"Yeah," he said, handing me a computer printout of his tax rolls. "There's a Methodist church camp up around Barber Lake, and they've got a few cabins they use in the summer."

"But they haven't used it for a couple of years," I said, "because the kitchen burned down."

"I know," he said, pointing to the second entry on the page. "The only other thing is the university's science camp. They've got three or four cabins up by the ski area that they let geology students use once in a while. They're empty most of the time, though."

"I know where it is," I said, picturing the location of the cabins, about a half mile off Highway 130 in the woods near the Libby Creek Recreation Area.

"It's a nice place."

"It sure is," chirped Tina, who'd come back from lunch in time to catch the tail end of our conversation. She looked like she was in a much better mood now that her tummy was full.

"You've been there?" I asked.

"Sure," she said. "My boyfriend and I rented one of the cabins for a weekend last winter. They're really cool. Double beds, fireplaces . . ." Her emphasis was definitely heaviest on the word *beds*.

"You rented one?" I asked anxiously. "How can you do that?"

"You just talk to the secretary in the science department," she explained. “If they don’t have any students using the cabins, they rent them out cheap.”

It took less time to drive to the University of Wyoming science building than it did to get down the stairs of the county building and out to the cruiser, but I had to wait for fifteen minutes until the department secretary got back from the student union, where she’d gone for her coffee break. A competent-looking woman in her late thirties, she was initially reluctant to give me any information, but she gave in when I showed her my badge.

“I hope there’s no trouble up there,” she said doubtfully, pulling a file from the middle drawer of her desk. “We make them sign a waiver of liability, but it still wouldn’t look good if—”

“All I want to know,” I assured her, “is whether any of the cabins are rented now. The university doesn’t have a thing to worry about.”

“In that case,” she said, handing me a small sheaf of papers held together by a clip, “we’ve had one of them rented for several months. It’s scheduled to be vacant by November fifteenth.”

The papers and carbons she’d handed me were a rental agreement and waiver, giving the occupant the right to stay in the university’s cabin for $150 a month. The agreement was dated June 15.

It was signed by Gene Matthews.

The name of the sheriff who killed Gordon Kahl.

Forty minutes later, I was back in Victory having a loud argument with my physician, Dr. Fast Eddie Warnock—a fidgety-looking man with a plump face, receding hairline, and big, startled-looking eyes behind round wire-rim glasses. Warnock’s a nice guy and usually fairly easygoing, but I could tell he didn’t care much for blackmail.

We were in his office, where I’d found him reading the latest issue of the *New England Journal of Medicine* and listening to some reggae music on his desktop tape player. Warnock’s been in Victory for a little over a year, working—not too happily—in a government-funded program to entice young general practitioners to serve small rural communities like Victory and Medicine Bow. He hasn’t been in town long enough to learn to like the place, but he’s been around long enough to put himself in at least one compromising situation.

"I can't do it, Harry!" he said. "I told you, you've got a bad sprain. You should stay off it. I'm not giving to give you a shot so you can keep running around."

"I need drugs," I told him. "I've got something I have to do, and I can't be limping around. Give me the damned shot, and I'll rest later."

"You don't get it," he said impatiently. "Pain is our friend. Pain tells us something is wrong. Pain makes us take it easy. If we deaden pain, we can hurt ourselves worse without knowing it."

"Give me the shot, Eddie."

"No, I won't," he said. "I'd be neglecting my responsibility as a physician. You could sue—"

"I won't sue, Ed. Promise." He wasn't buying it, so I started playing hardball. "Do you remember last summer when you were coming home from that dinner banquet in Laramie?" I asked. "Three sheets to the wind? Driving seventy. Downtown? I pulled you over?"

He blinked suspiciously behind his thick glasses. "Yeah, I remember," he said testily. "So what?"

I smiled serenely. "What did I do?"

"You drove me home," he said.

"What *should* I have done?"

The question seemed to hurt him, since every muscle in his face tensed. "I don't know. What?"

"I should have arrested you," I said. "Did I do that? Make you spend the night in jail? For your own protection?"

"No, and I appreciate it," he said. "I've never been that—"

"Did I say anything to anyone about it?" I broke in.

"No," he admitted, "but that's—"

"Then give me the shot, Ed—you owe me. And while you're at it, give me a syringe and an extra dose for later."

"Well," he said unhappily, "I suppose I could give you a half cc of lidocaine and a half cc of DepoMedrol. That should take care of it for a few hours."

"How numb will it be?"

"Numb."

"Better double it, then."

"Come on Harry, that's—"

"I've heard of lidocaine," I said, cutting him off, "but what's the other stuff, that Depo—"

"Steroids," he explained, "to help reduce the inflammation."

"Steroids?" I asked him, cracking a little smile. I had what I needed; no use ending our visit on a sour note. "Won't those make my *cojones* shrink?"

"Maybe a little," he said angrily. "But I wouldn't worry if I were you, Harry. You've got plenty of balls to spare."

19

You can sneak out of town in a Chevy Citation. You can sneak out of town in a Honda Civic. You can always sneak out of town in a Ford Taurus. On a Sunday morning when most people are still in church, you might even be able to sneak out of town in a red Camaro if you don't squeal the tires. But you'll have trouble every time if you try sneaking out of town in a squad car, especially if the town you're trying to sneak out of only has three major streets and everybody in the place is looking for you.

Fast Eddie's office is a block off Main on the southern tip of Victory, and I'd parked behind his building while I was inside convincing the good doctor to make my living a little easier through creative pharmacology. When I came out, carrying the blackthorn walking stick over my shoulder and basically dead below the waist, I could look across the six-car parking lot and see the backs of the businesses and offices along Main Street. In between those buildings, I could see little snatches of the main drag itself, and I didn't like what I saw there one bit. All told, there must have been fifty-seven varieties of cop on Main Street, some of them lollygagging beside vehicles from the sheriff's department, some keeping warm inside Ford sedans driven by agents from the DCI, some just walking up and down by twos, window-shopping in the storefronts and shooting the breeze.

I didn't want to talk to any of them. What I wanted to do was slip through town undetected and undisturbed, head up into the mountains on Highway 130 until I came to the university's science camp, and have a little talk with Kit Duerr. I'm sure any of the lawmen in Victory that afternoon would have been more than happy to come along if I'd asked them, would probably have demanded to come along if they'd known where I was going, but I was afraid our conversation would be inhibited if I brought too many associates.

The fact is, I wanted the Posse gunman behind bars as much as anyone did. But I wanted a shot at putting him there myself, even if it meant breaking the cardinal rule of police procedure: never go into a dangerous situation without plenty of backup.

With the clarity of hindsight, I know I was making a big mistake—but that afternoon, I'd been almost thirty-two hours without sleep. I was full of medication. I'd been battered, bashed, and bruised. I'd rolled down a cliff and frostbitten a couple of toes. I'd been shot at, and I watched one of my best friends get shot. I wasn't operating at peak performance.

That's why I decided to steal a car.

Granted, boosting a car in Victory doesn't take a great deal of skill, since most people leave their keys in the ignition, but the car I was planning to swipe would be just as easy, since I had a spare key in my pocket. Across the parking lot and halfway down the narrow alley that runs behind the buildings on Main, I could see the backside of the Silver Dollar and there—right by the metal Dumpster where I'd parked it six weeks ago—was the lime-green 1957 Jeep wagon Curly had purchased on impulse off a used-car lot one afternoon when we'd been in the city shopping for fishing paraphernalia at the West Laramie Fly Store. The shark at the dealership was asking $1,200 for the classic wreck, but Curly got it for $900 when we found some rusted holes in the quarter panel big enough to put a fist through. Since we'd taken his car to Laramie, I drove the Jeep back to Victory for him and parked it behind the Dollar, where he intended to leave it until he could find somebody to do the necessary bodywork on the cheap.

Luckily for me, I'd neglected to give him back the key, and as I slipped behind the big steering wheel and adjusted my bottom around a spring poking through the cracked leather seat, I chuckled at the poetic irony of my crime. Out of a job less than two hours, and I already had a new career as a car thief. And what better way to initiate my new enterprise than plundering a vehicle belonging to the man who'd fired me?

The old Willys looked like a dog, and it was in serious need of a valve job, but it started on the first crank, its tired cylinders clacking away like an ancient sewing machine. I didn't think the racket was loud enough to be heard inside the bar, but I still kept my eye on the back door as I backed out into the alley and jammed the stiff transmission into second gear. The old battlewagon groaned at the effort, but by the time I'd reached the end of the block the cold, rough-running motor was smoothing out. I rolled the window down to vent some of the noxious fumes that were leaking into the cab from the Jeep's decrepit exhaust system, pulled my hat low on my forehead, scrunched down in the seat, and turned left onto Main. There were cops everywhere I looked, but none of them gave me, or my antique chariot, a second glance as I rumbled out of town, heading into the mountains on Highway 130.

From the outskirts of Victory, the highway climbs almost straight up into the Snowies, taking you from about 7,500 feet above sea level to the 10,847-foot summit of Snowy Range Pass in under ten miles. By the time I was a mile out of town, the old Jeep was wheezing like a four-pack-a-day smoker and spewing a long screen of hazy black smoke out the tailpipe. I was burning about a quart of oil per mile and I had to stay in second gear in order to avoid rolling backward. There was no way in hell I could make the pass in that car, but I didn't have to. The ski area is only about three miles out of town, and the turnoff to the university's science camp is just beyond that.

I thought about Duerr while I drove, tried to figure out what made him tick. The gregarious, successful persona he'd shown to the public in his football days, and later as the retired star, didn't seem to jibe with the mental picture I had of people drawn to causes like the Posse's. I pictured those people as quieter, more introspective, maybe less worldly. I pictured them tucked away in a little backwater, simmering over the injustices of life until their desperation drove them to bolder action. I did not picture them nursing their idiotic racial grudges, plotting the overthrow of the United States government, then going on television with John Madden to discuss the intricacies of that year's football season.

I could maybe understand why Duerr had been drawn to the Posse in the first place. Posse sympathizers had become his surrogate parents after Duerr's own parents died. I'm sure they had plenty of time to indoctrinate their son-by-default before the shoot-out that took Kahl's life. Maybe Duerr embraced the Posse's dogma to fit in, to win their acceptance, their love.

I could even understand why Duerr might have become militant after Gordon's death. He'd already lost his parents, and here the government was, tearing his world apart again. I could understand his urge for revenge, to carry Gordon's torch.

What I couldn't understand was how Duerr had managed to maintain that hatred and his secret activities in the Posse in the years since Gordon's death. He'd been living two distinctly separate lives: the public life of the national sports hero, and his private life as a member of a vitriolic and violent underground—and no one had been the wiser, not even the powerful Federal Bureau of Investigation. I didn't know how he'd managed to pull it off, but I was discovering I felt an increasing admiration for his abilities. He was either a hell of an operative, I decided, or pathologically insane. Maybe he was both.

It didn't take long to reach the dirt road leading to the camp's cabins, and when I pulled off the blacktop, I nosed the Jeep to the side of the road and killed the engine. With the overheated motor steaming as it cooled and twisted shadows from the lodgepole pines falling across the roadway like camouflage patterns, I tried to figure out how I could approach Duerr's cabin without being noticed. The university's four cabins are spread out at intervals of a hundred yards, the first one less than two hundred yards from where I was parked but well hidden by dense forest. I knew that Duerr was holed up in the second cabin, well out of sight and easy hearing. The best approach, I knew, would be to leave the Jeep and walk in. That way, I could use the woods as cover and pinpoint Duerr's location before he knew I was around. My leg wouldn't take the strain of that hike, though, so I decided on a compromise.

I'd drive to the first cabin, stash the Jeep, and hoof it for the rest of the way. There was a greater risk he'd hear me coming, but it was the best I could do. For safety's sake, I always leave the chamber below the hammer of my revolver empty, but before I restarted the engine I slipped the sixth Magnum round into the cold cylinder. Then, I broke the chunky shotgun open, checked the load, and laid the weapon across my lap. If Duerr surprised me again while I was in the car, I wanted to jump out holding enough firepower to cut him in half.

Considering what I suspected about Kit Duerr, I suppose I should have been pretty scared about then. Although I hadn't allowed the thought much breathing room, I figured he wasn't the type who would surrender peacefully, and there was a good chance that one, or both of us, would come to a hard end. But the truth is, I felt remarkably calm as I started the Jeep and pulled out toward the first cabin. As a homicide detective, I'd put myself in more than a few dicey predicaments over the years, and there comes a time when you've committed to a course of action and you just have to see it through. There's time to be afraid beforehand, and if you make it out alive, there's plenty of time to be frightened afterward. But when the action is going down, you don't have the luxury.

Not that I intended to give him a sporting chance to hurt me. If he pulled a weapon, I was prepared to kill him. If he looked like he might pull a weapon, I was prepared to kill him. If he tried to run, I was prepared to kill him. If I found him sleeping in his bed, I'd whack him over the head with the shotgun, and then I might not have to kill him.

One way or another, though, he was going in, and I was the one who was going to take him.

I figured I owed Sonny and Ellen and Frankie and Tad and Alex—and myself—at least that much.

I drove slowly as I approached the first cabin, picking my way through the deep ruts in the snow. The road had seen considerable use since the last snowfall, and the icy furrows grabbed the front tires of the Willys, making it hard to steer. When the cabin appeared in the trees to my right, I cramped the wheel hard and gunned the engine enough to pop the vehicle out of the troughs and in between the brush that marked the boundaries of the narrow drive. From where I sat, the noise of the tires crunching through the frozen crust of the snow cover sounded loud enough to wake the Old Man of the Mountains, and I breathed a sigh of relief when I finally pulled up at the side of the building and killed the rattling motor. There was no way to really hide the vehicle, but at least it was out of the sight line of anyone coming from Duerr's direction.

Larry Calhoun, who'd been in all of these cabins while making his valuations, had told me they were virtually identical in size and layout, so before I started through the woods toward the one Duerr had leased, I took a couple of minutes to look the place over.

It was a basic post-and-beam cabin, built from logs likely cut in the area, maybe as a WPA project in the mid-thirties. About sixteen by thirty, it had a rough wooden door in front with large windows covered with gingham curtains on either side. There was a small porch at the front with firewood stacked chest high at one end and a swinging wooden love seat suspended by chains at the other.

I climbed up on the porch and peered inside, cupping my hands at the side of my face to cut the glare coming off the glass from the late-afternoon sun. The cabin was basically a one-room affair with a small kitchen area at one end, a double bed covered with an old-time floral design chintz bedspread in the middle, and a couple of overstuffed chairs at the other end, one of them on each side of the stone fireplace. There were braided rugs on the plank floor and alpine scenic photographs on the walls. In the far corner, on a stand beside a driftwood lamp with one of those goofy lamp shades with a panorama of the Tetons, was a small black-and-white television set outfitted with a pair of bent rabbit ears that probably didn't do much to improve the reception. There was a back door on the right-hand side of the bed and another door on the left heading to a tiny bathroom.

While the place was wired for electricity, there were no phone lines, so communication in or out would be impossible, unless you had a CB radio or cellular phone.

All in all, it was a nice little spread—quiet, warm, and homey. A perfect retreat for students who need time to study with a minimum number of distractions, or someone who wants to get away from the world without giving up too many creature comforts. If I had known about these cabins before, I might have rented one of them myself. The price was certainly right.

When I was satisfied, I checked the safety button on the sawed-off, turned up the collar of my hunting jacket, and cut off into the woods to the south of the road leading into the camp. In the best of times, woods like those are hard walking because of the underbrush and down timber. But throw on a thick snow cover to hide most of the deadfall, add in a nearly useless leg and a foot that felt like it had swollen to about twice its normal size, and you'd almost need a timed-action camera to measure your progress.

Duerr's cabin was about a hundred yards down the road, around a little bend, and up a slight incline. As I glimpsed toward it, holding on to branches and tree trunks for balance, I tried to stay about fifty feet inside the tree line. It was far enough to allow me to approach without being seen by anyone inside the cabin, but close enough that I could still see the road. Although I didn't see any human tracks in the woods, the snow was crisscrossed with wildlife sign, and in the short distance between the first cabin and Duerr's, I saw fox prints, as well as tracks made by snowshoe rabbits, deer, elk, and a small bear, who was probably looking for a protected place to hibernate for the winter. At the base of an old pine, I found a weathered antler shed by a four-point mule deer, its pointed tines reaching skyward like sharp, bony fingers.

It took better than a half hour before I saw the cabin, sitting in a shady hollow dotted with chokecherry bushes and red willow. The snowmobile was nowhere to be seen, but parked at the side of the building was an old four-wheel-drive Toyota Land Cruiser with the front wheels chained.

I hunkered down at the base of a tree and scanned the cabin for signs of life. With the harsh glare coming off the front windows, I couldn't see inside, but there was no smoke coming from the chimney and no sounds, no radio or television, to suggest that anyone was home.

I felt a stab of bitter disappointment as I realized that I might be too late. Duerr would have found it nearly impossible to escape from Victory after the troops had arrived to seal it off that morning. But between the time he'd left Frankie and me on the mountain and the time I'd hiked out to call in reinforcements, he'd had plenty of time to make a clean getaway. For all I knew, he was already in Denver, drinking a cold beer and enjoying a good laugh at our expense.

I watched the cabin and stewed over that unpleasant image for the next hour, by which time the sun had dipped behind the mountain to the west, dousing the little hollow in shadow. The temperature hadn't risen above zero all day, but within minutes after the sun was no longer around to offer its meager warmth, it dropped another five degrees. In another hour, it would be at least ten below and I'd be nothing but a big, frozen lump sitting out there in the dark. I didn't know for sure what I wanted to do, but I knew that whatever it was, I had to do it soon.

With the glare finally off the windows, I could see the rough outline of shapes inside the cabin, but I saw no movement, and with the exception of the chorus provided by a gaggle of hungry sparrows, the woods were silent as a vault.

Fast Eddie's dose of lidocaine had been fine while it lasted, but it was already wearing off, and my knee hurt as I duckwalked thirty feet closer to the cabin, where I crouched behind a clump of bristly sagebrush and fumbled underneath the snowpack until I came up with a handful of gravel.

I saw this trick in a movie once where the good guy wanted to get the bad guy outside, and did it by winging a rock at the bad guy's front door. When the bad guy came out to find out what made the noise, the good guy jumped him. I figured that was as good a plan as any, so with the shotgun in my left hand, I wound up and pitched the rocks at the front window of the cabin, where most of them clattered against the window at the right of the door like hailstones. The rumpus scared hell out of the sparrows, who flew off in a swarm, but that was all it accomplished.

Wherever Christian Duerr was, I didn't think he was inside the cabin, but I still wanted to make sure.

With the safety off and the huge bore of the shotgun holding on the front door, I scrabbled out from my hiding place and headed toward the front porch as quickly as I could, my eyes sweeping the front of the building and the periphery for movement, my breath coming in quick, ragged puffs. I stopped at the first step, the old wooden plank creaking as it took my weight. Someone had left a double-bladed ax leaning against the woodpile and a heavy pair of work gloves lying atop a small stack of kindling. The air on the porch was heavy with the sweet petroleum stink of the kerosene-soaked wood shavings in the two-pound coffee can at the right side of the floor. On a mat at the left side of the door was a large pair of buff-colored men's work boots, their scuffed toes and insteps splotched with dark stains that might have been blood but might also have been motor oil.

I made it across the porch in one giant step, and with my back pressed against the knobby logs of the wall between the door and the window, poked my head around to look in through the glass. While the first cabin had been clean and tidy, this one was obviously still in use. There were grocery bags on the floor of the kitchen and a stack of dirty dishes in the sink. There was a plate littered with bread crusts and orange peels and several mismatched coffee mugs on the wooden table. In the middle of the cabin, the bed was an unmade riot of jumbled comforters, pillows, and sheets. There was a large, military-style footlocker in front of one of the overstuffed wing chairs beside the fireplace, and leaning against the other was a black M16 assault rifle.

When I'd seen enough, I reached across the front door and tried the knob. It was locked but not by serious hardware. I could have broken the door open with one good jolt from my shoulder, but I decided to let it go because there was nothing to gain by forcing my way inside.

Duerr had been staying at this cabin, I was certain of it, but I'd missed my chance to bring him in alone. Now I knew I had to do what I probably should have done to start with—let Keegan and Aaron Cohen know I'd found his hiding place. If I hurried, I figured I could be back in Victory in a half hour or so, and we could all be back here a little after dark.

When I came down off the porch, my head was turned to the right, in the direction of the camp's three remaining cabins. The growing dusk had stripped the color from the forest, and for a moment, I thought I saw the gray silhouette of a man watching me from the woods. By the time I realized it was nothing but a deformed scrub pine, I was too late to protect myself from the blur of movement coming at me from around the corner of the cabin.

His kick caught me squarely in the kneecap of my sprained leg, and it made a loud, wet-sounding pop as it collapsed. I remember grunting in pain and surprise, and I think I must have dropped my shotgun, because before I could fall, a pair of strong hands were clamped around my gun hand and were swinging me in a whiplike arc toward one of the eighteen-inch logs that support the porch.

There was no way to stop myself, and I hit the log face first. When my nose shattered, it sounded like someone crushing walnuts beneath the heel of a boot, and the last thing I remember seeing as darkness began to fade the edges of my vision was a bright red splash of blood on the weathered pine.

When I came to, I was lying facedown on the braided rug in the cabin, my cheeks wet and sticky. I was breathing through my mouth and I could barely see because of the tears in my eyes.

I raised my head to see Duerr sitting on the arm of one of the living-room chairs with his leg crossed, examining my revolver. The shotgun was laying across his lap.

When he heard me groaning, trying to push myself up to my hands and knees, he stood, and with a curious smile on his face, kicked me full in the mouth.

Then, he grabbed the hair at the back of my head and pulled it until I was looking into his cold eyes.

"Tell me this, Starbranch," he asked, almost cordially. "How many times do I have to kill you, anyway?"

20

Sometimes, your mind plays some damned silly games with you. I was stretched out on the cold floor of the cabin, in too much searing pain to move, watching Duerr as he popped the blunt-nosed Magnum rounds out of my .44 one at a time, knowing that as soon as he decided to kill me—which he was surely going to do—there was absolutely nothing I could do to stop him. And while I considered that sad turn of events, I probably should have been making my peace with God, or with myself, or whomever it is you're supposed to square accounts with before departing this life. Instead, the one thing that kept running through my mind was the fun Sally Sheridan would have writing the account of my demise—"Ex cop, car thief, caught with pants down."

And to think that just that morning I'd been a hero.

The absurdity of the whole thing hit me about then, and I started laughing, the kind of laugh you try to stop by holding your breath, but it builds up in your belly, works its way into your chest, and finally gushes out in a giddy rush—although in my case it must have sounded extra silly, being filtered, as it was, through the bloody gap where my $2,500 bridge used to be.

"Do you see something funny here?" Duerr asked, tossing the .44 Magnum onto the chair behind him and pulling a fifteen-shot, 9mm Beretta from the brushed leather holster he was wearing on a web belt under his thick parka. I couldn't answer him though, because I was having some kind of nervous meltdown and cackling even louder.

I stopped as soon as he bent down and touched the barrel of the Beretta to my forehead.

"You're one strange motherfucker, Starbranch," he said, thumbing the black metal hammer of the weapon into firing position. There was no expression on his face. No anger. No triumph. No anticipation. No joy. Nothing. "Stupid and very strange."

"Sorry," I said, wiping the blood from my lower lip and looking down the barrel of the Beretta to the trigger, where Duerr's index finger rested heavily. "It's just I thought it would be different."

"What?"

"This." I shrugged, sweeping him and the room with my eyes. Since breathing through my busted nose was impossible, it sounded like I had the world's worst head cold.

"You mean you thought you'd sneak in here and catch me? Be a big hero?"

I didn't answer.

"Well, there wasn't much chance of that," he said, keeping the pistol pointed at my head as he stood up. From my horizontal vantage point, he looked about three stories tall and as solid as a boxcar. "I've been following you around the woods for the last hour and a half. I especially liked the part where you threw the rocks at the window. Where'd you see that one?"

"Rio Bravo," I snuffled. "John Wayne. Dean Martin."

"Figures," he snorted, giving the top of my head a halfhearted kick. They say you don't hear the noise of the gunshot that kills you, but I imagined that if he shot me in the head at point-blank range, I'd see some pretty spectacular neurological fireworks as the hot slug zipped through my frontal lobe. He stood over me for thirty seconds or so while I waited for the show to start, my eyes scrunched together so tightly that little trickles of tears started running down my cheek, my arms rigid at my sides, my fists balled. Instead of shooting me, though, I heard his footfalls as he walked away from me into the kitchen. When I opened my eyes, he was at the sink, filling a blue-speckled ceramic coffee pot with water. The Beretta was back in its holster.

"Your leg hurt?" he asked, looking at me over his shoulder.

I nodded weakly that it did.

"Good," he said simply. When the pot was full, he dumped a handful of coffee grounds directly into the water and set the pot on the stove. Cowboy coffee. "I'm pretty sure it's broken."

Although it made me dizzy to do it, I raised my head high enough to look down my torso and see he was right. Below the knee, my leg was pointing inward at a thoroughly unnatural angle, and when I tried to move my foot, nothing happened. I laid my head back down on the floor and tried to catch my breath, which was coming in wheezy gasps. In spite of the chill in the cabin, my forehead was covered in clammy sweat.

I recognized the symptoms of shock, but there was nothing I could do about it. I seriously doubted Duerr would run out and call me an ambulance.

"You wouldn't happen to have some bourbon around here?" I asked, the back of my throat gummy from all the blood that was seeping down it from my mouth and nose.

He threw his parka across the back of one of the kitchen chairs. "I know you're a drinking man," he said. Underneath his coat, he was wearing a plaid wool shirt that was tight across his thick chest, blousy where it gathered above the belt line of his narrow waist. The Beretta was riding butt first on his left hip, and on his right, he was carrying a bone-handled Kodiak hunting knife in a tooled leather sheath. He looked a hell of a lot more dangerous than he had at the Silver Dollar, when he was dressed like a Detroit pimp. "But no, I don't have any alcohol around. At least none I want to share.

"And besides," he said, turning his back to me again in order to rummage through the canned goods stacked neatly in a cabinet above the sink, "you won't have to worry about that pain for long, anyway."

There was a second holster nestled in the small of his back carrying a .45 Colt automatic, a newer version of the military handgun I'd taken away from Harley Coyne the night before. I wondered if it was the same gun he'd used to kill Tad Bauer and Alex Thibault. I imagined it was.

When he found what he was looking for, a can of tuna, he opened the container with the blade of his knife, pried the lid back halfway, and began eating the oily fish with his fingers. The mere smell of food was enough to make me gag, but he ignored me as he brought his snack into the sitting area, where he parked himself back down on the arm of the chair, nibbling thoughtfully while he looked out the window at the darkening woods.

"They'll be coming for you," I told him finally.

He nodded that he understood, wiped his fingers on his pants leg. "The Jew?" he asked.

"Cohen? Yeah, Cohen is here. But so are about a thousand other cops. Why don't you just give—"

He laughed out loud. "Oh, that's rich, Starbranch," he said. "And what happens then? He's forced to shoot me 'resisting arrest' like they did Gordon?"

I propped myself on an elbow. "Nobody's gonna shoot you," I said. "We'll just take—"

He didn't let me finish. He pulled the Beretta from his holster and aimed it at the middle of my chest. "Save your breath," he snapped. "You know as well as I do that fuckin' kike wouldn't let me leave here alive. Neither would you if you had the chance. Cohen and the rest of the mud people have to kill me, because if they don't, I'll kill them."

"Mud people?"

"People from the slime," he said. His brown eyes sparked with sudden hatred. "Jews, niggers, spics, all those people who—"

"Oh, Christ!" I moaned, laying my head back on the floor. "Go ahead and shoot me if you're going to, but spare me the asshole lecture."

"It's not a lecture," he said quietly. "What do you think I am? One of those shave-headed morons in a motorcycle jacket, standing on the steps of the capitol building yelling at the faggots in the St. Paddy's Day parade? You think I'm the kind of person who paints slogans on the walls of Jew businessmen? The kind who kills some spic's chickens like that stupid Alex Thibault? I'm a soldier, Starbranch. I'm just telling you the way it is."

With that, he walked to the front door, opened it, and stood looking down the road in the direction of the highway, the Beretta hanging loosely in his right hand. In counterpoint, the first fragrant steam from the brewing coffee was beginning to percolate through the cabin. It was a happy, comfortable smell that seemed out of place, but I embraced its familiarity like an old lover. Maybe there was some way out of this after all, I thought, looking at the M16 leaning against the chair, if only I could keep Duerr from killing me until I figured out what it was. He certainly didn't consider me a threat, or he'd have killed me already, and perhaps I could use that to my advantage. I'd underestimated him often enough in the past weeks with deadly results, and maybe I could get him to do the same for me.

I thought briefly about making a grab for the M16 while his back was turned but abandoned that foolhardy idea almost as quickly as it popped into my head. If he saw me going for the gun before I had it cocked and ready, I was screwed, and there was no way I could move my aching bones fast enough to surprise him.

The only thing I could do was try and buy a little time until an opportunity presented itself, the only problem being that I didn't know him well enough to predict what might work.

"Do they know who I am?" he asked casually as I was still trying to invent a scenario that didn't end up with me playing the role of corpse. His question caught me by surprise, so I stalled.

"Huh?"

"You heard me," he said, turning back into the cabin. "Do they know who I am?"

I couldn't think of a compelling reason to lie, so I didn't. "Yeah," I said, "they know who you are. And so does nearly everyone else in the country. It's not like you're gonna be able to hide."

He didn't respond, just nodded his head like he'd known the answer all along. Then he reholstered his automatic and walked into the kitchen, leaving the front door open so he could hear the engine noise of any vehicles coming up the road. "Well, I guess I won't be living the life of a football hero anymore," he said over his shoulder. His voice had a bitter edge. "Too bad, too, 'cause I love football. Only job in the world they pay you a fortune to hit niggers all day."

I watched Duerr carefully as he poured himself a cup of black coffee—he didn't offer me a drop—and blew along the rim of the steamy mug until it was cool enough to sip. I decided Carrie had been right when she said he looked like Harrison Ford, or even Tom Berenger. Both of those men are considered handsome, but only because the sum of their often flawed and broken parts adds up to a rugged, congruous whole. It was the same with Kit Duerr, except for his eyes. Those eyes were the eyes of a stone killer—ruthless, intelligent, brutal, merciless, and utterly without soul.

I wanted to ask him where his hate came from, how a man with so much going for him could throw it all away for such a degenerate cause. I wanted to ask him how he could have lived such opposite public and private lives. I wanted to ask him if he really believed the Posse dogma, if he thought he was really fighting for a better world. I wanted to know how he could kill with such cold brutality. I wanted to plumb the depths of his insanity, but I didn't think he'd be an eager participant in that conversation. I kept my silence and watched him drink.

When Duerr finished a half a cup, he brought his mug with him into the sleeping area and sat it on an end table while he bent down and pulled three orange ripstop-nylon duffel bags from under the bed. The first of these he began packing, slowly and carefully, with shirts and jeans he'd stored in the footlocker. He didn't pack like I do, by stuffing everything in the bag until there's no more room. He filled his duffel one precisely folded article of clothing at a time.

When he finished with his clothes, he used the second bag for his personal items: his razor and shaving foam, his toothbrush, his tape player, and his eclectic collection of reading material. His taste in music was white-bread country—Randy Travis, Hank Williams, Jr., George Jones, and The Judds. But his traveling library was anything but light reading. Along with his well-thumbed paperback copy of Niccolò Machiavelli's *The Prince,* were paperback editions of Theodore Dreiser's *Sister Carrie,* Ayn Rand's *Atlas Shrugged,* Carl Jung's *Psychology and Alchemy,* Friedrich Nietzsche's *Beyond Good and Evil,* Charles Darwin's *The Origin of Species,* and Karl Marx's slim volume of *Communist Manifesto.* When those were laid out in neat rows, he topped his stack with a hardback edition of Adolf Hitler's *Mein Kampf* and a thick, black, leather-bound Bible.

He used the third duffel for his personal arsenal, at least the weapons he wasn't carrying on his person—an Ingram Mac 10 and several hundred rounds of ammunition, an Uzi, a snub-nosed Smith & Wesson .38, and a black, foreign-looking .22 with a silencer, an assassin's weapon. He tucked an ugly K-Bar survival knife with a wicked, serrated edge in at the side of the bag, and almost as an afterthought, squeezed in my .44 and the sawed-off before zipping the duffel closed. I didn't know where he was planning to go, but I didn't think he'd get that last bag past security if he was thinking of catching a plane.

Then—I kid you not—he walked back into the kitchen, pulled a bag of birdseed out of the cabinet under the sink, walked out the back door, and spent the next five minutes filling a feeder nailed to a tree so the damned camp robbers and sparrows wouldn't get hungry in his absence. All of this without so much as a word to me, which, in its own way, was more humiliating than the beating he'd given me not so very long before. Call it the sin of pride, but I've always held a fairly good opinion of myself. In his eyes, though, I was insignificant. So impotent, so useless, so feeble and powerless that he could turn his back on me as if I was already dead.

When I remembered how this would likely end, with me looking into the muzzle of his automatic as he laid it between my eyes and finished me in the same way he finished Tad Bauer, I began crawling, one fingertip at a time, toward the M16. I'd made it less than a foot when he came back inside and caught me.

"I don't think so," he said, throwing the empty seed bag on the counter. I stopped creeping toward the rifle and watched helplessly as he crossed the small room in three long strides and snatched it out of reach. He jacked a round into the chamber, seemed to hold a momentary inner debate, then carried it into the kitchen and leaned it against the doorjamb. Then he pulled his parka from the back of the chair and slipped it on, leaving it unzipped so he'd have easy access to the pistols. He was leaving, and I didn't believe he'd let me hang around to tell the tale.

If I was going to die, though, I didn't want to go without having a couple of questions answered. I didn't want my ignorance nagging me through eternity. "I know you killed Sonny," I croaked. "But I can't figure out why. What could that poor scarecrow of a man ever do that would make you think you had to—"

Duerr dismissed my question with a wave of his hand. "He was a casualty of war, Starbranch. And so are you."

"No," I said shakily. "I meant *why*. You're gonna kill me, at least you can tell me that."

His face seemed to soften as he considered my request and decided, finally, that he had nothing to lose by granting it. "Jacob Haines," he said, lowering himself into the chair backward so that his arms were draped across the backrest. "He's why."

I recognized the name of the judge who'd been kidnapped by the Posse earlier in the summer, but it didn't answer my question. I shook my head in confusion.

"You don't get it, do you?" he asked, one corner of his mouth twisted in sarcastic acknowledgment of my ignorance. "You never did."

"I guess not," I said. "I thought it was all about the weapons."

"Oh, shit," he snorted. "It *was* about the weapons, but it was about Haines, too. It's about a revolution, Starbranch. One you didn't even know had started."

With that, he stood up, pulled the Beretta from the holster, and thumbed the hammer back, his head cocked toward the open front door. When all he heard was silence, he took a step in my direction, brought the automatic up to firing position as he moved. He aimed the muzzle at a spot just an inch below my hairline.

Duerr's face was a blank mask, but at least he didn't shoot. He held his aim for about thirty seconds and then his face cracked with the trace of a cold smile. "You know," he said. "I've got a couple questions of my own."

I shrugged, forced myself to a sitting position, but blood drained from my head so rapidly I thought for a second I might faint. I kept my broken leg as straight as possible and splayed my arms behind me for balance. My stomach was rolling, and I swallowed hard to keep its contents down. "What can I tell you?" I asked weakly.

"Why'd you keep on with this? The feds were here, so you didn't have to. Why didn't you just let it go?"

I thought about it for a second, and then gave him the answer I'd come to understand myself over the past few days. "Because I needed you," I said.

There was a question in his eyes, but he didn't interrupt. He just waited quietly for me to continue. "I'd forgotten a lot of what being a cop is all about," I explained. "I needed you to remind me. That's why I couldn't ignore it."

He thought he knew the truth when he heard it, or at least what the person speaking believed was truth, so he nodded his acceptance of my answer.

"But why did you come here alone today? I figure you found me through the rental, but you didn't have to come here alone. You could have got an army . . ."

The answer to that one wasn't pretty, but it was simple. "Revenge," I said. "You shot my friend, tried to kill me."

"Revenge is for fools," he said, easing the hammer of the Beretta back down into the at-rest position. I couldn't argue with the statement, so I didn't even try.

It was rapidly growing dark inside the cabin, and I watched him quietly, nursing my aches and pains, while he stepped over to the kitchen table and lit a single candle in a dish with a lucifer match he struck against his belt buckle. When its small yellow flame was going, softening his features as it danced, he walked past me to the duffel bags he'd left on the bed and grabbed the one he'd filled with weapons. Quickly, he unzipped the bag and groped around inside until he came up with the Smith & Wesson revolver. This he carried back into the kitchen, the .38 in his left hand and the Beretta in his right, and eased himself back down on the kitchen chair. When he was comfortable, he rested the Beretta in his lap, pulled a single stubby cartridge from his jacket pocket, and snapped it into the cylinder of the .38. When the weapon was loaded with its single round, he gave the cylinder a jaunty spin and placed the revolver beside him on the table.

"All right," he said evenly. "I have a proposition. You answered my questions, so I'll answer one of yours."

He didn't have to ask twice. "Why did—"

"Hold on," he said, cutting me off with a casual wave of the automatic. "After that question, we'll play a short game. I'll answer as many other questions as you want . . .

"But," he said, nodding at the revolver on the table, "after the freebies, every question costs. One question, one spin of the cylinder . . . sort of a cross between Russian roulette and 'Jeopardy.' We stop when you die, or I get bored, whichever comes first. What do you say?"

I saw a movie once, *The Deer Hunter,* where this loony, stressed-out Vietnam vet spends half the film playing Russian roulette with a bunch of equally crazy Asians. They were all loony, so of course they enjoyed it. But as far as I could tell, the game Duerr was proposing might be kind of one-sided, since he was the only crackbrained lunatic in the room. Still, I didn't have a hell of a lot of choice, because I doubted the cavalry would arrive in time to do me any good. I cast a furtive glance at the open door, hoping to see the telltale flickering of headlights against the tree branches that would tell me help was on the way, but all I saw beyond the doorway was gloom.

Duerr read my mind and told me what I already knew. "You're past the point of rescue, Starbranch," he said. "It's just you and me, so what's your pleasure?"

"Do I get to shoot you if you give the wrong answer?" I asked hopefully.

" 'Fraid not," he said, just the trace of a smile crossing his lips. "My game. I make the rules."

And how're you gonna quibble with that?

Lacking any sort of long-range plan, I came up with a spur-of-the-moment short-range alternative. I'd just keep him talking for so long on my first two free questions we'd never get around to number three. It was a half-baked tactic but the best I could do on short notice. "All right," I said, scooting myself backward until my back was against the bed. "But first, you mind if I get a little more comfortable? Sit on the bed?"

He nodded his permission, and I spent the next minute or so heaving myself off the floor and into a sitting position at the edge of the mattress. I pulled my mangled left leg into the least painful position I could find, which was still pretty damned agonizing. Fast Eddie's knee dope had all but petered out, but I had a spare dose in my pocket and wondered briefly whether Duerr would let me use it. In the end, I didn't bother asking. He was already starting to look a little bored.

"First question," I said. "What did Jacob Haines have to do with Sonny's death? Was he involved with Haines in some way?"

"That's technically two questions," he said, reaching across the table to pull the candle closer. "But since you're new at this, I'll let it go.

"To answer though, I've got to tell you a story that starts last summer, when old man Bauer bought the Posse all that hardware you found on the mountain. We needed that stuff for the revolution, but we couldn't take it directly to Idaho, because there were too many feds around. Then, somebody remembered that the Bauers had a big place in Victory, and since Tad was hanging around trying to get involved anyway, it seemed like a good idea to bring it out here and wait until we could distribute the weapons safely. The Jew and his pal turned up right away, but there were only two of them, so it wasn't a big deal. The guns were stored in the hayloft of the barn, and all we had to do was sit tight."

While Duerr talked, he used his index finger to wipe imaginary smudge marks off the glossy black barrel of the automatic. That same handgun is currently the weapon of choice in police departments around the world because cops started noticing a few years ago that the thugs and dope dealers they were going up against were a whole lot better armed than they were. They turned in their single-action .38 service revolvers and bought new Beretta or SIG-Sauer 9 mms because they hold fifteen rounds in a standard magazine. A 9mm doesn't have the stopping power of the heavier, slower .45, but it carries so many bullets there's more margin for error.

"The whole thing," he continued, "started going sour around the middle of July when a couple of Posse farm boys thought they'd start the revolution a little early by kidnapping Haines and turning him into a political prisoner. They were bringing him cross-country in a van, heading for Idaho, but they stopped in the middle of Nebraska to let the good judge take a piss, and shot him in the back when he tried to run away. They didn't know what to do, so they rolled him up in a carpet . . . and turned up at Tad's the next morning.

"We buried him about five hundred yards from where Toms found the bones of that woman. And that's the last we thought about him till October, when we heard Sonny Toms had discovered a body on or near Tad's property—"

"But those bones belonged to a woman . . ." I protested.

"We didn't know that," he explained. "For all we knew, he'd found Haines."

"So you went out to talk to him?"

"Yeah, I did just that."

"What were you driving?"

"Tad's girlfriend's car. She left it at the estate while they went on a date and mine wouldn't start. Why do you ask?"

"Never mind," I said. "I didn't mean to interrupt."

"Anyway, I got there, and the old coot wouldn't talk. Not at first anyway. Later, after I skinned him and broke his fingers, he told me why. He'd broken into your office, Starbranch, and taken that woman's jawbone. Then, he'd gone back out to the mine shaft and picked up the rest of her. She was in a cardboard box in his bedroom, for Christ's sake. He was afraid I'd take her away from him—which I did. I took her with me when I left and dumped her in a culvert."

"And you killed him because he could identify you," I broke in. He scowled at the interruption so I held my hands out, palms forward, to show him it wouldn't happen again.

For a few minutes, I worried that I might have already pushed him too far. Duerr's face was brooding as he toyed with the safety lever on the pistol, absentmindedly flicking it off and on. When he got tired of that, he stood up and poured himself a tall glass of cold water at the sink, draining it in a single long gulp. Finished, he licked his lips and sat back down.

"Ellen Vaughn had nothing to do with it then?" I asked.

"Nope." He laughed. "But it's pretty funny she got arrested for it. Like I said, Anthony Baldi is an idiot." The laugh dissolved from his face. "That was one question," he said. "Let's hear number two."

The pain was rattling the nerves of my leg so rambunctiously that I was having trouble concentrating, so I tried to shift it to a more agreeable position while I thought. I moved it by picking it up gently in both hands and setting it back down again as tenderly as possible. It was swelling worse than ever, so badly I thought the tightly wrapped athletic bandage might actually be cutting into my skin.

"Tad Bauer," I said through clenched teeth. "Why'd you kill him?"

"Ultimately," Duerr said, "because he was stupid. He thought the revolution was a game, for Christ's sake. He and Thibault thought it was about painting slogans and killing chickens. Things that draw attention." He skipped a beat. "They didn't have a clue."

Duerr paused as if trying to remember the sequence of events.

"He'd been nervous ever since we buried the judge, and we'd been arguing about him getting out for a couple of months," he continued. "But he really started getting scared after Toms's body was found, and the sheriff showed up with all those deputies, even though I told him there was nothing to worry about, no way they could trace it back to us. Baldi was incompetent, and I'd already checked you out. I didn't think we had much to worry about."

"What pushed him over the edge?"

"Two things," he said. "First, he convinced himself that his girlfriend knew too much, so he threatened her, which got him arrested by you and Bull. After that, he made us move the weapons out of the barn and up to that springhouse. Second, that newspaper article. The day that came out, he started demanding that we move everything again, get it all out of Wyoming. I'd been watching him, tracking his movements, because I thought he was crazy enough to try and move them himself, but there came a time he wouldn't listen anymore, said I had twenty-four hours to get rid of them, or he was gonna do it for me. I tried to impress on him that the weapons stayed where they were until the Posse said different, but it wasn't any use. He told his pet baboon to throw me out . . ."

There was ice in Duerr's voice when he went on. "And I shot the both of them."

In my years as a homicide detective, I'd heard more than my share of killers admit their crimes, some of them almost consumed by guilt and remorse, others, the more tightly wrapped specimens, nearly giddy with excitement. In all that time, I'd never run across any like Kit Duerr, who described the cold-blooded slaughter of human beings with the same emotional detachment most of us use to report a trip to the market for a dozen eggs. Their deaths simply hadn't touched him, at least not so it showed. I wondered how he felt, looking into their dead faces after he took their lives. I wondered if their ghosts ever came back to him in the night.

I closed my eyes to rub my temples, and when I opened them again, Duerr was pointing the cocked .38 at my right eye.

"Now," he said, his voice almost a whisper. "We do a little business."

The candlelight was skittering off the polished chrome finish of the revolver like sunbeams on a tranquil pond, but the black maw of the muzzle seemed to swallow light, to suck it in like a black hole at the edge of the universe.

Of all the images stored in the human mind, the one we call up for inspection least often is the image of our own deaths. And when we do, we always envision our deaths at some time in the very distant future. We believe they'll be peaceful and without pain. We believe that when our time comes, death will take us asleep and fulfilled, dreaming in our own beds, our loved ones nearby. It is our ability to postpone that inevitability, at least in our own fancy, that allows us to function on a daily basis, permits us to live with hope and optimism, anchors the fragile tether of our sanity.

I saw my own death in the muzzle of Duerr's revolver and had to look away, down the darkly glowing barrel and into the eyes of the face behind it. For ten seconds, I held his gaze, trying to find in their icy depths some trace of humanity, a flicker of spirit that would forge a psychic connection between us and by doing so, give my death some meaning. Nicole's face flashed through my mind, the remembered fragrance of her favorite perfume. I saw my oldest son, Robert, and felt a wave of sadness that I was about to die without his forgiveness.

The hammer fell, a clap of metallic thunder, the noise of a steel bear trap springing closed.

My shoulders sagged and the deep breath I'd been holding burst out of my broken mouth in a rush. I felt light-headed and there were black spots dancing in my vision. But I was still alive. The hammer had fallen on an empty chamber. For the time being, I'd beaten the odds.

Duerr placed the revolver on the table and filled his hand again with the automatic. "Your turn," he said.

"You bastard," I murmured, my relief giving way to a rush of anger.

"Maybe so," he said. "We don't have to do this anymore if you don't want."

"Of course I don't want to do it anymore," I said. "I didn't want to do it in the first place, but I didn't have a choice."

"You had a choice," he said. "And now, you're entitled to ask another question. . . ."

I felt so weak, so drained, that I was having trouble staying upright on the bed. To moor myself, I hooked the heel of my right foot behind the wooden railing at floor level. It wasn't much, but it was enough, and by pressing down on the railing with my good leg, I found I could relieve some of the weight and pressure from my broken one.

When the dizziness had begun to pass, when my heart rate and respiration were a bit closer to normal, I leaned forward, wiping a gob of thick, congealing blood from the tip of my nose with the back of my hand. I didn't have a tissue or a handkerchief, so I wiped my hand clean on his blanket.

"That wasn't supposed to happen, was it?" I asked. "The Posse didn't order Tad's killing. You were in deep shit . . ."

"They didn't understand," he said, his voice clipped and clearly agitated. "They lost sight of the cause."

"Who lost sight of it? Tad?"

"He was nothing," Duerr spat. "A dilettante. A dabbler. He was weak. His death changed nothing. The weapons were protected, safe. I told the Posse not to worry, but his old man—"

"Told them he was cutting the money off," I said, finishing his thought. "You knew he was going to do that, didn't you? You talked to him when he came to Victory?"

"I should have killed him, too," Duerr said. "But I let him go. . . ."

"And the Posse cut you loose. . . ."

Duerr slapped his free hand against the tabletop, the force of the blow causing the assorted dishes and cups to jump several inches in the air. The candle bounced out of its dish and rolled across the table, its tiny flame sputtering valiantly. He grabbed it before it reached the edge and jammed it back in the dish.

"Yeah, Starbranch. Money talks. They cut me loose."

I didn't know how to respond, so I said nothing, just sat quietly looking into his empty eyes. You could get lost in those eyes, I decided, drown in them, fall in, sink to the bottom and not come to the surface for three days. I wanted him to go on, but he didn't. Instead, he stood up—the Beretta in one hand, the .38 in the other—and walked to the front door, squinting into the darkness of the woods toward Victory. Outside, the early-evening breeze ruffled the bare branches of the aspens and willows nearest the cabin, a noise like water whispering in a swift stream.

It was cold in the cabin, well below freezing. I cast a longing glance over my shoulder at the empty fireplace, shivered, and pulled my coat around my throat. Then, I yanked a little of Duerr's bedding across the tops of my legs, rubbing my thighs to keep the circulation in my legs moving.

"I was the only one," he said finally, still standing with his broad back to me in the doorway. "The only one who kept the faith."

When Duerr turned back toward the kitchen, storm clouds had gathered on his face, and his voice had grown harsh and bitter.

"I told them it didn't matter that the old man's money was gone," he said, crossing back to the table. "There are plenty of others out there who'd give as soon as we showed them what the revolution was about, as soon as they saw the truth of the cause, saw the flames of the first great cleansing fires.

"William Pierce wrote that it will take eight years of war before our soldiers overturn this corrupt government, purge the Jews, the niggers, the slants, and use our nuclear arsenal to burn Israel to dust. And in any just war, there are bound to be false starts and setbacks. Bauer's death was a minor setback, nothing more. But they didn't want to listen. I was relieved of duty, Starbranch, told to disappear, told that someone else would come to move the weapons. . . .

"So I decided that if I was the only patriot, I'd show them what it meant, and my actions would give others the courage to go on."

Before I could speak again, Duerr pointed the .38 at my skull.

Thumbed the hammer back.

And pulled the trigger.

I felt my bowels loosen and tightened my stomach muscles instinctively as the firing pin fell on a second empty chamber.

"You're a lucky man, Starbranch," Duerr said, replacing the Smith & Wesson on the table. "But I've got to tell you, your odds are getting worse. Next time . . . one in four."

My face flushed with relief, then humiliation as the warm dampness soaking my crotch began to spread, then absolute rage. No matter what, I promised myself, I would not give Christian Duerr the opportunity to play his psychotic game again. I hooked the heel of my foot a little more firmly behind the bed railing and began testing my weight against it. If I pushed off from the railing like a diver going off the high board, I thought it would give me enough leverage to stand and perhaps move forward. I had no idea what that would accomplish, but it gave me some comfort to know I had one trick in my bag, even if it was picayune. I pulled the bedding off my legs and pushed it aside.

"All right, asshole," I said, placing my hands beside me on the bed and leaning forward. "My turn. I want to know why you shot Frankie Bull and tried to kill me. We'd already found the weapons, so there was nothing to gain by killing us. Your secret was out, so—"

"I'll tell you," Duerr snarled, gesturing toward me with the barrel of the Beretta. "I did it because I wanted to. Because I wanted to exact payment for the loss of the weapons. Because you and Bull were the final chapters of my story here in Victory, and I wanted to close you out. . . ."

Duerr stopped speaking and his face hardened. "Fuck it," he whispered. "I'm bored with this shit." He brought the muzzle of the pistol to my face and aimed down the barrel. He was going to kill me. No doubt about it. With no time to think, I screamed in fury and launched myself off the bed toward him. I began to stumble as soon as I came down on my broken leg, but my forward momentum carried me on, my hands reaching out for his eyes like talons. He fired when I was less than three feet away, the blue flame from the muzzle a wicked lightning bolt that connected his hand and my left shoulder. I felt the hot slug rip through me like a superheated railroad spike, felt the power of the blast begin to spin my body in midair.

We collided with the force of a train wreck as I crashed into the back of his chair. I tumbled against him, and he shoved me away, sideways into the table, which collapsed in splinters as I smashed through it to the floor. I rolled twice, and when I came to rest, my back was against the kitchen sink.

I don't remember grabbing it during my fall, but when I looked down at my right hand, I was grasping the .38.

In the kitchen, the first flames from the overturned candle were already licking their way across the jumbled tablecloth, caressing the gingham curtains. Across the room, where he'd come to rest, Duerr was looking at the pistol in my hand as he pushed himself to his feet. He'd lost the Beretta in the pileup, and he was reaching for the .45 he'd holstered in the small of his back.

"Don't try it," I grimaced, the .38 unsteady in my hand. From my position on the floor, with the reflection of the flames shimmering across his face, he looked like an angry god.

"Get real, Starbranch," he said, drawing the Colt, pulling back the slide. "Like I said, the odds are in my favor. And besides . . . I hear you always miss."

With that, he smiled. Began to raise the automatic.

I tried to focus my aim. Pulled the trigger, expecting to hear only the metallic sound of the hammer falling on another empty chamber. Instead, the gun shot blue flame from the muzzle and bucked violently in my hand. The bullet took him in the middle of his left breast pocket, the report deafening in the small room.

There was a look of absolute surprise on his face as he staggered backward for three or four steps—his hands shaking so badly he dropped his pistol—to the far side of the cabin and sank slowly down against it, leaving a wide trail of blood on the rough log wall.

With his heart exploded, he was already dead . . . but his body didn't know it.

For a brief moment before he crumpled sideways, our gazes locked.

The amazement in his eyes gave way to hatred, the first honest emotion I'd read there.

"Not always, you son of a bitch," I said. "I only miss when I *want* to."

21

For most of the next twenty-four hours, I was in a wondrous stupor induced by massive injections of the kind of high-octane drugs doctors keep locked away in hospital vaults for their very best customers.

Occasionally, I'd pick up snatches of conversation, the words coming from the ether like radio waves. The discussions were in English, but a discombobulated kind of English that was impossible to understand, sometimes loud, insistent, and demanding, sometimes spoken with the feathery softness of whispering silk. For the most part, I simply tuned it out.

There came a time, though, when I noticed something out of the ordinary, a narrow rent in the darkness I'd been inhabiting through which a band of bright yellow light was streaming, like light leaking into your bedroom at the bottom of a closed door.

I concentrated on that light, opened my eyes, tried to focus. Although the view was hazy, like looking through a camera lens coated with petroleum jelly, what I saw was truly amazing. With the inverted pink heart of her naked fanny pointing toward me like an invitation, the woman standing a few feet away from me raised her leg and rolled her stocking off the tip of her toes. Tossing the hose aside, she arched her back and stretched like a cat, running her fingers through her mane of red hair, her uncovered breasts firm and round and yummy. Then, she picked up a long, cotton nightgown from the bed at her side and pulled it over her head, tugging it over the curves of her full hips.

That's funny, I thought, as I closed my eyes and slipped back into the dreamy darkness of the void. Nicole always used to sleep in the nude.

When I opened my eyes again, I was not treated to the sight of my ex-wife doffing her undies. Instead, what I saw was the owllike face of Fast Eddie Warnock, who was holding my eyelid open with the thumb of one hand and using the beam of the penlight he was holding in the other to bore a tunnel directly through my brain.

"Oh, Jesus," I croaked. "I'm in hell."

"He's awake," Fast Eddie, grinning from ear to ear, said to someone standing behind him. "But I couldn't make out what he said. Could you?"

"Well, of course I couldn't," grumbled Edna Cook, who elbowed the doc aside with a sharp jab to the ribs. "His throat's all hinky. He needs a drink."

While Eddie scowled and rubbed his midsection, Edna—who was wearing an oversize man's flannel shirt and whose wiry hair looked like she'd styled it in a wind tunnel—held a glass of ice water equipped with one of those bendy straws to my parched lips. I sipped gratefully, felt the cool water sluice down my throat, washing away the accumulated sludge and sediment that was gumming up the machinery of my voice box.

While I drank, I took stock of my surroundings. I assumed I was in Ivinson Memorial Hospital in Laramie, but I couldn't remember getting there. My left arm seemed to be bandaged to my body, and there were tubes leading from my right arm to an IV stand on that side of the bed. In the periphery of my vision, I could see a heavy white bandage across the bridge of my nose, which was so stuffy I was forced to breath through the gaps in my teeth. Gaps in my teeth? Traveling south, I discovered I could wiggle the toes of my right foot, but my entire left leg felt like it was encased in lead. With great effort, I raised my aching head a couple of inches off the pillow and took a fearful look in that direction. I'm no expert, but I'd say they'd used enough plaster on the cast to make a damned statue.

"How bad?" I asked Warnock, plopping my head back down on the pillow. The small effort of raising it high enough to look at my toes had worn me out.

"You were lucky," he said. "You lost a lot of blood, but the bullet was through and through. Clipped a lung, but we got it pumped back up. You're gonna be sore up there for a while, might even have a little trouble moving your left arm on account of muscle damage."

He gave the cast on my leg a thoughtful rap with his penlight. "This is a different story. We set the break, but there's still plenty of torn ligaments and such. Later on, you might have to have surgery. You might not, but either way, I wouldn't count on running any marathons."

"I need to get out of here," I said, making a grab for the IV lines, which I had every intention of ripping out of my arm. What I planned on doing after that, I had no idea. I figured the bed was on wheels. Maybe I could kind of row my way out of the hospital using the bed as a canoe and the IV stand as an oar. Edna slapped my hand away before I could shove off.

"Cut that out!" she snapped. "You just lay back and be quiet."

I did what I was told, looking past the two of them to the other side of the room. There was another bed, but it was empty except for a small leather overnight bag at the foot. Beyond that, the window ledge was a jungle of floral arrangements—carnations, mums, roses, greenery, and a whole bunch of stuff I couldn't name but which looked nice on account of the fall colors.

Edna followed my gaze and nodded her old head in admiration.

"They been deliverin' this stuff all day," she said. "We finally told 'em to spread whatever else comes in around the rest of the floor. I never knew you had this many friends . . ."

"Nicole," I rasped, motioning for another shot of ice water.

Edna brought the glass to my mouth again, but this time the straw caught on something that caused my whole upper lip to burn. Cautiously, I explored the painful area with the tip of my tongue. Stitches. Lots of them.

"She was here all night," Edna said. "Slept in your room, but she left about a half hour ago to get herself some lunch. She'll be back shortly, if you can stay awake. . . ."

Much as I wanted to, I didn't know if that was possible. My eyelids weighed about three pounds each, and it was nearly impossible to keep them open.

"Listen, Harry," Eddie said, scribbling on the chart he'd taken from the railing at the foot of my bed. "You and I need to talk specifics about your recovery, but that can wait till tomorrow. In the meantime, there are a couple of cops outside who've been waiting to talk to you all day. You feel up to seeing them for a couple of minutes? If not, I'll tell them to go away."

"Keegan?" I asked drowsily.

"Yeah, that's the one. And another guy. Looks like a mongoose."

Aaron Cohen, I thought. "Sure," I said. "Send 'em in."

Cohen was wearing a sharply creased blue suit, a red tie, and a starched oxford shirt so white it seemed to glow. Ken, who was still wearing the military fatigues I'd seen him in—how long ago had I seen him?—had sprouted wrinkles in his wrinkles. There was a heavy salt-and-pepper stubble of beard poking out from the entire lower half of his face, and his eyes looked like he'd been smoking Panama Red. His hair is so short it's tough to mess it up, but even that looked like shit, with a big flat spot on the left side where the hair looked like it had been ironed to his skull. He didn't smell so hot, either, but I pretended not to notice.

While Cohen lowered himself into the blue Naugahyde chair at the far side of the room, Keegan hiked himself up onto my bed, took one look at the little card on my bedside table that said no smoking, and fired up a cigarette. When he spoke, there was a distinct lack of sympathy in his scratchy voice. "That was one stupid fucking stunt," he grumbled. "I take back all the nice things I ever said about you." To emphasize his point, he flicked his ashes in my water glass, where they drifted slowly to the bottom.

He was right, so there was no reason to argue, and I was too tired to explain. I just nodded that he was right. "How'd I get here?" I asked meekly.

"Sheer goddamned luck," he said. "You burned that cabin to the ground, and one of the deputies smelled smoke . . . went to investigate, and found you laying outside in a snowdrift. Had a damned syringe stuck in your shoulder. What the hell was that anyway? Did Duerr try to drug you after he shot you?"

"Lidocaine," I said.

"He shot you and then gave you a painkiller?"

"Nah, I must have given it to myself. I don't remember."

Keegan softened a little then, poured me a fresh glass of water in a clean glass, waited until I'd drunk my fill.

"Maybe you'd better start at the beginning," he said, pulling a notebook from his vest pocket. "Just the basics. We'll get the details later."

It took me a long time, but I was finally able to tell them how I'd found Duerr through the university's rental, driven out to the cabin, and been surprised. Cohen, who was listening intently, became even more interested when I got to the part about Judge Haines.

"Did he tell you where he buried him?" Cohen asked, rising from his chair and crossing to my bed.

"Not specifically," I said. "Just the general area."

"With all this snow," he said thoughtfully, "we won't be able to find him till spring. But at least we can quit looking for him until then. . . ."

He crossed to my bed, put a hand on my shoulder and smiled gently. "I guess the Bureau owes you a debt of gratitude, Harry," he said. His dark eyes looked almost soft. "I know I do." It was as close to an apology as he'd ever come. I accepted it with a nod.

When Cohen sat back down, I took them through the rest of the story, the game of Russian roulette, Duerr's account of his murders of Sonny, Tad, and Alex. I told them Duerr had exonerated Ellen Vaughn. When I was almost to the end, I reached out and grabbed Keegan's sleeve. "I had to kill him, Ken," I said almost plaintively. "He was going to . . ."

A grim smile creased Keegan's square face. "We understand," Keegan said, closing his notebook. "The son of a bitch got what he deserved."

"You brought his body in?" I asked weakly.

Keegan nodded his head yes. "He was real light, Harry," he said wickedly. "Mostly charcoal."

They finally let Curly in to visit on the third day, and he came bearing the best get-well gifts I'd gotten so far—a thick cheeseburger, a bag of greasy fries, a double-thick chocolate malted, and a half-pint of brandy. He was carrying the contraband in a huge shopping bag that was also stocked with magazines, paperback mysteries, and a $2,500 repair estimate for the Bronco.

"Leon Spinks," he said in mock horror as he came in, scooched himself up on the bed.

"What?"

"Leon Spinks," he said, nodding at the gaps in my teeth, the bandages on my swollen and crooked nose. "You look just like Leon Spinks."

"Suck a fart, Curly," I grumbled, smiling as broadly as my wounded mouth would allow.

He started pulling goodies from the bag, stacking them on the table.

"I told them to go ahead and fix your car," he said, uncorking the booze. "I also paid your rent, which Edna claims is a week overdue. . . ."

"That's funny," I said. "She's been in here to see me every day, and she never mentioned it a single time."

Curly shrugged and took a deep pull from the brandy bottle, passed it to me, and I did the same. It burned going down, but it quickly mellowed in my stomach, put the world in a slightly more cheerful perspective. I peeled back the wrapper on the burger with my good hand and took a greedy bite, which I had to spit out immediately because my mouth wasn't up to chewing solid food. I was forced to content myself with dumping a third of the remaining brandy in my milkshake and sucking the adulterated nourishment through the straw.

"I don't think I have to tell you I'm glad to see you kickin'," he said. "You have no idea how pissed I would have been if you'd screwed around and gotten yourself killed."

"That's why I stayed alive," I said. "To save myself from having to face your legendary temper. . . ."

"Yeah, well, I'm sure you'll have the chance to see it one of these days. I hope you don't mind, but I put an ad for some temporary police officers in the *Laramie Boomerang*. You know? Till you and Frankie are back on your feet? We've already had several responses. I'll bring the resumes in for you to look at tomorrow."

"I don't know why you'd do that," I said, licking brandy-flavored chocolate malt from my lip. "I seem to remember I'm unemployed."

Curly looked genuinely perplexed, held the brandy bottle up to the light, as if to see if there was anything foreign floating around in there. "Where'd you get an idea like that?" he asked.

"You fired me, Curly. Right before I stole your car."

Curly clucked sympathetically. "I gotta talk to Fast Eddie about your medication," he said. "Whatever he's givin' you, it's causin' you to hallucinate. I did no such thing, and the Jeep's right where it's always been. . . ."

I looked over Curly's shoulder to see Nicole standing in the doorway, listening to our conversation. When he noticed me smiling at something behind him, Curly turned around and waved her in. "We gotta watch him, Nicole," he said, trying unsuccessfully to hide the brandy bottle under my blanket. "He remembers conversations that never happened, and I think he's hiding liquor in here somewhere."

Nicole laughed happily while Curly dug around in his jacket pocket, came up with a hot pink marker, and wrote his name in illegible hieroglyphics on my cast. "There," he said, smiling with satisfaction as he finished with a flourish. "The first one to sign it. God, I always wanted to do that. . . ."

"Curly?" I asked as he was heading for the door.

"Yeah, what is it, Chief?"

"Thanks."

"Don't thank me. I get a discount on the booze. . . ."

"No, thanks for—"

"De nada," he said. "Just hurry up and get better. I can't carry too many deadbeats on the city payroll."

When he was gone, Nicole planted a nice wet kiss on my forehead and sat down on the edge of the bed. "He's a good friend," she said. "He's been beside himself, calling here every couple of hours . . ."

"I know," I said, showing her the contents of the shopping bag, pulling back my blanket to let her see the bottle of brandy. "And he came bearing presents. What more could a man ask for?"

She smiled mysteriously and shrugged out of her coat as she walked across the room to the chair, which she scooted across the floor until it was in front of the door. It wouldn't stop anyone from getting in for long, but it would slow them down. Satisfied with her fortifications, she came back to the bed, took the brandy bottle and drained it. Then, she lifted my blanket, ducked her head underneath and found, don't ask me how, the only part of my body that didn't hurt.

An FBI agent from the Chicago office named Skip Wiley called at 10:00 in the morning one week later, the day before I was scheduled to go home.

I'd just finished a game of checkers with Frankie Bull, who'd been moved into my room to keep me company while we recuperated. When the phone rang, I was lying on my bed, trying to scratch my broken leg by jamming a wire coat hanger inside the cast. The pain from my wounds was controllable, given sufficient quantities of dope, which I demanded every two hours like clockwork, but the itching under the cast was driving me crazy.

I thought the call was probably from Ellen Vaughn. A sheepish and embarrassed Anthony Baldi had let her out of jail as soon as I'd told my story to Ken Keegan and Aaron Cohen. She'd left for California three days before and had promised to call as soon as she was settled.

That's why I was surprised to hear a man's voice on the other end of the line. "Mornin', Chief Starbranch," Wiley said, his voice tinged with a southern drawl. Maybe Missouri. Southern Illinois. "I talked to a friend of yours a few minutes ago. Aaron Cohen?"

I grunted to acknowledge I knew the name, waited for him to go on.

"Look, Mr. Starbranch," he said finally, "I'm sitting in the middle of a Chicago police station right now, where I've been all night. A real curious thing has happened, and Aaron Cohen thought you'd like to know about it. You'll be hearin' this soon enough, but Aaron wanted me to be the one who told you—"

"Told me what?" I broke in.

"Magda Bauer," Wiley said. "She killed Wolfgang last night. Shot him six times while he was sleeping—"

"Christ, why'd she—"

"Because she finally figured it out," he said. "She called the police right after she did it, and we've been questioning her all night."

"Figured what out?" I asked. "That Wolfgang was ultimately responsible for Tad's murder?"

"That was half of it," he said. "The other part . . . well, the other part is pretty weird."

"I'm listening."

"Okay," he said. "Those bones that guy found on the mountain out by you?"

"Sonny Toms?"

"Yeah, him. Remember the newspaper stories about his murder?"

"Sure, why?"

"It seems Magda read 'em while she and Wolfgang were in Wyoming. And the more she thought about it, the more convinced she got that the bones belonged to someone name of Felice Ramirez. Young girl. Worked as a maid for the Bauers in the early fifties, right before she and Wolfgang got married."

"All right," I said. "I'm with you so far."

"Magda says she always knew Wolfgang and the Ramirez woman had an affair once while he was out there with the family . . ."

"Yeah," I said, encouraging him to go on.

"But for all these years, she's assumed Wolfgang just broke it off when his father caught wind of the deal. Can't have the son shacking up with some Mexican, you know. Anyway, the family never heard from the woman again, so Magda—"

"Thought she'd just gone away," I said.

"Well, she had gone away," Wiley said. "Permanently. The way she figures it, Felice told Wolfgang she was pregnant, and he had to marry her to make it right—"

"So he killed her," I said.

"That's Magda's theory," Wiley said. "Stuck her body in that mine shaft, and nobody was the wiser until last month."

"She confronted him?" I asked.

"Yeah, she confronted him," Wiley said, "and he denied it."

"She didn't believe him, I take it."

"Not at all," he said. "She told me she shot him because no man who kills both his children can be allowed to live. She admitted to everything when the police came. Told them the whole story as calmly as you please. . . ."

"Where is she now?" I asked. "Can I talk to her?"

"I don't think so," he said. "They just carted her off to some psychiatric ward for observation."

"She's been charged?"

"Nah, not yet," he said. "And to tell you the truth, I don't know if she will be. With Wolfgang's history of abuse, I'm sure she can make a hell of a case for self-defense. I think the prosecutor I talked to this morning knows that. He's definitely sympathetic."

"I don't know what to say," I mumbled distractedly, leaning back on the bed. "I guess it makes sense . . ."

"Maybe to you," he said. "I think the whole damned bunch of them are insane."

As I hung up the phone, I looked at the ceiling, saw reflected there the images of the Mystery Madonna's bones, alone and almost forgotten in the dusty mine—the hands of the small fetus in her skeletal womb pressed against its tiny temples—and Tad, who died hard and bloody, trying to stuff his innards back in his ravaged body.

I shuddered, chased the visions away, put on my headphones, and turned the Boss up loud.

You got off too easy, Wolfgang, I thought bitterly.

In a just world, a perfect world, the best of all possible worlds, she'd have been able to kill you twice.

EPILOGUE

Curly and I were on the river as the sun rose, and it took us nearly four hours to fish the first three-hundred-yard stretch of the Little Laramie, because it's hard to make good time in the Rockies when you're using a cane. It had been almost six months since Kit Duerr smashed my knee, but on top of the damage I'd done to the same knee the year before in a skiing accident, the joint was pretty much ruined. Oh well, I thought, at least I could buy dashing canes, maybe even get one of those romantic jobs with a flask in the handle like Lord Byron, not that I was drinking much those days.

To the east, the Laramie River Valley looked like the hills of Killarney, lush and emerald green, the grass ripe with the promise of May. To the west, the mountains were still buried under their deep mantle of snow, Brown's Peak and Medicine Bow Peak cold and forbidding in their icy magnificence. To the northwest, I could see the outskirts of Victory a few miles away, nestled in shadow between the flanks of the Snowies and Bald Mountain.

Where we were, on the flats, the sun was bright and shining, a beautiful late-April day, the air thick with the smell of juniper and willow, Nelson larkspur, Fendler's meadow rue, American bistort, and Parry goldenweed. I stood on the bank of the river, tying a Golden Ribbed Hare's Ear on the end of the leader, watching Curly fish a few dozen yards downstream.

After sticking his entire face in the water to see what was going on in the food chain, Curly was trying his luck with a Royal Coachman, laying down his two-pound leader with deceptive ease. By the fifth cast, he'd hooked a trout, not a big one from the looks of things, but big enough to keep him occupied and happy. When he'd nursed the eight-inch rainbow to the bank, he kept the fish in the water while he gently held its belly and pulled the barbless hook from its mouth, letting it go back to whatever fishy enterprise it had been engaged in when Curly came along to ruin its morning.

I finished tying the Hare's Ear, made a graceful cast, and laid the fly upstream near the end of a shallow riffle, then watched the water pull the fly quickly through the fast water and into a small pool. When nothing happened, I zinged the fly back in about the same place, but six inches closer to the far bank.

By the twenty-fifth or thirtieth cast, I had gotten myself tangled twice in the brush and lost my fly both times. I looked downstream to see what Curly was up to, but he had meandered out of sight.

At this point, most fly fishermen would give up and try a new spot, but I was just hitting my mental cruising altitude, my brain quietly disengaging from any mundane distraction that might intrude on the perfect harmony cooked up when you mix a nice run of trout-producing water with a sunny morning and the companionship of a good friend.

Within the next hour, I pulled four brookies from the run and let all of them go, but I was convinced there was a bigger fish lying under the overhanging bank at the far side of the pool, tucked back in the roots and submerged branches, the first faint pangs of hunger reminding him that he'd missed breakfast.

I made a half-dozen more casts before he hit, the big rainbow rising to the surface at the edge of the cutbank, just where I knew he'd be, barely breaking the water with his bullet-shaped head and ducking back under the surface with my fly in his underslung jaw. He didn't even realize anything was up until he was nearly back to his hiding place, where I joined the battle in earnest, holding the rod tip-up and setting the hook with a sharp tug on the line. And then he was off, heading downstream like a silver racehorse, hugging the bottom of the river and stripping line from my light reel with remarkable ease.

I let him take as much as he wanted, applying a little extra drag as the yellow line whizzed through my left hand.

Hooking a good trout on a two-pound test leader is a little like trying to rope a steer with a piece of baling twince. If you stop his run too forcefully, the line will snap and he'll only be a memory. If you're patient and make no mistakes, you stand about a twenty-percent chance of keeping the fish on the line until he tires enough so that you can bring him to the bank and declare victory.

Fifteen minutes later, it was nearly over for both of us, the only question being which one would go belly-up from exhaustion first. I'd been up, down, and through the same forty-yard length of the Laramie a half-dozen times, and while my hook may have drawn first blood, the fish had gotten in a few decent licks himself. It isn't easy to scramble down a rocky riverbank on a cane, and I'd fallen at least twice. The right knee of my blue jeans was gone and there was an ugly-looking scrape turning red and purple on my kneecap from a spectacular fall I'd taken when my ankle—now twisted and throbbing—had gotten stuck between two rounded stones below water level.

He gave up before I did, though, and allowed me to horse him into the shallows at my feet. I held the rod tip high, ran my hand down the line and into the cold water until I felt the thick body of the fish. He was too tired to fight anymore, barely wiggled as I lifted him gently from the water—I guessed he weighed three pounds, maybe more—and slipped the hook from his jaw. Bending down again with the trout cradled in both hands, I eased him back into the water and ran him back and forth until he'd caught his breath. Then I let go. He stayed where he was for a few long seconds, motionless save for his slowly fanning gills, as if he didn't understand what was happening, that he was free. When that fact registered on his fishy brain, he gave a powerful flick of his tail and swam away slowly, his dorsal fin just clearing the ripples, back toward the same small pool where this little adventure began.

I watched him until the sun dancing on the water made it impossible to see him anymore. Then I sat down on the bank to catch my own wind. I reached in the pocket of my fishing vest for a smoke, fumbled through the pack until I had one free, and put it to my lips. Before I could light it, though, I was overcome by a wave of good intention. I crumbled the smoke and tossed it in the bushes, then I followed that with the whole pack. Time to quit, I thought for the twelve-thousandth time this year. If I failed this time, I decided, I'd break down and ask Eddie Warnock for some of that nicotine gum, maybe some patches. Maybe gum and patches at the same time. Cop a good buzz.

Feeling incredibly self-righteous, I broke down my gear, dug my lunch out of my backpack, sat about twenty-five feet from the riverbank facing away from the Laramie, and munched as I watched a small herd of pronghorn antelope graze across the prairie, their white rumps like moving flowers among the sage.

It was good, sitting there in the sun, my only companions the meadowlarks singing in the sage and a gray jay who was hopping around expectantly for the scraps of my meal. I ignored him, lay back on the warm earth with my hands under my head, and watched the high clouds scudding across my field of vision. After a while, I closed my eyes and drifted, thought about life.

All in all it had been an interesting six months since the day I killed Kit Duerr and ended that chapter of violence in the mountain community of Victory, a little like one of those good-news, bad-news stories.

The gunshot wound in my chest had healed nicely, but I'd been off my feet for the better part of three months while my leg mended. Fast Eddie said I still needed surgery, but I'd been putting it off because Eddie said there was some risk the leg would be worse after surgery than it is now. Maybe in the late fall, I thought, after the tourists had gone home. Maybe never.

Frankie Tall Bull recovered from his wounds much faster than I recovered from mine, and was back to work at least two months before I was able to hobble in. He'd sold a couple of sculptures, however, and had taken calls from buyers interested in more. If his work started catching on, I figured I could keep him in Victory for another year, tops. Then I'd have to go looking for a new police force.

I'd spent a wonderful holiday with my family, and Nicole and I had tried another reconciliation during the period of my recovery. It wasn't long, though, until the same old problems started pushing us apart. Nicole and I love each other, but she will never move to Victory, which she says is too small. I, on the other hand, never want to leave. We see each other every couple of weeks, but there's a tentative quality to our encounters, as if we're both afraid of wanting each other too much. Maybe we'll find some sort of compromise before it's too late for us. Maybe we won't.

Trouble is, I was changed by the murders of Sonny Toms, Tad Bauer, and Alex Thibault. Changed by the Posse Comitatus and Kit Duerr. Before those events, I'd always thought of Victory as my place of escape, a quiet, unchallenging community to hide in while I repaired my damaged soul. I imagined that after I was healed, I could go back to my family, to Denver, to my old life. Now, I realize Victory is a destination, my home, a place worth fighting for. I've found a real sense of duty, obligation, my life's work. I've come to terms with my future here now, and I intend to stick around and protect Victory from further harm, protect it from the Kit Duerrs of the world, protect it from the ugly force of violent change.

In that regard, I'm already a little late, since Victory was changed by the Posse and the murders as surely as I was. In a way, we lost what remained of our innocence. There's less trust in town now, and lots more people than usual are still going armed. We watch outsiders with a little more suspicion; we're a little more on edge. We know what's out there now, know it can reach out and touch us at any time. Most of us lock our doors at night.

People want to be ready—and with good reason, it seems. Three weeks after I killed Kit Duerr and took the Posse's cache of weapons out of circulation, I received an unsigned note in the mail. The envelope bore an Idaho postmark, and I believe it was sent by members of the Posse Comitatus. "Thanks for doing our job by killing Duerr," it read, "but remember we're still around."

A month after that, I received word from Aaron Cohen that suspected Posse members had purchased a ranch just over the Albany County line and are using the land as a training ground for urban terrorists. The Hispanic deputy sheriff who regularly patrols that area was warned to keep away from the property or risk being killed.

So far, both sides are keeping their distance, but I figure it's just a matter of time before it comes to more senseless violence and brutality. There's too much hatred in America these days for things to end any other way. The bloodshed in Victory the previous fall was just another skirmish, and I wondered how my friends and neighbors would react to the war.

I considered that foreboding prospect while I drifted there on the warm ground, and didn't hear Curly as he ambled up from the river, carrying a sixteen-inch rainbow in the crook of a forked green stick. "The wife's dinner," he explained, plopping himself down beside me, water oozing from his tennis shoes, which he prefers over hip waders because sneaks will never fill up with water and weigh you down on the bottom while you drown.

I sat up, ran a hand through my hair, cracked a canteen, and took a long sip of cool water.

Curly took my measure and grinned. "Man, you look awful," he said. "What happened? A tree jump out and mug you?"

I turned my face toward the midday sun, stretched my tired legs. "That's about right," I said. "Big, testy son of a bitch with an attitude. How was the fishing?"

"Sixteen," said Curly. "Three keeper size. You?"

I conjured my best poker face, looked him in the eye. "The biggest rainbow trout I've ever seen on this river," I told him. "At least a five-pounder, maybe six. Jumped right out of the water yelling, 'Take me, Harry!' "

Curly clucked like my mother used to do whenever I told a whopper. "You keep him?" he asked skeptically.

"Nope."

He helped himself to one of my liverwurst sandwiches, bit into it like a hungry bear. He chewed for a while and then produced a flask of expensive Scotch from his fishing vest to wash it down. He unscrewed the lid, drank deeply, smacked his lips in appreciation. "Then I say your whole tale is bullshit." He grinned. Passed the flask to me. I took a long swallow.

The Scotch burned its way to my belly and chased away all thought of the Posse Comitatus, the shambles of my personal life, the sense of foreboding I'd been feeling about the future, wrapped me in its comforting, alcoholic glow. I laughed happily, lost in that perfect, fleeting moment. "Maybe so," I admitted drowsily. "But when you come right down to it, Curly, my best stories always are."